Praise for Misty Evans'
I'd Rather Be in Paris

"...fast action, scary situations, fabulous settings, and knock-your-socks-off love scenes..."
~ *Camellia, Long and Short Reviews*

"...what an exhilarating read...had me gasping aloud. Misty's books are some of the best I've read."
~ *Abi, The Romance Studio*

"...a fantastic suspense story...I look forward to the next book in her series."
~ *Minx, Literary Nymphs*

"In the shadowy cut-throat and high-tech world of covert ops, I'd Rather Be In Paris is a breath of fresh air—exciting and dangerous, but inhabited by unique and sympathetic characters...If you've been missing Alias, you need to read Misty Evans."
~ *Sean Ellis, author of The Shroud of Heaven*

Look for these titles by
Misty Evans

Now Available:

A Tickle My Fantasy Story
Witches Anonymous

Super Agent Series
Operation Sheba (Book 1)
I'd Rather Be In Paris (Book 2)
Proof of Life (Book 3)

I'd Rather Be in Paris

Misty Evans

A Samhain Publishing, Ltd. publication.

Samhain Publishing, Ltd.
577 Mulberry Street, Suite 1520
Macon, GA 31201
www.samhainpublishing.com

I'd Rather Be in Paris
Copyright © 2010 by Misty Evans
Print ISBN: 978-1-60504-445-3
Digital ISBN: 978-1-60504-471-2

Editing by Sasha Knight
Cover by Anne Cain

First Samhain Publishing, Ltd. electronic publication: March 2009
First Samhain Publishing, Ltd. print publication: January 2010

Dedication

This book, like all my stories, is dedicated to Mark, my real-life hero. You have pulled me up by my stilettos and set me back at my computer more times than I can count. For indulging my fashion addiction as well as my writing obsession, I offer all my love, forever and a day. *Je t'adore.*

I figured writing the second book in my Super Agent Series would be a piece of cake—my blonde roots were showing. Writing the second book in a series is more like climbing Mount Everest AFTER swimming the Pacific. I rewrote and rewrote and lost my voice along the way. *Merci beaucoup* to my partner in crime, Donnell, for telling me the truth and then becoming my personal 9-1-1 as I retrieved my voice—and my self-confidence—as a writer.

Deep gratitude also goes to Angela, for reading every revision with enthusiasm, and to Nana, for forcing me to up the ante for my characters and tweaking my dialogue so I sound much younger and hipper than I am.

As always, a high five to my incredible editor, Sasha, for challenging me to bring my A-game. *Tu es magnifique!*

Prologue

The betrayal began at four-o-three a.m. in an abandoned two-story farmhouse ten kilometers southwest of Paris.

Betrayal was an old friend of Zara Morgan's. Her mother betrayed her talent and prima-ballerina status to marry a millionaire. Her father, in turn, betrayed her mother by having an affair with the stock market as well as another woman. At fourteen years of age, Zara's own body betrayed her youth, training and determination, leaving her with a ruptured Achilles tendon and the shattered dream of restoring her mother's honor in the world of dance.

So when the guileless tone of Alexandrov Dmitri's voice raised the hair on the back of her neck, the foreign intelligence officer recognized the sound of betrayal, the feel of it in her bones, even before her brain processed his words coming through the small speaker of her laptop. Tim Owens, her friend and fellow CIA operative, had been betrayed by the most-wanted criminal in Europe.

Zara knew you couldn't defeat betrayal by wishing on a star, praying to God or pretending it didn't exist, and as the next few minutes ticked by, her pulse throbbed in a synchronized dance with fear. She could sit in the specially equipped gray van hidden alongside a row of trees and let the coming hours play out like a *mise en scène* inside the farmhouse, or she could place a call for help.

At four-o-five, she called Langley.

An hour later as she waited in the airless van for the cavalry to arrive, she speculated at the reason for her racing pulse. It wasn't just Dmitri. When Commander Lawson Vaughn arrived with his rescue team, betrayal would again be her friend. She could feel that in her bones too.

Vaughn was all the things she wasn't. Older, experienced,

solid as granite and tempered like fine steel. Disciplined. Intense. Deadly.

The first time she'd seen him at the Agency's training camp in Virginia, she was two days from graduating from the Farm. He was between rescue missions. He'd seen her watching him as he practiced hand-to-hand combat with another man on his team. The piercing assessment in his return gaze left a cellular imprint in Zara's body she couldn't shake. Didn't want to. His intense eyes haunted her even now, months later, a thousand miles away from that moment.

From the speaker Dmitri's bored voice turned sharper, more demanding. He tired of the game he himself had initiated. "Tell me where my merchandise is, Agent Owens, or I will break the bones in each and every finger you have."

Zara gripped the console bolted to the floor and leaned toward the small speaker. A ball of fear pinged around her stomach.

"Your porn library?" Tim's voice held measured sarcasm. Sarcasm Zara appreciated. It told her Tim was still mentally strong enough to fight. "Or your collection of feather boas?"

The sucking sound of a fist hitting soft flesh rang in the van and she flinched. Tim's groan filled her ears and she resisted the urge to throw her hands over them like she had done as a child when her parents' raised voices had sent her running to her room. How could this happen? How could this simple, straightforward field assignment go so horribly wrong?

Power, greed, lust...the basic motivators of betrayal were the same for fathers, mothers and criminals alike.

Dmitri chuckled. "Your agents stole my missiles." He paused, and in Zara's mind, she saw him taking a draw off the ever-present Dutch cigarette between his lips. She could hear him exhale. "I want them back and you know where they are."

No, he doesn't. Zara knew a rich Saudi prince expected Dmitri to deliver the cache of smart missiles and the technology to build more in less than six hours. Dmitri was under the gun, and now so was Tim, but Tim didn't know the whereabouts of the missiles.

He and Zara had been hunting down a turncoat spy in the Paris Embassy. An asset had led them to the farmhouse with the promise of evidence. Instead of finding the informant waiting for him, however, Tim had found Dmitri, a black market arms dealer the U.S. had been trying to arrest for months.

Trying and failing.

In the van, sweat soaked the back of Zara's white shirt. Her boss didn't want the French involved in Tim's rescue for reasons beyond her clearance level, so he'd called in Pegasus, the CIA's paramilitary team. Although the five-man squad had been on assignment in Germany, Vaughn had assured her Pegasus would arrive before sunrise.

Zara checked her watch. Sunrise was less than fifteen minutes away.

Fifteen minutes.

The speaker popped as Dmitri snapped his fingers. "Break his fingers." Another draw on his cigarette. "Slowly."

Zara dug her fingernails into the console's cheap laminate as the sounds of a scuffle and the clear ring of popping bone echoed through the receiver. Tim's cry of pain froze her blood and the ball of fear in Zara's stomach grew. As a young girl, her mother's sobs on the other side of her bedroom wall had triggered the same feeling. Helplessness.

She stared at the speaker, her heart in her throat. Where was Team Pegasus? Where was Lawson?

Sitting in the cramped van beside Zara, Annette Newton reached across the mess of wires and gadgets and squeezed Zara's arm. "There's nothing we can do, Zara."

An FBI analyst who worked with the CIA's counterterrorism team on European operations, Annette had come along to record the informant's information for French Intelligence as well as the CIA. Now she was recording Tim's torture.

Zara rubbed her stomach and motioned at Annette's matching laptop. "Call Pegasus again. Hurry."

As Annette placed the secure call, Zara looked at the picture of Dmitri taped to the side of her computer screen. The ice-blue eyes stared back at her, mocking her inexperience. Even before Tim had walked into the trap, Dmitri had garnered the Number One wanted position on Zara's personal list of international bad guys. His criminal network inside Paris and throughout Europe was responsible for the deaths of hundreds of innocent people and yet he was as elusive as the smoke from his cigarette. While Tim had kept Zara in the background learning to cultivate assets, she'd become obsessed with the terrorist no one could catch.

Now Dmitri had fallen into her lap, but she would gladly let him walk away if she could save Tim.

You won't get away with this, she challenged his image. *I won't let you.*

Annette caught Zara's eye. "No answer. They must be out of range."

Another cracking noise issued from the speaker. Another scream of pain.

"Out of range?" Zara's heart beat like a bird trapped inside her chest. "They should be in the field by now. How they can be *out of range?*"

Annette remained calm in the face of Zara's frustration. "The satellite might be down due to the storms throughout Europe or the signal is being blocked by the French."

French Intelligence wanted Dmitri as bad as the U.S. did. Or so they claimed. "FI okayed our presence. Why would they block our communications?"

"Maybe it's not FI. Could be the National Police or *gendarmerie.* French agencies are a lot like ours. They don't always play well together and they certainly don't play with us. It happens."

Zara rubbed her stomach again as she heard another of Tim's fingers pop. She wanted to scream along with him. "I shouldn't be letting this happen. I should do something to stop Dmitri. Flynn would."

Conrad Flynn, the new Director of Operations, was a god in the international spy world. A god always on her case, drilling her to be assertive but not too aggressive. It was a tightrope every spook danced on. A rope strung hair-trigger-tight for spooks like Zara in Flynn's secret army.

Annette fingered the keys on her laptop. "Director Flynn has years of fieldwork and experience with guys like Dmitri. You don't."

Flynn had plucked Zara from the other Farm graduates and put her through several weeks of his own special training program. She was one of Flynn's new army of spies. An army few people, including Annette, knew anything about due to the delicacy of the job. "Flynn trained me. I should know how to get Tim out of this situation..."

Dmitri's voice hissed from the speaker and both women fell quiet. "If you do not tell me what I need to know, I will shoot you and leave you for the rats to eat. They start with your eyeballs and your testicles..." His voice trailed off and amused laughter of the men in the room filtered through. "Think about it, Agent Owens. You have five minutes before you become rat meat."

Five minutes? Zara glanced at her watch. Ten agonizing minutes to sunrise. Dmitri now planned to kill Tim, not just torture him.

In five minutes.

Closing her eyes, she offered up a prayer to her god of a boss back at Langley. She needed to channel Flynn and she needed to do it now. *Move*, his voice commanded in her head. *Take control.*

But how? What would *he* do in this situation? The three point triangle he always preached appeared in Zara's mind— *delude, deceive, distract.* Her eyes flew open.

The only way to defeat betrayal was to meet it head on. She would have to distract Dmitri until Vaughn arrived. Glancing at her watch, she set the timer. Then she reached behind her for the gun in the waistband of her pants.

Annette raised an eyebrow and Zara pointed at the satellite phone. "Keep trying Vaughn."

As she checked the clip in the compact SIG Sauer 9 millimeter, she scrambled to the end of the van, grabbing a bug bot—one of the tiny microphones the CIA's geek squad handed out like candy—from a cache of electronic equipment by the door.

Annette swiveled her chair to follow Zara's path. "Where are you going?"

"Vaughn said he'd be in position by sunrise, but Tim doesn't have that long. I'm going to distract Dmitri until Pegasus gets here."

Annette's forehead creased in a frown. "And get yourself and Agent Owens killed in the process?"

"You got a better idea?"

"Yeah, wait for Vaughn."

Zara shook her head. "Tim's as good as dead right now if I wait. We don't even know for sure Vaughn and his group are in the field. I won't risk Tim's life because of a nonfunctioning satellite dish or a pissing match between *Sûreté Nationale* and French Intelligence." She pushed open the van door. "I have to do something and I have to do it now."

"Zara—"

Closing the door on Annette's high-strung voice, she slipped out into the shadowed countryside.

The manic bird continued to beat against her rib cage. She leaned her back against the van for a moment, trying to draw in a deep breath. Was she about to make matters worse?

How could they get any worse?

Ignoring her jack-hammering heart, she secured the bug bot in the lining of her bra and buttoned the top two buttons of her shirt. A storm moving in from the west buffeted her with wind. Strands of hair whipped around her face as the air cooled her back where the sweat-soaked shirt clung to her skin. Shoving the stray hair behind her ear, she scanned the horizon and wondered if this was her first *and* last mission for the CIA. Wondered if she could save Tim or if they'd both end up rat meat.

Zara secured her gun back in her waistband before swinging her leg over her motorcycle sitting next to the van. She kick-started the engine and shot out of the woods headed for the farmhouse. It was time for a personal face off with betrayal.

At five fifty-six a.m. Lieutenant Commander Lawson Vaughn pulled himself forward another inch on the ground and listened to a dove welcome the approaching sunrise with a low call. The night was not yet in full retreat, and in five minutes— technically four minutes and ten seconds—Lawson and his four-man squad were going to use the fading darkness and the approaching storm to take the terrorists in the rambling white farmhouse by surprise.

Rescuing a hostage was delicate work done with a sledgehammer. Time-consuming preparation for split-second decision making. Careful, deliberate negotiations laying a trail for guns and brute force.

In his career, Lawson had saved fourteen men, six women, three children and half a dozen bystanders. He kept track of those he lost too. Some people couldn't be rescued, couldn't be saved, no matter how hard he tried. The towers fell before his plane touched down. The cancer spread during the third course of treatment. The person had a death wish.

Every rescue op contained variables. Some were

controllable and he could plan for those. Relentless training covered the rest. What delicacy couldn't handle, the sledgehammer would.

Team Pegasus had already completed the delicate part of this mission, moving through the field south of the house with deliberate care. Each man had become a shadow in the night as they covered a half mile of dense trees, checking every inch for tripwires and infrared alarms. Now within a few yards of the house, they had found nothing except a one-man security patrol walking the grounds.

Careless of you, Dmitri. A spot between Lawson's shoulder blades twitched. Alexandrov Dmitri was nothing if not paranoid. The terrorist did not make mistakes when it came to security. So why had he seemingly failed to do so this time? Why pick an abandoned farmhouse in the middle of rolling hills to take a spy hostage instead of driving thirty miles farther south to his compound?

The cricket chorus was dwindling, and the first streak of sunrise broke the horizon even as the storm moved in. Dark clouds hung just above the horizon and the wind had kicked up hard enough to bend the trees over Lawson's head. At this point, it was a waste of time to analyze Alexandrov Dmitri's poor decision-making skills. The plan was straightforward. The suits in the States and here on the ground in France had concurred on all the important facts. Pegasus was activated.

In four minutes, Lawson had to get his men into the farmhouse, cover the CIA asset and arrest Dmitri. Agent Morgan's intel report stated there were four terrorists inside with Owens. Now one was out doing guard duty, leaving Dmitri, his lieutenant and another man inside. Even if Dmitri had something up his sleeve, Team Pegasus was skilled and experienced. Neutralizing four terrorists would be a simple takedown.

In his peripheral vision, Lawson saw his point man, Johnny Quick, retreat several feet and tuck his body into the shadows of the barn as Dmitri's security patrol sat on the porch step and lit a cigarette. The barn's floodlight illuminated the drive and a portion of the house. After a moment, Johnny gave him the clear sign. Lawson's other men, Teddy, Rooster and C.J., waited impatiently for his command. Like him, they were raring to go, even though the last mission was only hours behind them.

15

Every dove call, every blip of his digital watch, fine-tuned Lawson's attention.

Above the rustling tree leaves, he heard the drum of a motorcycle engine. The guard on the porch heard it too, rising to his feet as the cigarette dangled from his mouth and his rifle came up. Ten seconds later, a finely tuned Ducati shot up the road with a woman driving it. Strands of long blonde hair blew out behind her as she ignored the driveway, hopped the ditch and jerked the bike into an abrupt skid ten feet from the cigarette-smoking terrorist's feet.

The cigarette fell and the rifle locked into place.

"Dmitri!" Her voice echoed off the house and into the woods as she killed the bike. She dropped the kickstand and raised her hands in the air.

Zara. The sledgehammer landed right between Lawson's shoulder blades.

Zara had no time to think or plan what was coming. The guard's gun was trained on her. She ignored him and his command to fall to her knees as she kept her focus on the living room picture window and yelled again. "Dmitri! I know where your missiles are. I'll take you to them."

The guard grabbed her by the back of her shirt and pulled her away from the bike. She let him push her to her knees, the end of his AK-47 digging painfully into her back. He yanked her gun from her waistband and ejected the clip. It bounced on the ground to her left.

A second later, the door to the farmhouse opened and Dmitri stood in its frame, his face in shadows.

Cold fear ran over Zara's skin like gooseflesh. He said nothing, nor did his lieutenant behind him. For several heartbeats, she knelt rigid, willing him to take her bait.

A modicum of guarded relief flooded through her when he ambled down the porch steps in his expensive Italian loafers. But the relief changed course as he crossed the yard to stand in front of her, the paleness of his eyes evident even in the half-gray light of the approaching sunrise. His gaze cut to the road behind her, to her Ducati and back to her face.

Through the years, Zara had perfected a myriad of personas to deal with her family, the press, the public at large. Like the different ringtones on her cell phone, she had one for her father, one for the coworker who made a pass at her in the halls of Langley, one for the psychiatrist who administered lie detector tests. It was a crucial skill in her line of work.

Dialing up her impersonal, model-spy face, she willed her voice to stay calm, sound cool. "I know where your weapons are. I'll take you to the cache myself." She paused before offering him the key to success. "If we leave now, you can make your deadline to your buyer."

Dmitri said nothing, only cocked his head a millimeter to the side, studying her as if she were a curious oddity. Strands of his dark hair rose and fell on the wind. His gaze flickered over her, lingering for the briefest of seconds on the gold chain around her neck before lazily climbing back to her face. Another slight nod and the guard hauled her to her feet.

"Are you a complete fool?" he said in French.

It wasn't the question she was expecting, but she didn't miss a beat. Seconds were passing. "*Non,*" she answered him face-to-face. She switched to English. They would do this negotiation on her terms. "And neither are you. Accept my offer and let's get out of here. Prince Abkhahar will not wait one minute past the deadline."

Dmitri's gaze bore into hers. He switched to English as well. "Do you know how much I hate Americans? American women. American spies." He spit on the ground at her feet.

Thunder boomed in the distance and Zara jumped. A flicker of amusement danced in the madman's eyes. She used the gall it ignited in her stomach to stay focused. "Business is business. Abkhahar needs those missiles to funnel to Hezbollah. You fail to deliver them and he'll kill you. If you're ever going to be the ruling tycoon in the international world of black arms dealers, you need this deal to go down smoothly and on time." She met his gaze without flinching. "I can make it happen."

"Tell me where the cache is, and you can go free with your comrade."

She didn't actually know where the cache was. Even if she had, Dmitri would never let her and Tim go once he had the location. "I take you to it or there's no deal."

He stepped forward, his face far too close for comfort. He was handsome in that French bad-boy way. Many women found the combination of devilish looks and cruelty appealing. Zara found it repulsive. "Do you know who I am, spook?"

Terrorist. Assassin. Certifiable nutcase. A ruthless businessman who enjoyed the sport of killing whether it was to further his political agenda, his philosophical views or just for the act itself. He loved cat-and-mouse games, toying with his prey until it was exhausted mentally and physically before he lost interest and finally had it killed. Rarely did he pull the trigger himself unless it was to purge one of his own men. He didn't trust many people and occasionally, even those in his inner circle were eliminated without hesitation.

Yes, Zara thought, *I know* exactly *who you are.*

But she also knew who she was.

She raised her chin a notch. "You're wasting time. Deal or no deal?"

The corner of his mouth lifted in a comma at the challenge. Seconds ticked by in unison with the beat of her heart, but this time when the thunder boomed again, closer, she didn't move a muscle.

Dmitri snapped his fingers at his gun-toting guard. "Bring the car around."

"Let's take my bike. It's faster." She motioned at the others. "Your men can follow in the car."

Dmitri glanced at her bike and did an abrupt nod of his head, but her success was again short-lived. "Bring me Owens," he said to his lieutenant. The man left the doorway.

The hair on the back of her neck stood up again. Her bones vibrated. "Why?"

This time Dmitri smiled fully. He reached out a finger and touched the chain at her neck. "A little game I like to play."

Tim staggered down the porch stairs in front of Dmitri's lieutenant and another guard. His hands were tied behind his back. His face was bruised, haggard. When his eyes met hers, she saw a spark of admiration mixed with surprise but he shook his head at her in disbelief.

He doesn't believe I can pull this off.

Glancing at Dmitri, Zara could see he was thinking the same thing. He pulled a heavy black gun out of his shoulder holster and held it out to her, butt-end. "Kill him," he ordered.

The model-agent persona faltered. Dmitri was demanding she exterminate his witness. He was ordering her to kill her senior case officer. As a wave of panic threatened to undo her, her Farm training kicked in. *If I can just grab his gun...*

Dmitri's guard cleared his throat, reminding Zara his rifle was locked on her chest. Her gaze flew to Tim's and true panic squeezed itself like a python around her heart.

Her mouth dry, she forced her attention back to Dmitri. Flynn's advice rang in her head. *Don't let him make this personal. Stay detached.* "I don't play games."

With swift movements, Dmitri grabbed her hand and smacked the gun into it. Then he twisted her around, wrapping his left arm around her rib cage and slamming her back against his chest. He turned their bodies in unison, pulling the gun up to aim at Tim.

The contact was brutal and she jerked hard, but Dmitri's arm was a vise. He rested his head next to hers as lightning cracked above them. The smell of cigarettes, expensive cologne and male sweat mixed in her nose. His hand closed around hers, forcing the gun to point at Tim's head.

"Let me help you," he murmured in her ear, seductive as a lover. "Ready?" He trapped her finger on the trigger. "One, two—"

Beep. Beep. Beep. The timer on Zara's watch went off.

Chapter One

CIA Headquarters, Arlington, Virginia
Two months later

"Alexandrov Dmitri." Michael Stone, the Deputy Director of the CIA, pushed a button on the remote control in front of him and a giant picture of the terrorist's face appeared on the sixty-inch projection screen on the far wall. "French Intelligence has informed us he was released from Moulins, the high-security prison he was being held at, early yesterday morning. A judge reviewed his case and deemed the American evidence against him was invalid."

The instant Zara heard Dmitri's name she was transported back to France. The skin on her right cheek prickled as if his breath were a ghost touching her there. She brushed her hand across her cheek and shivered. Fear and anger warred inside her. Another betrayal.

"Last night," Stone continued, "Jon Vos Loo, the renowned biochemist, escaped from the same prison. The French believe Dmitri orchestrated the escape and the two may be partnering up."

Across the table from Zara, Maureen Tolland, a member of the Department of Homeland Security, spoke up. "To do what?"

A new picture filled the screen. This one showed the photo of a laboratory. Stone stood and shrugged off his suit jacket, his broad shoulders seeming to relax a bit at the freedom. "Odds are Dmitri recruited Vos Loo to set up a lab. Dmitri wants to supply various terrorist groups with biological weapons. With the continuing war on Iraq, these groups are piggy-backing on anti-American sentiment and launching their own agendas into the limelight. Most of them already have an array of black-market weapons and are now looking for unconventional ones."

Zara wished, not for the first time, Lawson had put a bullet in Dmitri's head. "He's an opportunist," she volunteered. "What his fellow terrorists are willing to pay for, he's willing to provide."

Maureen made a note on the papers in front of her. "What does Dr. Vos Loo specialize in?"

Annette, the FBI agent who'd worked the Dmitri operation with Zara, answered, "Anthrax, botulism cultures, aflatoxin, you name it. Ricin was his last interest."

Stone nodded at Annette. "What else do we know about him?"

Well-versed in European criminals, she continued. "Dr. Vos Loo is a trained geneticist who emerged from Russia after the Cold War. He's worked for several governments developing biological weapons." She checked her laptop's screen. "Yugoslavia, Saudi Arabia and Sudan. But as far as we know, he's never hooked up with any non-state-funded terrorists like Dmitri."

"What was he in prison for?" Maureen asked her.

"Murder." Annette scanned the document on her screen again. "He fed his girlfriend a dose of botulism for touching something in his lab. His sentence was for life in maximum security."

Another shiver ran down Zara's spine. While a terrorist could take out a building with a bomb and kill dozens if not thousands of innocent people, a psychotic biochemist could wipe out the entire human race with a dropper full of toxin before anyone saw it coming.

It was important to impress upon the DHS agent how dangerous this potential partnership could be, but first she knew she had to give Maureen the actual logistics. "An untested source with good access inside the prison notified us three weeks ago that Dmitri and Vos Loo were spending time together, checking out the same books from the prison library and bribing guards to pass messages back and forth between their cells. A woman who had been visiting Dmitri, Varina Scalfaro, began visiting Vos Loo as well. Varina has loose ties to several criminal organizations in Europe."

Stone's pacing slowed as he joined Zara in connecting the pieces of the puzzle. DHS needed to be on board with what they were going to propose. "We think Dmitri offered to help the doctor escape in return for his participation in Dmitri's new network of terror."

The door to the conference room opened and Zara's boss, Conrad Flynn, blew into the room with his usual air of controlled impatience. The head of the spy group gave her a lazy wink and nodded at the others as he dropped a Day Timer and some dark blue files on the table.

"What'd I miss?" He pulled out a chair and plopped into it, turning to face Michael Stone with a direct stare that made Zara want to duck out of the line of fire.

Stone crossed his arms and returned Flynn's piercing gaze. His tone was curt with warning. "Nice of you to join us."

Zara knew Flynn hated the never-ending meetings his role as Director of Operations dictated. He hated being in the office at all. She felt a kinship with him since she hated it too. The field was where she came to life, where all covert agents let the blood in their veins run wild with daring and anticipation. She was cut from the same cloth as Flynn. A cloth that seemed to rub against Stone like sandpaper.

Everyone inside Langley knew Flynn and Stone had issues. Big ones. Rumor had it the tension between them was over a woman. For a split second Zara wondered what it was like to have two incredible men like the rock-solid deputy director and the sexy spymaster fighting over you.

But only for a split second. She had no interest in relationships. No time, either. Her career was all that mattered, and stopping Dmitri now topped her to-do list.

"Zara?" Flynn lifted a brow at her.

Jerked out of her daydreaming, she straightened her back. Busted. She looked into Flynn's dark eyes and swallowed hard. *Don't stutter. Dial up competent intelligence officer.* "Alexandrov Dmitri was released from Moulins yesterday after a French judge reviewed his case and dismissed it on a technicality."

Making a production of taking a pen out of his jacket pocket and writing a note, Flynn muttered, "That's what happens when you give a French terrorist back to his own government for punishment instead of taking care of him yourself."

The gazes of everyone in the room ping-ponged between Flynn and Stone. Flynn was a firm believer that counterterrorism only worked when diplomacy took a backseat.

Office politics here or in her father's boardroom were the

same. *Stick to the facts, ignore the emotions.* She pretended not to notice the tension. "A few hours later, his prison buddy, Dr. Jon Vos Loo, escaped. Vos Loo's a biochemist who likes to cook up nasty stuff. Deputy Director Stone believes there's a connection."

Flynn rocked his chair, gave Stone an *I told you this would happen* look and jutted his chin at her. "And what do you think?"

She glanced around the room at the men and women gathered there. It was a powerful group but not one of them had ever done counterintelligence in Europe face-to-face with a terrorist with the exception of her boss. They believed in diplomacy, even when it failed, and squirmed at military interventions. Zara believed in taking out sponsors of terrorism, period. That's why she belonged to Flynn's lethal and efficient counterterrorism team. Some people might call her a vigiliante, but those same people might owe their lives to her ability to take out a known terrorist before he struck again.

Stone had been a Marine in his pre-Agency days and Zara respected that, but it was to Flynn that she directed her comment. "I'd wager my father's well-diversified stock portfolio they're up to something ugly. With Vos Loo's skills and Dmitri's connections, they could have a profitable network for the production and distribution of biological agents running within a week. Two, tops."

Flynn nodded, then put Stone on the spot. "So what are you doing about it?"

Maureen leaned forward. "What are the French doing?"

"We've heard the usual rhetoric from the French," Annette answered. "They believe both men have gone to ground. Dmitri's freelance men are missing in action, as is Scalfaro. The whole operation seems to have disappeared."

"Forget the French." Flynn waved his pen in dismissal. "There's obviously a corrupt official inside their judicial branch if a terrorist like Dmitri gets out of prison on a technicality. And they've no doubt got a problem with their intelligence group as well if Dmitri helped Vos Loo escape. If you're worried about these two teaming up, then *we* need to find them."

All attention shifted to Stone. He avoided meeting Flynn's eyes, instead studying the picture of the lab still on the screen. Stone preferred diplomacy, but would do whatever it took to protect his country. He pulled out his chair at the head of the table and sat down. "I agree."

Maureen glanced at her notes. "I agree as well, but I'm curious about what happened at the farmhouse earlier this year. Why did Dmitri believe Agent Owens knew where his missiles were?"

It was the same question Zara had pondered herself. When she'd asked Tim about it, he waved it off, swearing he had no idea, and she'd ignored the uncomfortable tingling inside her. "Tim and I were working on flushing out the mole in the Paris Embassy. Tim had nothing to do with the operation to confiscate Dmitri's weapons."

Maureen frowned at her. "But according to the transcript I read, you told Dmitri you knew where the missiles were and you offered to take him to them."

Zara shrugged. "I was bluffing."

"Bluffing?" Maureen snorted. "Why would you bluff about such a thing under those circumstances?"

"Under those circumstances?" Flynn glared at her, the lion ready to defend one of his pride. "Those circumstances dictated her actions or didn't you read Zara's report?"

Maureen met his glare for less than a second before pointing at Annette. "I'd like to hear the tape that corresponds to the transcript I read. Did you bring it? Start where Zara confronts Dmitri."

She doesn't believe me. Zara glanced at Flynn for help as Annette tapped the keys of her laptop. He made a small, almost unnoticeable gesture with his hand, telling her to relax. *Don't let her think she's getting to you.* The next second she heard her voice coming from the room's speaker system.

"Dmitri!"

As the recording played out, Zara's insides turned to Jell-O. Staring at the conference table and gritting her teeth, she struggled to keep her model-agent persona intact as she relived those awful moments. She clasped her hands in her lap as she listened to Dmitri's cold, calculating voice trade jabs with her.

"...a little game I like to play..."

"...I don't play games..."

In her mind, she saw the farmhouse, saw Dmitri's ice-blue eyes. It was as if his arms were around her again, his finger trapping hers on the trigger of his gun.

...beep, beep, beep...

The alarm on her watch had given her the microsecond of surprise she needed to throw all her weight to her right hip and jerk Dmitri's hand to the left. He pulled the trigger, but the bullet went astray and dropped his lieutenant instead of Tim.

In the same instant, Lawson Vaughn and his Pegasus team had emerged from the forest surrounding the farmhouse, one man killing both guards, another training his weapon on the lieutenant who writhed on the ground. Still another man moved in to cover Tim.

Zara had gone dizzy with relief. *Tim's safe.*

At least that part of her plan had worked. All she'd had left to figure out was how to save herself...

"...drop your weapon...let her go..."

Vaughn had aimed his weapon at Dmitri's head and the terrorist responded by shifting her to shield him from the deadly gun.

Dmitri's lips next to her ear, his smoky breath had brushed her cheek as he chuckled. He forced the big black gun to her neck and all sensation had left her hand. She'd locked her knees and clamped her jaw, beseeching Lawson with her eyes. *Please...*

Someone tapped a pen on the table, jolting her out of the memory. Flynn was frowning at her as if she'd missed something. Something important. Silence blanketed the room. She searched the gazes of the people staring at her. Was the tape done? "Sorry...I...uh..."

At the slight shake of Flynn's head, Zara closed her mouth. "As you can see"—he shifted his focus to Maureen—"Agent Morgan had a handle on Dmitri then and she still does. She understands what makes him tick. She knows how to manipulate him."

Maureen made a disgusted noise in her throat. "She took a huge risk—"

"And it paid off," Flynn interrupted. "Anything less and Tim Owens would be nothing but a star on the wall downstairs."

Silence once again reigned as Flynn and Maureen stared each other down. Zara tried to ignore them.

Michael Stone broke the tension this round, rolling up one, and then the other, of his shirt sleeves with slow deliberation. "The purpose of this meeting was to determine whether we go after Dmitri and Vos Loo and see if we can pick up their trail. Is everyone in agreement that when we do find them, we'll take action?"

Zara, Annette and Flynn nodded in unison. Maureen drew in a deep breath, pressed her lips into a thin line for a long moment. "Agreed," she said, reluctance ringing in her tone. "But what action we take needs to be decided now as well."

Stone shook his head. "We can't make that call until we know what they're doing."

Flynn shifted his attention back to Zara, his dark eyes dancing with mischief. "You up for fieldwork again, Tango?"

Flynn had christened her with the nickname Tango after her daring rescue because she'd danced with Dmitri and lived to tell about it. Not something any other American or French intelligence operative had ever done.

The nickname had caught on like wildfire. Rubbing the spot on her neck where Dmitri's gun had been buried, she met Flynn's gaze. He was offering to put her back in the field. Send her back to Paris. Give her the chance to hunt down the man who still appeared in her nightmares. There was no need to call forth any of her personas. She answered him with the determined part of her true self. "I'm ready, sir."

Stone closed the folder in front of him and toyed with his blue CIA coffee mug. "At this point, Zara, we're still speculating about Dmitri's plans. We have no real reason to doubt the French aren't doing everything they can to recapture both him and Vos Loo."

Zara didn't miss Flynn's eye roll as Stone continued, "But as we've discussed, the scenario seems too coincidental to ignore. The situation is delicate and must be handled with care. I'm willing to put you back in Paris to see what you can find out, but with a partner. Someone with tracking skills and on-the-ground experience." Stone shifted his gaze to Flynn. "Director?"

Flynn rubbed his knuckles across his chin. "I suppose I could get away for a few days."

Stone set his mug down with a hard thunk. "The Director of CIA Operations does not do fieldwork."

Flynn winked at her from across the table. "Of course not." He pushed back his chair and began gathering his files and Day Timer. "Come on, Tango. Let's go find you a partner."

Zara grabbed her pen and notebook and hurried to follow Flynn out the door.

Chapter Two

Lawson shut the door of Director Flynn's office and nodded a greeting. "You paged me? Is Agent Morgan in danger from Dmitri?"

Flynn motioned him to the chair across from his own behind a massive oak desk cluttered with papers. "Only if she does something asinine like the farmhouse incident."

The farmhouse incident had been added to the never-ending war stories folks in the CIA loved to tell over and over again. Shortly after Lawson had returned to the States from Paris, the story had grown to epic proportions, much of the gossip warped. Today, when he'd heard Dmitri had beaten the French system, a knot had formed in his stomach. Zara Morgan was an obvious target. "I can't believe she did what she did."

Flynn shrugged. "She saved Owens' life. Gotta give her credit for that."

"With respect, sir, my team saved Owens' life and Zara's for that matter. She had no business leaving the tech van."

"Not true." The challenge in Flynn's voice was subtle but clear. "Contrary to popular belief, Zara is one of the CIA's brightest new operatives. She passed the Farm at the head of her class, and while she didn't have the right kind of experience to deal with Dmitri face-to-face when he pulled his stunt with Owens, she showed more guts and cunning than spies who've been in the field for years."

"Still—"

Flynn raised a finger to silence him. "I assure you, Commander, she can jump out of a helicopter with an M16 slung across her back as easily as you can and look more graceful doing it. She was a star ballerina in her younger life."

A mental image of Zara with an M16 in her hands tested the bounds of Lawson's imagination. She was a fighter—he'd seen that when he rescued her—but she was hardly a seasoned soldier like the majority of spooks he worked with in the field. His mind found it much easier to imagine her dancing across a stage than taking out terrorists. "How did she go from tutus to machine guns?"

"I believe it was *Swan Lake*."

"Excuse me?"

"She was fourteen. Her partner didn't support her weight properly during a jump and she was injured. She never performed onstage again."

While she had certainly attracted his attention, Lawson still couldn't figure out how an ex-ballerina had attracted the CIA's. "Surely you didn't recruit her for her dance skills."

Flynn chuckled. "You might be surprised what I look for in a recruit and I wish I could take credit for finding her, but Stone did when he was still DO. She practically grew up in Europe. She fits in. She'd make a good Secretary of State if you ask me."

Zara was beautiful and...cultured, he'd give Flynn that, but a field operative taking out terrorists? It just didn't compute. Unbidden, the image of her jumping the ditch on the sweet Ducati flashed in his mind. She certainly hadn't looked like a ballerina then. "Is she one of your army?"

A tiny tic jumped under Flynn's left eye. "She's gutsy and I like her. Let's leave it at that."

Arguing with him was a battle Lawson wouldn't win, so he stowed his misgivings. If she was part of Flynn's black ops team, there was more to her than met the eye, and Lawson hadn't made it this far without knowing how to pick winnable battles.

Tapping his thumb against his thigh, he reined in his doubts but not his worry. "She sent Dmitri to prison less than a month ago. The son of a bitch might be looking for her."

"At this point, we believe Dmitri is too busy with his other prospects."

"Have you at least informed her he's escaped from prison?"

Flynn stared at him for a several seconds before a faint smile broke the flat line of his lips. "I do believe you have a soft spot for my foreign intelligence officer, Commander."

Lawson fought not to break eye contact. He didn't know why he was here, why Flynn was baiting him. The leader of the spy group was an ex-Navy man like himself, and an ex-SEAL on top of it. He had great respect for the retired spy, but even after contracting with him for several recent missions, he still didn't understand the way the man thought. "You said you had an assignment for Pegasus."

"Not Pegasus." Flynn leaned back in his chair. "You. Deputy Director Stone and I agree you are the best man for this job."

"What kind of job?"

"I'm sending Zara after Dmitri to see if she can figure out what he's doing with his friend, Vos Loo. You're her new partner."

A nerve in Lawson's shoulder twitched. Zara and him? She wouldn't even give him the time of day. "You can't be serious."

Reaching into a desk drawer, Flynn removed a plane ticket, a passport and a brown envelope and pushed them across the desk. "Your plane leaves Dulles at nineteen hundred hours. Your cover, money and written orders are all here."

Lawson stared at the plain envelope for a moment while his brain puzzled out Flynn's motivation. "You want me to tag after your agent in case she goes wacko again."

Flynn narrowed his eyes. "You've built your career on tracking people, Commander Vaughn. I want you to assist my intelligence officer in whatever capacity she needs to find Alexandrov Dmitri and Jon Vos Loo, and I want it done as quietly as possible. We, meaning everyone from President Jeffries on down to yours truly, do not want the French to know we're sticking our noses in this." He pointed at the brown envelope. "After you commit the assignment to memory, destroy the orders. This mission should be untraceable."

"Meaning you want deniability if Zara screws up."

Flynn gave no acknowledgement. "Contact with this agency should be kept to a minimum, but if you need analytical or technical assistance, Special Agent Annette Newton and Del Hoffman in case management will be available to you 24/7. Yvette LeMans will be your initial contact in Paris. Start with her. She will give you the details about Dmitri's release, Vos Loo's escape and the current police investigation."

"And who is her allegiance pledged to?"

Flynn again ignored his question. "This is a special assignment, Lawson. It could open doors for you."

"What about Tim Owens? Isn't he available?"

"Owens is under deep cover in another country and doesn't possess the skills I believe are necessary for this." Flynn rocked his chair. "Give Tango guidance with the operational plan, but work *with* her. I expect constant feedback and cooperation from both of you, but no unnecessary heroics on your part."

Lawson stood and grabbed the brown envelope. "Which translates to, don't play Superman unless your spook needs someone to save her backside again."

"Her backside, her front side, it's all in excellent shape and I want you to keep it that way." Flynn winked at him. "Off the record, you know who her father is?"

Again Lawson wondered about Flynn's thought processes. "Charles Morgan, the finance mogul."

"Charles Morgan, friend and consultant to Titus Allen. They go way back."

Politics. Lawson tried to avoid them as much as possible, but he knew how the game was played. Allen was the Director of Central Intelligence. Next stop President.

Flynn smiled benignly. "Anything happens to Zara, Titus will help Chuck mount our two heads on the study wall at the Morgan mansion." He stood and extended his hand to Lawson. "Good luck. I'll expect your initial report by twenty-three hundred hours tomorrow."

After Vaughn left his office, Conrad sat at his desk and stared at the closed door. Vaughn was a good Navy man. Experienced, a little hyper, but a productive, no-nonsense contractor. Conrad liked him.

Conrad liked Zara too. She'd been his first real test as Director of Operations. Stone had almost had his ass over the farmhouse incident, but, as usual, Conrad put his head down, dug in his heels and saved both himself and Zara from losing their jobs. It didn't hurt that her father was friends with Titus. It also didn't hurt that Titus had fond feelings for Conrad and wanted to keep him at Langley.

Zara was a doer and that's what Conrad liked. She didn't sit on her hands and analyze everything to death. She saw a chance and took it. She looked at a problem and figured out what she could do to solve it. She never said, "That's not my job," or looked the other way. Her inexperience at the farmhouse had in no way stopped her from taking a chance with Dmitri. She had balls the size of Texas and that was the first requirement to be a great spy. After all, he'd been the best in the field in recent years. He should know.

Zara Morgan was a Conrad Flynn in the making. *A Mini-Me.* Conrad smiled to himself.

Rocking his chair absentmindedly, he thought about Zara's future. He was already grooming her to rise high in the shark-infested waters of the CIA. If she could keep her wits about her on this mission and work in partnership with Vaughn, she had a real chance of becoming a senior case officer. Then he'd put her under Ryan Smith's tutelage in Europe and see how far his best friend and head of the European directorate could take her. With her black ops training, the terrorists didn't stand a chance.

Thinking about strong women, Conrad picked up his secure line and dialed his wife's cell number. When she answered, he told her, "I'll probably be going to Paris in a few days. Will you go with me?"

Julia's pause was brief. Her usually calm, collected voice took on a note of excitement. "Paris? I might be persuaded."

A former CIA operative and one of their top analysts, she now worked exclusively for the FBI. Lucky for him, she was in town for a training op and then she was off for a few days. He'd score points if he could whisk her off to Paris. She was fond of the place. "You, me, a bottle of champagne and that little B&B you love. It will be perfect."

"As long as there's shopping."

Conrad cringed, but said on a sigh, "Of course."

"Michael's okayed your leaving town?"

Not giving one good goddamn whether Michael Stone would agree to his leave or not, Conrad lied. "Of course."

Julia, of course, knew he was lying. "We'll talk about it tonight."

"Tonight." Conrad said goodbye with a smile on his face.

He was fond of Paris too.

~ ✧ ~

Geneva, Switzerland

Alexandrov Dmitri filled his lungs with crisp night air and leaned against the second-story balcony railing. After the sharp metallic smell of bars and the stench of doomed men, he fed on the fresh air like a vampire on blood.

His eyes followed the landscape, rising with the hills in the distance. The tips of the trees pointed like a forest of arrows at the belly of the late fall moon. He dropped his focus to the fleur-de-lis pattern on the wrought iron gate in the garden below the balcony, its pattern mimicking the tall evergreens. A smile formed on his lips and he took a cigarette from his inside jacket pocket and lit it. Like the moon, he was flaunting himself to the world, daring the poison arrows pointing at him to let loose and stop him. And like the moon, he hung just out of reach. With his latest transaction complete, he knew no one could touch him now.

His cell phone vibrated against his chest and he pulled it out, drawing deeply on his cigarette at the sound of the woman's voice on the other end. "You're marked."

Marked. He found he cared little. "What about the princess, does she know?"

"Yes."

Shifting the cigarette into the corner of his mouth, Dmitri breathed deeply again. No wonder the night air was so tantalizing—it carried the smell of fear. He fingered the slender gold chain wrapped around his wrist. "Good. And what is your employer doing about me?"

"Sending a two-person team to track you down."

"Only two?"

The woman snorted softly in his ear. "At this moment, you aren't even a blurb on the President's Daily Briefing memo."

Dmitri pulled the cigarette out of his mouth, exhaled and threw it into the garden below. "That will change one of these days quite soon."

"You'll like the man they're sending. He's found you before."

"Ah, him," Dmitri said and nodded at the moon. "I'm looking forward to our reunion. Who is assisting him?"

"The princess."

Dmitri fingered the chain again and thought of Zara Morgan's fragile throat. Imagined the feel of it under his fingers.

He could almost see her eyes bulging, feel the scrape of her fingernails on his face as she fought for her life. "I will enjoy that reunion as well."

Chapter Three

Fluid was the word that surfaced in Lawson's mind as he watched the woman glide toward him. Soft red silk flowed over every curve of her body like a quiet stream over polished rocks. She strolled through the busy terminal on matching red heels with the confidence of a pampered rich girl.

As she moved through the lines at the Air France counter, through the security check and then to the waiting area at the gate, she was noticed, admired and envied. Every man in the place, including Lawson, wondered what she looked like under the dress.

As comfortable in her own skin as she was in the second skin of the silk dress, she ignored the attention and sought out a quiet corner with an empty chair where she set her black and white satchel on the floor and sipped from her Starbuck's cup.

She now sat directly across from him, her eyes, so damned blue and intense, stared at him over the rim of the cup. Blonde curls feathered her face like delicate fingers, calling subtle attention to the classic cheekbones and tiny chin. Gone was the conservative suit she usually wore at Langley and in its place, the dress and four-inch heels. The change was uncanny. The attention she was drawing to herself, unnerving.

"Hello, Commander," she murmured from across the narrow aisle. Black lashes formed a protective screen over her eyes as she circled the rim of the cup with her finger. "I'm told you were assigned to be my partner."

Two seats down, a balding man in a powder blue suit lowered his *Washington Post* a half inch and stared at Zara with open interest. A college student in surfer shorts and an NYC T-shirt closed his cell phone and did the same. A nerve danced in Lawon's jaw even as he tamped down the heat stirring low in his stomach. What the hell was she doing? Had she lost her freakin' mind? Did *covert* mean anything to her?

He stood and pulled her out of her plastic airport seat. "Let's get you a drink."

She raised the Starbuck's cup to him along with her chin. "I have a drink."

He snatched the cup out of her hand and dunked it in a nearby garbage can. "I'll buy you another." Grabbing his carryon bag and hers with one hand, he took her by the elbow and steered her toward the nearest coffee bar with the other.

CNN flickered on a TV in the dimly lit bar. Midweek, international flights at that hour were few and the place was mostly empty. A businessman sat at one end of the bar, Bluetooth in his ear and a laptop taking up space beside his Perrier. A young mother feigning interest on the latest scandal in Washington flashing across the TV screen rocked a baby dressed in blue as she fed him a bottle.

Lawson scanned the room just like she did as she slipped into a corner booth. Catching the attention of a female employee working the counter, he held up two fingers. "Coffee," he said over the din of piped in music and the news. Light from the TV bounced off the clerk's multiple piercings as she gave him a seductive smile and a nod.

Zara had spoken to Lawson a total of two times since that morning in France. After handing Dmitri over to his second-in-command, Johnny Quick, Lawson had checked her over from head to toe. She'd tried to brush his physical assessment aside, but he'd been thorough, picking grass out of her hair with the same diligence he used to check her vital signs and examine her bruised rib cage. His gentle touch was in stark contrast to the powerfully hard look in his eyes. She knew that look. He was angry because she'd scared him.

While her fingers trembled, his were steady. While she blubbered incoherently from shock, Lawson remained businesslike. At least until it came time to hand her over to a medical doctor in Paris. If it was possible, his intensity ratcheted up a notch.

But he didn't talk to her, only to the doctor, as if she were a four-year-old. She should have cared, should have pushed him and his meticulous concern away, but due to the shock or the drugs or the feeling in her bones, she closed her eyes and let the wave of his vigilant duty take her under.

Back at Langley, during her reckoning period with Flynn, both he and Annette mentioned Lawson had discreetly checked up on her. But when Zara had come face-to-face with him in the halls of CIA Headquarters, he'd still been businesslike, reserved. He didn't seem like the type to seek out glory, but she wondered if he expected her to fall at his feet with gratitude or shower him with praise for saving her life. She'd tried to thank him, but for some reason the words wouldn't come. Each time she'd looked in his eyes, the rescue at the farmhouse flashed through her mind like a storm. If he had intercepted Dmitri five minutes sooner, she would have been saved from creating the distraction that shaved ten years off her life from pure fear.

The intercom above their heads announced a boarding call while Zara watched Lawson watch her. He reminded her of a chess piece with his strong chin, unsmiling mouth and detailed cheekbones. A knight carved out of stone.

Not a knight. A king. His features were exactly the way she remembered them, not to mention his eyes, the color of aged moss, which were now locked on hers. Energy hummed around him and her pulse danced under her skin as she tried to read his mind. Flynn's orders or not, she wasn't leaving the country to hunt down Dmitri with Lawson unless he passed her personal test.

He leaned over the table between them, his eyes snapping with controlled anger, and lowered his voice to a growl. "Didn't Flynn explain to you that tracking Dmitri is a *covert* operation?"

Point one to the commander. Zara fingered the bracelet on her left wrist, willing herself not to smile, and matched his lowered voice. "I don't need Director Flynn to explain anything to me concerning Alexandrov Dmitri. Having firsthand experience with the jerk, you can bet I know what I'm doing."

His attention dropped to the silk fabric clinging to the deep V of her cleavage. "That dress is like a matador's flag. Dmitri will spot us coming a mile away."

On purpose, she widened her eyes. "You don't like the dress?"

He loved the dress, she could tell. His gaze slipped over her arms and her cleavage again. She watched him wrestle with telling her the truth, and then she saw his expression change.

Whoa, not allowed. He cleared his throat, looked away and looked back. Again, his voice lowered, so much so, she could barely hear him. "The less attention we attract, the better."

Enjoying the fact her blatant sexuality could throw the king off his throne, she shrugged one shoulder. "Maybe, maybe not."

The woman behind the counter knocked on the top of the bar to gain Lawson's attention. "Order's up." The coffees sat side by side. She toyed with one of her earrings and eyed him with open interest as he paid her with crumpled bills from his pocket. He returned with the steaming cups in hand, seemingly oblivious to the attention.

"I prefer cappuccino," Zara said.

Lawson slipped into the booth and waited for the clerk to busy herself again before he spoke. "You want to tell me what you're up to?"

He wasn't one to play games. Her life as a spy was one continuous game, but she liked that he didn't want to play with her yet. She dropped the practiced innocence and the flirting, but kept her voice low so it wouldn't travel. "Come on, Lawson. I'm a spy. This is called subterfuge. Surely you're familiar with the term."

Sitting back in the booth, he crossed both arms over his sizable chest. In the diffused light of the table lamp, his hair reminded Zara of her mother's Russian sable cape. He smiled without the slightest hint of amusement. "Enlighten me, Miss Morgan."

After all they'd been through together, he never called her by her first name. "Dmitri and his group of thugs have disappeared with Vos Loo in tow. It's going to take something important to lure Dmitri out of his hiding place. Or maybe something less important, but equally challenging. A dare he feels confident enough he can pull off without getting caught."

Lawson continued to scan the bar as if paranoid someone was listening. "Dmitri won't surface for anything right now. Too much heat on him."

"I don't think so. He's got French authorities in his back pocket. If I know Dmitri, and I do, he's feeling pretty invincible right now."

She took a sip of her coffee and grimaced at the bitter taste. Her fingers rifled through several pink and blue sweetener packets in a plastic holder on the table before she selected one and dumped the contents of it in her coffee. In case the bartender glanced over, she smiled at Lawson, doing her best girlfriend impression. "He's outsmarted us, gained his freedom and acquired a new playmate who will net him more power and money than he's ever had before. He's in control of the gameboard and everybody knows it."

Lawson stared at her with his unwavering gaze and caught the gist of her plan. "You want to act as bait and get Dmitri to come after you."

Actually, it was the last thing she wanted to do, but Lawson didn't have to know that. "If he really believes he's untouchable, he might risk snatching me out from under everyone's noses just to see if he can. He doesn't like loose ends and he enjoys revenge. A lot."

"And what if Dmitri succeeds?" he said deadpan. "What if you flaunt yourself in front of him and he takes the bait?"

She looked him in the eye and flashed him a condescending smile. "You'll rescue me like you supposedly did the last time."

Lawson picked up his coffee. "Supposedly?"

"I rescued myself and we both know it."

He stopped the cup halfway to his mouth. "You almost took a bullet to the brain."

There it was. Lawson's version of the farmhouse incident. She hadn't talked about that night with anyone at the Agency but Flynn and Stone and yet the gossip around Langley always had Lawson rescuing her and getting all the credit for Tim's safe rescue as well. "But I didn't. I used my defensive skills and got away from him."

"You almost got Owens killed."

She willed her voice not to rise with emotion. "If you had been there sooner, I wouldn't have had to create a distraction. There wouldn't have been a farmhouse incident. I wouldn't have a reputation like I do now."

He set the cup down without drinking. "Pegasus was in position and ready for the takedown. Communications were the issue, not my team, and if you had waited a minute or two longer—"

"Tim would have been dead. I had to create a distraction but, just so you understand, I would *never* have let Dmitri kill Tim or force me to kill him. I had a plan. You just showed up before I put it in play. Your timing could use work."

Lawson didn't move a muscle but anger and disbelief emanated from every cell.

How does he do that? She fiddled with another pink packet and rushed on before he could ask her about the specifics of her nonexistent plan. "I doubt Dmitri's still in Paris. He's probably not even in France."

Lawson shifted gears with ease, sinking back in his seat with slow deliberation. His voice was still hard to hear, but now it was laced with curiosity. "Where else would he go? His home base has always been France."

A faceless voice announced another boarding call over their heads. "But Vos Loo's isn't. Del Hoffman and I did some research on Doc this afternoon. He's traveled a great deal and lived in several major European cities. Amsterdam, London, Geneva, Nice. He may still have private labs in some of his old stomping grounds. Even if he doesn't go back to one of those labs, he'll have to stay in an urban area for contacts and supplies."

Lawson tapped a thumb on his coffee cup, seeming to mull over her logic. "So instead of tracking Dmitri, we track Vos Loo. Check out his past haunts. He can't build a lab from scratch without supplies. We find out who his suppliers were in the past and see if he hits them again."

"Exactly." Zara nodded. He was passing her test with military-like efficiency. "Where Vos Loo is, Dmitri is."

"But for now, we start with Paris and we do it my way." He glanced at her cleavage again. "No matador tricks."

His way?

Before she could protest, he jabbed the table with his fingertip. "Once we're on the ground in France, we follow the French investigation and pick up our own leads. When we locate Dmitri and Vos Loo, I'll notify Director Flynn and we'll proceed as instructed. If Flynn and Stone want to apprehend the two terrorists, that will be my job, and my job only. Your job is to assist me with research and analysis. You can also help me with my French."

"Whoa." She held up a hand. "I'm in charge of this operation. You're assisting *me*."

"I'm the expert at tracking down criminals."

"But I—"

Lawson pointed his finger at her. "You're the spook.

Hoffman claims you're the expert on Dmitri in or out of Langley. He says you know more about Dmitri than him and Special Agent Newton combined."

"I do, and that's why—"

He shoved his coffee cup aside and her words with it. "You're also the only living person I've got with experience dealing with this asshole. Finding Dmitri won't be easy, even for me, but I can find him"—Lawson sliced his hand through the air and tapped the edge of it on the table—"here, where he is right now." He pointed a finger at her again. "You can figure out what he's doing and where he's going. That's why Flynn's got us working together."

Irritation, or possibly the coffee, burned a hole in Zara's stomach. "I'm perfectly capable of handling this mission on my own."

Lawson's face told her he thought differently. "My part of this mission is crucial to your success. Without me, you won't find Dmitri. We work as a team, we succeed. Either one of us goes off like a loose cannon, we fail." He paused as if to give his next words weight. "I expect your full cooperation."

While she silently seethed, she knew he was right. If she wanted to stop Dmitri, she had to find him first. If she wanted to return to the field full time, she had to make this partnership work. Flynn was counting on her. She wouldn't let him down.

Clenching her teeth to control her emotions, she glared at Lawson. "Awfully sure of yourself, aren't you, Vaughn?"

He didn't so much as blink. "I'm one hundred percent sure of myself."

The look in his eyes said he was less sure about her. Way less sure. He considered her reckless, and it galled her, but she had to let it go. For now.

Still she wondered...if he thought she was reckless and unfit to be his partner, why was he sitting across from her? "Why did you agree to this assignment?"

It was his turn to feign innocence. "I'm just a soldier following orders."

"Baloney. You're one of the government's special army. You don't partner up with rookie field operatives who have bad reputations."

He was quiet a second too long. "Your boss has absolute confidence in you."

41

There it was again, the part he left unsaid. "But you don't, because of the farmhouse incident."

The shift in his countenance was subtle—everything he did was subtle—yet she would guess her behavior in Paris wasn't the only thing causing him to doubt her abilities. The air around him, already charged with electricity, crackled. "Everyone working for the Agency has a rookie incident in their background. Most, however, are not pampered rich girls from the Upper East Side trying too hard to prove themselves in the real world."

Zara sucked in a breath. White-hot anger popped in her veins like fireworks. "Pampered rich girl?" She didn't bother to keep her voice lowered. "That's how you see me?"

Something flickered in his eyes. Amusement? Challenge? It rang in his voice too. "Flynn says you'll prove me wrong on this assignment."

"You're damn right I will." It was her turn to point a finger. "I take my job just as seriously as you do."

The intensity in his gaze, in his face, evaporated for a second. As if it was all in good fun, he smiled at her, for real this time. "Good."

Feeling like she'd been had, Zara glanced around the dimly lit bar, trying to regroup. The bartender once again watched Lawson with unabashed admiration. Zara made snake eyes at her. *Back off.*

Lawson sat silent, waiting. But for what? For Zara to laugh it off? Slap him on the back? Yell at him?

Flynn had trained her better. She could control her emotions just as effectively as Lawson. The cards were all out on the table, and at least now she knew how he worked, how he viewed everything.

*Pampered rich girl...*she'd show him. Forcing herself to close the door on that observation, she searched for a different subject. Glancing down at her bracelet, she remembered a question she'd meant to ask him. "I lost my gold chain that morning at the farmhouse. You didn't find it lying around, did you?"

Back to business, he shook his head and glanced at his watch. "Our plane will start boarding in twenty minutes. You need to change into something less"—he paused and scanned what he could see of her dress again—"memorable. Please tell me you have one of those conservative office suits with you."

Leaning forward like she was about to share a secret, she crooked her finger at him. Like a magnet drawn to steel, he responded, bringing his face a few inches from hers. His dark green eyes searched hers and her pulse kicked hard.

"For the record," she said, ignoring her pulse and making her voice sticky sweet, "in the real world no one tells me how to dress."

She was surprised to see him nod. "I'll remember that."

Reestablishing control was good. "Also for the record? The red dress was a test." She gestured toward her carryon.

Watching her rise, he handed her the bag and then grabbed his own. "A test?"

"You don't really think I *want* to attract the attention of a psychotically deranged man, do you?"

"You did it before."

Right. "Yeah, that's a pampered rich girl for you."

There was another one of his cryptic pauses. He shifted the carryon bags. "So did I pass?"

"Yes," she admitted. "That test you passed."

"*That* test? There's more to come?"

She smiled knowingly and left him standing there to wonder.

He followed her out of the bar and to the entrance of the women's restroom, laying a hand on her arm to stop her before she entered. When he spoke, he lowered his mouth to her ear. "From here on out, you need to be hyperaware of your surroundings. Make sure you know where every exit is and don't let yourself get backed into a corner. Pay attention to the people around you, and even when your pants are literally down, don't leave yourself open to an ambush. Got it?"

Zara almost laughed. Hadn't she survived the Farm, survived Dmitri and sailed through Flynn's special training? She leaned away from him. "Is this your James Bond mode?"

"I'm serious."

"So am I." She removed her arm from his grip. "Save the paranoia for Paris." Using her rear end, she pushed open the restroom door. "I know what I'm doing."

She didn't miss the slight narrowing of his eyes in disbelief.

Chapter Four

Once Zara disappeared into the restroom, Lawson pulled out his digitally encrypted cell phone and dialed up his favorite technical support dweeb. "You owe me twenty, Yankee," he drawled when Del Hoffman answered.

"She agreed?" The twenty-five-year-old snorted. "I can't believe Tango's partnered with you, Rebel."

"Flynn's orders, like it or not."

"Zara has Flynn wrapped around her pinky. You will be too, before you know it."

"Got a twenty says different."

"You're on."

"Meantime, hack into the personnel database and send me her Agency bio."

"That's classified. I'll get fired."

Lawson knew Del liked a challenge. "Only if Flynn catches you."

Del snickered. "What are you looking for?"

"Not sure. She's one of Flynn's army. I want to know everything there is to know about her."

"Everything you need to know about Zara you learned at the farmhouse."

That's what I'm afraid of. "Is her backstop identity ready?"

"Affirmative. Zara Morgan, aka Sara Lerner, is your stereotypical Paris Hilton clone, only way classier thanks to yours truly. I made her way smarter too. Harvard MBA, a few Trump-wannabe ex-lovers, and a weakness for—" His voice broke off. "Oh, yeah, Ding Dongs and Dom Pérignon."

In Lawson's mind, an image of Zara wearing nothing but her red shoes as she licked filling out of a Ding Dong caused the heat hibernating in his lower gut to flare to life. What he could do to her with a little champagne and chocolate...

He rolled his shoulders and shook off the image. This was business. He couldn't afford to get distracted. "Just be sure it's close enough to her real life so she doesn't forget something and screw up her cover accidentally."

"Jeez, Law, you sound like Flynn. Her cover will hold up to intense scrutiny and isn't that far off the mark. Even her first name is almost identical so she won't slip up. Besides, you forget who your new partner is. Tango's in a class by herself when it comes to this stuff."

A good reason to learn all he could about her. "I owe you, Hoffman."

"Yeah, no kidding. If Flynn finds out I hacked into personnel—"

"You're too good to let that happen." Lawson hoped that was true. He didn't want Del to lose his job. On the other hand, he never worked with an unknown. For all he knew about Zara, he didn't know enough, and that was a surefire way to die young. "If you get in trouble with Flynn over stuff you're doing for me, I'll take the heat for it."

Zara shook out the coffee-colored microfiber pants she had rolled up into the equivalent of a Tootsie Roll and examined them in the restroom stall. There were two articles of clothing she never traveled without—this pair of pants and her Prada Sport perforated-leather bomber jacket. The pants never wrinkled and the jacket, while no one believed it, folded down into a compact pancake and always looked great with anything she wore.

Slipping the pants and a white shirt on, she pushed away the nervousness that had been winding its way through her bloodstream since Annette had told her about Dmitri's release. She realized it wasn't just about proving herself to Flynn. The real reason she couldn't blow this assignment was Dmitri and Vos Loo. They were bona fide threats to the world at large. For the mother and child in the bar, as well as all the other innocent people who could be harmed, Zara had to stop them.

Slipping off her red heels, she traded them for a pair of low-heeled brown pumps. Giving her shirt a final smoothing, she shrugged on the bomber jacket, rolled up the red Prada dress—*forgive me, Miuccia*—and rearranged the items in her Kate Spade signature bag.

After leaving the stall, she stopped at the sink and examined her reflection in the mirror. She didn't look attention-getting anymore. A few more simple changes and she'd be a completely different person than the one who entered the restroom. She went to work on her face, brushing her hair out with her fingers and securing it behind her ears on both sides. After wiping off the red lipstick, she applied a flesh-tone gloss. Rummaging through her bag, she found her reading glasses and added them to her face. All in all, her appearance was much more understated and much less memorable. She'd certainly pass Lawson's critical eye now.

Even though he'd admonished her about the red dress, he'd had a hard time keeping his eyes off it, and that, Zara knew, gave her an advantage with her partner. He was going to be a challenge with his *I'm in charge* attitude, but he was a male. She knew how to use her feminine assets to gain the upper hand if necessary, and like any woman, knowing her physical attractiveness could make him do a double-take secretly pleased her.

The boarding call for her and Lawson's flight came over the speaker. Zara pulled her cell phone out of her bag and dialed quickly. Two minutes later, her call to Paris was complete, her plan in place. She would work with Lawson, stop Dmitri and prove to Flynn she was the best counterespionage spy he had, all in one operation. She was Zara Morgan, after all.

Smiling, she nodded at her image in the mirror. *Let's dance.*

Chapter Five

They were in the air less than an hour when Zara fell asleep beside him, an abbreviated dossier of Dmitri on her PDA. Lawson turned off the device and stuck it in his pocket. The faint smell of jasmine drifted up from her soft, warm body, catapulting him back to the summer nights of his childhood and the perfect white flowers blooming under a full southern moon outside his bedroom window.

His memory was a funny thing these days. His childhood friend Tucker was smiling and laughing beside the creek instead of sitting in his bedroom in a daze after the water snake's poison had caused permanent brain damage. Lawson's younger brother David was making tents in the woods with their father's old tarps instead of leaving their ramshackle house in a suit and tie for a job in the big city.

Drawing another deep breath of the jasmine into his nostrils, he deliberately closed the door on Georgia and the past and instead watched Zara's eyes move under her eyelids.

She was a wild child inside the pretty, tidy-looking package. A soft target under the polished shell exterior. And even after all he'd done for her, she still didn't like him.

That was too damn bad. Now that he'd made up his mind, he had a job to do and no one was going to stop him. He'd known women like her before and he knew how to handle them. Knew what fed their egos and busted their superior attitudes into a thousand jagged pieces. He knew how to look through the suit and the heels and the perfectly coiffed hair, find the crack in the shell and capitalize on it if necessary. Zara's crack had been easy to locate and he'd already sprung it wide open. *Pampered rich girl.*

Ignoring his physical attraction to her wasn't easy, but she *was* Zara Morgan. Born with a silver spoon in her mouth and accustomed to a lifestyle he could only imagine. What he knew about her world could be held in the heel of one of her red shoes. Even if they hadn't been working an operation together, she was so far out of his league he shouldn't even be looking at her, much less thinking about her in and out of that damned red dress.

Lawson could scale an installation and bypass any type of security known to man to get inside it. He could play MacGyver and build a radio from gum wrappers and duct tape. He could map out an escape route for a downed Army crew behind enemy lines or go in and rescue the men himself. But he didn't know a salad fork from a dinner fork or what type of wine you drank with fish. Hell, he didn't even drink wine. He drank beer, *Budweiser thank you very much*, and he drank it straight from the bottle.

He wasn't rich, cultured or Harvard educated. He was Lawson Vaughn, a soldier just like his daddy and his daddy before him.

Ignoring the in-flight movie, he hauled out his laptop and stretched one leg into the aisle of first class. Flynn wasn't expecting a progress report for a few more hours, but Lawson had nothing better to do than watch Zara sleep. God, he hated paperwork but it was imperative he keep Flynn happy and out of his hair. He'd swamp the head of the spy group with reports if that's what it took.

Plucking at the tiny keyboard, he tried to find the right keys to make coherent words. His deft fingers could crack a safe, communicate in code, sew stitches in skin to close a wound and find the exact spot that drove a willing woman right over the edge, but type a memo? Jesus, he'd rather be shot at sunrise.

He paused in his pecking and grimaced in frustration, scanning the keyboard for the key he needed. He had to use phrasing Flynn would like. Bullshit words and sentences that made it sound like there was a plan and the plan was being followed and these outcomes were expected. Yada, yada, yada. The more details the better.

He did have a plan, of course, and it wouldn't take a genius to implement it. Outcomes were more difficult to pin down because of the nature of the job, but they weren't impossible to hypothesize since he had quite a bit of experience in tracking people. This was the first time, however, his partner was not only inexperienced in his line of fieldwork but also a woman. There was nothing wrong with a female partner if she had the right training and experience and could detach her emotions from the job at hand. Flynn insisted Zara had the training, but she didn't have the experience, and Lawson had witnessed how a few simple words, or lack of, could trigger her emotions.

So why did I take this job? Why am I determined to play with fire?

Even though Flynn had strongly requested Lawson accompany his intelligence operative on this mission, Lawson could have said no. The halls of Langley were filled with men like him. The FBI, the CIA, the NSA—all of them had people as qualified as he was for a mission of this caliber.

He glanced at his new partner sleeping beside him, her dark eyelashes lying against her smooth skin, her lip gloss faded. The truth, he knew, wasn't anything grand or noble or listed in his current job description. It wasn't even based on his natural male attraction to Zara.

The truth, he forced himself to admit, was the one thing Conrad Flynn warned him not to fall prey to. The little boy from Georgia was all grown up now, but he still wanted to play Superman. Still wanted to save the innocent, rescue those in danger and make the bad guys eat dirt.

Turning back to his laptop, Lawson rubbed his eyes and typed three sentences, full of bullshit details, yes siree. Flynn would love it. He typed another sentence and glanced again at his partner.

As soon as he had her in Paris, he'd tuck her away in some quaint little dive and give her this part of the job to do. He'd load her down with paperwork and a bunch of other useless, but safe, jobs. As long as she was safe, Flynn would stay happy. As long as she was busy, she wouldn't get in his way.

He had a terrorist to hunt down and he didn't need Zara Morgan's *help* to do it.

Chapter Six

Lawson stared at the black car and the uniformed chauffeur waiting for them beside the curb in total disbelief. "What the hell is this?"

Zara greeted the chauffeur in rapid-fire French, and he nodded regally as he took her bag out of her hand. "*This* is a Mercedes Benz, Lawson," she said in that professional-suit voice she had. "I arranged transportation for us."

Gritting his teeth, he set his leather bag on the concrete and pulled Zara aside. "What did I tell you about this operation? Remember *covert*?"

She looked up into his eyes and smiled like a Cheshire cat. Like she enjoyed eating him one feather at a time. "Would you relax? I told you, I know what I'm doing."

This is another of her stupid tests. Out of the corner of his eye, he saw the chauffeur reach for his bag. "Don't touch that."

Maneuvering around Zara, he grabbed it himself. The chauffeur raised one haughty brow before giving a pert nod and stepping off the curb to shut the trunk of the car. Lawson returned to face Zara, hanging the strap of his bag on his shoulder. "This is *not* low profile."

She cast a glance around at the other travelers loading their luggage into taxis and private vehicles before bringing her gaze back to him. "The only thing attracting attention is you."

As the driver extended one hand to her, she stepped toward the car. In one graceful motion, she slid into the backseat, her legs disappearing from view as she glided across to the other side. The chauffeur turned to Lawson and raised his eyebrow again. "*Monsieur?*" His gloved hand directed Lawson to the backseat.

Lawson hiked the strap of the bag higher on his shoulder.

Men and women scurried past him, luggage, purses and children in tow, looking for shuttle buses or hailing taxis. No one appeared to be paying them any attention, and why should they? In Paris, as in most international communities, climbing into the back of classic Mercedes to be chauffeured around the city was as second nature as brushing one's teeth.

If the CIA had taught him anything, it was that there was *always* someone watching. His best move was to follow Zara's lead for the moment. Shifting his bag again and reining in his impatience, he nodded to the driver and dropped onto the gray leather seat next to her. He set the bag on his lap and blew out a controlled breath.

She flashed him a triumphant smile. "There, that wasn't so hard, was it? Albert will have at us at the hotel in about forty-five minutes."

If Zara had hired a car like this with its own driver just to take them across town, Lawson knew he wouldn't like the lodging she had arranged. "And which hotel would that be?"

Albert slid into the driver's seat and put the car in drive while catching Zara's eye in the rearview mirror. She nodded at him. "*L'Hotel Ambassador.*"

A muscle twitched between Lawson's shoulders. This was definitely a test. "The Ambassador," he repeated as the driver maneuvered the car into the busy airport traffic with ease. "You booked us into a four-star hotel?"

"Well, of course." Her tone suggested he'd lost brain cells in the air. "Where did you expect me to stay when I'm in Paris?" She cast a quick glance at his face, turned to her window. "The George V is luxurious but it isn't the same since they remodeled it. Besides, you'll love the Ambassador. It's decorated in vintage 1920's art deco and their restaurant has the best espresso in the whole world."

Lawson tightened the grip he had on his bag and lowered his voice. "Did you register under your real name?"

Zara lowered her voice to match his. "We're registered at the Ambassador under Sara and Isaac Lerner, the brother and sister team Annette set up. We're in Paris looking to expand our American security business. I arranged separate suites joined by a door. Kitchenettes and king-size beds, but no whirlpool tubs." She glanced at him again and held his gaze. "I wouldn't want you to get too comfortable and enjoy yourself."

He forced his attention away from her teasing baby blues to look out the tinted windows of the Mercedes. She was playing him big time. He would put a stop to it, but not in front of the driver.

Zara touched his hand where it gripped the bag, and he swung his attention back to her face. The eyes were wide again, the smile practiced. She knew she was causing him internal turmoil and she was enjoying it. "I've got everything under control."

That's what scared him.

L'Hotel Ambassador du Paris

Sometimes it was nice to have money, Zara decided as she pulled the sheer shower curtain partially around the claw-footed tub and sank down into the hot water. She released her breath and sighed. The water was infused with avocado and lemon bath crystals, and she drew the brisk scent deep into her lungs hoping the refreshing smell would perk her up. The past fifteen hours had yielded little sleep and an overdose of adrenaline. She'd plunged herself back into the world of espionage, and the thrill screamed through her nerve endings like a roller-coaster ride.

As she leaned her head back against the bath pillow, she let her feet float. Her pink toenails bobbed above the water. She'd made it to Paris, gotten herself and Lawson checked in, deposited him in the suite next door and unpacked the few essentials she'd brought from her travel bag. Then, out of Flynn-ingrained, paranoia-induced habit, she'd double-checked the window locks and even looked under the bed. Lawson might not give her credit for being a good spook, but she was. He'd learn that soon enough.

Once her room check was complete, she'd washed out the microfiber pants and her panties in the sink. They were now hanging over the shower curtain above her head to dry.

Before the showdown at the farmhouse, Paris had been like her second home. It had seduced her with its style, its art and its history. Even now, the city wove a spell around her with its clashing mix of vintage and modern, the smell of fresh pastries and musty museums, and the clichéd air of promised romance. The naysayers could be damned in Zara's book. Paris was still the most dramatic and seductive city in the world.

So even with her heart pounding at the thought of being so close again to Alexandrov Dmitri, she had moved from airplane to car to hotel as though she owned the world. With the grace her mother had instilled in her. With her chin up and an air of self-confidence that at moments was completely faked. As usual, it had worked like a charm. No one questioned her, doubted her or called her bluff.

Except Lawson. He'd kept his mouth shut during the drive to the hotel and the check-in, but his silence and clenched jaw spoke volumes. She might be a natural blonde but she wasn't stupid. Her partner was wound tight and he didn't like her tests one little bit.

Zara dialed up Tchaikovsky on her iPod and stuck the ear buds in her ears. She cupped her hands and pulled the warm water toward her chest. Back at Langley, she'd found out a few things about her rescuer through the Agency grapevine. Annette had told her stories about successful rescues and extractions attributed to his Pegasus team, but it was Lawson who got the most acclaim. According to Annette, he was a quiet, competent, loyal warrior who always got his man.

Or woman.

Watching a drop of water fall from the gold-plated faucet, Zara hummed along with the music in her ears. Once he let go of his pseudo-spy complex and realized they were safe, he'd be okay with everything. After all, what human being in his right mind would refuse a night at the Ambassador?

The rooms were stylishly decorated, comfortable and conveniently connected. She and Lawson could come and go from each other's rooms without anyone seeing them and it made sense Isaac and Sara Lerner, the owners of a successful security consulting business, would stay in an upscale hotel.

Yes, she was sure once Lawson had a chance to rest up, he would realize the Ambassador was the perfect place for them to stay while they figured out what Dmitri was up to. Along with that, she hoped he would also realize what an asset she was to the Agency. Not that she cared what Lawson thought, but the desire to prove to him she wasn't going to let Director Flynn down sat like a rock in her chest. She knew this world as well as any and could take care of the behind-the-scenes details like accommodations and transportation *and* help Lawson track down Dmitri.

Zara smiled and closed her eyes. Once Lawson saw her in action, this partner thing was going to work out just fine.

Chapter Seven

This partner thing was not going to work out.

Lawson paced the pale gray carpet of his suite—she'd reserved freakin' *suites*—and cursed himself for being such an idiot. Flynn could spout Farm skill and achievements all he wanted, but Zara didn't understand the first thing about clandestine operations. From the moment he saw her jump the ditch at the farmhouse on her Ducati, he'd known she was an in-your-face type, not a smooth undercover operative. You didn't sashay into town, throw a bunch of money around and call dubious attention to yourself, unless that was the intended cover. Which it never was, because, contrary to Hollywood's propaganda, playing James Bond wasn't cool, it was deadly.

Running a hand over his face and through his buzzed hair, he looked around the suite again. The Ambassador was a nice place. Way too nice for someone like him. Everything from the funky wallpaper to the oddly shaped blond furniture made him squirm. He wouldn't know Retro from Victorian when it came to decorating, unless it was something straight out of the eighties. Even then, if it didn't look like it belonged in a college dormitory or his mother's house where everything had country geese on it, he was screwed.

Pacing into the kitchen area of the suite, he pulled a bottled water out of the tiny refrigerator. Good God there was even a miniature two-burner stove along with everything else. A microwave, coffee maker and some contraption that looked like a juice machine.

He tipped his head back and drank half the bottle in a couple of gulps. All this...*stuff*. It was enough to give him a headache.

Over the past ten years, he'd practically existed on MREs, meal-ready-to-eat hash, and slept more often than not on the ground. Which was pretty much the way he liked it. None of this pansy-assed *stuff* for him. He was a soldier through and through. The tougher the conditions, the more uncomfortable the surroundings, the better he liked it. Got him in touch with his inner self in a way nothing else could, and he was proud of that. Jimmy and the rest of Pegasus would piss their pants laughing if they saw him drinking Evian water and lounging in any hotel, much less the Am*freaking*bassador in Paris.

Lawson finished the water and threw the empty bottle in the sink. Enough with Zara's silly tests and hotshot attitude. He had to get her straightened out. Even with their cover identities, they had to leave this place and find something more suitable. He had to make her understand their success depended on her following his instructions, not going off on her own.

First he needed to arm himself. In his line of work, walking around without his gun was like walking around with an arm missing.

He grabbed his bag and retrieved a Nintendo DS, a hairdryer and an electric razor. Within a minute, he had recovered all the parts to his Beretta from their secret hiding places. Another minute and the gun was reassembled and loaded.

A man in his position couldn't be too careful. He never traveled commercial flights armed. It called too much attention to him and wasn't worth the effort. But he always had his gun's components in his carryon, within easy reach and at his immediate disposal. The stricter airport security measures now in place didn't faze him in the least. One of the best things about the Agency was its techno geeks. Those guys spent thousands of hours figuring out ways to hide weapons in plain view—the closest thing to James Bond Lawson had witnessed during the past year of contracting with the CIA.

Under normal circumstances, he would have assembled the gun in the car when he and Zara left the airport. He hated riding through Paris unarmed, but the chauffeur deal had thrown him a curve ball. He wasn't about to sit in the backseat and put a gun together with Albert as witness.

Lawson stuck the gun in the waistband of his jeans at his back. Then he reassembled the dryer and DS and threw both back in his bag. He passed the super-sized bed and knocked on the suite's connecting door. His side was unlocked, the security chain dangling.

"Za—" He checked himself. She was Sara now. Setting his hand on the doorknob, he called her by her cover name. "Sara?" When she didn't answer, he knocked again, sharper this time. "Sara?"

Still no answer. The spot between his shoulder blades twitched. Not a lot, but a definite twinge.

Probably she was just in the shower and couldn't hear his knock or his call. Still, he removed the gun from its hiding place at the small of his back and angled his body against the door, listening for any sounds on the other side. Paranoia was entrenched in his system and Lawson swore by it. So far it had never failed to keep him alive.

Turning the doorknob with slow precision, he was both relieved and annoyed to find it unlocked from the other side. Besides setting Zara straight about her role in the op, he needed to give her a lesson in security procedures. He moved with natural stealth and a moment later was standing next to her bed. The whole suite was a mirror image of his room.

The contents of Zara's carryon, with the exception of the red dress, were sitting in a haphazard pile on the end of the bed. Lawson's brain automatically logged everything. Wallet and passport, three lipsticks, travel-size bottles of shampoo and conditioner, cell phone. Several pairs of lacy underwear and a slip of a nightgown. Other miscellanea including breath mints, antiseptic hand cleaner, two paperbacks, a hairbrush and a nightlight.

The red dress was neatly pressed out on the other side of the bed. The matching shoes stood side by side in the closet, while the black shoes had been discarded nearby on the floor, one lying on its side.

Lawson checked the door to the hallway and found it locked, the security chain in place. *Good girl.* At least she got that part right. Next he checked the windows. They were locked and intact. He let out the breath he'd unknowingly been holding.

As some of the tension left his body, he crossed the living room area and pulled up short at the bathroom door. It was partially open and he listened for sounds. No shower, flushing toilet or running hair dryer. No noise at all. Zara had to be in there, but why the hell wasn't she answering him?

Leaning closer to the door, he tried to pick up the sound of movement. After listening for a full minute, he still didn't hear a thing. As the faint smell of something citrusy filtered to his nose, he called to her again and tapped his knuckles on the bathroom door. "Sara?"

Silence.

Damn, he had to make sure she was all right. Holding his gun up and ready, he pushed the door open in a slow arc.

Like a magnet, the bathtub drew his eyes. A sheer shower curtain fell from a gold-plated oval rod and partially obscured his view. The tub was a large cast iron claw-foot, deep and flared around the edges, much like the one he and his brothers and sisters had bathed in as children, sometimes all five fitting in the big tub at once.

Light from the wall sconces bounced off the gold-plated fixtures and Lawson noted Zara's pants and a pair of red lacy panties hanging from the shower curtain rod. Red. His brain stuttered for a split second before he catalogued the panties for further thought later. As he took another step into the room, he tilted his head to peek into the tub, an odd mixture of concern and fear driving him. Had she indeed fallen and knocked herself unconscious?

The first thing he saw was her left foot propped at the end near the faucets. His eyes traveled from her pink toenails up the length of her shin and to her bent knee. Her skin looked tan against the bright white of the bathtub porcelain. "Sara, are you okay?"

She didn't move, didn't respond. He took a step closer and followed the line of her thigh to the point where it broke the surface of the water. Her other leg and stomach were under the two feet of water in the tub and his eyes automatically jumped to the point where her chest rose back out of the water.

His attention paused, but only for a second, adding another element to his catalogue to review later. He forced his gaze up to Zara's face.

Her head was on a satin bath pillow, her chin tilted down into her collarbone, her eyes closed and her lips parted. An iPod lay on a stack of towels behind her head, ear buds disappearing under her hair. One of her hands rested on her chest, the other was in the water on her stomach. The rhythmic rise and fall of her chest made the twitch in his shoulders relax. She was asleep.

Jet lag was a bitch for most people. Zara had logged less than an hour of sleep on the plane. She was now dead to the world with music playing in her ears. No wonder she hadn't heard him call her name or knock on her door. He replaced the Beretta in his waistband and crossed his arms over his chest.

The steam from the water had relaxed her curls and several hung over her forehead. Her face in sleep looked years younger, almost girlish. If it wasn't for the curves and muscles below that face...

As his eyes fell to her breasts, his brain yelled at him like a drill sergeant. *Get out!*

He pulled himself up short but not before his groin tightened.

The iPod's screen lit up for a second and then blacked out as it shut off. Lawson turned to escape and the floor creaked under his foot.

A sigh escaped from Zara's open lips and he froze. The hand on her chest slid down past her breast and into the water. She shifted her body, raising her chin and bunching up her shoulders.

And then she opened her eyes and looked straight at him.

"Oh, my God." She sucked in her breath. Instinct made her cover her breasts as she sat straight up. One ear bud fell out.

Averting his eyes, he mentally cursed himself. "You fell asleep in the bathtub. I knocked and called your name several times but you didn't answer."

Why did that sound so lame? He chanced a quick glance at her face and saw her eyes were huge. The look she gave him set off a warning in his brain. It wasn't modesty or even disgust. She looked at him as though he were some asshole about to do her harm.

She pulled the other ear bud out, and he backed toward the door, damning himself again for entering the room in the first place. "Must be serious jet lag that had you sleeping so hard. That and the music."

The look of fear vanished with the blink of her eyes. She snugged her knees to her chest and wrapped her arms around them, clearing her throat. "Jet lag. Yep. Knocks me for a loop every time."

"It does a lot of people."

"Yes, well, I appreciate your concern, but as you can see, I'm all right. Naked and embarrassed, but all right. Could we dispense with further conversation until after I get some clothes on?"

He jerked his gaze away from hers and again pinned it to a spot on the far wall. Back to business seemed like the course to take. "We need to discuss my op plan for the next twenty-four hours. When you're dressed, come to my room."

Without waiting for any reply, he walked out.

Well, wasn't that too weird for words? Zara shook her head and tried not to laugh from nervous embarrassment.

Dread, shadowy but keen, had quivered in her veins for long seconds before she'd snapped out of her sleep-induced confusion and realized Lawson was standing over the tub and not the terrorist from her nightmares. Still, waking up to Lawson's presence in her bathroom wasn't exactly pleasant either. Startling, yes. Pleasant, no.

Being a dancer, she'd grown up with her body on display, and, like all athletes, understood how important her body structure was to her success. In ballet, the lithe, agile body of a ballerina was the focus. From the top of her head, literally, to the tip of her toes and fingers, a ballerina's every movement was observed with a critical eye.

Lawson had obviously gotten an eyeful, but his intense attention had shown none of the desire she'd seen in the airport bar, more like a touch of concern and a boatload of irritation.

Angry, just like he'd been at the farmhouse, the airport and on the drive there.

A cold chill shook her body, and she massaged her stiff neck. She didn't doubt his reasoning for being in there. The jet lag had definitely zonked her out and she could well imagine his concern when she didn't answer his calls. She only wished she could have fallen into that wonderful sleep in bed instead of in the tub, avoiding her stiff neck and keeping her modesty intact.

As she pushed herself out of the bathtub, she reached for a plush Egyptian cotton towel from the towel warmer and dried herself with brisk strokes. Grabbing another, she wrapped that one around her and drained the tub. He could be angry all he wanted, but he'd soon find it didn't help their mission. If he wanted to wrap up this assignment quickly, he'd need to focus on something besides staying aggravated at her.

A new thought made her straighten up. Maybe she'd make him so mad, he'd quit as soon as he located Dmitri. Then she'd finish the op all by herself.

A grin tugged at her mouth, even as her stomach did a nervous hop. Stopping Dmitri alone could bring her the glory she craved. It could also bring her face-to-face with her own mortality again.

In the adjacent room, she slipped off the towel and smoothed expensive collagen cream over every inch of her body, including her face. For now, she had to string Lawson along. Once he located Dmitri, however, all bets were off. She'd play it by ear and when the time was right decide if she should continue on alone.

And when the job was over, she'd have to find time to stop by Dr. Messine's shop and pick up another bottle or two of the expensive cream.

After brushing her hair, she donned a pair of underwear, a T-shirt and one of the hotel's lush robes. She finished up with a layer of lip gloss and slipped her cell phone into the pocket of the robe.

With nothing left to do but go see Lawson, she snugged the robe's belt a little tighter. It was too late to be embarrassed about him seeing her naked in the tub. She just hoped she hadn't been snoring.

Chapter Eight

Geneva, Switzerland

"They landed in Paris two hours ago."

Dmitri took the cell phone away from his ear, folded his royal flush and left his men to their pot of bullets. On his way down the hall, he passed the office where Jon Vos Loo bent over a small black notebook. The little weasel of a scientist was taciturn, but at least he was quiet.

Continuing down the hallway, Dmitri turned into the spacious and well-equipped private gym, empty at this hour. He closed the heavy door behind him and sat on one of the weight benches. "Where are they?"

The woman's voice was edged with impatience. "The Ambassador. The man is meeting Yvette Lemans to start the investigation."

Dmitri's mind raced with all the possibilities before him and stopped at the most tantalizing. "I have been waiting for this."

"I'll update you as much as possible. Things are a close hold here."

Dmitri grunted, ended the call and placed another. "I have a job for you," he said to the woman on the other end.

Varina Scalfaro released an exaggerated sigh. "You're beginning to annoy me."

Dmitri tsked at her as he stood and crossed to the gym's mirrored wall. He examined his image in it, enjoying the way the muscles in his naked chest flexed with his movements. "You'll like this job."

There was a long pause. "It will cost you."

He ran a hand through his hair and saw the 18 karat gold chain wrapped around his wrist catch the light. He twisted his wrist back and forth, watching the reflection. "Name your price."

Lawson was bent over a map spread out on his bed and talking to someone on his cell phone when Zara entered the room. He raised his head, looked her over from head to toe, and then went back to his map.

Feeling dismissed, she wandered to the desk in the corner of the suite and picked up the room-service menu. She was hungry and she bet he was too. Scanning the menu, she made a simple list. Toast, some eggs, a couple of pastries, juice and coffee. Using the hotel phone, she dialed the front desk.

A minute later, she hung up and turned to find him glaring at her. "What are you doing?"

She tucked the room-service menu into the top desk drawer and ignored the demanding tone of his voice. "I ordered food. I'm starving and figured it would be safer to eat here at the hotel than go out."

His hands went to either side of his waist and he took several steps toward her. Then he pulled the chair out from the desk and motioned her into it.

She knew what was coming from the look in his eye. She stayed standing.

He crossed his arms over his chest. "We need to get a couple of things straight. First, we can't stay in this hotel. It's not Agency-approved and it's goddamned expensive to boot. Flynn will cut my balls off if I turn in an expense report with a freakin' four-star hotel on it." His hands went back to his waist as he paced to the bed. "Secondly, you have to quit going off on your own and doing shit like this—making hotel reservations, hiring chauffeured cars—hell, you might as well put that red dress back on, climb the Eiffel Tower and shout, 'Here I am, Alexandrov. Look at me.' You're advertising yourself and our mission. Not smart."

Zara's spine stiffened. She was growing increasingly tired of his attitude. "Put your ego on chill mode for a minute," she said, keeping her voice even. "I'm paying for the room and Albert is one of my father's Paris employees who are well compensated for their discretion."

Facing her, Lawson planted his feet. "Yeah, well, in case they didn't teach you this in Spying 101, this"—he motioned around the room—"is not how you run a successful undercover operation."

She bit the inside of her cheek to curb the tart reply on the end of her tongue. It came out anyway. "The name of the class is Introduction to Covert Ops, not Spying 101."

"Smartass."

"Comes with the territory."

She saw the flicker of something in his eyes, just like she'd seen at the airport. Amusement again? She had to keep the upper hand, but how?

So far, he'd been a logical guy, so she'd give him logic. "As owners of a successful security consulting business, I hardly think Isaac and Sara Lerner would stay in the equivalent of a Motel 6 and hire a taxi to tool around town in."

"That's not the point." He paced forward and towered over her. "One undercover assignment does not make you an expert in this kind of operation. Your inexperience could get us killed. From this moment on, I call the shots. With everything. No exceptions. You don't so much as take a piss without my okay. Got it?"

Oh she got it all right. Staring up into his eyes, she got his meaning—he wanted her to feel intimidated. Well, to hell with that. She'd grown up with Charles Morgan for a father. She'd trained under Conrad Flynn. She knew how to handle overbearing men. Pushing herself up to her toes, she glared back at him, doing her darnedest to look intimidating right back.

Which of course was hard to do since Lawson stood almost six inches taller than her, and she had to crane her neck even on tiptoe just to look him in the eye.

Planting her fists on her hips in a mocking gesture, she stood her ground. "Newsflash. You may be the expert at undercover ops, but I'm the expert on Paris and Alexandrov Dmitri. You said it yourself at the airport. Your French sucks. I'm the one who can read the street signs, the menus and the newspapers, and I'm staying here at the Ambassador for the next twenty-four hours *at least* so I can recoup from the plane ride, eat a decent meal and shop for some appropriate clothes for Sara Lerner. If you don't like that, you can get yourself another partner. And if Director Flynn doesn't like it, he can fire me and then he can kiss my pampered, rich girl derriere all the way back to the United States."

She took a breath, dropped back down to her flat feet. "At which time I will personally call in a favor from my friends in Washington and stop Flynn's forward career path in its tracks before he can say 'I Spy'."

Lawson looked down his nose at her for a long moment and then dismissed her show of bravado with a soft chuckle. "You could do that? Wreck Flynn's career with a phone call?"

Of course not. Flynn was the King of Operations. He was the *God* of Operations. Titus Allen, the DCI and her father's closest friend, was Conrad Flynn's biggest fan.

"Of course," she lied.

Lawson now looked at her with curiosity. "I like the good Director. I respect him."

"I do too." She gave him a pert nod. "So let's not go there."

A knock came from the door and Lawson went into business mode again, removing a gun from his waistband. She watched bemused as he crossed the room like a SWAT officer moving in for the kill. A bellman in the hall called out "room service" in French and Lawson checked the peephole before moving off to the side of the door.

She reached for the door knob, sending him an annoying look. "It's just our food."

He grabbed her wrist, his fingers a band of steel. "Tell them to leave it in the hallway."

This constant paranoia was too much. She jerked her arm out of his grasp. "What about his tip?"

"You can add it to the bill when we check out."

"*Mon Dieu*," she murmured. Shaking her head, she called out Lawson's instructions to the waiter. Through the peephole, she saw the man walk off, mumbling and cursing about *les américains stupide.* Zara didn't blame him.

She slipped the deadbolt off the door. "He's gone. You can quit with the Mel Gibson thing."

Lawson lowered the gun to this side. "What?"

Rolling the cart into the room, Zara inhaled the smell of steaming espresso and freshly baked croissants. *Ahhh...*

"You know." She lifted the lid off one of the blue and white china plates. Her mouth salivated at the sight of the fluffy yellow eggs underneath it. She glanced at Lawson's gun. "*Lethal Weapon?*"

He slid the gun into the waistband of his jeans and relocked the door. "I was going for Clint Eastwood."

Surprised he might actually have a sense of humor, she snorted and handed him a cup of coffee. "You are so *not* Clint Eastwood."

Lawson took the cup from her and sipped. "I think you're trying to bruise my ego."

Rolling her eyes, Zara began shifting the room-service plates, napkins and silverware to the breakfast bar. "Let's eat before the eggs get cold. You can fill me in on the...what did you call it? The op plan?"

"Operational plan." He followed her to the bar and straddled a stool. "It's a blueprint for our mission."

Sometimes playing the dumb blonde came in handy. It made people relax and she knew if she was actually going to get out of the hotel room and do some terrorist hunting, she had to get her *partner* to do some serious relaxing. Fast. She had her own op plan. Feed him, make him laugh, and play up to his alpha ego.

"Dun dun dun dun dun dun dun dun," she started humming as she slid up on a barstool next to him.

He quizzed her with a look.

"What?" she said. "Isn't this where I start humming the *Mission: Impossible* theme song?"

"James Bond, *Lethal Weapon*, *Mission: Impossible*. What are you, the spook of pop culture?" A faint smile moved the line of his lips before he scooped up a mouthful of scrambled eggs. "I've already been in contact with our source here in Paris. I'm meeting with her in a couple hours to see what she's got on the prison break and the French investigation."

"Her?" Zara chewed a bite of toast. "Okay. I've got some questions for *her*."

Lawson swallowed. "You stay here and work on getting us a couple of rooms at a cheaper hotel. I'll handle the source."

Yeah, she'd get right on that. Checking herself before she lipped off again, she set her toast down and wiped the corners of her mouth with her napkin. "You're not taking me to meet this source? I thought we established *I'm* the expert in this

Lawson continued to shovel eggs into his mouth. "The source doesn't know you're here and that's the way I plan to keep it. She can give me what she's got and I'll bring it back to you."

Exasperated, Zara picked up her coffee cup and cradled it near her chest. She turned her barstool an inch and watched Lawson finish his eggs. There was no way she was getting left behind. "Your French obviously stinks. What if you can't read the street signs and get lost?"

"I don't get lost."

"Never?"

Lawson shifted to face her and their knees touched. "No. Never."

Zara felt a flutter low in her stomach. He was so sure of himself. It was annoying and yet sexy at the same time. *Play up to his ego.* "That's impressive."

"One of my many skills." His gaze dropped to her lips for a split second before looking away. A slow smile spread across his face as he picked up a piece of croissant.

Lawson Vaughn flirting with her? No way. Yet, she knew it for what it was and immediately suspected he might be trying to play her as much as she was trying to play him.

What exactly made him tick under his well-developed tough-guy exterior? He had a core made up of honor and responsibility, strength and courage. She'd seen all that in person. But what about the rest?

Dropping her gaze, she eased the barstool so she was again facing her plate. She set the coffee down and picked up the piece of toast. "Your family must be very proud of you."

Out of the corner of her eye, she saw him shrug. "I don't see them much. My brother David died in the towers on nine-eleven. My dad lost his fight with cancer about five years ago and since then, my siblings and I have drifted apart. We all love our mother, but it seems like Dad was the glue holding the family together after David was killed."

Zara's throat tightened around the toast she tried to swallow. A sick feeling settled in her stomach. "I'm so sorry. That must have been terrible for all of you to lose them both so tragically."

Lawson was silent for several seconds and she stole a

67

glance at him. A muscle danced in his jaw.

"Mom took it hardest. Both David and Dad." He cleared his throat and sipped his coffee. "When Dad was diagnosed with the Big C, she quit her job to be with him and help him fight it. She put all her energy into keeping him alive and then, later, into keeping him comfortable."

"She must have loved your dad very much."

"After he died, she didn't know what to do with herself, and she was thousands of dollars in debt from his medical bills the insurance company wouldn't pay. We kids had to pitch in and help her out. I'm the oldest so I took over getting the bills paid off. My youngest sister got her an apartment and a job working part-time at a local grocery store. The others do what they can, helping with her living expenses and getting her to the doctor to keep her diabetes in check. She's only sixty-three years old, but you'd think she was eighty."

Lawson tossed the last of his coffee into his mouth and swallowed it. "'Two peas in a pod', she used to say."

He left his stool to grab the plate of croissants and the coffeepot. After bringing both back to the bar, he set the plate down and refilled Zara's cup along with his own before straddling his barstool again. "You're right about the coffee. It's pretty damned good."

The seriousness of the moment was gone. Zara took one of the sweet pastries drizzled with glaze and bit into it, letting him change the direction of the conversation at his own pace. She knew it wasn't always an easy thing to talk about your family. Wiping her lips with her napkin, she said, "How many siblings do you have?"

"Two sisters, another brother besides David."

"Four siblings. What was that like growing up?"

Lawson grinned. "Tiring. Being the oldest, I had to run after the younger ones all the time. They were always getting into something they shouldn't have been and fighting with each other. Drove me crazy."

"Good experience for raising your own kids."

Lawson shook his head. "Nah. I've done my parenting gig for this lifetime."

"You don't want to have kids?"

"No."

"Never?"

He shook his head and took a bite out of a croissant. "Never."

At the height of her parents' fighting, she'd vowed never to have kids either. She'd been eight. In later years, however, when she saw her mother and father holding hands at a fundraiser or drinking coffee on the veranda of their condo, she reconsidered her decision. But only briefly in those moments when her parents appeared at peace with each other after so many years. Deep inside her, she'd always believed it was her fault they'd fought the way they had. Even as an adult, she still believed it.

Lawson drained his cup again and stood. "I'm going to jump in the shower and try to catch some sleep before I meet with our source."

Zara pushed her plate back. She had a few things to do before she tailed him. "Okay," she said in her most complacent voice as she slid off her own barstool. "I'll put this outside for maid service."

"Don't let me chase you off. Finish your breakfast."

She stacked Lawson's plate on top of hers. "I'm done."

"You should get some sleep too." He took the plates out of her hands, set them on the cart and turned back to her. "This time use the bed though, okay?"

She gave him a *ha-ha* smile and picked up the coffee cups. "You've got no sense of adventure, Clint."

His smile held a hint of warmth. "I love adventure. The only thing sleeping in the tub gets you is a sore neck. That's not adventure." Moving toward the bathroom, he stripped off his shirt and threw it on the nearby loveseat. Zara's pulse jumped. "Go get some rest, spook."

Rest, right. Setting the cups on the cart, she let her eyes move over his back as he walked away from her. Wide shoulders, defined muscles, and the indent of his back where his gun was still secured, all perfect. She watched until he disappeared behind the bathroom door, and then she stared at the door for another minute. When the sound of the shower slipped under the crack in the door, she pulled out her cell phone and started typing a text message.

The bathroom door cracked open and Lawson's head popped out. "Be sure to lock your side of the door."

Zara jumped, dropping the phone into the cups and plates. She shuffled them in a futile attempt to look busy. Then she checked herself. "You mean the door between our rooms?"

Lawson nodded, and she said, "Why?"

"For a security consultant, you suck." Humor flashed in his eyes.

"*Security,* right." Zara gave him a thumbs up. "But what if you want to visit and I have the door locked?"

"It won't stop me."

Zara called up the dumb-blonde persona again. "It won't?"

"No. In fact, it won't really stop anyone, but it will slow them down long enough for you to reach your gun."

"I don't have a gun yet. Flynn made me leave mine behind. I'll need to secure a new one here in Paris."

"I'll get you one."

How nice of him to offer. "I'll do it myself, thanks. I prefer small ones. Subcompact so they'll fit in my handbag. I'm thinking a SIG Sauer would be good."

"You could fit a machine gun in your bag." He laughed as he pulled his head in and closed the door.

Zara smiled to herself and fished out her phone. She'd fed Lawson, let him think he was in charge and got him to relax and tell her a little about his family. She'd even made him laugh. She just hadn't gotten him to change his mind about staying at the Ambassador or to relent and take her with him to meet the source.

She rubbed the back of her neck and shot a glance at the bathroom door again. No big deal. Her fingers flew over the keys of her phone. She'd just revise her op plan.

Because no one could stop her from enjoying at least one night at the Ambassador, and no one could stop her from doing the job Director Flynn had sent her to do.

No one. Not even the skilled rescue hero Lawson Vaughn.

Chapter Nine

Café Toulouse, Rue Marbeuf

"*Darling,*" the woman said, gliding toward Lawson with her arms extended. She had waist-length black hair, dark skin and perfect red lips. He had no choice but to accept her embrace which included her lips skimming each of his cheeks. Yvette LeMans took his arm, her ample bust pressing into it, and led him through the busy pub to a small table in the back. If anyone was watching, they would think he was a lover she was trying to keep secret.

"What of the security business, Isaac?" she asked as if interested. "Quite profitable these days, no? Americans scared of their own shadows?" She laughed low in her throat and smiled up at him. Her accent was European, but indistinguishable as to country. She could have been French or Italian or Swiss.

Lawson played the part of the gentleman and pulled a chair out for her while his attention swept the room and the customers. "Business is good," he said, taking a chair for himself. The position gave him a panoramic view of the restaurant and the doors. "And yours?"

Yvette looked him over with her almond-shaped brown eyes and produced two cigarettes and a lighter. She handed the lighter and one of the cigarettes to him and placed the second stick in her own mouth. "I have more than enough business these days." She thrust her face forward for him to light her cigarette. Continuing to play his part, he obliged. She drew a deep breath and held the smoke in her lungs. "Your friends keep me busy."

A waitress appeared and Yvette ordered a beer and a glass of wine. Lawson laid his cigarette on the table, unlit. As the waitress left, Yvette's sloe eyes again scanned his face and body.

She braced her elbows on the table and leaned forward, the cigarette held between two slender fingers. "The one you come for is not in Paris."

Lawson purposely smiled at her as though he was enjoying this secret meeting and the fact she was tantalizing him with her double D's. "Where is he?"

"That is your job, no? To find where he is?"

When he frowned at her, she took another pull on the cigarette and waved it through the smoke as she exhaled. "Honestly, darling, if I knew I would tell you. What I do know is he is not here in Paris."

"How do you know?"

She laid her left hand across the table, running her fingernails down his forearm. "I have the information you want back at my flat. We will go there and I will show you everything."

If he'd been a different man, he might have toyed with the idea of taking what she was offering. The petulant mouth, the sexy accent, the ripe body. Yvette's looks no doubt made sane men trip over their own feet. He should have been flattered at her invitation to hook up, instead he felt annoyed. Sean Connery had said it best in his movie, *Entrapment.* "Rule Number Two, never trust a naked woman." Only idiots and fools mixed business with pleasure—no matter how tempting the pleasure might be—and Lawson didn't place himself in either category.

The waitress deposited their drinks on the table, and Yvette made small talk with her for a minute. When the woman walked away, Lawson said, "I asked you to bring the information to this meeting."

Yvette widened her eyes. "Your friends asked for so much, Isaac. Newspaper clippings, pictures, blueprints of the jail. I would need a briefcase to carry it all in. It would have been conspicuous." She sipped her wine and stubbed out her cigarette. Lit the one he'd left on the table. "We will go back to my place and I will give you what I have. Then we can discuss what happened with the prison break. I can translate the news pieces for you and explain anything you do not understand."

Damn. Lawson twirled his beer bottle in circles. There was nothing that annoyed him more than a woman with her own agenda, especially when it interfered with his. "You were to put the information on a flash drive for me, Yvette. Next time, follow orders."

"You don't want to go back to my place?" The petulant lips popped out even further. "*Ça va.* I will pick up the information and bring it to your hotel. *Où est l'hotel?* You would like that better, no?"

No, he would not like that better. Not with Zara there. The hotel offered him better cover for his backside, but bringing the risk of trouble to Zara was out of the question. "We'll go to your place, but I won't be staying. You'll give me the information and then I'll leave. I don't need a translator and I don't need your advice about the situation."

She sat back in her chair and raised one beautifully arched eyebrow at him. He wondered how many times she had practiced that in the mirror. "*Excusez-moi.*" Her gaze flickered over the bar. "I was trying to be of assistance."

Lawson twirled the longneck again. Why was he suddenly so blessed with female help? Tapping his thumb on the bottle, he gave Yvette a charming smile. "Finish your smoke. Then we'll go back to your flat."

Zara glanced down the alley at the BMW motorcycle and its rider hidden in the shadows. Lawson had been inside the Café Toulouse for ten minutes for his meeting with his informant. She couldn't go in without showing herself to him, even if she snuck in the back door. The place was too small and too open.

She had what she wanted anyway. She'd seen his source through the window as Yvette greeted him like a lover. No wonder he hadn't wanted Zara with him. Yvette was a welcome rendezvous. How had he met her? What had the two of them worked on together before? It was obvious they shared a past.

Leaving the café's shadow, she made her way to the adjacent alley and the motorcycle rider. There were few people she trusted more than Lucie. Still, she was trying to be discreet. "I need another favor, sis."

Straight blonde hair fell in a cascade to the woman's shoulders. "*Mais oui!* Avenue Montaigne?"

"How did you know?"

Lucie laughed. "Always there is the shopping with you."

"It's not for fun. It's for work. I need dress pants and a jacket."

Lucie ran a hand through her hair and slid a helmet over it. "You know I will do anything for you, little sister."

Eight months was all that separated them. Zara climbed on the back of the bike and embraced Lucie in a strong hug. Love for the half-sister her parents chose to ignore rose in her heart.

"You are here to look for Dmitri, yes?" Lucie glanced at Zara in her small round rearview mirror. "You are okay with that? Not scared?"

Dmitri's release had made international headlines, so Zara wasn't surprised her sister knew the monster was out. Yet Lucie's question caught Zara off guard. Of the few people who knew what had happened with Dmitri, most, like her mother and father, chose to act like nothing had happened. Zara knew it was because they loved her that they couldn't stand to think about the dangers she encountered in her job, especially specific confrontations like the farmhouse.

With Lucie it was different. Lucie understood betrayal and its effects as well as Zara did. As young girls, they had secretly shared their fears, their loves, their mutual need to embrace all of life in long, handwritten letters. In her teens when Zara had fought with her parents over being a ballet star, Lucie had supported her with endless emails. As an adult, she had never shied away from talking about the dangers of Zara's job. She was the only person Zara had discussed the fear she'd felt when Dmitri had forced the gun to point at Tim. The fear when he'd turned the gun on her. Lucie was the only person to see her cry after it was over.

Registering the concern in her sister's eyes, Zara felt the sharp sting of tears behind her own. She forced a smile and threw her arms around her sister again. "I'm okay," she said into Lucie's hair. "And I'll be even better with a new pair of shoes on my feet."

Lucie laughed and handed her a helmet. "*Entendu!* Avenue Montaigne, here we come."

~ ✧ ~

Lawson walked beside Yvette as they headed south on *Rue Marbeuf*. His eyes shifted constantly behind his sunglasses, taking in the parked cars along the street, the bicycles zinging by and the other pedestrians sharing the sidewalk. Appearing to listen to Yvette's nonstop chatter as they crossed the street, he checked second-story windows and rooftops and picked out landmarks to help him remember his way back. What he'd told Zara at the hotel was true. He never got lost. Like a human version of a Global Positioning System, he had the natural ability to figure out the lay of the land and know his position in relationship to it at all times. His military training had honed the skill, giving him a definite advantage tracking and retrieving people in the field.

Yvette laughed at some joke she had made and leaned into him, putting her arm around his waist as a lover would do. Lawson rested his arm around her shoulders. He hated playing stupid games, pretending to be someone he wasn't, but it was necessary all the same in case someone was watching.

Yvette was more at ease playing the game than he was, and since she was his blue-chip asset at the moment, he would take her lead. Once he had the information on Dmitri and Vos Loo, he and Zara could sort through it and put the next stage of the op plan into play. Yvette could go back to spying for the CIA or French Intelligence or whoever the hell was paying her, and Lawson could wash the smell of her oppressive perfume from his clothes.

Halfway down the next block, Lawson heard the rumble of a bike coming up behind them. *BMW Sport.* Another skill of his, deciphering the sounds of different cycles. This one more personally satisfying. Tuning into the hum of a bike was like tuning into the hum of a woman's body when it was rocking against his own. Pure heaven on earth.

He couldn't stop his head from turning to find the bike. The black and grey machine shot past him on the street, two riders weaving around a Renault. Laughter drifted back to him. The passenger turned her head and looked over her shoulder in his direction, the ends of her blonde hair lifting and falling under her helmet.

All of Lawson's senses went on high alert. She was familiar, and even though he couldn't see her eyes because of her helmet's visor, he was sure she was staring straight at him.

Two seconds later, she and the bike were out of sight, and Yvette tugged on his arm like a child. "*Ici*, Isaac." She motioned for him to follow her down an alley.

Lawson stared at the street where the bike had disappeared and let his mind replay the bike and passenger. The sound of her laughter...the easy grace with which she turned and looked at him...

"Holy hell," he muttered.

His partner was on the loose again.

Chapter Ten

L'Ambassador

Zara held the door as a bellhop brought in a set of boxes and bags containing purchases from hers and Lucie's shopping trip. Thank goodness the stores they'd visited provided free delivery. There was no way she could have gotten everything strapped on to the motorcycle.

"Oh, *oui.*" Lucie grabbed a bag from the bellhop's hand. "The skirts."

Her sister pulled two denim skirts from the bag and dropped the tissue paper they were wrapped in on the floor. She threw Zara's at her, holding the other one up to her face and kissing it. "*C'est superbe.*"

Laughing, she dug in Lucie's Louis Vuitton handbag and found several euros to tip the bellhop. He thanked her and backed out of the room.

The past hour with Lucie had made Zara lighthearted. She had bought a few items using Lucie's credit card since she couldn't use her own, promising to repay her sister before the bill arrived in the mail. She also offered to buy Lucie several items to make up for the favor, and it looked to Zara, as she scanned the pile of clothes and accessories on the bed, that Lucie had gotten the better end of the deal.

Lucie had quizzed her relentlessly about the mission. After several lies failed to pass the Lucie bullshit meter, Zara had finally broken down and explained she was on assignment with Lawson, but left off the specifics. Lucie had crowed in delight— Zara had told her about the Pegasus team leader in one of the novel-sized emails they exchanged every week. When Lucie wove extravagant fantasies about Lawson, Zara dropped the subject.

Now she wondered where Lawson was as she watched

Lucie shimmy into her skirt. She'd been sure he'd beat them back to the hotel, but she and Lucie had been back for fifteen minutes and he had yet to show up. She glanced at the clock. He'd been gone over three hours. She remembered the way he'd been walking down the street arm in arm with that woman.

Source, my sweet fanny. Lawson was having an afternoon in Paris to remember. How dare he accuse her of not understanding what covert meant.

"Zara?" Lucie said. *"Qu'est-ce qu'il y a?"* What's the matter?

She shook her head. It was time to kick Lucie out and get back to business. She wanted to talk to Annette and see what she'd found out about Vos Loo's past lab facilities. "Nothing. Look, I hate to cut this short, but I have to get back to work."

Lucie looked crestfallen. "Five more minutes? We haven't seen each other in months."

Five minutes. What would it hurt? Zara checked her watch and sighed. "All right. We have to sort out my pants and jackets anyway."

Lucie made a shooshing sound. "Forget the business attire." When she said *the* it sounded like *zee.* "Put on your skirt and pair it with"—she reached forward and grabbed a crocheted halter-top off the bed and threw it at Zara—"this." *Zees.*

Zara held the two pieces up to her body and looked down at the combination. Definitely not Sara Lerner material, but definitely Zara Morgan. "What about shoes?"

Lucie dug through a pile of boxes on the floor. "Shoes? *Non.*" She gave Zara a wicked smile. "Boots, *ma petite.* Boots!" In her hands she held up long doeskin boots in shocking hot pink.

Feeling her fingers itch in anticipation, Zara studied the wicked things. "Those are yours, Lucie."

Her sister crossed the room and held them out. "Try them on. If you like them, we will buy another pair, *d'accord?*"

Zara slid a hand over the soft suede. A grin tugged at her lips. *"Peut-être."*

Perhaps.

Lawson heard muffled female laughter coming from Zara's suite when he entered his room. The same laughter that had drifted to him on the streets of Paris and continued to echo in his ears an hour later. Locking the door behind him, he ignored his partner's giggles and headed for the desk in the corner. First things first. He threw down a thick bundle of newspapers and booted up his laptop.

While he waited for the welcome screen to appear, he removed the watch from his wrist. A little tool from Hoffman, the watch had 128MB of memory and could store data, music and photo files. Pulling a slender USB cable from the rubber wristband, Lawson attached it to the USB port on the notebook. In less than a minute, the files he'd copied from Yvette's personal computer were now on his.

Next he removed a sleek black pen from his jacket pocket. He turned the digital camera on and listened to the voice function tell him the camera was out of memory. He'd used the pen to photograph pictures and copies of the prison blueprints Yvette had refused to part with. The pen held only 32MB of memory, but contained a real built-in stylus so it could be used in every situation without suspicion.

A strange woman's voice emanated from the other room, rattling off something in French. She followed with a catcall and Zara admonished her. Both women giggled.

She won't be laughing when Flynn finds out his little soldier is compromising this mission.

Lawson shed his jacket as the camera downloaded images to his notebook. While he had what he wanted and was done dealing with Yvette, the rest of the task was still daunting. He had to begin checking out Dmitri's old haunts and find Vos Loo's past labs and suppliers, but even that seemed easier at the moment than reining in his partner.

He stared blindly at the notebook's screen. Who was the woman in Zara's room and what had Zara told her? *Christ Almighty, how many freakin' ways do I have to explain covert missions?*

Was this yet another test?

A multitude of things could go wrong during any operation. That was a given. Some were controllable. They could be avoided, or at least planned for in advance. Other problems came out of nowhere and blindsided you. Depending on how serious they were, you could devise a new plan, or you could roll over and play dead, aborting the mission.

Lawson had never aborted a mission.

But he had also never encountered a partner like the one next door. She kept blindsiding him with her boldness. It was like they were working two entirely different missions. He wasn't ready to give up yet though. He would never give up.

Zara was impulsive and had a streak of defiance in her, but so did he. Like a headstrong three-year-old, she just needed a strong hand to guide her and set limits. He could do that. His four younger siblings and quite a few younger non-coms could testify to Lawson's ability to teach common sense and mold a person's character. Even the four other members of Team Pegasus would admit their success in and out of the field had been largely due to Lawson's leadership skills.

Sitting forward, he skimmed the files he'd downloaded making sure everything he needed had transferred. Satisfied with the results, he made a copy, removed it and secured the tiny flash drive in a secret compartment in his travel suitcase. Then he shut down the notebook computer, checked the gun at the small of his back and strode across the room to the Zara's door. Raising his hand to knock, he stilled when he heard the strange woman's voice on the other side say, "Ooh, la, la, *ma cheri*. You are the bomb!"

She's a bomb, all right.

Lawson took a step back and rolled up the sleeves of his shirt. *And somehow I have to find a way to defuse her before she goes off.*

"Sara." He rapped the door with his knuckles. "Open up."

He heard her whisper on the other side, "Oh no. Help me, Lucie. Pick up this stuff."

Shuffling sounds and more whispers filtered through before he heard the chain slide free of its lock. At least she'd followed *that* order.

Zara popped the door open a crack and smiled up at him. "Hi. I didn't realize you were back."

He peered over her head into the room beyond and saw a lithe blonde snatch a pair of bright green underwear off the desk and hide them behind her back. She caught him watching her and offered a coy smile and a tiny wave. Lawson dropped his gaze back to Zara's. "Explain."

The gears in her head turned before she answered. "I did a little shopping while you were gone. I needed clothes to wear on this trip and you told me not to use chauffeured cars, so I called Lucie to take me. We were just trying on some of our purchases."

He shoved the door open, grabbed Zara's arm and pulled her into his room. "Do you remember the conversation we had—" He stopped short, looking her over from head to toe. "Jesus, what the hell are you wearing?"

She jerked her arm out of his grasp, took a step back and followed his gaze down her body. "I splurged on the skirt. They were having a great sale at MaxMara's and, well, I couldn't resist."

The skirt? Lawson dragged his eyes up from the pink stiletto boots, taking in the amount of thigh between them and the miniskirt, and forced himself to look at the article of clothing in question. The skirt's frayed hemline stopped two inches short of being decent, as his mother would have said, and did a fine job showing off Zara's incredible thighs. The waistband rode low on her hips and Lawson's eyes were immediately drawn to a small diamond navel ring in her bellybutton.

He clenched his jaw and tried to control his very male reaction. "Where exactly do you think you're going to wear that?"

Zara crossed her arms underneath her breasts. "Wherever I darn well please."

"Not on this operation."

She tapped one foot on the floor. "Well, of course not on *the operation.* I bought clothes for our stay here and I bought the skirt for later, when I get back to the States. The boots and tank top belong to Lucie."

Lawson ran a hand over his face and rubbed his eyes, trying to keep them off the boots. He had to admit he was disappointed the boots weren't going back to the States with the skirt. This had to be another damn Red Dress test. "And who exactly is Lucie?"

"If you'd stop being such an ass," Zara said, strutting toward the door, "I'd introduce you to her."

He reached out and caught her hand, pulling her back to him. "Did you just call me an ass?"

Zara turned to face him and the stilettos brought her face four inches closer to his. She raised her chin and looked him in the eye. "Yes." No further explanation offered.

He couldn't believe she'd used a cuss word. "Here I thought you were too prim and proper to swear."

Zara blinked as confusion creased her brow. "Are you teasing me?"

"No." He rubbed his thumb over her wrist where he still held on to her. Her pulse jumped under his fingers. Another crack in the veneer? "I've never heard anything stronger than 'darn' and 'baloney' pass your lips."

Her eyes narrowed a fraction. "I can out-cuss you anytime, anyplace."

Was she challenging him to a swearing match? Obviously, she'd forgotten he was ex-Navy and a Special Forces commando to boot.

And, quite honestly, just being a man gave him the upper hand in the swearing department. "Is that so?" he egged her on. "Shall we test your theory?"

Her breath hitched and determination pinched her lips into a thin line. "I know at least a hundred swear words in six different languages," she bragged. "Top that."

Up to that moment, Lawson hadn't been worried about winning a swearing contest against anyone, especially not a girl. His vast repertoire of swear words was a thing of beauty. But when Zara's challenge registered, he mentally used a few of his favorite four-letter words on himself. English and Spanish were his only fluent languages which meant he'd just lost this bet.

To a girl no less.

To a freakin' girly-girl standing there in freakin' hot pink knee-high stiletto boots.

Jesus, what was his world coming to?

He let go of her wrist. "Why am I not surprised?"

A triumphant smile lit her face. "Is that a concession?"

It was, but damned if he'd admit it. He took a step back and set his hands on his hips. "Let's get back to why you were out riding around town on a motorcycle and going shopping when I specifically told you not to do anything but find us a different hotel."

Her smile faded a bit but not her bravado. "All the cheaper hotels in town are booked solid for some convention or something. We have to stay here at the Ambassador for now and I had to shop. Besides, you never said I couldn't go shopping."

Lawson didn't remember any discussion about shopping, period. "I told you not to even take a piss without my permission."

"Yes, you've repeatedly stated this is an undercover mission, but there you are, meeting your Eurotrash girlfriend in broad daylight in the heart of Paris and spending the afternoon with her. Walking right down the street with your arm around her, in fact." Her hands went to her hips, matching his. "At least I was doing something productive that pertained to this mission."

He couldn't believe it. He was getting reamed out by this inexperienced, immature spook. It was enough to make him want to shake some sense into her. "The woman you saw me walking with is the source Flynn set up for us to contact. Her name is Yvette LeMans."

Zara pointed a finger at him. "Correction. *You* contacted her. I was denied that opportunity, and after I saw you with her, it became clear why." She dropped her finger and turned her back on him, reaching for the doorknob. "If you wanted to bang your *source*, Commander, all you had to do was say so. It's not like I'm going to tag along to watch."

Without thinking, he grabbed both of her arms, swinging her back around to face him. Her eyes went wide as he pulled her close. "Jealous, partner?"

She pushed her hands against his chest. "Don't flatter yourself. Why would I be jealous of a woman like that?"

Lawson couldn't stop himself. He brushed one palm up her naked spine to where the halter top's strings were tied together and enjoyed the way she sucked in her breath. "Eurotrash?"

"*Sex and the City*, season one, episode five. She sleeps with men who have small dicks and large bank accounts. They fly her to St. Tropez, buy her diamonds and clothes, and she makes them think size doesn't matter."

His pop-culture princess was at it again. "Which we both know is a lie."

She held his gaze. "Maybe. Maybe not."

"So what would be Yvette's attraction to me then?" He tried to sound serious. "I'm certainly not the kind of man who can fly her off for a weekend in St. Tropez."

A heartbeat passed between them. "I imagine a constant diet of small dicks would leave any woman wanting something more..." she paused and fidgeted slightly in his arms, "...satisfying."

Lawson let go of a deep laugh. All his earlier irritation melted right there. He had to stop flirting with her, but he just couldn't help himself. She kept jeopardizing his mission, but she was good at this cat-and-mouse game and it had been a long time since he'd allowed himself this much fun. How she'd ever made it into Flynn's army, he'd never understand. "What you saw was just an act. Yvette is definitely not my type."

He expected her to ask him what his type was, but instead, she wrenched herself out of his arms. "Yeah, well, her perfume stinks. You need a shower." She reached for the door handle again. "Once you're cleaned up, come over and meet my sister. I think you'll like her."

He missed a beat. "Your what?"

"Lucie, my sister. Half-sister actually."

Zara's employee file Hoffman had sent listed her as an only child. "You don't have any sisters. Or brothers for that matter."

"Oh yeah?" She pointed at the door and lowered her voice. "Maybe you'll want to tell that to Lucie. She can show you the paternity test if you like."

"Tell me she doesn't know why you're here."

The Cheshire-cat smile lifted the corners of her mouth. "She knows everything."

"Great."

"Oh, come on." She punched him on the arm. "She's my sister. You can trust her."

Lawson held her gaze. "Trust is something that's earned. In my book it isn't given away to strangers, no matter how good their references."

Zara stared back at him. "You trust me, though, right?"

Did he? Could he honestly say he trusted this woman, who consistently ignored his orders, went off on her own and played games with him at every turn? Who drove him crazy every time she walked into the room? He made a fist and playfully returned her arm punch. "Maybe," he said. "Maybe not."

She sized him up. "This is some partnership we've got here."

You said it, Lawson thought, and followed her to meet her sister.

Chapter Eleven

Zara let out a deep sigh and pinched the bridge of her nose. Her eyes blurred after hours of reading news clips and staring at the information on Lawson's laptop. Dmitri and Vos Loo's biographies and business histories had long since run together in her brain, and she'd spent the past hour playing twenty questions with Lawson trying to develop leads they could begin checking out the next day.

It was almost the next day already. Zara rubbed her eyes and stared again at the mugshots of the two terrorists on the screen. Her head hurt and all she wanted to do was shed her T-shirt and jeans and sink between the crisp white sheets of the bed in the other room.

But Lawson was still going strong. He was pacing again between the breakfast bar and the loveseat, barking questions into his digitally encrypted phone at Del on the other end. Zara wondered if Del was as tired as she was.

"I need maps and blueprints of Vos Loo's lab sites," Lawson said into the phone. "Cross-reference them with any of Dmitri's past hangouts and fax them to me." There was a pause. "Not soon enough. I'll be heading out at 0800 hours. I need them before then." Another pause. "I also need some wheels. Not a rental. Untraceable."

Zara stood and stretched and thought about Lucie. As Lawson had ushered her out the door, Lucie had grabbed her pink boots, declared Lawson *ravissant, mais embêtant*—gorgeous, but boring—and kissed Zara goodbye with a promise to pick up her shopping purchases the next day.

"No, line it up from someone else. I don't trust her... Yeah, that'll work... Thanks, Hoffman." Lawson tossed the phone on the loveseat embroidered with varying shades of red roses. Plopping down next it, he ran a hand over his face. "Let's talk about the night of the farmhouse incident."

Zara sat in the matching chair and pulled her feet up underneath her. "Who did you just tell Del you didn't trust?"

Lawson sat forward, propping his elbows on his knees and resting his chin in his hands. Exhaustion showed in his eyes. "Del wanted me to go to Yvette for a car. I don't trust her any further than I can spit. She'd probably have the damned thing bugged or put a tracking device on it just for fun."

"You don't trust Yvette to get you a car, but you trust her to give you accurate information about Dmitri?"

Lawson was silent for a long moment. "She's Flynn's asset. Why would she feed us false information? It would only come back to bite her in the ass and sever her lucrative relationship with the CIA."

"I doubt she needs the CIA to support her lifestyle. She's probably only working for us so she can brag to her friends she's a secret agent. It's probably a great, sexy line when she's hooking up with a new sugar daddy."

Lawson frowned. When he didn't say anything, she motioned to the papers strewn across the coffee table and desk. "We have a ton of data here, but as far as I can see, none of it gives us any idea where Dmitri and Vos Loo are *right now.*"

"The more information we have, the more complete the picture is. That helps us find our quarry."

"But your information came from a source you don't trust. Are you willing to wager our mission's success on Yvette?"

A muscle in his jaw jumped. "Jesus." He stood and paced to the desk, leaning over the chair to stare at the computer screen.

Zara yawned. "There was an untested source inside Moulins Prison who told us about Dmitri budding up to Vos Loo before the escape. What about that source? Maybe he could help us."

Lawson straightened. "The guy was a prison guard who was killed during the riot Dmitri staged for the escape. The pilot of the helicopter who picked up Vos Loo at the prison was also conveniently killed once he landed twenty miles away. Del couldn't track him to any known terrorist group. Apparently he was nothing more than an independent contractor."

Dmitri was very adept at tying up loose ends. "What about money? Dmitri's got to be leaving a money trail of some sort.

Building a lab like Vos Loo needs is a pricey undertaking."

"French Intelligence has frozen Dmitri's bank accounts here in France."

She was running out of options. And brain cells. "Director Flynn thinks French Intelligence has a mole. Is anyone investigating that group for links to Dmitri?"

Lawson shrugged. "Out of my scope. I assume Stone and Flynn are examining that angle and a few other ones as well, but I honestly don't know how broad this operation is. It obviously doesn't rank up there with finding, let's say, bin Laden."

Zara rose out of the chair to take a turn at pacing. "So let's think like Dmitri. What would we need to set up a lab?"

"Money."

"Back to that. If I was Dmitri stockpiling money to set up a biochemical lab down the road, I'd keep it in an offshore account or a Swiss bank where it was accessible but virtually untraceable."

"Has Dmitri ever lived or worked outside of Europe?"

"He was born and raised here in France and detests non-European cultures. Thinks they're dirty and uncivilized. That doesn't mean he wouldn't use a bank in the Caymans if he had to, but I'd bet anything he keeps his money in a place closer to home."

"His French accounts couldn't have been his only resource. He's too smart for that."

Zara returned to the chair. "He's most likely using Switzerland. A good country for him to hide his money in and a great place to live. A European melting pot where both he and Vos Loo can walk, talk and conduct business without anyone giving them a second glance."

"Hoffman says Vos Loo had two labs in Geneva back in the '90s." Lawson rifled through some papers on the desk and pulled one out. "One was part of a legitimate research company called ChemTech2000. The other was a private research lab he shared with another biochem doctor. Three years ago, they were making a form of ricin that could be released from an airborne weapon."

Propping her feet up on the coffee table, Zara rubbed her eyes again. "Geneva has emerged as a global player in biotechnology and pharmaceuticals over the past ten, fifteen years. There's a large network of research facilities and universities dabbling in healthcare and life sciences."

"Vos Loo's own little Petri dish of contacts and suppliers."

"Exactly." Lawson was quiet, and Zara closed her eyes. She had to get some sleep or she would be worthless when he woke her up in six hours. "So what's our plan for in the morning?"

"I want to check out the farmhouse and see if I can find Dmitri's compound south of there."

She forced her eyes open. "*We*. We will check out the farmhouse and the compound. I'm going with you whether you like it or not."

His jaw muscles worked but he didn't say no.

"What about Geneva?" she asked.

Lawson looked at the paper in his hands again. "It's a good lead, but we need a concrete link to it before we leave here and move our base of operations. Del and Annette can work on that. Meanwhile, I want to examine Dmitri's compound before we leave France. And I want to get you outfitted with a gun."

Even a gun couldn't motivate her at the moment. Dragging herself out of the chair, she gave Lawson a thumbs-up sign and plodded across the room to the door linking their suites. "I'm going to bed. What time do we start tomorrow?"

He pointed at the computer. "I need you to type a report for Flynn first."

"Director Flynn is not at work right now."

"I want you to type it now so he'll have it first thing when he comes in to the office. It's the only way I can keep him out of my hair, so before you sneak off to La-La Land, type." He pulled the chair out and motioned for her to sit.

Zara looked him straight in the eyes. "Tell me you're kidding."

"Nope."

"Because I'm the female in this partnership, typing responsibilities just naturally fall to me?"

He raised his brows. "Men suck at typing. Women don't. It's in your genes. Since you're the better typist, I want you to type the reports to Flynn from here on out. My time and skills are better used elsewhere."

Her mouth fell open. "That's just sexist and...and..." She set her fists on her hips. "And wrong. I'm not your secretary and I'm not about to type up a report for you and let you sign your name to it. Get real!"

"What are you getting so uptight about? It's a freakin' report."

She couldn't believe what she was hearing. "Type your own damn report. I'm going to bed."

Lawson's husky laughter stilled her hand on the doorknob. Looking back at him, she saw a truly rotten smirk stretch across his face. "Gotcha," he said. "You failed my test."

She stared at him in disbelief. He was teasing her again. While she didn't like it, she had to admit anything was better than Military Man. "I stand by my earlier judgment of your character," she said, keeping her face serious. "You're a bona fide asshole, Commander."

He tipped his head and his face went serious. "And you, Agent Morgan, are a thorn in my side, but we can learn from each other. I can teach you how to stay alive in the field."

"That's what the Farm was for."

He looked her over from head to foot. A spark of lust flared in his eyes. The same spark she'd seen at the airport. The one she'd seen a few hours earlier when he'd gotten a good look at her in her miniskirt and Lucie's boots. "You can teach me the finer points of playing James Bond."

Zara's chest tightened. What was going on here? "Yeah, right." She laughed, trying to sound casual. "You are so *not* James Bond, Lawson."

When he spoke, his voice was low and edged with a roughness Zara recognized as well. "That's too bad, 'cause you'd make one hell of a Bond girl, Z."

She stood stock-still for a second, her gaze locked with his. "I'm the spook, remember? I'm *007*. So in that case, *you're* the Bond girl."

When Lawson laughed, she smiled coyly before walking out.

Chapter Twelve

He should have been sleeping. Or at least trying to come up with a solid piece of evidence pointing to Alexandrov Dmitri's whereabouts. But the day's events kept circling in Lawson's mind like a carousel, spinning up, down and around in a cacophony of light and sound. Lying in the too-big bed, he stared up at the ceiling and went through them all methodically again. He stopped at each incident during the day and waited for his gut to react, for the twitch between his shoulders to signal where he needed to probe deeper.

The only time either reacted was when he thought of Zara. He couldn't get the images of her out of his mind. The fantasy red dress. The sight of her sleeping in the tub. The way she sat on the motorcycle. Those damn pink knee-high boots.

He threw the sheet off his naked body and shifted in the bed to try and get comfortable. He could still see the confidence in her eyes when she'd bested him at swearing without uttering a single cuss word and then the defiance in her whole body when he'd insisted she play secretary. He remembered the feel of her eyes on him every time he moved, and the sexual tension flowing between them whenever he teased her. He was keeping her off-balance which was good. She was throwing him for a curve every time she looked at him with those big baby blues.

Her sister Lucie had the same eyes. It was downright weird how much the two of them looked alike. Not quite twins, but damned close. There were men who would wet themselves just fantasizing about a pair of women like them. Lucie was taller and thinner than Zara and walked with her hips leading the rest of her body, but overall the sisters were more alike than different. Zara had explained that Lucie was the product of a brief affair between Zara's father and a Dutch woman that occurred before Zara's mother, Olivia, got pregnant with Zara.

Lawson stuck his hands underneath his head. The only thing nagging at him besides his attraction to Zara was the thing she'd said about trusting Yvette's information. Lawson had believed Yvette was a reliable source because of Conrad Flynn.

Since when do I take anyone's word for gospel? While the DO sat behind his oak desk at Langley, Lawson was in Paris putting his ass on the line. Zara's too. He couldn't afford to trust the wrong person, even if that person was his current employer.

Forty minutes later he was climbing the fire escape to Yvette's flat under the cover of night. He entered through a bedroom window she'd carelessly left open. The scent of her perfume, clouded with the smell of stale pot, candle wax and sex, greeted his nose.

The room was dark but his eyes adjusted quickly as they took in two sleeping forms on the bed. What a surprise, Yvette wasn't alone. The man in bed with her was lying flat on his stomach, snoring lightly. Lawson drew a knife out of the sheath attached to his leg and moved toward his source.

The prick of the knife's point against her neck brought her instantly awake. Her lips parted on a sharp intake of breath and he saw the white of her eyes as they widened in fear. "Tell me," he whispered an inch from her face, "why I shouldn't slit your throat?"

When she didn't answer, he sank his free hand into her hair and pulled her head back to expose more of her neck. He didn't like playing hardass with a woman, but this woman was messing with him and putting his life and the life of his partner in danger. In that case, all bets were off.

Yvette swallowed hard and grabbed his arm, but her strength was dulled from the marijuana. "Please." The accent disappeared from her voice. "Don't kill me."

"Give me a reason not to."

The man stirred next to her, and Yvette stayed silent until his snores filled the room again. "I told you everything I know," she whispered.

"Tell me where Alexandrov Dmitri is."

She shook her head. "I don't know."

"You told me he wasn't in Paris. You know where he is."

"Not him. I only know…"

When she didn't continue, Lawson turned the point of the knife just enough to break the skin underneath it. Yvette flinched. "There is a woman," she said, all resistance leaving her body. "Varina Scalfaro..."

Lawson needed sleep, but with less than two hours left before sunrise, sleeping seemed pointless. He stripped off his clothes in the bathroom and turned the shower on. When the water was hot, he stepped into the tub and stuck his head under it.

The human body was an amazing thing. The way it could heal even after being beaten, the way broken bones and burnt flesh could repair themselves with the correct medical intervention, the way the soul and spirit of a person could push the worst of physical experiences behind them and keep on living.

Terrorists were human too. Their bodies broke and bled like everyone else's. And sometimes their humanness was the one thing that betrayed them. Even the most die-hard, self-serving lunatic needed other human beings to survive. Basic human needs—food, shelter, water, sleep—had to be met. Money and other essentials had to change hands. An efficient organization had to have employees. The preacher had to have a congregation to preach to and the human ego had to be fed just like the stomach.

Tipping his head back, Lawson sluiced water out of his hair and reached for the soap. His partner was sleeping in the other room, and he was glad at least one of them would be fresh for the day. Zara wasn't at all what he'd expected. The pampered, spoiled rich girl image was a surface facade, and under it he saw the sparks of the operative Flynn believed she was.

He respected the fact she was facing one of her fears head-on. He didn't know any woman, and not too many men for that matter, who would willingly chase down the person who had tried to kill them. That kind of bravado made great fodder for movie scripts, but it wasn't even close to reality.

She was quirky, but underneath that was also a strength Lawson was beginning to admire. She was smart and she had balls. Bigger balls than most of the people at Langley. And all that strength and intelligence and courage was wrapped up in a sexy, sweet-smelling package sleeping twenty feet away.

The now familiar stirring in his groin brought him up short. He turned the cold water faucet further to the left and sucked in his breath at the cool blast. Better to concentrate now on washing his body than thinking about Zara. He had uncovered the link to finding Dmitri and Vos Loo and now he could complete the mission.

Then he could get back to the States and call up Johnny and the rest of Pegasus and have a couple beers with them. Tell them all about how he tracked down a couple of no-good terrorists and saved the world again. Lawson Vaughn, Superman. Make the guys laugh until they cried when he told them about chauffeured cars, four-star hotels, cussing matches and pink boots.

Sure they'd poke fun at him and call him a wuss, but, Lawson smiled to himself, every guy on the team would be jealous as hell. And that was just too good to pass up.

Chapter Thirteen

Zara hit the button on her tiny travel alarm before it went off. She'd slept deep for five straight hours, waking two minutes before the alarm was due to ring.

As she pushed the blankets off, she swung her legs over the edge of the bed and wiggled her toes. Then she stood and went through a light routine of stretches. She started every morning with ballet warm-ups to keep her body strong and graceful. The first few minutes of each day she could put everything out of her mind and just focus on the way her body moved.

After completing her routine, she grabbed the clothes off the bed she'd laid out to wear for the day and headed to the bathroom. She had at least twenty minutes before Lawson knocked on the door. He expected her to still be sleeping, but she was going to be up and waiting on him. Show him she was the early bird who nailed the worm and all of that. Maybe it was petty, but after yesterday, she was keenly aware of his competitive spirit. No way was she giving him the upper hand at anything as trivial as who woke up first.

Washing her face, she realized keeping her mind on Lawson prevented her from dwelling too much about the day's agenda. Visiting the farmhouse was definitely no trip to Berthillon—goodness, what she'd give for a bowl of their world-class ice cream—but Lawson had finally included her in his operation plan. He was taking her with him and that said a lot. She had to push the anxiety away. It was just a house, nothing a soldier in Flynn's army couldn't handle.

Be a man, she told herself as she smoothed lotion on her face. *You eat red meat, practice wild turkey calls and consider* Fight Club *a classic movie.*

Zara squeezed a line of toothpaste onto her toothbrush. She could be just as tough as any man. The act would distance her from the memories of the farmhouse and from the ice-blue eyes of Dmitri. From the feel of the gun pressed to her neck. She would just shut all of that out and deal.

She pulled her "I'd rather be in Paris" T-shirt over her head and hiked up her jeans. She was a good actress. Past experience showed she could pull off anything if she set her mind to it.

Finishing her makeup, she swept two coats of mascara on her lashes and applied a layer of lip gloss. Then she squeezed a dab of gel into her hands and scrunched her hair, taming a few flyaway hairs. Looking herself over in the mirror, she smiled. She wouldn't wait for Lawson to knock on her door. She'd one-up him and knock on his first. Wouldn't that tick him off royally?

Zara set her fists on her hips, puffed out her chest and frowned, doing her best tough-guy imitation in the mirror. "You're a beast," she said to her reflection.

She couldn't hold back and laughed out loud. Somehow she couldn't see any man on Team Pegasus wearing pink lip gloss, no matter what the op plan called for.

Turning off the bathroom light, she headed back into the main area of the suite which was still dark. She stopped for a second to give her eyes time to adjust.

A familiar voice came from her right, near the breakfast bar. "Do you talk to yourself often?"

Zara's hand flew to her chest. She snapped it back down to her side and glared at Lawson's broad shoulders outlined by the nightlight. "What are you doing in here?"

"Wake-up call." He moved into the kitchen and flipped on the overhead light. "Although it looks like you don't need one." His gaze flickered over her, stopping at her chest to read the words on her shirt. "What were you laughing about in the bathroom?"

The first rule of Fight Club is don't talk about Fight Club. Zara pulled her lips in between her teeth and bit down on them to keep from smiling. She turned her back on Lawson and walked to the closet. "How did you get past the chain on the door?"

"I told you that wouldn't stop me."

She grabbed her Prada jacket out of the closet and slid her arms into it. God, he was so darned sure of himself. And he was already one up on her for the day. She turned back to face him. "I want to know how you do that."

One brow rose, forming creases on his forehead. "Why? So you can figure out a different way to keep me out?"

"Yes."

Scoffing at her, he reached into her mini-fridge and pulled out two bottled waters. He tossed one to her. "Let's go to work."

She caught the water and then picked up her Kate Spade bag, sliding the water inside. "What about breakfast?"

Lawson pulled a granola bar out of his jean jacket pocket. "*Voila!*" He tossed that at her as well.

She let it fall to the floor. "We're in Paris and you want me to have a honey oat granola bar and water for breakfast? What are you, a prison guard?"

He leaned back against the counter, crossing his feet at the ankles and giving her a grin. "You can have a full course meal later. I want to get going. You're up for this, right? If not, feel free to stay here. There're plenty of reports to type."

Zara retrieved the granola bar and dropped it into her bag as she pushed the image of a warm, delicious street-vendor crepe out of her mind. She set her shoulders, refusing to let him sense any weakness. "All ready. Let's go."

"Good." He walked up to her and laid his arm around her shoulders, steering her toward the door. "Now, ground rules again. First thing you have to remember is I'm in charge..."

There it was. The farmhouse.

Zara was unprepared for the anxiety sweeping through her as she stared at the peeling paint and crumbling foundation. The past two months hadn't been kind to the abandoned building or its barn on the western edge of the property. Both were in disrepair.

She sat frozen in the passenger seat of the black Mercedes convertible coupe Lawson had *borrowed* from a friend. Apparently, the car was a loan from one of Yvette's gentleman friends. Seemed a certain international playboy was a bit tied up after the local police raided Yvette's flat and found a cache of drugs. An anonymous call had tipped the police off, and Yvette's friend wouldn't need his car for awhile.

Zara deduced her partner had a bit of a criminal bent.

Lawson shut off the engine. "I'm going to have a look around inside."

She was too if she could just get her legs to move. Staring at the spot where she'd held a gun pointed at Tim's head, she tried to still the tremors running through her diaphragm. "What do you hope to find?"

Opening his door, he glanced at her, then studied her more scrupulously. "Just stay here. I'll do a quick walk-through and be back in a minute."

He slid out of the seat and shut the door, and the tremors spread to her lungs as he sauntered up to the house. Fear, irrational and cold, spurted through her and she fought the urge to shout at him to be careful. In her mind, Dmitri was still there, haunting the house with his horrible dark energy.

Watching Lawson test the front door and walk inside, she forced herself to breathe. When nothing happened—no yelling met her ears, no guns were fired—she checked the time on her watch and ticked off the seconds one by one.

She should be in the house with him. Should be doing her job. But by the time the second hand had swept the dial three times, her heart was thudding harder. She'd replayed the memories of that morning in her mind over and over. Trying to block it out did no good. She could feel Dmitri's body hugging hers, could feel his breath on her cheek. When she thought of what could have happened if Lawson hadn't been there...

In a flash, time rewound. "Let her go," Lawson commanded, lowering his gun and taking a step toward her and Dmitri.

Zara flinched as Dmitri shoved the gun deeper into her neck. "Why would I?"

"The murder of an American citizen is a crime that will put you in prison for the rest of your life."

Dmitri stood silent. Lawson took another step forward. "My guess is you had your lieutenant do your dirty work here tonight and, so far, you haven't committed a crime that will get you more than a few months in jail. But if you kill her"—he glanced at Zara and back to Dmitri—"you'll be kissing someone's ass in prison on a daily basis until Hell decorates for Christmas."

Zara sensed Dmitri considering Lawson's words. She

clutched at hope.

But of course Dmitri was Dmitri. "Do you really think I will let you go?" he whispered in her ear. His soft, cruel laughter sent a shiver down her spine. "Stupid girl."

In that moment, Zara knew she'd truly lost the game. She hated losing. Anger boiled up inside her, along with desperation.

Without considering the consequences, she picked up her booted foot and slammed it down on top of Dmitri's, yelling like a banshee. He tried not to react, but grunted in pain nevertheless, bending forward enough for her to grab his arm again and use the momentum to jerk him off balance. As their bodies fell forward, he stuck his left hand out in front of them to stop the fall. Zara pushed the hand holding the gun upward. It went off, sending a bullet whizzing millimeters from her head.

She had barely hit the ground with Dmitri on top of her when Lawson slammed his own booted foot down on the terrorist's hand, breaking bones and knocking the gun clear...

As the second hand on her watch swept the twelve again, Zara blinked back to the present. Lawson had said he'd be back in a minute. How long did it take to do a quick walk-through? Her mind raced from one disastrous scenario to another.

Ridiculous, she told herself. Dmitri was off somewhere playing Mad Scientist. He wasn't anywhere near the farmhouse and didn't even know she and Lawson were on his trail.

She knew she was overreacting, but never in her life had she experienced such a physical reaction to her mind playing tricks on her. Not even when the doctors told her she would never dance again. Not even when she struggled through Interrogation at the Farm. Knowing something logically didn't make it any easier physically. As she parted her lips and struggled to take a deep breath, her fingers shook and her thighs spasmed.

Still Lawson failed to reappear. She had to quit thinking about Dmitri. Shut him out and turn on her inner actress. Pretend she was out for a drive in the country with a sexy man and...

It wasn't working. If she didn't do something soon, she'd lose it. *Move*, her brain commanded. *Take control*. Opening the car door, she forced her frozen legs to stand and then to defy their trembling weakness and walk toward the house. She intentionally avoided the spot where she'd stood with Dmitri.

"Lawson," she called as she climbed the porch steps. "Lawson!"

At least she was moving. Taking some control. She charged through the front door and flung herself into the living room, and there he was, half-running toward her, his face intense as always. She stopped dead still.

"What is it?" He reached for her. "What's wrong?"

His hands on her arms and the look in his eyes brought her back to reality. Drawing in a ragged breath, she mentally chastised herself.

Dmitri wasn't in the house.

Lawson was all right.

She was all right.

He rubbed her arms. "Jesus, Zara. Why were you screaming?"

"I wasn't screaming. I was...just...just..."

She froze again as reality hit home. How was she going to explain that there wasn't anything wrong? That her imagination had simply gotten the best of her? So much for acting like a man. She'd just pulled a classic hysterical-woman move.

"Crap," she said under her breath, jerking backwards and severing Lawson's hold on her. "Never mind. I...I was, uh..." she stammered again and clamped her lips shut. *Don't stutter.* God, she hated it when she did that.

Putting more distance between them, she swept her focus over the living room, and her breath caught in her throat. The furniture was covered in dirt and dust and cobwebs. She could suddenly see Dmitri and his men, moving like ghosts before her. She could see Tim tied to a chair, being beaten. She moved to the window and saw herself in the yard, Dmitri's arm around her, his gun pointed at her neck...

Chapter Fourteen

Stupid, stupid, stupid, Lawson chastised himself as he propped Zara against the trunk of the hundred-year-old oak tree and patted her face. What had he been thinking, bringing her back here?

It hadn't been necessary. He'd figured the farmhouse wouldn't give him any clues to Dmitri's current whereabouts. He'd brought Zara for his own purposes.

Lawson knew men who seemed stable until coming face-to-face with their past tormentors. He wanted Zara to look at the place she'd been held hostage and face the demons he knew lurked under her bravado. Her psych exam and therapy at Langley vetted her clean, but that meant nothing in the field. He needed to be sure she was stable if they came face-to-face with Alexandrov Dmitri.

He never dreamed his bold, in-your-face partner would react by passing out. She'd panicked, pure and simple. And he was indeed the asshole she claimed he was.

"Wake up, Zara," he said. "Come on. Open your eyes."

She blinked several times and held onto his arm as she sat up. "What happened?"

"You fainted. How do you feel?"

She was silent for a minute and then she said, "Stupid."

"Yeah, well that makes two of us. I shouldn't have brought you here, Z. I thought you could handle it, but you're not ready for this yet."

Her whole body stiffened, and she dropped her hand from his arm. "My blood-sugar level is low, that's all." She brushed at dirt on her leg. "Sometimes I pass out when I haven't had enough to eat. Our morning rations were a bit meager."

She wasn't going to admit she was rattled by being there. He had to admire her spirit. Patting her leg, he stood up. "Wait here. I'll be right back."

He hadn't gone five steps when she called to him. "Where are you going?"

"The car," he said over his shoulder. "I've got more substantial food in there. We better get your blood-sugar level back up to par."

He opened the trunk of the Mercedes and pulled out several bags along with a blanket. He hauled the load back to the tree, spread the blanket out and started unpacking.

Zara sat watching him. "We're about to have a picnic at the site of the farmhouse incident. How quaint."

Lawson handed her a bottle of Coke. Her fingers trembled when she took it. "I knew we wouldn't get back to town until late. I grabbed a few things for lunch. Since it's only ten o'clock in the morning, I guess we'll call this brunch instead."

Zara took a swig of Coke and unwrapped the loaf of bread he'd laid near her feet. "You got up early enough to go shopping? I'm impressed." She gestured to the food. "Where did you get all of this? One of the outdoor cafes?"

Lawson pulled his KA-BAR knife out of its holder and sliced some whitish-colored cheese from a chunky triangle. He passed the slice to her. "I took it from the hotel's kitchen."

"You stole food from the hotel?"

"You'd rather go hungry?"

Zara eyed the knife. "What is that?"

He cut off another slice of cheese. "It's a knife."

"It's a little over the top for slicing brie." Breaking the loaf of French bread in half, she handed a piece to him. "I assume you use it for more...military type stuff."

He sheathed the knife and took the bread from her hand. "Mostly to scare people." He tore off a chunk of bread and laid the cheese on top of it. After taking a bite, he tried not to make a face at the strong flavor. He'd take Velveeta over this stuff any day.

"Mostly, huh? So you've done worse than just scare someone with it."

He studied her face, still pale from passing out. "Do you really want to know the answer to that?"

She held his gaze for a long minute. "Just tell me you sanitized it before using it on my food. I mean, I'm not going to catch a disease or anything from eating this cheese, am I?"

If she ended up diseased, it wouldn't be from his knife. The cheese was another story. He picked it off his bread and frisbeed it into the yard. "My knife is cleaner than your mother's best silver, but that cheese is God-blessed awful."

Zara layered her cheese and bread like he had done and took a bite, still watching him. She swallowed. "My mother would no doubt argue with you about the cleanliness of her silver."

Lawson accepted the point without further discussion. He would expect the same from his own mother and her sterling flatware from Walmart. They ate for several minutes in silence and Lawson saw color return to Zara's cheeks. "So Tim was your field officer?" he asked. "What was he like?"

She shot a nervous glance at the house and then turned her head the opposite way to look out at the road. "Funny guy. Always cutting jokes. He had me meet him at The Louvre in front of Mona Lisa's portrait once." A faint smile passed her lips. "It was the first time he'd seen it and he couldn't get over how small it was. There he was trying to have this big cultural experience, as he called it, and Mona turned out to be small. He felt cheated."

"Size matters," Lawson said, giving her a grin.

Zara ignored him. "Tim was a good case officer, but he worked too hard at keeping me safe. I wanted to develop some assets who had contact with Dmitri, and I had hopes of personally infiltrating his network down the road. Tim supported my plan in theory, but wouldn't let me actually do anything."

Lawson knew the feeling. He wanted to keep her safe too. She seemed to trigger a man's natural desire to protect her.

He pulled a plum out of one of the bags and handed it to her. "You were pretty inexperienced to try such deep cover, weren't you?"

She took the plum and gave him a frustrated look. "No, I wasn't. You have to quit doing that."

"Doing what?"

"Undermining my skills and abilities."

Nodding, he wiped a second plum off and eyed it before he looked at her. "You're right." He bit into the plum, chewed and swallowed. "I'm not used to working with women."

"Obviously." She stared at the farmhouse. "However, I am embarrassed I freaked out and then passed out. Very female. Very wrong. I'm usually cooler than that under pressure."

"It's okay to be scared of Dmitri, Z. He's one bad dude and you got to find that out up close and personal."

She sent him a harsh look. "I'm not scared…" She shook her head, took a deep breath and eyed her plum. "Okay, that's a lie. I am scared of him. A little." Glancing up, she fidgeted. "I still have nightmares. Ones where I end up killing Tim or Dmitri kills me. I want to nail his ass for those alone, not to mention all the other stuff he's done. All the rotten crimes he's committed."

"Did Tim ever talk to you about the other operations he was working on? He was in Italy quite a bit, right? Did he ever say anything about the Italian mafia?"

Zara's forehead wrinkled and she bit into her plum. She chewed and swallowed. "What has that got to do with tracking down Dmitri?"

"Humor me a minute. Did Tim mention any names or specific operations?"

She shook her head. "He never talked specifics, but I know the group he was trying to infiltrate was part of the Italian mob, and they were branching out into France. Their drug business was in a slump and they were putting some of the smaller suppliers out of business in an effort to create more demand for their own drug supply. Along with that, Tim said the group was recruiting chemistry students and disenchanted research scientists to develop different recreational drugs they could mass produce and market through their already well-established channels."

Recreational drugs. Made sense. Recreational drug use in the States and Europe was still dominated by softer drugs like pot, but more and more kids were expanding their drug repertoire to include amphetamines and ecstasy. "When it comes to hedonism," Lawson said, "recreational drugs will always be a lucrative market with kids."

Zara finished her plum and washed it down with a drink of Coke. "Kids? How about adults? Many of them experimented at some point and still use common stuff."

Lawson snagged an apple out of his bag and buffed it with his shirt. "Did Tim ever talk about a female asset?"

"Not that I recall. Why? Is there something you aren't telling me that has to do with Tim and Dmitri?"

He watched her over his apple as he bit into it. The sun was cutting through the leaves of the tree, dancing in her blonde curls. "There may be a link between them, yes."

As Zara thought it over, he took another big bite and tossed the rest of the apple on top of the discarded slice of cheese. He brushed his hands over his jeans. "Our Eurotrash friend told me about a prostitution ring run by the Italian mob that caters to the rich and famous...playboys, royalty figures, actors and self-indulgent millionaires. Apparently Varina Scalfaro actually does the recruiting and manages it all. Part of the services her girls offer includes drugs. Cocaine, pot, ecstasy. Whatever the client wants."

"Top-class prostitutes, high-quality drugs and discretion. A profitable combination."

"Yep. The clients not only become repeat customers for the girls, but they also have a source for drugs they can count on."

"What does that have to do with Dmitri and Tim?"

Lawson shrugged. "Maybe nothing. I don't have a complete picture of Tim's job assignment, but I believe he might have been trying to infiltrate this ring. I also know Varina visited Dmitri and Vos Loo in prison, but I don't know why. Annette claims she disappeared after the prison break along with our two guys. Either she's jumped ship from the mafia to a terrorist organization or she's creating a link between the two."

"For drugs? But Vos Loo's into creating biochemical weapons, not an ecstasy replacement."

"Maybe some of Varina's clients want both."

"And you think Tim may have tried turning her into an asset he could use to get inside information on the organization and its clients?"

"She who holds the balls holds the power."

Thinking it over, Zara shook her head. "What could Tim or the CIA have offered Varina to make her give up that kind of information about her employer?"

"Maybe they threatened to prosecute her and throw her in prison."

"What person in their right mind would be more scared of the CIA than the Godfather?"

She had a point. "We obviously have some research to do while we're looking for Dmitri." He stood and began gathering up the bags and blanket. "In the meantime, as long as we're out here in the middle of no man's land, you're going to get some shooting practice in."

Coming to her feet, Zara brushed her butt off. "You got me a gun?"

Lawson reached into the inside of his jacket and pulled out a Glock 22 and several clips of ammunition. He showed the gun to her. "Think you can shoot this one?"

She screwed up her face. "Did you steal this too?"

"For someone who's broken the law more than a few times, you sure are hung up about *my* conduct."

She squinted at him. "How would you know I've broken the law?"

He shrugged and she looked him over head to toe. "You read my agency bio, didn't you?" she asked.

Grinning, he held the gun out. "Do you want it or not?"

She took it and turned it over in her hands before she raised her gaze to his. "You were a juvenile delinquent, weren't you?"

Lawson smirked. "Damn close."

With Lawson's coaching, Zara was field stripping, loading and shooting the Glock with accuracy and consistency in under an hour. The only time panic struck was when he'd stood behind her as she aimed at the human outline he'd drawn on the side of the barn.

He'd repositioned her arms with his, that's all. But it was enough. They had already shed their jackets and his front had been flush against her back. Her flimsy T-shirt did little to block the heat coming from his body. With his voice rough and sexy in her ear and his arms wrapped around her, she'd had a hard time concentrating on his words. Not because Dmitri had held her in a similar manner, but because Lawson was so damned attractive. Fighting her female reaction to his nearness, she'd ignored her pounding pulse and put all of her energy into following his instructions.

It paid off too. Keeping her mind focused on the gun and shooting her barn-board target made her fear and anxiety about Dmitri fade away. In its place, anger and revenge blossomed. She blew chunks out of the pretend man on the barn and every shot sent confidence pumping through her veins.

Every nod of Lawson's head made her flush with triumph.

Under his intense scrutiny, she didn't have time to contemplate what she was doing or what the future held. She had to keep her mind clear and her aim true. She suddenly wanted to impress her teacher.

Even though her bones vibrated with certain betrayal.

She fired off another series of bullets, finishing her last clip, and lowered the gun to her side. The Glock sat differently in her hand. Her weekly target practice in Virginia had kept her arms toned, but they were going to be sore later. Her hand was going to be stiff.

Lawson walked up to the barn and fingered the holes in the imaginary man's chest. She'd made the first ones with the previous clip and widened them with the latest one.

"That's good," he said, walking back to her.

She couldn't keep the grin off her face. He took the gun from her hand and dropped both it and his on the ground near the big oak tree. Then he turned back to her. "Now we're going to brush up on your self-defense training."

Her grin faltered. Self-defense training meant body contact. Self-confidence drained out her toes. "Why?"

"Because you may need it."

He took a step toward her and she instinctively backed up an equal distance. "Dmitri comes near me, I'm just going to shoot him."

He curled a finger and motioned her to come to him.

She shook her head no.

A grin crooked his mouth. "Scared of me, Z?"

Truth be told, she was a little scared of him. He sliced cheese with a knife the size of Cuba and carried a loaded gun everywhere he went. He teased her relentlessly and turned everything into a competition. "I'm not scared of you," she lied. "I just don't see the point."

He moved so fast, she barely had time to register his intent before he had her by the arms, spinning her around and backing her into his chest. Her instincts and previous training kicked in automatically and she jerked forward, bending at the waist and trying to pull him over her back. They fell together into the grass, him twisting his body so he took the brunt of the fall and landed underneath her.

She kicked her heels down hard, making contact with one of his shins, and heard him grunt, but her satisfaction was short lived. A second later, she was on her back and he was lying on top of her, his hands pinning hers to her sides.

He gave her a smug smile. "Not bad."

His heart beat a sharp staccato against her chest, tripping her pulse into its rhythm. Strong muscles in his legs sandwiched hers and Zara knew with sudden sureness that even with Flynn's training, she was too soft to be any real challenge to Lawson Vaughn.

Which was exactly what he was thinking too. She willed her body to relax and gave him a sheepish smile. "Guess I am a little rusty."

He released her arms and shifted his weight off her. "We'll fix that. I want you to know how to handle yourself in any"— Zara jerked her knee up and connected with his balls—"*umph.*"

He rolled away, cursing, and she jumped to her feet and stood over him. "That's worth at least two points," she said. When he swerved toward her, she sidestepped him. "Now if I really wanted to hurt you, I'd plant one foot in your face and one in your kidney and then I'd grab my gun, load it and shoot you in the head."

Lawson rose in slow motion to his feet, staying bent at the waist. His voice strained to rise above a whisper. "You never cease to amaze me."

She started to say that was because he didn't give her enough credit, but before she could utter a word, he swept her feet from underneath her and she landed hard on the ground.

"Hey!" She gasped as he flipped her over onto her stomach. His knee dug into her back and the next thing she knew he had her wrists pinned behind her. She tried to rock him off, but his body weight kept her from moving at all.

His deep chuckle rippled over her skin. "Say Uncle," he demanded.

Zara considered her options. She could not let him beat her. Injecting resignation into her voice, she forced a heavy sigh. "Uncle."

Releasing her wrists, he helped her stand. She hung her head as though out of breath and laughed like it was all a big joke. Then she balled her right hand into a fist and swung at Lawson's stomach.

This time, though, he expected it. He knocked her fist away, grabbed her arms and brought her up against him. "Not bad for a girl," he said.

She glared up at him. "You haven't seen anything yet."

Chapter Fifteen

Zara let herself into her suite and closed the door behind her. She threw the lock, dropped her bag on the floor and leaned against the door with a sigh. She was tired and dirty and hungry from the past eight hours with Lawson and all she wanted was a hot shower and a nap before the two of them hit the city for dinner.

He'd promised to take her anywhere she wanted to go. She smiled at all the possibilities as she kicked off her shoes and hung up her jacket. She'd done well with the target practice and, while Lawson had kicked her butt through most of the defense training, she'd still managed to make him sweat. More than once, she'd even had him breathing hard. He'd thrown a lot of tough scenarios at her and there had never been any question she wouldn't fight back with every ounce of female determination she possessed.

Before she took a shower, she needed to make contact with Director Flynn. Using her cell phone, she typed a text message. *So far, so good. Plenty of bread crumbs to follow. Mother Goose is demanding but manageable.*

Stripping out of her sweaty clothes, she dropped them on the floor as she made her way to the bathroom. Her partner had revealed a lot during the past few hours. On the drive back to Paris, he'd told her a few things about his independent contracting jobs, most of which were classified.

The majority had come through the CIA, but he'd also contracted with several other government agencies. He'd worked with Navy SEALs on black ops to retrieve nuclear warheads as well as with the East Coast FBI Hostage Rescue Team in a couple of delicate situations involving kidnapped children.

Team Pegasus was his pride and joy. He had personally recruited the men and trained them himself. Today, he was training her.

She caught sight of herself in the bathroom mirror. Even though her hair was matted and her face had dirt smudges on it, her cheeks were flushed and her eyes were shining. Tiredness aside, she felt emotionally and mentally revived, like waking from a deep sleep. She'd faced the ghosts that haunted the farmhouse and still went on to eat a picnic lunch in the yard. She'd blasted the snot out of the side of the barn and practiced self-defense in the exact place she'd been stripped of some of her dignity. Today, she'd taken her dignity back.

The sound of a bike bell came from her phone. Opening her messages, she read Flynn's reply. *Keep Mother Goose happy, but find Big Bad Wolf. No retreat. No surrender.*

The last two sentences were Flynn's code for *eliminate threat.* Zara sighed to herself and responded. *No retreat. No surrender.*

Turning on the shower, she pushed terminating Dmitri from her mind—ugly business, but incredibly necessary to protect innocent people—and concentrated on the coming evening. Lawson had dropped her at the hotel so she could get cleaned up while he went to return the Mercedes. She wanted to pick a nice place for them to eat, but it couldn't be too fancy or even hint at romance. Cloth napkins, a breathtaking view of the city's lights, a dinner cruise on the Seine, all out. She needed casual but hip. Maybe a café in the Latin Quarter on the Left Bank, near the Sorbonne. The two of them could blend in with the young professionals there, and maybe after dinner they could visit a wine bar or a shop or two.

She hopped into the tub and started washing her hair. Her arms were fatigued from the target practice and self-defense training, but she welcomed the heaviness. It reminded her of the feel of Lawson's hands on her body as he guided her through different fight scenarios. Of the solid wall of his chest planted against her back and the feel of his fingers on her neck, wrapped around her wrists, grasping her hips. He was hard muscle, rogue confidence and brute strength with just a touch of Southern gentleman thrown in when she least expected it. She would have sworn the only reason he'd offered to take her out to dinner was because he blamed himself for causing her so much anxiety she freaked at the farmhouse and passed out on him. *Farmhouse Incident II.*

Finishing the second rinse of her hair, Zara saw movement in the bathroom on the other side of the shower curtain. Her heart leapt into her throat and she froze.

The shadow of a man appeared on the curtain again, his hand rising to pull her protective screen back. She reached for the only weapon she had—her shampoo bottle. When the man jerked the curtain open, she threw the bottle at his head.

He flinched and grunted as the small bottle hit his paunchy cheek and fell to the tile floor. He was under six feet tall, and with the bathtub raising her up five inches off the floor, Zara was staring directly into his small, piercing black eyes.

Her reflexes still heightened from her afternoon of training with Lawson, she swung her flat hand at his ear and made contact. He let out another grunt, shaking his head and calling her a choice name in Italian. But he didn't stop his advance. When she took another swing, he grabbed her wrist in mid-aim and jerked her out of the tub.

Off balance, she slipped on the floor and went down hard on her knees. Pain shot up her thighs and she grabbed her attacker's legs to keep from falling over. They were as solid as the pink marble columns on the ground floor of the hotel. He didn't budge an inch.

As he sank a hand into her hair, he twisted her head to the right. A sharp sting ran from her ear down to her collarbone like fire. She grabbed his hand with hers, trying to ease the pressure on her scalp and keep him from snapping her neck. He hauled her up by her hair and propelled her through the bathroom door, where she fell in an unceremonious heap in front of a pair of three-inch black Dolce and Gabana slingbacks.

"Darling," the woman said, and Zara raised her gaze from the shoes, up the fishnet-stocking-covered legs, past the woman's black skirt and silk blouse to look at her face. Highly glossed red lips smiled down at her with unqualified disdain. "We need to talk."

She'd seen the woman's face on the street, smelled her musky perfume on Lawson's clothes. Yvette LeMans.

Time to play dumb blonde. "Who are you? What are you doing here?"

Yvette walked to the coffee table where the contents of Zara's purse had been dumped out. "That is exactly what I was going to ask you." She picked up Zara's alternate-identity passport. "Sara Lerner," she read from the inside and glanced between the picture and Zara's face. "This is you, no?"

A chill rolled over her and Zara wrapped her arms across her breasts and awkwardly stood. "I'm afraid you have me at a disadvantage." She looked down at her naked body. "In more ways than one."

The man moved behind her and she tensed, but a swift shake of Yvette's head stilled his threat. Yvette's focus slid down her body, and Zara forced herself not to squirm under the woman's assessing gaze.

She tilted her head and dropped the passport back on the table. "No wonder Isaac was not interested in my help. He has you."

"I don't believe *help* was what you were offering."

One corner of Yvette's red mouth lifted. "*Touché.*" She motioned toward the man. "Get her a robe." A moment later, Zara wrapped the plush white robe around her and tied the belt.

Yvette lit a cigarette. "Isaac didn't mention he was traveling with a companion. Where is he, by the way?"

"Out."

The woman took a drag on her cigarette and blew the smoke toward Zara. "His little prank this morning annoyed one of my most affluent clients, which in turn has angered one of my business partners. I like him, you know? But his prank has cost me some business and I cannot let that go..." She raised her hands, palms up. "How should I say it? Unpunished?"

Zara's heart skipped a beat. Where was this discussion going? "Look," she said, in her best woman-to-woman, help-me-out-here voice. "I haven't had a decent meal in almost three solid days. Isaac promised to take me out to dinner, and I really need to get back in the shower and finish getting ready because, short of an act of God, I'm eating something delicious and fattening tonight and getting a full eight hours of unadulterated sleep. As you can see, Isaac's not here. In fact, he's returning the car he borrowed from your friend. I'll be glad to tell him you stopped by, and I'll have him call you later, after we eat. That way, I get what I want, and you get what you want. *Comprenez-vous?*"

Yvette smiled at Zara through a faint cloud of smoke. "You have *verve*. My client enjoys young, athletic types full of insolence. You will make the perfect conciliatory gift for him, and I will teach Isaac a lesson at the same time."

She nodded at the man standing behind Zara. Beefy hands grabbed her shoulders.

"Get dressed," Yvette said to her, and the man pushed her toward the closet. "Wear the Prada and make it quick."

This just cannot *be happening.* Zara shrugged out of the man's hands and faced Yvette again. "I'm not going anywhere with you. Not tonight. Not ever."

Sighing, Yvette ground out her cigarette on Zara's passport. "Your attitude annoys me."

She was annoyed? "No one tells me what to do or what to wear." *Except on occasion, Lawson.* "Especially some high-priced Eurotrash slut like you."

Yvette circled the loveseat to stand in front of her. "You do not seem to understand the situation here. You now belong to me. You will do what I tell you to do or you will meet with unpleasant circumstances." She flicked her gaze to her mercenary.

Zara pulled herself up to her full height and set her hands on her hips, mostly to hide the fact they were shaking. "Actually, I understand quite well. You think because you sleep with rich, powerful men you own the world. Guess again, *cherie.* If you think I'm going to help you get your fat ass out of trouble with your pimp, you're not only wrong, you're stupid."

Yvette's open hand flew at her face. Zara blocked it. Yvette's eyes widened a fraction, and before she could speak, Zara delivered a full-fisted blow to her mouth.

She stumbled backward, losing her balance on her D&G's and emitting a low howl of pain.

The man was quick, but not quick enough. Zara jumped out of his reach, lunging for the door to the hallway. Fighting Yvette was one thing. Guido, the bodyguard, was a whole different story.

She was two steps into the hallway when Guido's hand clamped down on her shoulder, spinning her around. She let out a karate yell and flailed her arms at him, making contact with his head a couple of times before one of his giant mitts smacked her on the side of the head. Her ears rang and her vision blurred, and she dropped to the floor, the robe falling open.

She almost missed the familiar creak of the hinges coming from the door at the end of the hall. As she raised her head to call for help, Lawson appeared, dropping his leather bag to the floor. His other hand aimed a gun at Guido's head.

"Back off," he said, soft and businesslike as he took a step toward Zara, "or you'll be dead before you blink."

The door to the suite across the hall opened and a bald man stuck his head out, saw Lawson's gun and retreated back inside. Zara scooted over to the wall, yanking the robe closed and trying to stay out of the line of Lawson's gunsight.

Yvette sauntered out of Zara's suite and stood by her bodyguard. She reached under the man's jacket and pulled out his gun, letting it dangle at her side. She sucked on her bleeding lip and smiled at Lawson like he was her long-lost friend. "Darling," she cooed. "I've been looking for you."

Lawson ignored Yvette and kept his eyes and his gun trained on Guido. He took another step toward Zara. "You all right?"

No, she wasn't all right. She was tired, hungry and pissed off. Her vision was blurry and her knees were starting to swell. Her dinner plans were ruined and she hadn't even had a decent shower. All in all, she was feeling pretty darn cranky.

"You know me." She eased her body up and leaned on the wall for support. "I live for this stuff."

She wasn't sure but she would have sworn the corners of Lawson's mouth twitched. Great. She was on the verge of hysterics and he was amused.

"I see you're out of jail already," he said to Yvette. "You should be more careful about the company you keep."

The woman smirked and made sharp clucking sounds. "You have stepped on the wrong toes, Isaac. I must correct this and make amends with my client. I had planned to have Giovanni here beat you to a pulp, but now I think I will take the girl instead. Is she weaned yet?"

"What?" Hot anger shot through Zara's veins. She pushed off the wall to face Yvette and blinked several times to clear her vision. It almost helped. "Are you calling me a baby?"

When Yvette dismissed her with an exaggerated eye roll, the urge to go for her neck rose like molten lava inside Zara. "This *baby* is the one who fattened your lip, or have you forgotten that already?"

Yvette raised the gun and pointed it at her forehead. "I have had enough of you. Shut up."

Zara couldn't suppress the little squeak that escaped her lips as she jumped backwards.

"Put the gun down," Lawson said from behind her. "Or you'll be the first to die."

From the nearness of Lawson's voice, Zara knew he'd shifted his position to get a better shot at Yvette, but standing smack dab between two loaded guns was worse than playing Russian roulette.

Yvette was silent for a moment, seeming to think Lawson's demand over as she held Zara's gaze. Her face remained impassive, but Zara saw something flicker in her eyes a second before her finger moved on the trigger.

Diving for the floor, Zara threw her arms over her head. Yvette's gun went off twice. Or maybe it was Lawson's. Zara wasn't sure until a second later when Yvette's body dropped to the floor next to her, and she saw a bloody hole where the woman's left eye had been. Yep, definitely Lawson's gun.

Scuffling noises came from behind her, and she looked up to see Guido—Giovanni—and Lawson circling each other. Why didn't Lawson shoot him? Glancing around, she saw Lawson's gun on the floor at the end of the hallway. *This just* cannot *be happening.* How in the world had Giovanni disarmed Lawson?

In the next second, Giovanni lunged and Lawson blocked the man's fist from connecting with his stomach. Then Lawson spun and kicked out at him, knocking him down.

Zara scrambled out of the way as Giovanni fell across Yvette's limp body, but when she saw him reach for his gun, still in Yvette's grip, she yelled, "No!" and dove for it too.

He was closer, but Zara was faster. She knocked the gun out of Yvette's hand and sent it spinning across the floor. Giovanni roared another choice Italian expletive at her and smacked her across the face. She fell backwards, stunned again from the man's strength, but before she could sit up and clear her head, a gun went off. She opened her eyes to see Lawson standing over the man's lifeless body.

He pulled the end of his T-shirt out of his pants and wiped the gun down, dropping it on top of Giovanni, whose blood poured out, soaking the carpet.

His face was grim as he offered her his hand. "Get up."

Rubbing her cheek, Zara let him pull her to her feet. She swayed slightly when he let go to run down to the end of the hall and retrieve his gun. He snatched his bag off the floor and swung the strap over his head to settle it across his chest. "Hotel security will be here any second. We've got to go. The police won't be far behind."

"But," Zara began as he grabbed her arm and pulled her toward the door to the stairs, "what about my stuff?"

"No time." He jerked the door open and pushed her through.

She seized the handrail to stop her forward motion. "Lawson, I don't have any clothes on."

He slipped his arm around her waist and dragged her along beside him as he descended the stairs. "The robe will do."

Her feet barely touched the stair treads. She shoved him away with all her strength and started back up the stairs. "I am *not* leaving without my jacket and my bag!"

"Zara!" His voice boomed in her ears as she ran back through the door. "There's no time."

Behind her, he cursed and then she heard the sound of his footsteps following her. Blinking to clear her vision, she ran as though the devil himself were after her.

Chapter Sixteen

Right Bank

Zara was looking for a miracle. She passed the red BMW 5-series and cupped her hand around her eyes as she looked in the window of a Renault. She wasn't even sure what street she and Lawson were on, just that it was semi-residential, there were hardly any pedestrians out and there was a nice restaurant nearby. The tantalizing smell of roasted chicken drifted down the street, causing her stomach to growl. The one thing she *was* sure of was a woman running around in a white bathrobe in Paris at nightfall was bound to draw attention. She had her bag with her Prada jacket, gun and miniskirt stuffed inside it, and she had sneakers on her feet, but she didn't have time to change. She needed to find a car and she needed to find it fast.

A police siren blared a few blocks south, and Zara moved onto the next car. Lawson was on the other side of the street, canvassing cars as well. He had told her to look for an older car without an alarm or tracking system that he could hotwire. Zara thought it was wiser to look for one with the keys hanging from the ignition. This was the Right Bank after all. Crime was rare, local drivers had already had several glasses of their favorite beverage and she and Lawson were in a bit of a hurry to get out of town.

The next car was a mid-nineties black Audi sedan with the windows down. Zara leaned in to look at the ignition, but it was devoid of keys. She smacked the door with her hand. She was supposed to be on her way to dinner right now. Instead she was dodging police with no underwear on.

The police siren drew closer. She moved onto the next car, a silver Porsche Boxster. Wouldn't that be sweet for a getaway car? Heck, at the moment, she'd be glad to use it for a changing room. She needed to ditch the robe and get her clothes on. Grabbing the door handle, she lifted. No luck. Doors were locked.

Letting out a sigh, she turned and looked across the street for Lawson. He was on the sidewalk, leaning against a light pole with his head down while a pair of lovers idled past him. The man's voice evoked soft laughter from his female companion.

Without warning, the police car she'd heard in the distance turned the corner at the end of the block and headed straight toward her. Lawson raised his head and their gazes locked across the narrow street. Zara swung away from the police car and backtracked to the black Audi. As if she owned the car, she opened the driver's door and slid inside.

The police car slowed as the officers swept the neighborhood. She tried to catch sight of Lawson, but he'd disappeared. She dropped her head and rummaged in her bag. Just as the police car pulled even with the Audi, she found the tube of lip gloss she'd swept off the coffee table into her purse. Flipping the window visor down to use the mirror, she jumped when the keys to the car fell into her lap.

Light from the police car swept across her face, and she opened the lighted mirror in the visor and began applying her lip gloss. At least she'd have color on her lips when they took her mugshot.

She could feel eyes on her and she glanced out the open window. The male officer driving the car nodded at her, and she gave him a flirty smile back. The car moved on and Zara dropped the lip gloss back in her bag, closed her eyes and breathed a sigh of relief.

When she opened her eyes again, she scanned the street for Lawson. She couldn't see him, but his intense, unwavering attention was there. In the rearview mirror, she watched the police car turn the corner and disappear from sight. She leaned out of the car window, put her index and pinky fingers of her left hand in her mouth and gave a sharp whistle. Then she started the car.

Ten seconds later, Lawson threw his bag into the backseat and slid in next to her. In the dim light from the street and the dashboard, she saw the grim set to his jaw. He looked her over and gave her a nod. She put the Audi in gear and took off down the street.

~ ✧ ~

They had just passed the city of Dijon and were sailing through the French countryside headed toward Geneva, Switzerland. Annette had left Lawson a message while he and Zara had been at the farmhouse that there was indeed some suspicious activity with lab equipment sales as well a spike in common antibiotics and antiviral medications being shipped into the area. It wasn't much, but since they were need of a new base of operations, it was good enough.

As mile after mile of dark road flew under the car, exhaustion made Zara's limbs numb. Lawson had been quiet, busy watching over his shoulder for any sign of a tail. She was functioning on autopilot, driving toward Geneva and the one place her gut was telling her she could find food and rest and safety. Her friend and ballet mentor Christian Bernier's house.

"Pull over," Lawson said.

She glanced down at the gas gauge. Still over half a tank. She looked around at the landscape and saw little in the way of civilization. "Why?"

Lawson grabbed his leather bag from the backseat and pulled out his phone. "I'll drive now."

She didn't want to stop, not even to change drivers, so she kept her foot buried in the gas pedal. "I don't think that's a good idea."

Lawson turned to her as he punched numbers into his phone. "You're exhausted."

True, but she didn't want to admit it. "I'm fine."

"You don't even know where you're going. Now pull over and let me drive."

Zara gripped the steering wheel tighter. "I do too know where I'm going and I will have us there in another hour or so. Quit worrying about me and place your call."

Lawson closed the cover of his phone with a snap. Zara could feel his gaze on her. "You did okay back there, but you're lucky Yvette's bodyguard didn't get to that gun first. Next time, stay clear so I can handle the situation. And next time, don't go back for anything."

She kept her attention on the road, letting his words sink

in. "If I hadn't knocked the gun away, you'd be dead and I be sucking some rich Italian asshole's dick right now. And I had to go back for shoes. I have limits, Commander. I don't run from the goddamn police barefoot."

Silence enveloped the car again and then Lawson's low laughter broke through it. "I see your swearing skills surface when you're under stress."

Her mother had taught her that a proper lady never used vulgar language, but at the moment, Zara didn't feel much like a lady at all. She should probably just keep her mouth shut. It was better listening to Lawson talk anyway. Kept her mind from overanalyzing their current situation.

"Did you really punch Yvette in the mouth?" he asked, a grin on his face.

"She was going to kidnap me and give me to the client you pissed off. I sure as hell wasn't going down that road without a fight. She tried to bitch slap me, so I punched her."

He reached out and ruffled her hair. "That's my girl."

She jerked away. "Don't call me 'girl'. I am *not a freaking girl*. I am a woman who has lived through more than her fair share of shit in this world, and I'm sick and tired of people insinuating I don't know my right from my left."

He dropped his hand and went into business mode again. "Zara, pull over. Now. I'll drive, and you get out of that robe."

Zara tightened her grip on the steering wheel another notch. It was solid under her hands, and she needed something to hang on to. "The only reason you want to drive is because your male ego can't stand a woman behind the wheel."

When he didn't answer, she shot a glance at him. His brows were drawn together and he stared at her, assessing her.

"I'm fine." She turned her gaze back to the road. "I want to drive."

"You are *so* not fine," he said, throwing her own phrasing back at her. "Quit trying to prove something here. You're scared and you're tired. Pull over and let me drive."

She jerked the wheel and sent the car skidding into gravel on the side of the road. A car behind them blared its horn as it passed. She slammed on the brakes and shoved the gearshift into park. Then she turned on Lawson. "I am not scared. I am not tired. I just want to get us to Christian's where we'll be safe. Then we can think through what happened back there and what we're going to do about it."

"Who's Christian?"

"A friend."

"Boyfriend?"

Zara threw her hands up in disgust. "No, he's not my boyfriend, and what difference does that make? You just killed two people and we're now running from the police in a stolen car. Christian has a house where we can hide for tonight, and right now that sounds a whole lot better to me than a jail cell."

"What are you so pissed about?"

"I'm not pissed!" As her voice rang inside the car, she forced herself to take a deep breath and calm down. "I'm just having a really, *really* bad night."

Lawson got out of the car and came over to her side. He opened the door and pulled her out of the seat, putting his hands on her shoulders. "I'm not going to let anything happen to you. I promise."

She looked into his face, and without warning, burst into tears.

Mortified at her lack of control, she brushed Lawson's hands off her shoulders and walked to the rear of the car. The tears rolled down her cheeks, and she pressed the sleeve of the robe to her face in an attempt to hide them.

"Hey." He came up behind her and rubbed her back. "It's not that bad. I've been in a lot tighter situations than this."

She shrugged his hand off. "You just killed two people and you think I'm overreacting?"

Lights from a passing car touched his face. He guided her to the other side of the Audi and leaned her back against the passenger-side door, planting his hands on either side of her.

"I didn't say you were overreacting." He dropped his face close to hers. "Yvette was going to kill you, plain and simple. I took care of her before she could do the job. At that point, it became necessary to stop Giovanni as well. If I'd left him alive, he could have followed us or reported back to Yvette's friends and then we'd have a classic Chinese goatfuck."

His gaze traced over her face. "Right now, we've dodged the police and whoever may follow up on Yvette's death. We need to get on the road again before we call any more attention to ourselves, and I need to make contact with Langley."

Zara wiped at her eyes again, took a breath and regrouped. As she was driving, her brain had red-flagged a couple things Yvette had said. "I think Yvette was tied in with the same group Varina Scalfaro is running for the Mafia. She kept talking about her clients and her business partner. I don't think Yvette's playing mistress for a handful of rich men solely for her own gain. I think she was actually running a prostitution ring in partnership with someone else, probably Varina." She hated herself for what she was about to say. "And in that case, I'm not sure what Director Flynn has up his sleeve."

In the deep shadows of the night, Lawson nodded. "We just ran out of people we can trust, didn't we?"

"What are we going to do?"

Lawson eased her to him. "Shhh. Don't cry."

"I'm not crying, you moron." She smacked his chest and attempted to push him away at the same time. Although she wasn't sure why she was pushing him away. She felt better when he was close. "I had dinner all planned out. We were going to go someplace nice, but not too fancy, because I knew you wouldn't like that, and...and... Damn it!"

Lawson smiled down at her. "So we have to take a rain check on the dinner thing. The mission isn't over yet. We've still got time."

"But I wanted to do it in Paris, and now we're fugitives on the run from there. We can't go back. Not even for dinner."

He pushed a stray hair away from her face and hooked it behind her ear. "When the mission is over, our names will be cleared. We'll have a proper dinner anywhere you want then, okay?"

She studied his expression in the dark shadows of the night. "If I didn't know better, I'd say you're trying to placate me. After the mission is over, we won't be partners anymore."

"That doesn't mean we can't have dinner."

Her pulse tripped over a couple of beats. "You want to have dinner with me after the assignment's over?"

He lowered his face and leaned his forehead on hers. "Jesus. I've spent the past twenty-four hours trying to come up with an excuse to do just that."

"We don't even like each other."

He brushed her lips with his in response.

A jolt of electricity shot all the way down to her toes. This could *not* be happening. "You *are* bent, Lawson Vaughn," she said, smacking his chest again.

"Then we make a good pair."

This time, his lips were more insistent against hers, demanding and possessive. Zara closed her eyes and kissed him back. One of his hands went to the small of her back, and he drew her in close to his body, pressing her against the car frame and sinking his other hand into her hair.

He held her head as he parted her lips with the tip of his tongue, and she let go of the last of her hesitation and *ahhed* into his mouth. She ran her hands under his jacket, and the solid muscles of his back tightened under her palms. Rising up on her toes, she pulled their bodies even closer.

She wanted to forget about Yvette and Giovanni. She wanted to forget about being on the run from the police and whoever Yvette worked for. She wanted to forget she and Lawson were running out of people to trust.

At that moment, in the darkness of the French countryside, she wanted to forget all of it, to give up control and forget about everything except the tough, sexy man holding her close.

Chapter Seventeen

He couldn't believe it. Zara was kissing him back.

When she rose up on her toes and sighed into his mouth, all his brain processes shut down. The kiss turned wetter, hotter and when her hands went under his jacket, pulling him in tight, his brain exploded in an array of fireworks.

Jesus, she wasn't just kissing him back, she was inhaling him.

This is wrong. She'd just been through a hell of an experience and here he was, jumping at the chance to wrap his arms around her and console her. He was taking advantage of her at a weak moment.

There's not an ounce of weakness in her.

Fury had crashed into him when he'd returned to the hotel and saw her at Giovanni's feet. He should have shot the bastard the minute he opened the stairwell door and walked in on the scene, but Zara had been too close to the guy and Lawson didn't want to risk hurting her. So he'd checked the anger and called on his professionalism to size up the situation and figure out the best alternative. He didn't know who the man was at that point and frankly didn't care. It didn't take a Harvard grad to know what Zara would suffer if the man kidnapped her.

Unfortunately Yvette's appearance had thrown him off, but only for a moment. She'd actually done him a favor. The second she'd pulled the gun on Zara, Lawson sent his professionalism packing and proceeded with his gut instinct. Zara now had another rotten experience to add to her collection but, by God, at least she was still alive.

Very alive, Lawson thought as she pressed her lower body to his, *and very willing.*

He broke the kiss and slid his lips to her neck. She tilted her head to give him better access, and he buried his mouth in the curve of her shoulder. She hitched her breath in that familiar way, and he enjoyed the response her body gave as she arched into him a little further.

A fleeting memory of her body moving against his during the self-defense session earlier in the day popped into his head, and he smiled into her neck. She'd been emitting that whole woman-in-charge aura since the minute they'd walked off the plane at Charles de Gaul. Even up to a few minutes ago, she'd been cool, calm and collected every step of the way.

It was bugging the shit out of her that he'd killed Yvette and her bodyguard, as evidenced by the fact she'd mentioned it twice already, but how many women would have enough sense after witnessing such a thing to go back into the hotel room and grab their running shoes? How many would then have sat in plain view of a police officer and applied lipstick with the nonchalance of a seasoned actress? And how many would have called his bluff about driving the freakin' car?

Jesus, he hated women ball-busters, but this take-charge woman was starting to grow on him. Hell, she wasn't just growing on him. At the moment, with her hands tangled in his hair and her tongue halfway down his throat, he was ready to drop her robe on the ground and let her drive more than his getaway car...

The sound of a motorcycle cut through the lust building in Lawson's body and he stilled, every sense on high alert. He raised his head and listened.

"Lawson?"

He put a finger to his lips and his eyes slid to the left, checking the dark highway. Traffic was light and the bike was still a half-mile away. No sirens, but something about it had his gut knotting and the spot between his shoulder blades twitching.

Police were in general easy to evade, and Yvette and Giovanni had both been free of identification so it would take awhile for their names to be reported. That should slow Yvette's business partner down considerably if he followed-up and looked for her killer. But there were always people watching. For all he knew, Yvette may have been a regular customer at the Ambassador. The hotel's manager may have had a direct line to Yvette's boss.

Lawson tried to place the make and model of the bike.

I'd Rather be in Paris

High-precision, high-speed. *Ducati.*

"Get in the car," he said and hustled Zara into the backseat. For once, she didn't protest or ask why. He ran around to the driver's seat and jumped in, jerking the car into drive and pulling onto the road in a spray of gravel.

Zara's voice sounded calm. Too calm. "Police?"

The motorcycle's headlight hit the rearview mirror. It was picking up speed. He planted his foot on the accelerator while he adjusted the seat to fit him. "Keep your head down."

The Audi was an older model, but the owner had kept it in good condition. It wasn't as easy to manipulate as the Duke but it was damn close. Germans, they knew how to build kick-ass cars.

"Damn it," Zara said from the backseat. Her head was down but Lawson saw clothing flying around.

"What?"

"I don't have any underwear."

He was pushing one hundred miles an hour on the speedometer and the bike was still crawling up his ass. The headlight in his mirrors blinded him enough to keep him from identifying whether there was more than one person on the bike, and more importantly, whether or not either of them was armed.

He heard the sound of a zipper from behind him, and Zara muttered something in French. Then the back window shattered and she screamed.

His blood ran cold. Question answered. The men on the bike were definitely armed. Swerving the car from side to side to make them a harder target to hit, he asked the real question burning in his gut. "Zara? Are you all right?"

The second it took her to answer was the longest one he'd ever endured. "I think so," she said, her voice still sounding unnaturally calm. "But there's glass everywhere. I'm afraid to move."

He let out the breath he was holding and zigzagged by a car in front of them. An oncoming car dodged out of his way, horn blaring, but the flustered driver blocked the motorcycle for crucial seconds.

He had two options. Evade the threat or eliminate it. "Get up here and drive."

127

"What?"

"Come on, you're a woman of action, right? You wanted to drive, so get up here and drive the damn car."

Zara's head rose from the backseat, her gaze catching his in the rearview mirror as she leaned forward. "Stop yelling at me."

Lawson reached back and grabbed her arm, hauling her into the passenger seat. She flailed and fumed and once she'd righted herself, he saw she'd exchanged the robe for her leather jacket and miniskirt. She tugged the hem of the skirt down and sent him a scathing look. "What exactly—?"

"Take the wheel. We're going to exchange places, okay?"

"While the car's moving?"

Lawson flipped the steering wheel up as high as it would go. He set her hand on the wheel. "You're going to slide on top of me, got it? Like you're going to sit in my lap."

Her hand tightened and Lawson saw her shift into spy mode. A second later, she climbed across the gearshift and slid between his legs.

"That a girl." He released the wheel and extracted his body from around hers. "Keep the car on the road, but don't make it easy for them to shoot us again. When I give you the signal, I want you to pull the hand brake and crank the wheel to the left like you're doing a hard U-turn. You're going to turn the car counterclockwise and land on three o'clock. The car will be blocking the road and I'll be facing the motorcycle. Got it?"

She dropped her hand and repositioned the seat, her eyes shifting between the rearview, him and the road ahead. "And what are you going to do?"

Lawson hauled the gun out of his waistband. "My Dirty Harry impersonation."

"Oh God." She gripped the steering wheel in a ten-and-two position. "We're going to die, aren't we?"

"No," Lawson grunted, checking the clip in his gun. "We are not going to die. Ready?"

The road ahead was empty of traffic. He moved to lean out the passenger-side window and Zara said, "Wait! What's the signal?"

"I'll yell 'go!'"

"My mother is going to spend the rest of her life scandalized because her only daughter died bare-assed in the middle of France in a stolen car."

But then she said, "I'm ready."

And Lawson yelled, "Go!"

The brakes kicked down and the tires screeched as she swung the car around, bringing it in a two-hundred-and-seventy degree arc. Lawson held onto the car frame and as he came around, he saw the Ducati's driver and passenger instinctively pull back in their seats as if the shift in their body weight alone could keep the bike from its forward trajectory.

Without hesitation, he raised his Beretta and fired.

The night was on his side. He and Zara were alive and both bad guys were dead. The road was empty for now, and the Duke was still intact. All in all, things were looking up.

Lawson removed the MP5 Heckler and Koch submachine gun from the dead man at his feet and dropped the strap across his chest. Shoving the gun around to his back, he dragged the body off the road toward the Audi. Once there, he grabbed his leather bag from the backseat and stuffed the body into the car.

Zara muscled the motorcycle into an erect position several feet away. "Where do you want this?" she called through chattering teeth. The temperature had dropped at least ten degrees in the past hour.

"Other side." He ran to the second body and hauled it to the Audi, depositing the dead man into the front seat. Now all the evidence was off the highway, except for some blood and brain matter mixed with bits of helmet. In another minute, the car was going to go up in a ball of fire, eliminating the dead men and the evidence that could link them to him and Zara.

Lawson searched Zara's purse for her Glock, her passport and the travel-size bottle of antibacterial hand soap she carried. The gun and passport he set on the trunk of the car and then he squeezed a big gob of soap out and briskly cleaned his hands with it. He wiped his hands on his pants and threw Zara's purse into the car through the missing back window.

"What are you doing?" She set the kickstand on the bike and marched to the back of the car.

Lawson picked up his bag and began strapping it on to the bike. "Your purse goes up with the car."

"What?" Zara looked between him and the car. "Why?"

"Those two." Lawson used his chin to motion at the Audi as he yanked a hankerchief from his bag. "They aren't the police, so who does that leave who wants to chase us down and shoot us? People from Yvette's world, that's who. And how do you think they found us?"

Zara thought for a second. "Tracking device? But how?"

"Yvette was intent on not losing you. She probably stuck it in your purse while we were out in the hallway dealing with Giovanni. Might be in your cell phone or your lipstick or actually inserted into the lining of the purse itself, but we don't have time to look for it." He walked to the trunk of the car and handed Zara her gun and passport. "The purse goes up with the car."

Lawson waited for the argument, but it didn't come. Zara stared blankly at the spot where her purse had disappeared. Then she took the Glock from his hand and turned away from the car, slipping the weapon into the waistband of her skirt. Straddling the passenger seat of the bike, she crossed her arms under her breasts and hung her head.

He couldn't help but think she'd given up too easily on that one, but he didn't have time to analyze Zara's mood. He stuck her passport in his jacket pocket and stuffed most of the handerchief into the Audi's gas tank. Leaving about half of the material hanging out, he used a lighter he'd found in the glove compartment to set the cotton on fire.

Running to the bike, he hopped on and started it, adjusting the MP5 so it sat across his stomach.

The compact German-manufactured gun fit perfectly in his lap and was small enough he could ride with it partially concealed under his jacket.

Accurate and reliable weapons, various versions of the MP5 were used by SEALs and other elite units around the world. It was lightweight even with a 30-round magazine in it and could fire parabellum 9 mm rounds at 800 rounds per minute as well as single-action fire.

With Zara's hands resting on either side of his waist, Lawson drove down the highway for several yards before circling back and getting a running start at the Audi. As he flew by the car, he riddled the rear passenger side with bullets. Zara flinched as the car's gas tank exploded like a giant Molotov cocktail behind them.

As he kicked the bike up a notch, he thought about how he never got to set off explosions anymore. Loud balls of fire rarely went hand in hand with covert missions. Too bad he couldn't sit back and enjoy this one.

Zara wrapped her arms around his waist and laid her head on his back. He glanced down at her bare thighs outlining his jean-clad ones and resisted the urge to pat one of them. Adrenaline still pumped through his veins from the night's work. He had a Ducati under his ass and a beautiful woman in a flip-and-go skirt and no underwear on the back. The memory of her soft lips and demanding tongue made Lawson draw in a sharp breath and smile into the night.

Explosions were damn good, but truth was, they were nothing compared to his Bond girl.

Slowing the bike, Lawson took the turn Zara pointed to. For the first time in his life, he wasn't exactly sure where he was or where he was going. Technically, he knew he was in Switzerland and heading south because the sun was rising on his left. Geneva was north and east. Guessing at the distance he and Zara had already driven, they had to be getting close to the Rhône. But at that moment, he was guiding the Ducati up a narrow dirt path, flanked on both sides with some kind of jagged rock wall and behind that, acres of forest. Birds chirped and called overhead as sunlight began to push its way past the dense leaves of the trees.

"Christian's house is just ahead," Zara said. "Up and over the next hill."

After the past night, Lawson had mixed feelings about hiding out at anyone's house. In their current state, however, he had little choice.

They needed to touch down somewhere and get their bearings. They needed sleep, a bathroom and some food. A hotel was out of the question, and while he could have easily stolen food and slept on the ground, he wanted his partner to have a real bed and something decent to eat. She wasn't complaining, and he appreciated that, but her silence told him all he needed to know. She was balls-to-the-wall beat.

They crested the hill and without warning the path widened and gave way to a breathtaking view of green lawn. Beyond the black wrought-iron gate, Lawson saw a nineteenth-century estate, house and gardens spread out over acres and acres of well-manicured land.

"Jesus," he murmured as he brought the bike to a stop. "That's not a house. That's a freakin' castle."

Zara slid off the bike and trudged up to the gate. A camera mounted on the stone column followed her progress. She pushed a button on a video monitor embedded in the column on the left side. A minute later, a woman's voice asked for identification. Zara gave a weak wave to the video camera. "It's me, Maria. Zara."

Several minutes passed and then Lawson heard a shriek. A husky shriek, if that was possible. Certainly not Maria. A voice, very male, said, "Zara? My Zara?"

A smile lifted the corners of Zara's lips. "Yes, Christian. Your Zara."

Another of those weird shrieks and then, "Perfect timing, love. Breakfast is on the veranda."

A loud grating noise came from the gates. Zara turned her smile toward Lawson and walked back to the bike. The gates swung out like giant arms reaching to gather the two of them into the estate.

Zara hopped up behind him and again laid her head on his back. Her arms snaked around his waist. "We're safe," she sighed.

Lawson eased the bike past the columns and followed the two-car-wide driveway toward the house. The gate screeched behind him and he shot a look back over his shoulder as the giant, cage-like arms closed. The spot between his shoulders twitched hard, and he forced himself to keep the bike rolling forward.

Chapter Eighteen

Villa de Bernier

Lawson watched as Christian Bernier grabbed Zara in a bear hug and swung her around in a circle. "Where have you been, love? It has been far too long since your last visit."

Bernier was five-ten with shoulder-length brown hair, wet from a shower or maybe an early swim. His long face held a straight slice of a nose. Zara laughed in his arms and Lawson instantly disliked him.

Depositing her back on the floor, Christian kissed her cheeks before he held her at arm's length to look her over. "You look like hell. Rough night?"

"Not one of my best."

Christian pointed at her feet. "White sneakers? Are you feeling okay?" He placed the back of his hand against Zara's cheek. "Running a fever? Been toking again?" He glanced at Lawson and made tiny hand gestures in the air. "A few ounces of pot and her fashion sense goes right out the window."

Zara smacked his arm. "Lawson, meet Christian, the best *instructeur de danse* in all of Europe. Christian, my friend Lawson."

Christian held out his hand. "Is that a gun under your jacket or are you just happy to see me?" He laughed and waved Lawson's scowl away. "Sorry, I couldn't resist. I don't get to do my Mae West impression very often."

He shook Christian's hand and was surprised by the man's strong grasp. Under the colorful silk robe, Lawson guessed he was built like rhino. "I have a gun, yes. Is there a problem?"

Christian raised a brow at Zara. "He's gorgeous, mysterious and he carries a gun." He pointed at a white wrought-iron table and chairs overlooking a kidney-shaped pool. A maid was arranging two more place settings on the table. "Why don't we sit down and you can tell me what happened last night over breakfast. Gunther is fixing omelets. Looks like you could use some nourishment, and I'm dying for a good adventure story."

"First," Zara said, "I need a toothbrush and a toilet."

Christian put his arm around her shoulders and faced her back to the open French doors. "Take the Tower Room for yourself and"—he threw Lawson a look over his shoulder—"put your bodyguard wherever you please. Sundries and toiletries are in the cabinet above the vanity in the bathroom. Help yourself."

"Thank you." Zara hugged him and crossed the threshold into the house.

"And shoes, love," Christian called after her. "Hit the shoe closet and find something decent for your feet."

Lawson picked up his leather bag. "The bike we rode in on needs to be kept out of sight for now. You got a garage or a barn?"

Christian rubbed the end of his chin between one slender finger and his thumb. "This story of yours is quite good, isn't it?"

Lawson held his gaze and didn't smile back.

Christian dropped the routine and nodded. "I'll have one of my men put the bike in the garage."

"Thank you," Lawson said before he went to catch up with his partner.

Zara stood in the columned Great Room and stared at the gold-framed Degas above the fireplace. In the group of ballerinas onstage in the picture, two seemed suspended in air. One in particular floated without effort.

Sunlight spilled through the arched windows on each side of the room. She felt jittery and wild from the past night's events. Like the woman in the pastel work of art, she too seemed suspended in air and time, wondering if, when her toes touched down again, she would land gracefully or fall. Her world at the moment was surreal. None of her personas seemed to fit.

Lawson's hand touched the small of her back and she jumped. "You're sure we're safe here?" he said.

"Yes."

The palm of Lawson's hand stayed possessively on her back, and she found herself relaxing into it a little as she kept her attention fixed on the ballerina's face. "Ballet has a basic law. *Aplomb*. It means perfect balance. It's what every ballerina strives for every minute of the dance, even when her feet aren't touching the dance floor."

"Do you miss it? Ballet?"

Zara thought about the music, the stage and the costumes. She'd been out of the dance world for years, but she did miss it on occasion. "Every movement of the ballerina is a story within itself. A story of dedication, persistence and love for the art. I think ballet is the most beautiful form of dance there is. Once it captures you, it never lets you go."

She shifted her weight and Lawson's hand stayed with her. It was so strange to have him there with her in Christian's house. Yet at the moment, it was comforting. A little too comforting. She slid sideways away from him. "Have you ever seen a ballet?"

He dropped his hand and assumed his usual crossed-arms pose. If she hadn't known better, she would have sworn she saw color flush the tan of his cheeks. "Not unless you count my sister Opal's dance recital when she was nine. Ballet isn't my thing."

But apparently blowing up cars, stealing motorcycles and shooting people were. He'd been quite adept at those *things*. "What do you do when your op plan goes so far off track?"

His attention refocused on the Degas. "You switch to an alternate one."

"Plan B?"

"Yeah."

"Do we have a Plan B?"

A beat of silence went by. "Sure."

She didn't believe him, but she did believe *in* him. She believed in herself as well. "Okay, then." She headed for the French doors which led out of the room to the Great Hall where they'd entered the house. "I suppose we should get cleaned up and have some breakfast with our host. Then you can fill me in on our alternate course."

Lawson followed her into the spacious entryway. Two matching staircases led to the second floor. Zara slipped off the Nikes and dug her toes into the plush red carpeting as they

135

climbed the stairs. "What do you think of the house?"

"I think being a dance coach pays pretty damn well."

She found the energy to laugh. "Like I told you, Christian is the best in the business. He handpicks the most talented young girls and boys in Europe and brings them here to study. They usually go on to successful careers in the most elite dance troupes. My mother brought me here every year to supplement my stateside dance education."

On the second floor, she led the way down the hall toward the west wing. Her eyes skimmed the familiar family portraits decorating the walls between rooms. "The house has been in Christian's family for over a hundred years, but Christian grew up in London with his mother. That's where he studied various forms of dance."

Lawson simply nodded, not seeming to care. Zara, however, needed to talk...about anything other than what had brought them here.

"His father was your kind of guy. An adventurer. He was always on safari in Africa or sailing the West Indies or some such thing. Got killed in a skiing accident in the Alps. Two months later, Christian's grandparents were killed in a car accident on their way back from the opera in Geneva. Very sad. At twenty-one, Christian inherited this house and the grounds."

She stopped in front of a set of closed doors. "At that point, he already knew he would never be an elite ballet dancer, but he had a choreographer's eye. He started working with other choreographers and coaches and found his niche. After a few years, he renovated a section of the east wing on the ground floor and put in a studio. The rest, as they say, is history."

Once she opened the doors, she crossed the marble floor of the sun room, taking in the view of the grounds from the towering window wall. She could see the water fountain in the patio below the balcony, a marble statue of Poseidon in the center. Beyond that was a formal garden adorned with more statues of gods and goddesses, an herb garden and a neatly trimmed boxwood maze.

"There's a bedroom and bath through there." She pointed to the door in the northwest corner. "You can clean up and stow your stuff."

She continued on her path to a different door. "I'll be upstairs in the Tower Room, through this door and directly up the steps. Think you can find your way back to the patio for breakfast?"

Lawson glanced over his shoulder at the way they had come. "Of course."

"I forgot. You never get lost."

"No."

Lucky you, she thought, and then before she could stop the words from coming out of her mouth, she said, "Do you ever get scared?"

"Everybody gets scared once in awhile. Mostly, I get..." he paused, "...concerned."

"Concerned? Sounds almost human."

One side of his mouth lifted. "Surprised?"

"Yes, and relieved. I was beginning to think you actually believed you were immortal."

"You only get one life, Zara. You can't shrink away from the challenges just because you're scared."

"Or concerned?"

He smiled. "Or concerned."

Even after the night they'd had, she could see the confidence in Lawson's eyes. She knew he wouldn't have killed any of those people if he hadn't thought their own lives were in danger. Yvette had pointed a gun at her head and Zara had no regret over the woman's death. The others had also meant her harm and she trusted Lawson knew the line between the good, the bad and the ugly just as well as she did. "I'm doing the best I can, but I have to admit, there were a few times last night I almost peed on myself."

His gaze dropped from her face, down her chest and stopped at her skirt. "I can't see the Zara Morgan I know ruining a kick-ass piece of clothing she just bought in some fancy French boutique because she was scared. That's like sacrilege or something to you, isn't it?"

A small laugh again passed her lips. Her real self stopped digging for a persona to hang on to. "Hell yes."

Leaving Lawson behind, she made her way up another set of stairs, this one narrow and circular, to her favorite place in the whole house.

After showering and shaving—without interruption for the first time in two days—she lathered herself lovingly with some expensive body lotion she'd dug out of an antique glass-fronted cabinet in the corner.

She felt almost normal again. Rummaging through another cabinet, she found a new, unwrapped Sanogyl toothbrush and some toothpaste and went to work on her teeth, even scrubbing her tongue. She rinsed and wiped off her mouth. Much better.

She scrunched her towel-dried hair before digging out a couple of tiny glass pots of rich eye shadow and a brush. More cabinets and drawers yielded more makeup brushes and bronzing powder.

Using a fat brush, Zara stroked the light bronzer on her cheeks and forehead to give her face a bit of color. Then she took the eye-shadow brush and dipped it in a pot of smoke-colored eye shadow, using it to line her upper eyelids along her lashes. Her tired eyes looked less tired. Now if she just had her lip gloss she'd be all set.

Of course that had gone up in the explosion with her favorite handbag and everything else, including her cell phone. Flynn would be expecting a message, but right now, she was glad she had an excuse not to send one. She was ninety-nine percent certain he would never betray her, but ninety-nine wasn't a hundred.

She forced her mind not to dwell on the explosion or the car chase. Like she'd admitted to Lawson, she'd been scared, but she'd also felt alive. Even though the tightrope under her feet had wiggled and thrown her off balance, she'd stayed on and rode it out. She'd survived.

Lawson's kiss had thrown her off balance as well. Boy, oh boy, the man could kiss. Another praiseworthy skill to add to his list. Too bad she couldn't explore that list a little more.

Zara always had nagging doubts about the men who romanced her. Some wanted to find out if she was a natural blonde, and once they knew, she never saw them again. Others wanted to sink their fingers into her bank accounts, give her investment advice or get her to invest in their capital ventures. A few were bold enough to use her to get to her father, skipping her modest assets to get to Charles Morgan's empire.

During her wild college years, she'd envisioned herself as a woman of the world, enjoying and partaking of the international male smorgasbord, but the truth was, casual sex wasn't her style then and it still wasn't now.

And that's where the problem was with Lawson and his wonderful lips. She could see him, pumped with adrenaline like he'd been the night before, stripping her naked in the heat of the moment. Raw and passionate head-banging sex up against a car.

She could also imagine him hiding her away and making love to her in a protective, gentlemanly manner. Passionate, but slow and tender and attentive to her every whim. His body comforting and reassuring her with his expert touch and luscious kisses.

He might even tease her into a sexual encounter just to take her mind off a bad situation or yank her chain. Sexy and provocative, he'd make her hate him for wanting him so much. As competitive as he was, he'd probably do everything in his power to make her come first so he could prove he was more in control than she was. The thought made her laugh out loud.

What she couldn't see, didn't want to imagine, was the future after the sex. After the mission ended and they were no longer partners...where Lawson told her he would call her for that dinner rain check, and she went around for weeks with her heart doing double-time every time her cell rang only to find it was her mother on the other end.

Where she primped every morning in the mirror just in case she ran into him at Langley. Where she deluded herself with imaginary conversations that would never take place and made up excuses for his absence.

He was attracted to her, his kiss had told her that loud and clear. But a kiss in the heat of an adrenaline-pumping getaway was just a kiss. It probably never would have happened if Zara hadn't broken down in the first place. He'd tried to console her and gotten carried away because of the heightened stress of the night.

She had too. That was all it was.

Hour by hour, though, Lawson was getting under her skin. He was forcing her to face her past and yet protecting her at the same time. Every time he looked at her or touched her, a strange drumming took up residence in her rib cage. A drumming she recognized as sexual attraction and something else she couldn't quite define.

She knew about hostage situations, knew about transference. Was it possible to have a crush on the man who'd saved her life two months ago? Was it the previous night's heroic acts making her feel this way?

No, it's not transference.

Sex with Lawson could be fun, but she couldn't do it. A short-term fling on this mission was out of the question. For her and for Lawson. It would undermine their professionalism and endanger the success of the operation.

Pushing him out of her mind, she considered what still needed to be done. First, she had to find some clean clothes and get some food in her stomach. Second, get some sleep. Sleep would give her perspective and help her figure out this mess.

The memory of Lawson's kisses surfaced again and a flutter drummed next to her heart.

Three, she added to her list, stay away from Lawson's lips.

Chapter Nineteen

Lawson finished his second cheese and walnut omelet and took a sip of coffee. Then he reached for his third croissant and buttered it under Christian's watchful eye.

Christian sat across the glass-topped table, a curious smile on his face, and sipped his own coffee. Lawson knew he should be more polite and make conversation, but at the moment he just wanted to keep eating. The food was delicious and he didn't know what to talk to Christian about anyway. Jobs? The man was a freakin' ballet teacher.

Sports? Was ballet a sport? Not to him.

Zara? No way. Lawson didn't know how much Christian knew about Zara's work with the CIA so that was not a safe topic.

Where was Zara anyway? It had been over an hour since she'd disappeared into the Tower Room. It didn't take that long to shower and brush your teeth. Lawson had been done and out in ten minutes. Of course, he'd been around his share of women, including his mother and sisters, and he knew how long it took a woman in the bathroom. It took as long as she wanted it to.

There had been times in the past few days when he'd have sworn Zara was a high-maintenance woman. She had some of the attitude and that girly obsession with clothes, but she wore almost no makeup and kept her hair natural. She actually seemed comfortable with her body and adamant he not instruct her on how to dress.

"Would you like another omelet?" Christian asked, interrupting his thoughts.

Lawson swallowed the last bite of croissant and his cell phone vibrated on on his belt. It had been going off for the past few hours, one reason he'd put it on vibrate. Flynn, Annette and

Del had left messages. None of which helped him and Zara in the least. "No, thanks, but I'd appreciate a glass of milk."

Christian raised a hand and the maid appeared. "Marie, bring a glass of milk for Mr. Vaughn."

As the woman nodded and walked back into the house, alarms went off in Lawson's head. "You know my last name?"

"In my business, people are my number one asset. I must know all about them to understand them. Who they are and where they come from, what their dreams are and, more importantly, what their fears are. Then I can give them what they want. Or"—he shrugged nonchalantly—"take it away."

Lawson wondered what *business* Christian was referring to. "Why would you know about me?"

"Because of Zara, of course."

Marie returned with Lawson's milk and he thanked her. She returned to her post out of earshot of the table near the veranda doors.

Christian sat back in his chair and fiddled with a heavy white cloth napkin. "I owe you a debt of gratitude for saving my Zara from that despicable excuse of a human, Alexandrov Dmitri, earlier this year." He smoothed the napkin into a triangle. "Whatever you want, Lawson, it is yours."

Lawson didn't like the way Christian constantly referred to Zara as *my Zara*, but now at least he knew the man was aware of what had happened. He raised his milk glass in salute. "The shower and the breakfast are more than sufficient payback."

The man's expression remained serious. "Alexandrov threatened someone I love very dearly. In my opinion, he should not be allowed to walk the Earth, but I am hardly in a position to mete out justice. Zara claims she is all right, and for that, I'm glad. So perhaps one day in your personal or professional life you will need certain information or a favor of some nature. You have only to ask me and I'll provide what you need."

Lawson finished his milk and stared out at the pool and garden around it. The sun was high enough now its reflection on the water caused the pool to look like a blanket of sparkling diamonds.

Wealth could buy a lot of things other than a cache of material goods. Loyalty, security, information. He wasn't sure how far to trust Christian, but his gut told him the man could be a valuable asset. He found he wasn't opposed to using

Christian's money or his love for Zara to help him track down Dmitri. Especially since his backside was a little vulnerable at the moment.

Setting his empty glass on the table, he turned his attention back to his host. It seemed like the time to find out if Christian Bernier could indeed help him. "Right now, I need to find Alexandrov Dmitri."

"His prison reprieve was well financed," Christian said without missing a beat. He lifted a porcelain coffee cup to his lips. "It should not be that hard to find out who provided such monies and follow the trail. The only reason the French authorities have not found Vos Loo is because the two men have bought themselves new identities."

It was no surprise that Christian knew about the prison break. It had made the *International Herald Tribune* in Paris and most of the British dailies as well. Lawson agreed with his theory on the new identities. "I think both men are here in Switzerland."

Christian nodded slowly, mulling the idea over. "Geneva?"

"Possibly."

Again Christian nodded, his gaze falling to the pool. "Private banking and an international community. Makes sense. But what does dear Alexi need with Dr. Vos Loo?"

"Vos Loo is a chemist. He specializes in biological agents."

Christian's attention returned to Lawson. "Weapons?"

"With the research universities and companies around here, Vos Loo has easy access to what he needs to create biological weapons."

"But for whom?"

"The Italian Mafia."

Christian's brows lowered. "You have names?"

"Varina Scalfaro. Yvette LeMans. A bodyguard named Giovanni. A customer or possible business partner of Yvette's named Rogan Janvrin who was arrested two nights ago for drug possession."

"Janvrin? The computer wizard?"

"You know him?"

Christian picked up a carafe and poured more coffee into his cup. "His wife. She's publicity chair for our local arts council which serves the Alpine Diamond—Geneva, Lyon, Basil and

Turin—helping local artists promote their work and bringing cultural events to the area."

"What can you tell me about Janvrin?"

"He was a technical prodigy hired by the Swiss Institute of Technology when he was eighteen to write software code for laparoscopic surgery simulators. He now heads The Image Medical Group's technology team. They specialize in virtual reality simulators for the medical field."

Lawson toyed with his knife, flipping it end over end. How did a computer geek fit in with a terrorist, a biochemist and the mob? "He apparently enjoys the company of women other than his wife. Recreational drugs too."

Christian's expression turned bemused. "What man doesn't?"

"Do you think his wife knows about his indiscretions?"

"She has quite a list of her own." His head came up and his eyes zeroed in on a spot over Lawson's left shoulder. "'She moved with a slowness that was a sign of richness; cream does not pour quickly.'"

Even before he followed Christian's eyes, Lawson knew the quote referred to Zara, even though he had no idea who it originated from. She walked through the veranda doors, smiling and saying something in passing to Marie. The maid dipped her chin and curtsied.

Zara turned her smile on the two of them as she walked across the patio toward the table. She looked refreshed, her skin flushed and her eyes bright again. She was wearing a pale pink dress with some kind of gauzy material over it which seemed to float around her knees. On her feet she wore a pair of ballet slippers.

Lawson heard the sound of Christian's chair scraping on the inlaid concrete, and he too pushed his chair back from the table and stood.

Christian stepped around him and reached for Zara's hand. Immediately, the show was back on. "Feeling better, love?" he asked as he led her to an empty chair between them.

"Yes." She lifted her face to Lawson's as she accepted the seat. "I hope you didn't wait for me."

Lawson sat and pushed his plate back, suddenly feeling a bit like a country bumpkin compared to the aristocrat next to him. "Sorry, I didn't. I was starving."

"Me too. I'm hungry enough to eat a cow whole."

Christian clucked his tongue and reached for the carafe of coffee. He poured some into a clean cup and set it in front of her. "Meat is bad for you, my dear."

Zara glanced at Lawson as she sipped the steaming coffee. "Christian's a vegetarian. No meat of any kind."

"Clogs the arteries and weighs the body down. Sure death to a dancer." He motioned to Marie and she scurried to the table. "Bring Ms. Morgan one of Gunther's fabulous omelets, *s'il vous plaît*, and some fresh croissants."

Marie hurried off, and Zara said to Lawson, "So what were you two talking about?"

Before he could answer, Christian jumped in. "Why, ballet, of course." He reached for a bowl of cut-up fruit and placed a spoonful of melon on her plate.

"Really?" She quirked a brow at Lawson. "Was Christian entertaining you with his great success stories?"

Lawson wasn't sure why Christian had lied about the conversation topic, but before he could decide whether or not to go along with it, Christian interceded again. "I was just about to tell your friend what an exquisite ballerina *you* were." He speared a piece of melon and looked at Lawson. "Her talent was exceptional. Guaranteed future with the Royal Ballet."

A flicker of sadness crossed Zara's face as she stared into her coffee. When she looked up and met his eyes, she smiled, brushing the sadness aside. "He says that about all of his students."

"I do not." Christian set down the fork and tapped his chest with his closed fist. "The dance was in Zara. Inside, you understand? It came from her heart. She is one of the few I have ever worked with who had pure, genuine talent. Just like her mother."

Zara unfolded her napkin and laid it on her lap. "I loved dance, but it wasn't meant to be."

Christian dished melon onto his plate. "*C'est vrai*, but you could have done it, Zara. You could have been greater than Olivia. If only she had not fallen in love with your father. But then, you would not be here, right? It is a shame for the ballet world both of you gave up so soon."

"My mother gave up ballet for love." Zara's voice was a fraction lower than Lawson was used to, but every bit as spunky. "You know I had an injury and decided I wanted to do something else with my life. Not the same thing."

Christian studied her for a long moment. "You were injured, this is true, but you defied the doctors and danced again."

"Not competitively."

He shook his head. "Your talent is wasted."

The urge to defend Zara rose in Lawson like a flash fire, but he saw her lips thin in resolve. She didn't need him to come to her rescue.

"I have many talents," she said, looking Christian squarely in the eye, "and none are wasted. You of all people should understand exactly what I'm doing and respect my choices."

Marie arrived with Zara's omelet, a basket of warm croissants and a carafe of fresh coffee. Zara thanked her and she nodded, picking up the empty carafe and returning to the house. Lawson watched Zara dig into her food.

Christian also watched Zara. "Your eye for design and costumes along with your own experience as a ballerina would make you a good choreographer. I could take you on as an intern and make you a great one." His arm flourished through the air. "You could start your own business and freelance or perhaps gain a spot with Mark Morris in America. He's almost as good as me."

She swallowed. "I won't give up my job with the CIA for ballet."

"Ha." Christian rolled his eyes. "The CIA. As if any such organization could compete with ballet."

The corners of Zara's mouth slid up. She gave Christian an endearing look. "The next time I have a few days to myself, I'll spend them with you, okay? Maybe I can help with one of your camps next year."

"I would love that!" He rose and pushed in his chair. "Now I must excuse myself. I have a few phone calls to make and other business to attend to. Marie will prepare your rooms, and you know you are welcome to use the pool and the riding stables and anything else that appeals to you. Lunch is on your own. Just tell Marie what you'd like and she will pass it on to Gunther. Dinner will be at eight tonight. Please dress for it." He took Zara's hand, bringing it to his lips. "I will see you then, love."

He nodded at Lawson. "The names you mentioned. I will investigate and see what I can find out."

Lawson nodded back. "Appreciate it."

He disappeared into the house.

"What names?" Zara asked.

Lawson's phone buzzed on his hip again. He turned it off. "He knew about Dmitri and Vos Loo. I told him we suspected they're connected to the Mafia. He asked for names and I gave him what we had. He thinks he might be able to dig up something for us."

Zara helped herself to a croissant and broke it in half. "Christian has a lot of contacts, but I don't want to drag him into this."

"The minute you showed up on his doorstep, you involved him. No one knows we're here and we won't be staying."

"If he starts asking too many questions, or asks the wrong people, he could end up in trouble."

"He's very shrewd and he wants to help. He has connections here in Switzerland. We need him."

Zara frowned, breaking a piece of bread off and dropping it into her mouth. Lawson shifted in his chair to stretch his legs. "Do you visit Christian often?"

Laying the corner of the croissant on her plate, she shook her head. "I came for a weekend right after I was stationed in Paris, but I never found the time to visit after that."

"Did you leave that dress here?"

Zara glanced down at the dress and back up at him. "This isn't my dress," she said in that don't-be-silly voice of hers.

"Then whose is it?"

"It's Christian's. He has a whole room of clothes and accessories like this."

Lawson didn't like the Technicolor images his brain suddenly conjured up. "Is Christian gay?"

Zara sat back in her chair and crossed her arms under her breasts. "Because he has a room full of women's clothes automatically makes him gay?"

"No, that makes him a transvestite, and yes, I do know the difference."

Zara gave him a disgusted look. "I didn't say he *wears* women's clothes. He's friends with several designers—Donatella

Versace, Ralph Lauren, Marc Jacobs. They often send him samples of their new lines, both men's and women's, and he keeps a variety of clothes on hand for his guests. The estate is like a mini-resort. He entertains all sorts of people. International dignitaries, movie stars, you name it. The clothes and shoes are part of the package. His guests love it and it's good for the designers too. He often makes sales. That's why they keep sending him their stuff."

Lawson grinned at her. "You didn't answer my question."

"What difference does Christian's sexual orientation make?"

"It doesn't." He shrugged. "I'm just curious." Which was an understatement. Lawson's gut told him Christian Bernier was totally infatuated with Zara. If it turned out the man was straight, he was going to have to punch him in the face the next time he called Zara *my Zara.*

"Last I knew," she said after a minute, "he swung both ways."

Not what he wanted to hear. "And do you ever swing with him?"

Her jaw dropped. "You think I would sleep with Christian? My God, he was my ballet instructor, and besides he's at least fifteen years older than me and—" She stopped and her eyes narrowed. "Are you jealous of Christian?"

Him jealous of a guy who taught ballet and walked around in designer-labeled clothes? No way. Hell, the guy didn't even eat meat. Lawson affected a disinterested face. "I told you, I'm just curious."

She leaned forward and pinched his leg, doing her Cheshire-cat impression. "Better be careful, Commander. I hear he loves tall, dark and dangerous guys like you. He's probably upstairs in his office right now figuring out how he's going to talk you into swimming laps with him so he can see how your package fills out a Speedo."

She was so cocky, Lawson chuckled. "You're supposed to be my partner. Can't you protect me?"

Now she laughed and he laughed with her, enjoying the moment's reprieve from their serious situation.

"I don't know." She tried to turn serious. "Are you going to stop bossing me around?"

"Whatever you want," he answered, bringing his face close to hers. He was pretty sure he meant it too. With every passing minute, he knew he'd do anything to keep the sadness out of Zara's face and make her smile. Jump tall buildings? No problem. Fly faster than a speeding train? Piece of cake. Reverse time and give Zara the chance to make Dmitri pay? He'd give it a shot.

Her eyes flickered with challenge. "You're on."

She stood, threw her cloth napkin on the table and looked down at him. "I'm going to go take a nap, but tonight after dinner I want you to come to the Tower Room with me. There's something I want to show you. And"—she winked at him conspiratorially—"you'll be safe from Christian there."

Lawson grabbed her hand, pulling it to his mouth and kissing the top of it like Christian had a few minutes before. "Bless you, love," he said in his best British accent.

She rolled her eyes and tugged her hand out of his. As she marched back to the house, he smiled smugly to himself. She had invited him to her room after dinner. Damn, that was a fine thing.

Pushing himself out of the patio chair, he stretched and watched the sun on the pool water again. He needed to call Hoffman and see what he could track down about Yvette and her relationship to Varina and the Mafia. Then he was going to grab some sleep. In the past forty-some hours, he'd had less than three hours, and if things went the way he planned, he wouldn't be getting much sleep tonight either.

Tonight, he'd be drinking a special brand of rich cream, and he'd be damned if he'd waste one single drop of that opportunity.

Chapter Twenty

Lawson spoke into his encrypted digital phone as he paced the bedroom. The room was an extension of the sunroom, marble floors, skylights, plants and eighteenth-century furniture. "Whatcha got for me, Del?"

The younger man snorted. "What I have is The Great Conrad Flynn and The Mighty Michael Stone crawling up my ass wanting to know where you are and what the hell you're doing. You haven't checked in for thirty-six hours and someone, presumably you, is leaving a mess of dead bodies all over France."

Del's voice was low and Lawson had a mental picture of him hunched down in his cubicle at Langley trying to hide from listening ears. "So why are you talking to me instead of patching me straight through to Flynn?"

"I'm giving you a heads-up. Flynn is one pissed-off camper. I can tell by the way he keeps pacing through the CTC and yelling at everyone. People are dead and you're MIA. If you don't give him the answers he wants to hear when you talk to him, my guess is he's going to pull you off the assignment."

Not if he can't find me. "Do you have the info on Vos Loo?"

"I emailed info about his Switzerland network to you five minutes ago."

Lawson pulled out a chair and sat at the desk in the corner of the room. "How much have the French authorities figured out about the dead bodies?"

"Everything. Flynn's having a tough time smoothing things over with them and keeping your and Zara's mugs out of the newspapers. Especially since the bodies were found outside your rooms at the Ambassador—what the hell were you doing staying at the Ambassador anyway?"

"Long story. Go on."

"They have an eyewitness who claims he saw you and heard the gunshots. The hotel's security cameras have you on tape, and when the local police started trying to trace Isaac and Sara Lerner, they turned it over to French Intelligence real fast. Flynn planned to visit Paris this week to do some sightseeing. Now he's coming in an official capacity."

Lawson tapped his fingers on the desk as his laptop received what Del was sending via satellite. "It was Flynn who established Yvette LeMans as my contact, but apparently she was buddies with Varina Scalfaro and tied to the Mafia with some kind of prostitution slash drug ring. Yvette showed up at the hotel with her Italian version of the Hulk, pulled a gun on Zara and tried to kill her. I'm not feeling the love here, Del."

"Back up. You said Yvette LeMans was at the Ambassador last night? What did you do with her?"

"Pay attention," Lawson said, scanning his computer screen. "I shot her and her bodyguard Giovanni."

"You're talking about the woman you left outside your room with a bullet in her brain?"

"Who are you talking about?"

Del cleared his throat and Lawson heard the faint clicks of his computer keyboard. "The woman you killed last night was not Yvette LeMans."

"Then who was it?"

"I'm sending you a JPEG file right now. Open it."

A minute later, a message with an attachment appeared in Lawson's inbox. He clicked on the attachment hotkey.

"Is that her?" Del asked.

Lawson looked at the sloe eyes on the screen and could almost smell the woman's perfume. "Yeah, that's her."

"My man." Del sighed. "The woman you killed outside your room at the Ambassador last night was the infamous Varina Scalfaro."

Lawson sank back in his chair. "Damn it." He stared at the screen and tried to process the information. "So where's Yvette?"

"I don't know, but if Varina was using her identity, I've got a twenty says Yvette's floating at the bottom of the Seine."

That was one bet Lawson wasn't stupid enough to take. "All right, listen, I've got a couple more names I need you to run for me. Varina was spending time with Rogan Janvrin. He's some kind of computer geek who works for the Swiss Institute of Technology."

"Watch your mouth. Computer geeks make the world go round."

"I also need information about a man named Christian Bernier. Lives in Switzerland, southwest of Geneva."

There was a pause, and then Del said, "Christian Bernier. Name's familiar."

"He's a dance guru here in Europe. Owns an impressive estate and entertains a lot of important people, dignitaries, expatriates, movie stars. Has an extraordinary collection of art work. I'm sending you a photo of a Degas painting and a couple of other pieces in his collection. I want you to track down where they came from."

"What does that have to do with Dmitri?"

"Nothing." Lawson rubbed his eyes. "Is Flynn worried about his counterintelligence spy?"

"That would be the second reason he's stomping on people around here."

Lawson didn't blame him. He'd do the same in Flynn's position. Zara was a unique operative and Lawson was starting to appreciate just how unique.

From the minute he'd blown up the car until they crossed the border into Switzerland, Zara had talked in fits and starts over the roar of the bike. She'd been scared, but she hadn't given into it. Instead she'd talked. He now knew her favorite movie was *The Wizard of Oz* and her stint in Girl Scouts ended when they kicked her out of her troop at the ripe old age of seven for refusing to wear the ugly uniform.

"Are you going to call Flynn and get him off my ass?" Del asked.

"Maybe," Lawson said, thinking it over. "But probably not."

He cut the connection before Del could respond and turned the phone off, setting it next to his laptop. He pulled out his handy-dandy spy camera, downloaded the images of Christian's collection of fine art and emailed it to the techie.

The next half hour he spent reading about Jon Vos Loo and trying to piece together the Plan B he'd told Zara existed. There was no Plan B, but the lie had relaxed her a little and seeing the worry line on her brow soften was worth it.

The stakes for this mission were getting high. It wasn't a simple tracking mission anymore. He and Zara were on someone's radar now and whoever it was wasn't fooling around. Lawson's gut told him Flynn was still trustworthy—the man had nothing to gain by screwing over his hired contractor—but in this business, it never hurt to err on the side of caution. For now though, it was in his best interest to keep Flynn out of the loop and pay the hell he was earning later.

Caution also demanded he put Zara on a plane back to Langley and finish the job on his own. She'd be safe, but after spending the last few days with her, Lawson couldn't imagine her living in the conservative Agency environment. She had too much substance and determination, too much intensity for close quarters. She'd handled the tough situations of their mission with the same style and grace as she'd handled the routine, and for that reason, Lawson would keep her with him. Along with the fact that, until he knew the identity of the people chasing them, he wasn't sending her anywhere alone.

At least that's what he told himself. In the back of his mind, he knew the real reason he didn't want to send Zara home to the States had nothing to do with her safety. She'd grown on him, and the thought of putting her on a plane and watching her fly out of his life made his gut contract like he'd been punched.

Shutting off his computer, he rubbed his eyes. Better not to go there, he told himself. Better not think about why his gut was reacting to her leaving so strongly. He was exhausted after the past few days with no sleep and too much adrenaline and his brain was starting to short out. That was all.

Without stripping off his clothes, he fell face down on the bed. A few hours of shut eye and he'd be fine. He'd be able to come up with a solid Plan B and figure out what to do with Zara.

What to do with Zara...

Before Lawson's eyes closed, his subconscious was already at work on several tantalizing possibilities.

Late afternoon sun poured through the single window in

the Tower Room when Zara woke from sleep. She stretched and peeked out through the layers of sheer tulle that fell from the bed canopy to see the miniature clock on the nightstand. It was five o'clock.

Lying back with a sigh, she snuggled further down in the pillows and closed her eyes again, enjoying the fresh lavender smell of the bed linens. That smell alone could transport her back in time to her teenage years and the ballet camps she had attended at Villa Bernier. Staying at Christian's had given her a sense of peace she couldn't find at home. She'd always hated the way her parents worried about what she was going to do with her life, even though she understood their concerns were natural. She'd been a bit of a challenge, and as she grew older, she understood more and more just how much her parents had done for her over the years in the name of love.

While Christian's love bordered on parental, he was more like a godfather, with a blind eye for her shortcomings and overindulgent with his praise. His unconditional love made her feel special.

Opening her eyes, she rolled onto her back. The Tower Room seemed completely out of place in Christian's villa which was one of the reasons she loved it. With the exception of the four-poster bed, everything in the room was miniature. The armoire, the dressing table, the trunk at the foot of the bed, the rocking chair in the corner. All that was missing was the White Rabbit. The walls were ballerina pink with white trim, the furniture was painted in various shades of pink and white, and the floor was covered in white marble that had veins of pink quartz running through it.

The room was part of an actual tower. It vaulted high above the rest of the villa like a castle turret. The stairs leading to the room continued their spiral up through the middle, ending at the roof and an amazing view of sky and land and water. You could see the Rhonê a few miles south. Zara could hardly wait to bring Lawson up there later. If the night were clear, a blanket of stars would reach down and envelop them.

A light rap on the door to the stairwell below brought her out of her daydreaming. Christian's voice called softly up the stairs. "Zara, may I come up?"

"One minute."

Getting up, she grabbed the sundress off the bed and slid it over her head. She smoothed the material down the front and sides and ran her fingers through her hair. Then she leaned over the stair railing. "Come on up."

Christian climbed the stairs and kissed her on one cheek. "You look refreshed. Did you snag a decent nap?"

"Yes, I feel much better."

"Good. Now you must tell me, are you in danger?"

There really wasn't anyplace other than the bed big enough for both of them to sit on, so Zara pulled the top sheet and comforter up and sat on top. Christian joined her. "I can't tell you much," she said. "I'm on assignment for the Agency as you probably guessed, and even if it wasn't confidential, I'm not sure I could explain exactly what happened last night or why. Things are rather..." she trailed off, searching for the right words, "...confusing right now."

Christian gave her an impetuous frown. "I thought you were working at Langley instead of doing fieldwork."

"My boss thought I was ready to return."

"Because Vaughn's your partner?"

"Because Alexandrov Dmitri is out of prison. I'm the expert on him."

He patted her hands. "I don't like it, but you're safe here and welcome to stay as long as you wish."

"You've always been here for me. How can I ever thank you?"

He grinned. "Dance for me, Zara. Come see the studio. I remodeled it last month. *C'est magnifique!*"

"I'd love to see it."

She put on her shoes and followed Christian down the spiral stairs, through the west wing, down to the first floor and into the east wing. As they passed the formal dining room and entertainment room, her pulse picked up at the thought of standing in the middle of Christian's studio again. So many years had gone by. Who would she see when she looked in the wall-to-wall mirrors? The girl of all those years ago or the woman she was now?

Christian opened the sliding doors with reverence. "The *pièce de résistance.*"

She stepped across the threshold and stopped, transfixed.

Just as Christian promised, it was magnificent. The whole

north wall had been taken out, and in its place, a wall of windows had been installed. Soft light from the setting sun bathed the room in a warm glow. The wooden floor was buffed to a perfect gloss, tempting Zara's slippered feet to glide on it. Doing a slow turn, she took in the fifteen-foot columns supporting the corners of the ceiling. On the columns, stereo speakers and spotlights looked down on the room. The east wall was mirrored and supported the long barre for warm-up exercises. A pile of ballet shoes and a box of resin sat in one corner, an upright piano in the other.

The wall at the far end was also mirrored but free of a barre. This was where the dancers practiced their techniques and learned combinations. Zara could imagine dancers doing *pirouettes*, *glissades* and *grand jetès* in preparation for a dance.

Continuing her turn, she saw giant black and white pictures of two of the greatest ballet dancers of all time, Anna Pavlova and Vaslav Nijinsky. The pictures hung on either side of the sliding doors, and Zara knew Christian had purposely placed them there to inspire each dancer who passed between them.

At the end of a practice, whether training or rehearsal, every ballet dancer was physically and emotionally drained. As they left the studio, seeing role models such as Pavlova and Nijinsky lifted their spirits and made the aches and pains and disappointments with their performance fade. Determination to improve their technique next time bloomed in their hearts.

The stars of fallen CIA members did the same for the men and women who worked at Langley.

As Zara gazed up at Anna Pavlova in her *The Dying Swan* role, the desire to dance again rippled through her muscles. "She's so beautiful," she whispered.

The tendon Zara had ruptured healed after time and physical therapy, but she could never again exert the pressure on it she needed to in order to perform the aerial jumps and demanding pointe work of a professional ballerina. Even jumps done close to the ground required a softness and elasticity her calf and ankle no longer possessed. The girl who had perfected *pliès*, *battements* and *ports de bras*, who had danced in front of the mirrors with her heart pouring out through every move, could never become a topnotch dancer like her mother.

Christian came to stand next to her, following her gaze to

Anna's picture. "Yes. Perfection."

Zara cut her eyes to him. "You always said there was no such thing as *perfection* in ballet."

"*C'est ne vrai pas.* Not true at all. I told you there was no such thing as a *perfectly executed dance.* There is a difference." He held out his hands in offering. "So what do you think?"

Zara looked around again and smiled. "It's stunning."

Christian returned her smile. "And are you tempted to dance here?"

Leaving him, she walked the perimeter of the room, feeling the floor beneath her feet and enjoying the view of rolling hills and forest outside the windows. Her heart fluttered. "Yes," she admitted.

He beamed at her from across the room. "Come," he said, walking toward her and holding out his hand. "Come to the barre."

Zara flushed, her heart beginning to pound. "I can't. It's been too long."

Christian took her hand and pulled her forward. "Your body will remember. Your muscles will remember. Relax and let them move."

Zara took one of her hands and laid it gently on the barre. As if they possessed a will of their own, her legs turned out at the hips and her feet moved into first position. It wasn't the young ballerina of long ago she saw in her reflection, but the woman in the mirror looked natural *á la barre* nonetheless. Her posture was straight but relaxed and there was a confident, more mature set to her chin.

Christian stepped to her side and smiled at her. "And begin," he said, falling into teacher mode. "*Demi-plié.*"

Begin, Zara's brain echoed. Her knees automatically bent.

Christian took her through the usual warm-up set of plies in all five positions. Then she went on to *tendues,* pointing and stretching her feet, and finally through several sets of *battements.* After twenty minutes, she was sweating and mentally cursing the sundress which limited her movements too much.

"Your muscles are strong," Christian said, "and your Achilles tendon seems very pliant. That's good, love."

She took the white towel he offered and patted her forehead

and neck with it. "I do yoga and some ballet stretches every day and strength training several times a week."

"While you are here, we will work on strengthening your feet and legs and begin drills. Keep you ready for that choreographer's spot."

"Christian, stop. I do not want a job in ballet, even as a choreographer. I'm an intelligence officer for the CIA. This visit is just a pit stop while Lawson and I regroup."

"Perhaps you should let Lawson finish the mission on his own. From what he has told me, I believe your life could be endangered if you continue."

"I'm a field operative. I won't back out now just because things got rough yesterday. Besides, Lawson needs me."

"I'm certain you excel at what you do, but Lawson lives and breathes this type of work every day. You do not. It would be like Lawson trying to do a *grand jeté* without ever learning to do smaller jumps."

Zara laughed at the thought of Lawson in tights. "Christian, *I* live and breathe this type of work. Just because I've been at Langley for the past few months doesn't mean I've lost all my field skills. In fact, the opposite is true. My boss taught me a variety of essential spy tricks."

Christian eyed her with keen interest. "I think there is something more going on here. You have a crush on Lawson, don't you?"

She threw the towel into the corner and turned her back on him. "Of course not. We're partners, nothing more."

"He doesn't seem like your type. You and Lucie are always attracted to the needy boys—the temperamental artists, the tree hugging environmentalists, the political reformists..."

Zara walked in front of the northern windows, watching shadows take shape below. He'd always been able to see through her lies, and protesting was counterproductive. Admitting some of her feelings here, in the sanctuary of his studio, seemed harmless enough. "I think what I feel for Lawson is a type of transference. He rescued me from a traumatic experience, so I've turned him into someone bigger than life in my head."

"You're attracted to him because he makes you feel safe."

"Sort of."

Doubt was clear in Christian's voice. "How interesting."

She turned to face him and saw his *get real* look.

"Okay, okay," she admitted. "That's crap and we both know it. The farmhouse incident left me questioning myself and feeling some guilt, but overall, the worst I suffered from my confrontation with Dmitri was a few bad dreams. Before this mission, Lawson's irritated me more than anything else. Everyone at the Agency thinks he *rescued* me."

"He did, my dear."

"No." Zara shook her head. "He helped, but I rescued myself. And I kept Tim from getting killed. I'd like just a *little* acknowledgement for what *I* did." She let her head fall back. "I was *not* rescued."

"Why did you agree to be Lawson's partner?"

"We were assigned to each other. Flynn gave me no choice in the matter."

"No choice?"

She faced him. "Why are you looking at me like that?"

Christian waved her off. "Your confidence is one of the things I love about you. I believe Commander Vaughn admires it as well."

She snorted. Paced the room. "The last few days I've gotten to know him—the man, not the hero everyone makes him out to be. He's not exactly what I expected." She walked back over to the barre, leaning her back against it. "I've never met anyone like him before. He's demanding, he's rude and he's competitive beyond words, and yet he seems to genuinely care what happens to me."

"Ah, he's your fantasy man."

It was Zara's turn to give Christian a *get real* look.

He leaned his back against the barre next to her. "Does he ever smile?"

"Smile?"

He shrugged. "He's very good looking. Sort of Bear Grylls only with more of a Mad Max edge."

"Bear Grylls? From the adventure reality show?"

"*Man vs. Wild.*" Christian gazed into space. "Think what I could do with Lawson in a black Dolce and Gabbana suit, a pair of Italian shoes, a little hair gel..." He pushed off the barre, his eyebrows shooting straight up to his hairline. "My God, he's my fantasy man too."

She threw her head back and laughed. "He's straight, Christian. Very, very straight."

"You don't think I noticed?" He grunted. "I mean, what am I? Instant oatmeal? I even did my serious, no-nonsense approach at breakfast this morning and I couldn't get a twinkle out of him. It appears he only has eyes for you."

Zara thought about that for all of two seconds before she blurted out, "That's silly."

But her heart thudded in her rib cage as she thought about Christian's description of her partner. Bear Grylls crossed with Mad Max. Oh that was *so* Lawson. She giggled low in her throat. Wouldn't it be fun to sic Christian on him? Just to make him sweat a little?

"You know," she said, taking Christian's arm and guiding him toward the open studio doors, "I'm sure Lawson has no clue how to dress for dinner tonight. Maybe you could pull something together for him out of your den of clothes. What do you think?"

Christian smiled down at her and waggled his eyebrows. "I think this is going to be absolute fun."

Chapter Twenty-One

A knock on the door brought Lawson instantly awake. His hand snagged the Beretta before his feet hit the floor. The room was dark. He wasn't sure how long he'd slept or where he was.

Christian Bernier's voice on the other side of the door brought things into sharp focus. "Commander Vaughn? A word, please."

He lowered his gun, rolled his head from side to side to loosen up his stiff neck and ran his hand through his hair. Before opening the door, he flicked on the bedside lamp. The clock read seven thirty.

In the doorway, Christian's intense focus swept over Lawson's disheveled hair and rumpled clothes. His gaze lingered a moment on Lawson's gun, and Lawson tucked it into his jeans at the small of his back.

"Will you be joining us for dinner?" Christian asked.

His stomach growled at the mention of food. He looked at his host, standing there in a dark purple smoking jacket and black cuffed trousers and wondered if he was already late for the meal. "Yeah, I'm coming. Give me a minute to clean up."

Christian gave a curt nod and once again sized up Lawson's appearance. "You'll find a package of knickers in the top drawer of the bureau." He pointed to a huge dresser in the corner. "After you shower, meet me at the other end of the hallway in the last room on the right. We'll dress you in appropriate eveningwear."

As Christian walked away, Lawson stared at the man's smoking jacket and gave an involuntary shudder. He could static-line jump from helicopters into enemy territory and not feel an ounce of fear. He could face gun-wielding terrorists and keep a level head. He could even endure his mother's and sisters' constant looks of pity and their interrogations about when he was going to settle down and get married without blinking an eye.

But the thought of Christian Bernier dressing him in anything, much less *eveningwear*, scared the shit out of him.

Ten minutes later, Lawson hesitated at the open door of the room as Christian bustled between a rack of suits and a built-in set of shelves nearby that held rows of black dress shoes. A man in a butler's uniform stood quietly next to a full-length mirror in the center of the room.

Lawson cleared his throat and Christian turned to look at him. A smile broke over his face. "Ah, yes. There you are. Come in, come in."

Shuffling his feet, he stepped into the room and shoved his hands into the pockets of his jeans. It wasn't that he was opposed to changing his clothes—his jeans and T-shirt were starting to smell pretty ripe—he just didn't want to end up looking like the cover of *GQ* magazine.

Or worse, like a bisexual European ballet instructor's bitch.

"Neck size?" Christian asked over his shoulder as he sorted through several neat stacks of white and black dress shirts.

The last time he'd worn a shirt that didn't come marked XL, he'd been a groomsman in his sister Angie's wedding. That had taken place almost nine years ago. "A T-shirt would be good. Extra large."

It was hard to believe Christian could convey a look of evil, but then again, the ballet instructor was a chameleon. He glared at Lawson, threatening dire harm.

"Seventeen, I think," he said, relenting.

Christian pulled a black shirt from one of the stacks. "You *think*?" The hint of disapproval in his voice reminded Lawson of his mother.

"It's been awhile since I've worn a dress shirt." He didn't like the defensive tone his voice was taking on. "Most of the time I'm lucky if my shirt isn't stained and my jeans aren't ripped in the crotch."

Christian made a disgusted noise. "See bear not score."

"What?"

"Never mind. We won't be doing any ragamuffin impressions tonight, Lawson."

Huh? "Look, I appreciate you loaning me some clean

clothes, but I'm not the kind of guy who wears..." he pointed at the suits, "...that. How about khakis and a polo?"

Ignoring his protests, Christian held the shirt up to Lawson's chest and eyed his neck. "Seventeen and a half will do." He tossed the shirt to the butler who disappeared behind the mirror with it. "Jacket size?"

Lawson shrugged.

"You're broad through the shoulders but narrow in the waist." He pulled a black pinstriped suit coat off the rack and held it out for Lawson to try on. "This is European cut. It will accentuate your assets."

"I don't do jackets."

Again, Christian glared at him. "Is that right?"

Reluctantly, Lawson sank his arms into the armholes and hefted the jacket up over his shoulders. It fit him perfectly but he itched wearing it all the same.

Christian tugged at the shoulders and smoothed his hands down the lapels, stopping to button the top button of the jacket. He tilted his head back and forth a couple of times and then unbuttoned it again, taking a step back to get a better view. "Do you know anything about women?"

Lawson knew a lot about women, but he couldn't fathom where Christian was going with this change of subject. He motioned for Lawson to take off the jacket. "Women are a mystery to those of us of the male species. But, my friend, I have worked with and studied them for years and there is one thing I know. There are women who will indulge your crotchless jeans and stained shirts because they are only interested in the physical attributes underneath them. And then"—he put his hands on his hips—"there are women like Zara."

Like Zara. Lawson let the words churn in his brain. Rich? Beautiful? Free spirited? Totally, one-hundred-and-ten percent out of his league? "We're partners on a mission. That's all."

Christian dropped the jacket on a sofa and walked to the mirror to examine his image in it. "Yes, so she claims as well. But let me tell you, my Zara is right now pouring herself into a white silk dress that will make your eyeballs pop out of your head. Her hair is perfectly coiffed and her face is flawless. Do you think you'll feel comfortable sitting across from her at dinner tonight in your jeans and T-shirt?"

The image of Zara in silk shot a jolt of heat straight

through Lawson's stomach. She looked good no matter what she put on for clothes, but he remembered the red dress she'd worn to the airport and his reaction to that had been less than subtle. Tonight she was in her element. The expensive house, the servants, the sophisticated clothes. The last thing he wanted to do was wreck his chances of getting laid because of his attire.

The butler returned with the black shirt, freshly pressed. He handed it to Christian, who laid it on the sofa beside the jacket. Christian attacked the rack of suits, flicking the hangered items past his nose. "Waist?"

Lawson sighed. "Thirty-two."

Christian pulled a pair of cuffed pants which matched the jacket off the rack and laid them next to the shirt. Before he was all done, a vest with matching pinstripes was on the couch along with black socks, a bow tie and a black belt. It looked like a freakin' tux. On the floor was a pair of dress shoes. Black.

"There." Christian surveyed his handiwork. "I'll give you five minutes and then I'll check on you. After dinner, we'll discuss what I found out about the names you gave me this morning."

"I'd rather talk about that now." Anything to delay putting on the monkey suit.

"Americans!" The word sounded like a particularly disgusting plague. "Abrupt and always putting business before pleasure." He strode up to Lawson and wagged a finger in his face. "A healthy tip for you, Commander—no matter your age or occupation, no matter what country you find yourself in or what matters are pressing on your mind, never, *ever*, keep a beautiful woman waiting. It's the rudest of moves."

Christian had officially turned into Mama Vaughn. Lawson dropped his head in resignation, knowing he didn't stand a chance. "Right," he said. "Dinner first."

Christian patted Lawson's cheek. "*Trés bien.* See bear score."

Lawson waited until the door closed behind him before he looked at himself in the mirror. Feeling suddenly self-conscious of his appearance, he ran a hand over his stubbly beard and brushed the hair off his forehead. He hadn't shaved in two days and his hair was a week past due for a trim. His eyes didn't look as tired as they felt, but he still looked like he'd been on a week-long bender.

He would put on the clothes, at least some of what Christian had laid out for him, but it wouldn't change anything. It wouldn't change the way Zara saw him or the way he saw himself. He'd still be Lawson Vaughn underneath the expensive clothes, and, while he hoped he might indeed score tonight, he wasn't part of Zara's world and he never would be. He wasn't going to change and become someone he wasn't for anybody, not even her.

Pulling off his shirt, he dropped it on the floor but kept his jeans on. He looked over the clothing on the couch and reached for the shirt. He'd wear a clean shirt to make Zara happy, but just the shirt and just for tonight. Maybe it would even be fun. He could turn it into a mental game he played with himself. He'd see how many times he could get her to smile over the next hour or so.

And then later, when she took him to the Tower Room, he'd do more than make her smile. He'd see how many times he could push her over the edge and get her to scream his name.

Before he left the room, he snagged the jacket for insurance.

Chapter Twenty-Two

It was a rare occurrence Zara found herself speechless, but speechless she was. Her mouth fell open as Lawson sauntered across the dining room toward her looking for all the world like he'd just stepped off a Paris runway.

A piece of his hair hung over his forehead and he'd left the suit jacket unbuttoned as well as the neck of his shirt, going sans tie. The frayed hems of his jean legs covered the black leather of the loafers he wore. The effect on the otherwise impeccable image was tauntingly sexy, as if he were as *dégagé* walking around in a three-thousand-dollar jacket as he was in his Levi's.

She grabbed her Waterford goblet off the table and took a long sip of water. Candlelight flickered over the Ceralene Laurier china, mimicking the flutter in her chest. Setting the crystal glass down, she forced her mouth closed and took a deep breath to try and slow her heart rate.

It didn't do any good. As Lawson crossed the Persian rug, his gaze trailed from her mouth, across her breasts and down her stomach and legs before coming back up. He offered her a casual smile, as if her appearance had no effect on him.

Liar. She saw the spark in his eyes.

Refusing to give in to her fluttering heart and dry mouth, she smiled as he stopped in front of her. She kept her voice matter-of-fact even though he was purposely invading her space. "Who are you and what did you do with my partner?"

He opened the jacket and looked down. "Clean up good, don't I?" As he leaned toward her in a conspiratorial manner, he whispered, "Not exactly my style, but I was hoping to impress you."

His clean smell wafted past her nose and she sucked in a breath. Her gaze dropped to the tantalizing triangle of skin above his open shirt. The four-inch heels of her shoes put her at the perfect level to see the pulse beating in the hollow of his neck. Checking herself, she bit the inside of her cheek and pretended to give him a critical once-over. "You look very...distinguished."

"I've been called a lot of things in my thirty-two years, but never *distinguished*."

"Clothes make the man they say."

"Clothes have nothing to do with what makes me a man."

Heat flooded her cheeks. A man's flirtatious conversation hadn't made her blush since she was in her teens. This wasn't just any man, though. This was Lawson. And discussing what made *him* a man was dangerous territory. Probably she should change the subject.

But she didn't. "Is that so?"

He touched her chin with one of his knuckles. "Yes."

Christian cleared his throat as he passed by them to take the chair at the head of the table. "You both look quite presentable. Now, may we move onto the food?"

Zara broke eye contact with Lawson, grateful to be saved from his penetrating stare and the unspoken challenge he'd just given her. Always the gentleman, he pulled out her chair and she sat.

As she unfolded her napkin and placed it on her lap, she absently listened to Christian describe the evening's menu. Sipping her Lillet aperitif, she felt Lawson's gaze on her from across the table and looked up to meet it. He flashed an insouciant grin at her, and the cool vermouth liqueur turned hot in her stomach.

Like the French women she'd studied for years, she took the art of seduction seriously. He wanted to flirt? Fine, she could flirt. Just so he understood she wasn't going to go gaga because he looked like a D&G ad come to life.

The man sitting across from her enjoyed the sport of competition. No matter what the game or how high the stakes, competition made him tick. However, in the game of seduction, Zara could flirt, tease and seduce with the best of them. She had no doubt she could wipe away Lawson's apparent indifference before the dinner progressed past the first course. *It's just for fun. Just another test. Let the seduction begin.*

Seduction started in the mind. Sipping her Lillet, she

turned her imagination loose and sent images of Lawson's lips, his bare chest, his strong hands floating through her brain.

As she licked moisture off her bottom lip, she shifted her gaze to look at him from under lowered lids. He felt her stare and glanced her way. Keeping her lips parted, she sucked a corner of the bottom one between her teeth.

He stilled completely, her message received loud and clear. Not a muscle twitched in his face or body, but the blasé persona morphed into something so hot, so carnal, Zara's breath caught in her chest.

Point one to the spook, she congratulated herself.

Chapter Twenty-Three

Lawson could not tear his attention away from Zara as the waitstaff entered and began setting trays of food on the table. When she gave him a coy smile, he knew he'd been had. Again.

Christian waved the staff off once the food was assembled. He passed a quiche to Zara. "To the French, cuisine is an art, not a science like Americans and Brits make it out to be."

Zara served herself and passed the quiche to Lawson. He mimicked her and watched to see which fork she picked up to eat it with.

The long mahogany table could seat twenty-five, but the three of them were contained at one end near the stone fireplace. A low fire burned behind the fireplace's iron grate, more for ambience, Lawson guessed, than for warmth. Ceiling fans oscillated in lazy circles high above their heads, creating a nice flow of air and making the tall candles on the table flicker. Along with the plates, wineglasses and assorted bowls between him and Zara, there were a variety of breads, spreads and a tureen of soup.

Zara took a bite of the quiche and a look of pleasure passed over her features. "The French have always enjoyed a predilection for fine food," she said, licking her lips. "During the Middle Ages, spices were favored, but during the Renaissance, the French replaced heavy seasonings with indigenous herbs."

Her words went in one ear and out the other. He nodded as if he cared about the French and their gastronomic history. At the moment, his mind was on other things.

If Christian hadn't been in the room, he would have been tempted to use the opposite end of the table to get busy with Zara right there. The soft lighting, the fireplace, the virginal white dress, the look she was sending him. She fit perfectly into this environment, and a desire to explore it all with her burned in his stomach. He wanted to lay her out on the table, slide the long skirt of her dress up and enjoy a different kind of feast. Drip wine on her breasts and cream on her stomach and taste the contrast of sweet and tart...

Christian interrupted his thoughts. "Throughout history, traditional regional cuisines have endured alongside the imaginatively creative new dishes by the country's top chefs. All are fabulous, but," he said, raising his glass of wine in toast, "the true connoisseurs of wine are the Brits!"

Zara raised her glass in salute. Lawson rushed to follow her. As the dinner continued with each course bringing a different variety of wine or beer, he struggled to keep up his end of the conversation.

The main course surprised him with both its food and its conversational turn. Small, whole-roasted chickens were brought out on a platter as well as lobster and stuffed crabs. "I thought you were a vegetarian," he said to Christian.

Christian shot a look at Zara, and Lawson instantly knew he'd committed a *faux pas*.

The man adjusted the scarf at his neck. "A good host does not project his own food preferences on his guests at a formal dinner. Tonight, Zara is my guest of honor and she loves seafood"—he raised his glass of Brut—"and champagne."

Zara raised her glass for another of Christian's toasts. Her cheeks were charmingly flushed, but Lawson knew it wasn't from the alcohol. He'd been monitoring her alcohol consumption. She'd passed on all the offered drinks except the aperitif and the champagne, preferring water with her meal.

The topic of discussion turned to politics as Christian told a story about a Russian ambassador he had met in Bern. The talk went from Serbs to Croats and then to Muslims. Zara brought up Afghanistan and terrorism. The invasion of Iraq. All of which brought a distinct tension between the two of them. Neither was shy about their political viewpoints.

Lawson was used to such conversations, had never found it particularly difficult to talk politics or defend America's position on anything. He'd been involved in a few "engagements" and had witnessed things that stopped his blood cold. He didn't like war any more than most people, but he did support his country and his president. It was apparent from the conversation Christian was one of the few Brits supporting the same agenda.

Zara did not. She and Christian argued political theory and Middle East history until Lawson wondered if World War III was about to break out right there at Villa Bernier.

Christian shook his fist and thumped it on the table, shaking the glasses. "Ah, this from you! I bet you didn't even vote during your last presidential election."

"I did too." She pointed her fork at him. "I voted against the man currently screwing things up if you must know."

"Ha! Probably only to offset your father's vote."

"Not true," she said with indignation. Then she sat back in her chair, a smile breaking over her face. "Okay, you got me on that. But still the world's thirst for war has to end. In the past two years, our government has identified dozens of significant international arms dealers and the terrorists they are supplying. Why are we not eliminating these people instead of inciting more problems?"

Christian turned to Lawson. "What do you think, Commander? Shall we send our guest of honor back to Paris where she can march on the *Place de la Concorde* and protest?"

Across the table, Zara arched a brow in challenge. Watching her become so riled up was fun. Even if he *had* personally agreed with her views, he would have played devil's advocate just to make her squirm.

"I think you've made some valid points tonight," he said and saw her mouth soften in triumph, "but I also think some of your views are simplistic and based on emotions instead of facts."

The smile faded. "Are you saying my emotions keep me from thinking logically about politics?"

Lawson shrugged. "You're a woman."

Her eyes narrowed at him and his lungs stopped on the inhale. "You can't be serious," she said.

Grinning, he finished his breath and took a sip of his beer, knowing his nonchalance was driving her as crazy as his playing devil's advocate. He was rewarded when she threw her napkin on the table and launched into a dissertation about the male species that was completely stereotypical.

And completely true as far as Lawson could see. After a minute, he glanced at Christian and both of them burst out laughing.

Zara stopped in mid-tirade and stared at him. "You're

yanking my chain, aren't you?"

"Me?" he said in mock protest. "Wouldn't dream of it."

Her napkin flew across the table and hit him in the face. "Men!"

He laughed and turned to Christian again. "What was I saying about emotional women?"

The next course was cheese and the talk turned to a safer subject: dance. Christian passed an immense tray to Zara and said to Lawson, "Did Zara tell you she's dancing for me again? She came to see my new studio this afternoon and couldn't help herself. You should have seen her. She's natural as can be. She should return to the world of ballet *tout de suite.*"

Zara selected a creamy-looking slice of cheese and glanced at Lawson before looking away again. He could have sworn she was blushing.

"That's great," he said without thinking.

"I'd like to set up a training schedule for her." Christian passed the cheese tray to him. "Three times a day for the next several months. Strength training and jazz classes. Within the next year, she could have many doors open for her again in the ballet world."

"Training schedule?" Zara's forehead creased in a frown. She shook her head. "We discussed this. I'm not taking up ballet again as a profession."

"But dance is your dream, love, I know it is. Not to be insensitive, but you are twenty-five years old. If you are going to get back into the dance world, time is of the essence. With my help, you can make it. You can stand on the stage and receive the applause you deserve."

Now it was Zara who pounded a fist on the table. "Wrong. Ballet was everyone else's dream for me. When I injured my tendon, I realized there was a whole world outside of dance. Working for the CIA *is* my dream."

Christian reached out to lay his hand on her fist. "Your commitment to your work and the CIA is commendable, but I'm positive Lawson is quite capable of finishing this assignment without you, and I know the CIA won't fall to ruins if you hand in your resignation." His gaze fell on Lawson. "Back me up here."

Lawson picked up his glass of wine and took a sip. Zara was glaring at him across the table, her face looking as set as it had the previous night when she'd been so daring in the hotel. So determined to grab her bag and get her shoes. She didn't need his opinion or advice, but...

But if she was as good as Christian said, should he tell her to go for it? Did she need his okay to...what? Quit the assignment? Was that the only reason she was arguing with Christian? If Lawson told her he needed her to stay with him until the mission was over, if he made her stay with him until they found Dmitri, would she be giving up a second chance at a childhood dream?

Could he tell her it was all right to quit, even if it meant he might never see her again? The thought made his jaw tighten.

Every moment of the last few days with her played on the mental movie screen in his head. Every defiant look she'd given him, every word of the verbal sparring they'd done, every sigh, every move. Thinking about finishing the mission without her, thinking about his immediate future without her made the wine in his stomach sour.

"All I know," he said, meeting her solemn eyes over the tops of the dwindling candles, "is Zara knows what she wants. She doesn't need either of us telling her what to do, Christian."

Her face softened in something akin to surprised relief. She raised her champagne in a small salute to him before taking a sip. Taking Christian's hand in hers, she squeezed it. "I love you, Christian. I truly do. But you cannot live your life vicariously through me. I cannot and will not ever be the fantasy ballerina you and my mother wanted. I'm a foreign counterintelligence operative for the Agency. I am working in partnership with Lawson to hunt down Alexandrov Dmitri and Jon Vos Loo who are dangerous and sadistic criminals. It's an important job and it's *my* job."

The dance instructor frowned but after a pause, nodded his consent. He pushed his plate back. "Then I suppose we should get down to business."

Zara paced the sitting room and tried to concentrate on what Christian was telling Lawson, but her nerves jittered under her skin, her emotions out of sorts. Whether it was caused by the tumult in Paris, her mixed-up internal clock or the champagne, she wasn't sure. All she knew was that she kept losing the thread of conversation.

The two men were seated in matching Queen Anne chairs, Christian looking perfectly at home, Lawson looking like a frog on a hot stove. He was sitting forward as though he were ready to jump and run, the Cuban cigar Christian had forced on him dangling from his fingertips.

Christian took a puff from his own cigar and continued talking about a group of the Italian Mafia that was considered extreme, even by the larger group's standards. "The older generation is dying off and taking many of their Old World ways with them. The younger generation has reorganized and restructured. The Family is now a more equal-opportunity employer and both sexes are attending Ivy League schools, trading companies on the New York Stock Exchange and developing a new business plan for the Mafia's future."

"What kind of plan?" Lawson asked.

"They're expanding their pharmaceutical and munitions rings. Looking for improved products to control the market and develop better ways to milk profits. Eliminating serious competitors and all the layers of middlemen is their key to market dominance, whether it involves drugs, guns, gambling or prostitution." He crossed one leg over the other. "They're also working outside those foundation markets. Telecommunications, private banking, life sciences, you name it, they're jumping into it with both feet."

Zara leaned on the back of the sofa. She could feel Lawson's gaze on her. "Dmitri and Vos Loo are involved in this?"

"You know I have an eclectic group of friends and acquaintances. I did a bit of digging with some names Lawson gave me this morning and came up with a theory for you. Alexi and company had help getting out of Moulins Prison, and from what I fished out, the most likely culprit to back them is Stefano Biaggio, a twenty-seven-year-old computer genius high in The Family ranks. Varina Scalfaro is his business partner and mistress. Rogan Janvrin is a close friend and possible business associate as well. The three of them have known each other since their Harvard days."

Lawson rolled the cigar between his fingers. "You said Janvrin didn't go to college."

"He wasn't a student. He taught a class for a semester on writing some kind of code for virtual reality applications. That's where Scalfaro and Biaggio met him."

Zara began pacing again. Even with her back to him, she could feel Lawson's gaze tracing its way down her spine. She shivered, her skin suddenly too sensitive under the dress fabric. "I still don't see what this has to do with Dmitri and Vos Loo."

His voice reached her across the room, but seemed too low and masculine for the current topic. "They have something Biaggio wants."

She turned to face him and saw he'd stood and was putting his cigar out. She tried to stay focused on the subject even as she assessed his profile with genuine female approval. "What would the mob need with an independent arms dealer and a biochemist?"

Laying the cigar in the crystal tray, Lawson stared at her for a moment, and Zara was sure from the glint of his eyes he wasn't spending much brain power thinking about terrorists. Her insides warmed. "That's what we're going to find out."

Without missing a beat, he turned to Christian and held out his hand. "The dinner was delicious, sir. I don't think I've eaten that well since the last time I sat at my mother's table."

Flustered, Christian rose out of his seat to accept the handshake. "I'll pass the compliment on to Gunther. He'll be quite pleased."

"Tomorrow I'll have a few more leads for us to follow, and I'd appreciate your help."

Zara smiled at the way Christian's face lit up. He patted Lawson on the shoulder. "Of course! Whatever I can do."

Lawson turned to her and Zara waited in anticipation of one of his body scans, but he held her gaze with his and smiled so faintly she almost thought she imagined it. "Good night, Zara. Sleep well."

She and Christian stayed quiet as he left the room and then they exchanged a look.

"Well?" Christian said to her.

"Well, what?" she countered.

"Go on." He made little shooing movements with his hand. "You played your part marvelously, and he took the bait. He's absolute putty in your hands, and I'm utterly jealous. You get to spend the rest of the night with a gorgeous, mysterious devil, and the most excitement I'll have is watching the BBC."

Was she really brave enough to go upstairs and invite Lawson to spend the night with her? "I'm not going to sleep with him."

"All the flirting during dinner and now you're not going to follow through?"

"No."

Christian took a puff on his cigar. "You're young, single and in the middle of a dangerous international operation. Why the hell not?"

It had been a long time since she'd gone after a man she really wanted. "The morning after?"

"God's sakes, woman." He rolled his eyes. "I thought I raised you to grab opportunity when it came your way."

"In a few hours, the magic of this evening will be over and I'll have to look Lawson in the eye again. Our working relationship will suffer."

"You're scared."

"I am not."

"Yes," Christian said, "you are. You're also a tease and you should be ashamed of yourself. Poor Lawson, I feel sorry for him."

Letting out a sigh, she kissed Christian on the cheek. "You're trying to live through me again."

"So humor me."

Laughing, she left him in the sitting room to go find poor Lawson.

Chapter Twenty-Four

The heels of her shoes clicked on the marble floor of the sunroom until she stopped and looked around for Lawson. This was where she figured he'd be, by the door to the Tower Room, but he wasn't there. She scanned the shadows cast by the wall sconces and moonlight, but she could sense as well as see her partner had not waited for her.

She folded her arms across her chest and tapped her foot on the floor. Well, didn't that just beat all? She'd told him she had something to show him after dinner and then she'd pulled out all the stops—the silk Valentino with its plunging V-neckline and open back, her hair immaculately swept up and off her face, her strategic placement of blush and perfume.

On top of that, she knew she'd sent Lawson all the right signals and he had sent her some very strong ones back. Even Christian had been sure of Lawson's interest. So what was the deal? Why wasn't he waiting for her?

Her foot tapped faster. Knowing Lawson, he'd played her over dinner like she'd been playing him.

He was the tease.

Her hands went to her hips and her chin came up. Well, she'd just show him. She marched over to the closed door of the Garden Room and knocked.

Two seconds later, he threw open the door, a towel in his hand. His jacket was off and his shirt was out of his waistband and completely unbuttoned. His feet were bare. Wiping water from his face with the towel, he smiled. "Well, if it isn't my favorite Bond girl."

Her insides turned to instant mush and her previous irritation evaporated. "Uh," she stammered. "I, uh..." *Don't stutter.* Clearing her throat, she started again. "Did you forget I wanted to show you something upstairs?"

Smooth. Real smooth. Talk about the lost art of seduction, she sounded like a pathetically bad actress in a porn movie. "The stars," she blurted out. "I wanted to show you the stars. Upstairs. On the tower roof."

One corner of his mouth quirked up. He threw the towel on the bed behind him. "Lead the way."

She was conscious of his eyes on her backside as she crossed the sunroom and took him through the door and up the spiral stairs to her room. Leaning over the railing, she pointed to the bed and told Lawson how everyone from Bianca Jagger to Princess Diana had spent a night there. He seemed unimpressed and she continued to climb. A few seconds later, she stepped onto the roof with him behind her and was pleased when she heard him whistle softly between his teeth as he took in the view.

It *was* stunning. The top of the tower stood out above a canopy of trees, which at night looked like chocolate pouring down into the valley. The waning moon lit the sky and the stars seemed to twinkle literally right above their heads. Although they couldn't see it clearly in the blanket of the night, the Rhône bubbled and gurgled in the distance. The air was cool and scented with rosemary drifting up from the gardens below.

"Doesn't it make you feel like a god?" Zara skirted the marble table and wrought-iron chairs in the center of the roof. She gave in to the urge to spread her arms and twirl under the moon. Dropping her head back, she laughed up at it. "Like you're above mere mortals?"

"It's incredible," Lawson said, coming up beside her. He captured one of her outstretched arms and drew her to his chest. "And so are you."

He stared down into her eyes and slid his arms around her waist. A low hum started deep inside her. As one hand touched her naked back, a shiver ran up her spine. He lowered his mouth to hers and took advantage of her parted lips. With her heart thudding, she stood on her tiptoes and offered more of her mouth to him. His kiss became instantly hotter.

For a moment, she let herself just stand there and enjoy Lawson's greedy exploration of her mouth, but then the vibration inside her turned erotic and demanding, and she kissed him back, wanting to consume whatever it was he was feeding her. Her bold self got even bolder, primal and wild.

She ran her hands inside his shirt, enjoying the ripple of muscles under her palms as he broke the kiss and sucked in his breath. He was so solid and strong, she wanted to sink her teeth into him.

Wrapping her arms around his neck, she pushed her body closer and he helped her, pressing on the small of her back to bring her into full contact with him.

She dug her fingers into his short hair, forcing his mouth down to hers. The kiss again became urgent and the heat in her stomach fanned out, spreading to her legs where they touched Lawson's, to her breasts buried against his chest. To her bottom that he was now cupping as he bent her backwards and slid his wet mouth down her neck.

His other hand held her head as he pushed her further back, the tip of his tongue touching the hollow of her throat. Her breath caught right there as she gazed up at the stars above them, and she held onto him for dear life. He brushed his lips back up to her ear and whispered her name, the heat of his breath sending another shudder through her.

He paused, looking down into her eyes. "Tell me what you want, Z," he said, his voice low and rough.

She answered him strong and clear. "I want you."

Lawson tipped his head, looking heavenward. "Thank you, God." He glanced down at her again. "Are you sure?"

Resting her hands on his gorgeous chest, Zara gave him a wicked smile. "It's stupid and completely unprofessional, but I've never been surer about anything in my life."

Lawson chuckled low in his throat. "From you, that's quite a testament."

Her heart was pounding with the sweet mixture of lust and dread and she wanted him to feel it. She took his hand and pressed it to her chest. He was heady passion wrapped around strength and kindness, a combination she couldn't have resisted even if she'd wanted to.

She didn't want to. Wherever Lawson was going to take her, whatever roller-coaster ride they were on, she wanted to go. She hoped somehow he would feel the pounding of her heart and understand.

He kissed her tenderly then, making love to her mouth under the moon and the stars. It was beautiful and romantic, but after a minute Zara wanted more. She didn't want him to treat her like she might break. She wanted him to treat her like the woman she was.

Sucking his tongue into her mouth, she teased him. A low moan sounded in his throat and the intensity of their kisses shot back up into the danger zone.

She moved his hand from her heart to her breast. His fingers closed over her and she sighed into his mouth. His hand felt good there, but it wasn't enough. She wanted it on her bare skin. As if he read her mind, he pushed the spaghetti strap of her dress off her shoulder, peeling the white fabric down to free her breast. He cupped it again. "Jesus," he whispered, "you're so soft."

The touch of his rough palm on her sensitive breast made the breath rush from her lungs. She tugged the other spaghetti strap off her shoulder, and he helped her pull the top of the dress down to her waist. His free hand closed over her other breast and his mouth again took hers. She slanted her head and fed him short hot kisses, running her hands over every part of his body she could touch. His hair, his face, his shoulders. She tangled her fingers in the short, curly hair of his chest and gently scratched her nails down his corrugated stomach.

His mouth broke free and he murmured in her ear, "Let's go back to my room."

The lust inside her was coiled so tight, Zara had almost forgotten where they were. "Why?"

"So I can make love to you properly." He took her hand in his and stepped back.

Even after everything they'd been through, Lawson still thought of her as a pampered rich girl. Someone who had to have a nice bed under her so she could lay back and let the man do all the work. Someone who didn't want her hair mussed up or her makeup kissed off.

The hell with that. She resisted, planting her feet, and tugged him back to her. She didn't want anything about this encounter to be proper. She wanted wild, sweaty, curl-your-toes, scream-your-lungs-out sex and she wanted it right there on the roof of Villa Bernier.

"We do it here, Vaughn," she said, licking her swollen lips, "or we don't do it at all."

He raised a brow at her challenge and his eyes did a slow sweep of her naked upper half. "I wouldn't want to ruin that pretty dress."

Zara thought about it for a moment, looking down at the folds of white silk covering her legs. It *would* be a shame to wreck such a wonderful dress, but...

"Forget the dress. I can replace it if necessary."

A sensual smile danced on his mouth and he stepped toward her. "You had to think about it."

She took a step back. "It *is* a Valentino."

"It could be a blue-light special and you'd still look like a million bucks." He took another step toward her and the same carnal expression she'd seen at dinner crossed his face. "Now take it off."

She licked her lips again and turned, presenting her back to him. "Unzip me?"

His fingers touched her back and before she could suck in her breath, the zipper separated and the Valentino pooled at her feet. A soft whistle emanated from between Lawson's teeth and she almost giggled.

He skimmed her shoulder blades with the tips of his fingers and slowly traveled down her spine to the top of her butt. "Jesus," he murmured into her hair, his warm breath falling on the top of her shoulders. "I never would have made it through dinner if I'd known you weren't wearing anything under that dress."

As he turned her around, she hugged his neck, bringing her mouth up to meet his and arching into him. He grasped her bottom and lifted her, and she wrapped her legs around his waist. One shoe and then the other dropped off her feet.

Walking her backwards a few steps, Lawson deposited her on the ornate Italian marbled tabletop, his gaze roaming over her naked skin. His hands followed, touching her all over.

Zara's lust was now tight inside her. A wonderful feeling, it was also terrifying and overwhelming in its intensity. She sat forward, grabbing Lawson's shirt and peeling it off his shoulders and down his arms. "Your turn."

He stepped back, stripped down to nothing and stood naked in front of her. Moonlight touched the tops of his shoulders. The Greek God statues in the garden below had nothing on him. His solid muscles and impressive proportions were enough to make a grown woman giddy with anticipation.

"I want you," he said, stepping between her legs and

bringing his face down to hers so their noses touched. "But I want to be damned sure this is what you want too."

She whispered against his lips, "This is what we both want. Get to it."

"Yes, ma'am." He kissed a trail down her neck to the pulse beating in the hollow. He continued his descent, kissing her nipples, then licking them and sucking each one into his mouth as his fingers slipped between her legs. She opened herself up to him and gasped as those fingers touched her with demanding strokes, making her greedy for more. She lay back on the tabletop, feeling the cool night air replace Lawson's mouth on her breasts as he let her go.

His attention traveled over her entire body and then he smiled. A smile so masculine the hairs on the back of her neck stood straight up. When he dipped his head and kissed her navel, goose bumps rose all over her body. She sank her hands into his hair, as soft as her mother's sable cape, and laughed into the night air.

A second later, the laughter stuck in her throat as Lawson moved lower. He spread her legs and kissed her between them, his warm mouth making her swear under her breath and grasp the edges of the table.

White-hot currents shot through her from head to toe, tingling her breasts, her stomach, her legs. She closed her eyes as Lawson used his tongue and mouth to pull moans from her and coax her toward orgasm. "I haven't even gotten to touch you yet," she whispered.

He withdrew his mouth a micron, his breath sending more goose bumps racing over her skin. "We've got the rest of the night, Zara. The op plan is for you to enjoy every minute of it."

Reaching down, she grabbed his hair and pulled his face up to hers. "It's been a long dry spell for me in this area. I want you inside me. Now."

He chuckled. "You're the boss."

"Finally, you let me be in charge."

As he moved away, she rose up on her elbows to see what he was doing. He snatched his pants from the ground and shoved his hand into one of the pockets. Withdrawing a foiled wrapper, he ripped it open and proceeded to glove himself with a condom.

"Do you carry condoms on every mission?" she asked

without thinking. Probably she didn't want to know.

"No." He returned to the spot between her legs. "There was a box in my top dresser drawer along with the packaged underwear. Extra-large, ultra-thin. *C'est très bien, non?*"

Zara laughed at his awful accent and wrapped her hand around him. "Ahh," she said, loving the way he felt. "*C'est très superbe!*"

Her body only accepted him so far before it resisted. She held onto his shoulders as he rocked his hips, slowly pushing his way farther and farther into her. Finally her muscles relaxed and let him bury himself all the way to the hilt.

"How's that?" he whispered against her cheek.

The nerve endings in her body screamed for more, and she shifted, grinding her pelvis into him. "Move." She grabbed his buttocks and pressed him down. "I need you to move."

He did, slipping in and out in a slow, even rhythm. She moved with him, but it still wasn't enough. She rocked her hips harder. "Stop teasing me."

Lawson rocked faster and harder as he delved into her again and again. She met each thrust with her own, her breath coming out in choppy gasps as the first wave of orgasm hit her. She threw her head back as wave after edgy wave rippled under her skin, sucking all the air from her lungs.

As her orgasm pulsed around him, he slowed the rhythm again, teasing out her pleasure. She clung to him and when his ragged breathing mixed with hers and he buried himself fully to her core one last time, she held him close and whispered his name.

In the aftermath, she stared up at the heavens as Lawson's heartbeat tripped hers into its solid rhythm.

Chapter Twenty-Five

He couldn't stop touching her.

Zara slept on her stomach in Lawson's bed, her head half-buried in the pillow, her backside completely uncovered by the sheet, affording him an uncompromised view.

The sun was rising, one strip of light running the length of her body, illuminating her face, one arm and a thigh. He lightly traced the landscape of her shoulder blades with his finger, watching her slow, steady breathing raise and lower her rib cage. His fingers walked down her spine.

Sex on the rooftop had been a fast and explosive couple of minutes that left him barely able to walk when it was over. He had wanted it slower, wanted Zara to be comfortable so he could take his time and draw out her pleasure. But she kept demanding a different agenda and he had to admit, in the end he hadn't minded a bit. The sex had been amazing.

Afterwards, he'd put her in the shower and washed her from head to toe, soaping her slowly and studying every curve of her body while he sorted through his feelings for her. At dinner he'd realized there was something more than physical attraction stirring his gut every time he looked at her. More than her big blue eyes and her even bigger attitude.

He liked the way she was up for every challenge he handed her. The way she refused to take his bullshit without giving a healthy dose of it back to him. The way she wasn't letting her past interfere with her future.

He liked how she defended her point of view with passion and substance. She knew what she was talking about whether the topic was fashion or war, and she could argue anyone into the ground about either.

He'd known before she knocked on his door last night that he wanted more than sex from her. The fantasy had already turned into something else. Something deeper and far scarier than anything he'd ever faced on any mission, air, ground or sea.

His gut had warned him one night with her wouldn't be enough. Their mission might last another week, maybe longer, but now he knew even that wasn't enough time. He wanted more. He just wasn't sure how much more, and he wasn't sure how much Zara was willing to give him.

He palmed one of her butt cheeks, and she grabbed his wrist, tried to push him away. Sleep made her voice husky. "Don't you ever rest, Vaughn?"

He kept his hand where it was and gave a little squeeze. "Never." He leaned over and planted a kiss between her shoulder blades.

She shivered under his lips. "You've got to get over this Superman complex," she said into her pillow. "You're killing me."

He planted another kiss on her back, lower. "Too much for you, huh?"

"That's not what I meant." She started to roll over, but Lawson moved down her body and pinned her legs underneath his arms. He placed his open mouth on one beautiful butt cheek and sucked her cool, smooth skin into it.

She gasped. "Easy," she said over her shoulder. "I don't like pain."

He moved his mouth to the other butt cheek and repeated the process, enjoying her wiggle as she tried to escape. Then he released her legs and, as expected, she rolled over and sat up. She stretched and pulled her knees to her chest.

He propped himself up on one elbow as she raked her hands through her tousled hair. "I would never hurt you, Zara."

Her hand stilled. She looked away from him, embarrassed, and scanned the room. Her attention landed on the Valentino hanging on the armoire. A tiny smiled curved her mouth. "You hung up my dress."

"I knew it was important to you."

Her gaze came back to his. "That's so sweet."

Lawson wasn't sure he'd ever been described as sweet—he sure as hell wouldn't want the guys of Pegasus to hear that— but coming from Zara it sounded nice. For her, he'd be as sweet as his mama's peach preserves. "My mother tried to raise me to be a gentleman," he said, putting a bit of southern Georgia into his words. "I guess her hard work must a done some good."

"Seems to me your mother did a fine job teaching you to be considerate of others." Moving toward him, she nudged his hand out from under his head and pushed him over on his back. She straddled him, leaning forward so her face was only a whisper above his. "Your benevolence is downright sexy. Makes me hot."

Running his hands over her thighs, he took stock of his benevolent arsenal. "Did I ever tell you about the time I rescued the president from a terrorist and stopped a ticking nuclear warhead?"

Zara shifted her hips and took him in her hand. "My hero." She brushed her lips over his, stroking him at the same time. "You deserve a special reward for all the good work you've done."

Her lips moved to his jaw, to the hollow of his throat, to his collarbone. Her velvet hand continued to stroke him in a steady rhythm. "In fact, I never thanked you properly for supposedly saving my life. You get *big* points for that."

"Supposedly?"

She kissed his bellybutton and proceeded to go lower. Lawson closed his eyes as her warm, wet mouth replaced her hand.

"No thanks necessary," he said, although he wasn't sure why he would say such a thing at the moment.

Her mouth left him. "Really? You don't want to be recognized for a job well done? You don't want me to make you feel appreciated?"

Jesus, she was such a tease. Of course he wanted her thanks if it involved her mouth returning to its previous spot. He drew in a deep breath and opened his eyes to look at her. He liked the way her blonde hair contrasted against his tanned legs and darker hair. "A man always likes to know he's appreciated."

Low, husky laughter matched the carnal female look she gave him. "Then lay back, Lawson, and relax, 'cuz I've got a boatload of appreciation to show you."

When it was over a few minutes later, Lawson was sure he'd just had something akin to a religious experience. Zara had done things that had both amazed and impressed him. He'd tried to give her back as much as he took, but it had been all he could do to remember to breathe.

He'd closed his eyes to block the beauty of her arched back and her compact butt riding him. He'd tried to concentrate on something besides how tight and warm she felt inside. He'd tried to shut his ears to her moans and whispers.

Even with his eyes closed and his mind trying to remember all the names of his pet dogs he'd had as a child, he just couldn't distract himself enough. So instead, he'd opened his eyes and enjoyed the view.

Now he was still trying to get air into his lungs as she slid her body next to him. "Jesus H. Christ," he mumbled.

Laying her head on his chest, she tangled her fingers in his chest hair and laughed. "Did you like it?"

"I think I just died and went to heaven."

"Good." She smiled against his chest before slinging one of her legs across his waist and running a hand over his biceps.

There would come a day in the not-too-distant future when she'd be out of his reach again. When they left this little fantasy land of Villa Bernier behind and returned to their normal lives. He would go back to tracking people down for the CIA or the FBI or whoever needed him, and she would probably be back in Paris running agents. The only way he'd see her again would be if he went to wherever she was.

And he would probably do it. At that moment he knew that even if Zara never wanted to see him again, he would still fly anywhere in the world to be near her. He would even force himself to sit through a ballet performance if it meant being in the same room.

Wrapping his arm around her, he pulled her closer. For now she was here with him and he could touch her and hold her to his heart's content. He wasn't the kind of man to let such an opportunity pass him by. "I can't get enough of you," he murmured into her hair. "I'm at your mercy."

She raised her head to look at him. "Really? Most of the time I can't decide if this partner thing is working for either of us."

"Sorry you came?"

"No," she said after a pause. "I'm not sorry at all."

Lawson rolled them both over. "I was hoping you'd say that."

~ ✧ ~

"Edgar Degas," Del said into Lawson's ear. "Pastel on monotype. Entitled *Ballet Scene*. Circa 1878-80. Whereabouts unknown according to Interpol. It's believed the painting was lifted from a private collection quite a few years ago. There's a similar history on most of the other pieces you photographed and sent to me."

Lawson drummed his fingers on the desk and listened to the shower running in the suite's bathroom. Zara was cleaning up after their last lovemaking session.

He shifted the phone from one ear to the other. "Christian Bernier's an art thief?"

"Not Christian." He heard Del shuffling papers in the background. "His father, probably his grandfather as well. Stealing famous artwork apparently runs in the family. Except Christian's clean from what I can tell. Never stole so much as a candy bar. He's just your everyday European millionaire who likes to run around in a leotard and keep the family's stolen artwork under wraps. The man has friends and acquaintances in high places, low places and everywhere in between. Makes the CIA contact list look like child's play. I'm guessing our friends at Interpol would love to get inside that house, though. What are you still doing there?"

"How do you know I'm at Christian's?"

Del laughed. "I've known exactly where you've been every step of the way. I just didn't tell you."

Lawson fingered his laptop and then the digital satellite uplink. "Bug's in the satellite, isn't it?"

"One in your phone too. They give out a random pulse even when they're not in use." Lawson heard Del shuffling papers again. "I've got info on Janvrin."

Del spent the next minute giving him Janvrin's résumé. Most of the information was identical to what Christian had already told him.

"I found him in bed with Varina a couple nights ago when she was playing Yvette's role," he told Del. "They'd had themselves quite the party. Blow, reds, some other stuff I can't even name."

"You call the cops?"

"My civic duty."

"Borrowed Janvrin's car?"

"He was going to be tied up for awhile. I didn't think he'd mind."

"Apparently he did."

Lawson heard the shower stop. "How about Yvette? She turn up yet?"

"No. Flynn's agent on the ground in Paris claims he talked to Yvette in person and gave her the Dmitri assignment Tuesday morning, the same time you were getting your end of it back here. That was the last time anyone saw her."

"Why didn't Flynn give me a picture of her? He could have saved me this freakin' mess. All I had was a phone number to establish contact."

"Flynn didn't have one. A lot of the field agents are reluctant to do photo IDs these days with the Internet and all. Makes it too easy for their likenesses to fall into the wrong hands at lightning speed. Besides, Yvette's been a reliable source for the Agency for years."

"Enough reason to take her out?"

"Could be, but why substitute Varina in her place?"

Lawson sat back in his chair. "To cover up Yvette's disappearance. Maybe Yvette knew more about Dmitri and Vos Loo's prison break than was healthy. Varina and friends didn't want that passed on so they got rid of her, but then they had to buy themselves time because they knew someone from the CIA was already on his way to meet her."

The bathroom door opened and Zara appeared, wrapped in a dark blue towel. Her hair was wet and her cheeks were pink from the shower. She smiled shyly at Lawson as she crossed the room to retrieve her dress from the bureau. His heart banged against his ribs like a sledgehammer.

"Forget the Yvette angle for now," he told Del. "I found out who was behind Dmitri and Vos Loo's prison break. Mafia guy named Stefano Biaggio. Ivy League education, friends and business cohorts with Varina and Janvrin. Sounds like he's good at thinking outside the box and probably has a hundred and one uses for a terrorist and a mad scientist. He could be our link to figuring this whole thing out."

"You think Dmitri's working for him?"

Zara lifted the dress off the bureau doorknob and headed toward the bedroom door to leave. He was out of his chair and reaching for her before he even thought about it. She grinned as he put his hand behind her and shut the door, sealing off her escape.

"If Biaggio financed Dmitri's prison break and subsequent disappearance," he said into the phone while he ran a finger over Zara's collarbone, "I'm sure he did it with a few strings attached. I want you to find out what you can about him and his business dealings."

"What about Dmitri? You still want to know where he and the doctor are hiding out?"

Zara pinched his waist and laughed silently as he jerked away from her fingers. He pressed her up against the door and stared into her eyes. "You got something for me?"

At that, she lifted her brows, and Del said, "My good buddy Annette figured something out. She said if she wanted to set up a lab near Geneva and was afraid to go back to her previous abode, she'd be looking for real estate. Something outside the city limits with no nosy neighbors nearby but with good access to the road for deliveries. With that in mind, she did some digging and found an estate forty miles north of Villa Bernier that meets those requirements and was recently purchased for large sums of cash. I sent you the address."

The spot between Lawson's shoulder blades twitched, but he ignored it as he dropped a silent kiss on Zara's lips. "I'll check it out today."

"Actually, you're not supposed to go near it. Flynn says you and Zara need to lay low until he can get things smoothed over with the Frenchies."

"Still got their undies in a bunch?"

"Try a complete wedgy, and they're sure we're the ones giving it to 'em. Stone's taken a lot of heat in the past twenty-four hours from everyone from the DCI to the President's National Security Advisor. Flynn's already in Paris kissing FI's ass."

Frowning, Lawson took a step back from Zara. Conrad Flynn did not kiss anyone's ass. "You're shitting me."

"I shit you not, my man. I got a twenty says you won't be on Flynn's Christmas list this year. He's blaming you for everything."

Zara laid a hand on his arm. He glanced at her and saw her brows knit together in worry.

Images of the previous night flashed through his mind and made the inevitable ugly confrontation with Conrad Flynn seem almost unimportant. Taking hold of Zara's hand, he winked at her. "I got a twenty, Del, says Flynn will be my biggest fan when this is all over."

Chapter Twenty-Six

Zara stared in disbelief as Lawson checked the clip in his gun and stuck it in the back of his waistband. "You're leaving?"

"I need to do reconnaissance on this property Del gave me while it's light." He shrugged on his jacket.

She'd spent all morning and most of the afternoon going over the information they now had about Dmitri, Vos Loo and the Mafia. Del and Annette had managed to inundate them with biographies and other data, including MOs on Varina Scalfaro, Rogan Janvrin and Stefano Biaggio. What they hadn't been able to supply was a theory on why this group of people had joined forces with an international arms dealer and a radical biochemist.

Brainstorming, Zara, Lawson and Christian had managed to come up with a few theories on their own. None of them comforting. Now, even though Director Flynn had given them explicit orders to lay low and stay out of sight, Lawson was about to go looking for trouble.

Zara didn't like it. She also didn't like that Dmitri might be so close. "I'm going with you."

"We've already been over this." Lawson stuck two extra clips of ammo into the inside pockets of his jacket. "Recon is my area of expertise. You stay here and see if you can solidify any of the theories we came up with on what Dmitri's doing with the mob. Meanwhile, I'll track him down."

"And if you find him?"

"I'll check out the house and perimeter for security and figure out a safe spot for us to set up surveillance tonight. I don't want us stumbling around in the dark setting off alarms."

"I know you're the expert on reconnaissance, but you always work with a team in the field. Pegasus isn't here, so I'm your team. You need me."

A faint scowl darkened his features. "No, Zara. I don't."

Even though she knew it was true, she was surprised at how much his words hurt.

He came around the bed and placed his hands on her bare arms. "Looking for booby traps and tripwires is dangerous work, even for a professional like me. You'd distract me and that alone could end up getting both of us killed. I know you hate sitting and twiddling your thumbs, but you've got to."

Taking a deep breath, she mulled over his words, both spoken and not. She could be a professional just like he was. She could ignore the butterflies zinging around in her stomach like little kamikazes that accompanied the touch of his hands. She could turn off the memories of the previous night and remind herself she still had a job to do. She could even chastise herself for thinking about putting Lawson in danger because of her own inexperience. She would stay put, even if twiddling her thumbs was out of the question.

What she couldn't do was feel happy about it. Being professional today, in her opinion, sucked the big one. But she dialed up her model-agent face and gave Lawson the answer she knew he wanted to hear. "You're the boss."

His eyes widened in surprise. Then he patted her arm and dropped a kiss on her lips. "I'll be back before dark."

She watched his back retreat through the bedroom door. "I'll be waiting."

Half an hour later, she shut Lawson's laptop and sighed in frustration. She didn't want to read about terrorists or Mafia henchmen anymore.

CIA operative or not, what woman could do terrorist intelligence analysis when she'd just spent the night before with a man whose touch made her toes curl? A man with integrity and charm and wit who made her scream with pleasure as easily as he made her laugh.

She didn't know exactly what was happening, but she'd fallen for Lawson Vaughn. Not love, just a different form of transference. Maybe it happened that morning when he'd told her he would never hurt her. Or at dinner last night when he teased her so unmercifully.

People who worked together, whether in an office or, like her and Lawson, in the field, experienced it all the time. Movie stars were a classic example. They'd work together on a set for six or eight months, get caught up in that other world and marry each other. A year later, they were at each other's throats in divorce court.

Flopping onto the bed, she closed her eyes. She could still smell him in the sheets, could still remember the feel of his body spooned around hers. How they fit together...

A knock on the door interrupted her thoughts. "Zara?" Christian's voice came from the other side. "Are you in there?"

Sitting up, she called back, "Yes. Come in."

He slung the door open and eyed her. "Are you coming out anytime today?"

"I'm working." She motioned at the desk. "Or at least trying to work."

"Mind in the clouds and all that after your night with the Commander?"

She sighed. "Afraid so. I can't concentrate."

Christian shook his head and clucked his tongue at her. "Sounds like you've got it bad."

"What should I do?"

"Dance."

Laughing, Zara grabbed a pillow off the bed and tossed it at him. "That's your answer for everything."

He caught the pillow and tossed it back on the bed. "It actually might help your brain work better if you get away from the paperwork and get exercise."

"Couldn't I just take a walk in the gardens?"

"Get your Balanchinian body down to my studio and warm up."

"I don't have a Balanchine-type body anymore."

Christian shrugged indifference. "Frankly, love, I don't care if you're built like Dolly Parton. If you can dance, you should dance."

So dance she did.

Dressed appropriately in a leotard and tights this time, she went through a repetitive but more serious barre routine. The day-after-day fine-tuning of technique in her youth had developed the correct memory in her muscles so now she could think less about technique and enjoy the physical feeling, the musicality, of the movements. Every movement, whether at barre or at center, possessed a basic rhythm that was somewhat arbitrary but entirely logical to her body. Every movement contained an energy she loved and understood.

"Placement," Christian barked, taking Zara's outstretched hand and turning it a centimeter to correct it.

She repositioned. Her mentor's teaching philosophy had not changed over the years. He still preached simplicity and purity of line to build strength and lengthen muscles. He still turned into Scrooge the minute he had a student in front of him.

But the chemistry between them had always worked to make Zara comfortable while at the same time challenged. He kept her interest engaged and nourished her desire to dance. In some ways, Christian was like Director Flynn. He knew what made her tick. She smiled at him in the mirror. He didn't smile back.

"You've always been a fantastic instructor," she said.

"The best." He still didn't break his concentration. "*Plié.*"

Zara performed as instructed. "You remind me of my boss at Langley."

"I suppose that's a compliment. *Plié.*"

Again, she dipped her body. "I think he's going to regret he sent me on this mission."

Christian let out a sigh of exasperation. "Do you remember when you came to me at ten and insisted you were ready to dance on pointe?"

She nodded reluctantly. "You told me no."

"Of course I did. You weren't ready." He crossed his arms over his chest and began to pace behind her. "The exercises of ballet are soundly scientific. When done properly, they build a beautiful, strong and symmetrical body. If not done properly or begun before the student is ready for that level of training, the same exercises can cause injury. I'm sure your boss wouldn't have sent you on this assignment if he didn't think you were ready." He faced her in the mirror again, arms still crossed. "*Plié.*"

Zara rolled her eyes at him and performed the simple exercise again. The pleasant ache between her legs reminded her of a different dance she'd enjoyed last night. Her mind wandered to where Lawson was and when he would return. Would they be doing surveillance tonight instead of enjoying bedroom activities?

Her heart sank a little and the feeling startled her. Since when did she prefer sex over catching bad guys?

She didn't have time to dwell on it. *"Tendues,"* Christian announced. Zara moved into position and pointed her foot.

"And one, and two..."

Before the end of the session, Christian put Christina Aguilera on the CD player, and while she belted out, "I am beautiful", Zara followed Christian through a series of simple combinations. They repeated the sequence a few times together before Christian moved off to the side to let Zara complete the song on her own.

Christina was singing the last chorus of the song when a deep pulsing vibrated the floor under her feet. She glanced at Christian and saw him lift his eyes to the ceiling. She stopped dancing and picked out the faint rhythmic thudding noise over the music. *Helicopter.*

The dancing forgotten, she followed Christian out of the studio, through the house and out to the garden. A hundred yards away, a helicopter sat on the immaculate lawn, the wind from its blades whipping and bending the trees in the orchard and causing goose bumps to rise on her skin.

As the blades began to slow, Annette jumped out of the helicopter, her hand on the hilt of the gun at her hip. Behind her, Director Flynn emerged.

A sudden tightness filled Zara's chest. Her boss stood still for a moment, bent slightly like the nearby trees, and adjusted his ball cap. Two suited men exited the helicopter behind him. Crew cuts, mirrored sunglasses and an air of authority, Zara immediately guessed they were cops from the CIA's Office of Security. Before the group took more than a dozen steps, Flynn and his bodyguards were intercepted by two of Christian's own security officers.

The conversation between Flynn and the security officers was animated. "That's Conrad Flynn," she said to Christian. "He's the Director of Operations for the CIA. My boss."

Christian was silent as his security officers checked IDs. "He's here for you and Lawson."

The tightness in Zara's chest threatened to cut off her breath. Lawson had told her the Ambassador had the two of them on tape, and Flynn was in France trying to smooth things over with the local authorities as well as the French Foreign Intelligence Service. She never dreamed he would follow their trail.

Christian walked out to the cluster of men, speaking first with his security officer before extending his hand to Flynn and then to Annette. Zara debated following him, but she stayed where she was. Flynn showing up was bad news and she refused to rush headfirst into that.

When she'd come back from France after surviving Dmitri, it was Flynn who debriefed her and walked her through her psych evaluations and therapy sessions. He accepted Charles Morgan's wrath over his daughter's near-death experience with calm reassurances. Flynn was one of the few people on Earth who believed in her spying abilities.

At least up until now.

The spymaster crossed the grass, taking off his sunglasses. "How you doing, Zara?"

She nodded at Annette and took the hand Flynn extended to her, matching his strong shake with her own. "Good, sir. I appreciate you sending me back to Europe."

Flynn's expression showed none of the anger she expected. "Perhaps we should keep you here."

The helicopter's blades had finally come to a stop and the pilot killed the engine, but the loud droning continued to echo in Zara's ears. "I'd like that."

"Is your partnership with Lawson working?"

"Yes," she said.

He studied her for a moment, waiting for more. She stayed silent. "Where is Lawson?"

Annette looked at the villa. "We need to bring both of you up to date on what's happening in Paris."

A need to defend her partner rose like a wave inside her. "Varina put a gun to my head and would have shot me if Lawson hadn't interceded. The other two came after us with similar intentions. He had no choice but to kill them before they killed us."

Flynn nodded a reassurance. "I assumed as much. Lawson has never taken a life without necessity. I'm glad I sent him along to cover your backside. I didn't need a dead officer on my hands."

Her stomach kicked. She saw the truth in his eyes before he looked away. Tasted betrayal in her mouth. "You never believed I could pull this off, did you?"

Christian stepped forward. "Perhaps we should continue this discussion inside."

Flynn ignored him and stepped closer to Zara so the two of them were face-to-face. "I believe you are quite capable of nailing Dmitri's ass to the wall, but not without causing a whole lot of other"—he searched for the right word—"issues."

"Issues?" She fought to control the shaking inside her. "What issues?"

"Look, I was just as crazy and headstrong as you when I started out, but I was also lucky I didn't get my head blown off. You take chances that would make Green Berets piss their pants. That can be good or bad. I enlisted Vaughn to be your partner to keep you from doing something completely stupid in your quest to find Dmitri and getting yourself killed. I have plans for you."

She took a deep breath and a step back. Anger boiled inside her, but being Flynn's star pupil, she was very adept at keeping a lid on it. "Lawson's not here right now, but he'll be back soon."

"Where is he?" Annette asked.

"He's following up on a lead."

Frowning, Flynn glanced at his watch. "He was ordered to stay out of sight." He shook his head in disgust. "He's the one I expected would follow orders."

Unlike me. Zara straightened her spine, her instinct to defend Lawson kicking in again. She knew Lawson would laugh at her for trying to protect him. "He may not always follow your orders, Director, but he does get the job done."

The corner of Flynn's mouth turned up. His previous irritation with her disappeared. "If I didn't know better, I'd think you had a soft spot for my contractor, Agent Morgan."

Annette cleared her throat and looked away. "I need Lawson's notebook computer. Is it in his room?"

Delude, distract, deceive. Without taking her focus from Flynn, Zara answered Annette, "He took it with him."

"How about tea?" Christian said from behind them. "I'll have Marie brew some right up and bring it to the drawing room."

Zara lowered her voice and glared at Flynn. "I don't have soft spots, Director."

Betrayal was a virus that seeped into your blood, tainting it cell by cell. It was a jailor imprisoning your heart one bar at a time. Flynn had once told Zara she could only be truly betrayed by someone she loved.

He was right.

Two minutes before midnight, she sat alone in Christian's library, trying to keep her mind off her partner. He should have been back hours ago, but she'd already learned that Lawson didn't operate according to any set timetable. If he were on the trail of the terrorists, he wouldn't remember his promise to be back before dark. He wouldn't care she was sick with worry or angry as hell. He was working. End of story.

She would have been the same way, she told herself, if she were the one doing surveillance instead of sitting there doing nothing.

"Here it is, love." Christian came in holding Lawson's laptop. "I was afraid that nasty Annette would sneak off and search his room. I hid it while Marie was serving tea just in case."

"Thanks," Zara said.

She opened the computer on the desk and inserted a flash drive into the USB port while she waited for the opening screen to appear. When it did, it asked her for a password.

While she tried to be mad at Lawson for convincing her to stay behind, she was just plain mad at herself. That wouldn't stop her from punching him in the stomach when he walked in the door for making her worry. For leaving her behind to deal with Flynn.

PEGASUS, she typed in the box.

Access denied.

RESCUE.

Denied again.

Lawson wasn't a spy. He wasn't a computer tech. He wasn't transporting any top-secret information on his laptop. Surely he hadn't used an encrypted password or anything too difficult to break.

She continued to play around with combinations of words and numbers she'd gleaned from his personnel file. His birthdate. His social security number. Nine-eleven.

Nine-eleven. She sat forward and typed, DAVID911.

Bingo.

Director Flynn and Annette had briefed her on the Paris fallout before they left to return to the U.S. Embassy there. Because tensions between America and France were already so strained, Flynn had insisted Zara and Lawson call it quits on the mission and return to the States before the two of them ended up in a Paris jail. He was doing all he could to smooth things over, but with the French, there were no guarantees. Even though two of the people Lawson had killed were known members of the Italian Mafia and high on the FI's Most Wanted list, there were still questions that had to be answered, actions to be accounted for.

"I can't protect you here," Flynn had told her. "Get back on U.S. soil so I can."

Zara didn't want his protection. She was close to finding Dmitri, and she'd argued with Flynn for over an hour about it. Unrelenting, he refused to give into her arguments. As soon as Lawson reappeared, they were to contact Flynn and he would have Annette personally accompany them back to the States.

Zara didn't know if Lawson would quit just because Flynn had told him to—he *was* a soldier and Flynn had picked him because he was good at following orders as well as tracking down missing people—but there was no way Zara was calling off the mission.

As the laptop downloaded Dmitri's and Vos Loo's files to the flash drive, she laid her head against the ornamental back of Christian's office chair. She would not quit looking for Dmitri even if Lawson did. Alexandrov Dmitri had to be stopped before he hurt more innocent people.

Even if it meant losing her job, she would do whatever it took to bring his illegal and immoral career to an end.

With or without Lawson's help.

Or Flynn's permission.

No retreat. No surrender.

From the start of her career, Zara had known the reason she excelled at operations. It wasn't something that could be measured by the Myers-Briggs personality test or labeled by personnel on her résumé. It had nothing to do with skills like language proficiency or accuracy with small arms.

The thing that made Zara good at her job was an intangible, mysterious and dangerous commodity. It was the one thing Conrad Flynn recognized in her that others didn't, why he'd selected her from a dozen equally qualified candidates to be one of his army. It was the same commodity terrorists, criminals and even saints and disciples traded on a daily basis.

The will to betray.

Because she had studied it, taken it into her body as well as her mind and absorbed its properties, she knew betrayal like she knew her own skin. She'd breathed it, cried it and fought it, until finally accepting it as a part of life. Her life.

When the flashdrive light went off, Zara removed it and slid it inside her bra. She clicked on Lawson's email files and scanned the subject headings. Only one caught her eye. *Ding Dongs and Dom.* Like most of the emails, it was from Del.

She'd figured out Lawson had read her classified personnel file. She'd read his, too, thanks to Annette. However, at the moment, the additional deceit sat like a brick in her stomach. She picked up the new cell phone Flynn had given her and IM'd Del.

I've composed an email to DO re Ding Dongs and Dom security breach. Suggest you turn in your resignation before I hit send.

She gave him a few minutes, knowing he might be away from his desk getting a fresh Diet Coke or attending a meeting.

A reply came faster than she expected.

Down on knees, begging forgiveness. Please don't send. What can I do to counter? Provide you with equal file?

Del knew how the game was played. What he didn't know was the classified file he sent Lawson was a dummy. Flynn had created it. Ninety-nine percent of it was accurate. The only thing missing was Zara's specialized training.

Just tell me why Commander wanted it.

The pause was lengthy, and she grew impatient. *My finger is hovering over the send key.*

Okay, okay. Official reason—he didn't trust you.

That was no surprise. Zara typed back, *Unofficial reason?*

Del's response was quick this time. *He's a man.*

The answer almost seemed cryptic but Zara knew better. All men seemed to want the same thing from her. *He wanted to sleep with me?*

A beautiful, sexy intelligence officer...don't we all?

Del's stab at humor left Zara cold. She logged off and set the phone down with shaking fingers.

"What is it?" Christian asked from the other side of the desk. "What did you find out?"

The only person who can truly betray you is someone you love. "Nothing," she told him as she shut the laptop.

Flynn had sent Lawson along to babysit her. Lawson had lied to her and had planned to seduce her all along. The distracting happiness she'd experienced earlier in the day vanished as if it had never existed. Without any effort, her mind slid into a dark, familiar place.

She would prove to everyone she was capable of stopping a terrorist all by herself.

"What are you going to do?" Christian asked as she rose from his chair and slipped her cell phone into her back pocket.

She didn't bother picking up the laptop. "I'm going to bed."

Chapter Twenty-Seven

Lawson reached for Zara even before he came fully awake. She wasn't there.

The whole time he'd been staking out Dmitri, he'd been thinking about her. About her husky laughter and her liberal politics and the way her muscles moved under her skin when she made love to him. About the way her eyes lit up when she was mad. About the way she curled into him when she slept.

By the time he'd finally made it back to Villa Bernier, he'd morphed into a man possessed. He hadn't been able to get her out of his head the whole time he was away and the only thing he wanted when he drove through Christian's gated entrance was to hear her say his name right before he took her to his bed and ravished her.

But she hadn't been waiting up for him and she wasn't in his bed. He'd taken the steps to the Tower Room two at a time, irrational fear making his stomach churn.

When he found her sleeping between the sheets of her own bed, relief brought him up short. He'd stripped down to his underwear and climbed in next to her, his first thought to wake her and satisfy the need building inside of him all day. But she was sleeping so good he didn't have the heart to disturb her. Exhausted from his own day, he pulled her against his body and was content just to close his eyes and listen to her breathe as he too drifted off to sleep.

Rolling over, he looked around the room through the gray morning light. She sat in the shadow of the miniature chest of drawers, her back to the wall.

"What are you doing over there?" he asked softly.

"Deciding whether or not to cut your balls off."

Rubbing his eyes, he sat up and swung his legs over the edge of the bed. He knew she wouldn't be happy with him this morning. "I'm sorry I didn't get back sooner last night, but I found Dmitri. Annette was right. He's camped thirty-six miles southeast of here, across the Rhône in a big estate like this one. Looks like he and Vos Loo are in business already. A truck carrying a shipment of what I think was munitions pulled in around seven o'clock last night. Two hours later, it left again, heading toward Geneva."

He shifted, stretching his arms and yawning. He was so damned tired. When he got back to the States he was going to sleep for twenty-four hours straight. "I'll send the pictures I took of the estate and the truck to Del. We'll see what he digs up for us and then we'll do surveillance tonight. I want pictures of Dmitri and all his friends before I sic Flynn on them."

Zara didn't say anything, just sat on the floor, her arms wrapped around her drawn-up knees. Lawson slid off the bed and walked the two steps over to her. The marble tiles were cool under his feet. Bending down, he put his face close to hers, but she wouldn't look at him as she fiddled with her gold bracelet.

He touched her cheek. "What's wrong, Z?"

She pulled away from his hand. "Director Flynn was here last night."

Lawson dropped his hand and rested his forearms on his bent knees. "Here? At the Villa?"

"He ordered us to quit the assignment and return to America. He says we'll end up in a French prison and then he'll have to wash his hands of us."

Lawson mulled the situation over in his mind. He understood the orders and Flynn's concern. He also understood what that meant to Zara. "I'll talk to Flynn. See if I can get him to give us a few more days."

"And if he doesn't?"

"I'll figure something out."

She was quiet for a moment, staring out the window. "I need to know something from you."

The tone of her voice, her delivery, made the spot between Lawson's shoulder blades twinge. "All right."

"At the airport you told me Director Flynn had the utmost confidence in me."

Lawson thought back to the airport discussion. "When Flynn recruited me to be your partner, he insisted you are one of his best field operatives."

"He recruited you to be my partner because he wanted you to babysit me. This is a test to see if I can do my job without doing something stupid like the farmhouse incident." She took a deep breath and toyed with the bracelet again. "What I want to know is what did Flynn promise you to get you to take this job?"

Lawson rocked back on his heels. "Do you really think I would take you on as a partner if I didn't believe you were key to the success of this mission?"

She studied him as if she were trying to read his mind. "Honestly, Lawson, I don't know what to believe. I have no doubt you could have handled this assignment just fine without me. You're like a one-man army. On the other hand, after all that's happened between us, I want to believe you at least *wanted* me for a partner, and I don't mean in bed."

For years while his comrades trained for combat search-and-destroy missions, Lawson and a handful of others trained for search-and-rescue missions. From the time he'd entered the Navy, it was the only thing he ever wanted to do. Help others.

Now when he looked into Zara's eyes, he realized she had the same need. She wanted to know she was helping him, helping the CIA and the United States, stop a couple of no-good terrorists.

It was something he admired, and so he told her the truth. "Flynn didn't promise me anything to get me to take this job. He said it could open some doors for me down the road, but I only took that to mean if I completed the mission successfully, he would send me on similar missions again. I never took it as a bribe to be your partner, and I don't believe Flynn meant it that way. Besides, I'm the one who's in trouble on this mission, Z. I'm the one who's got the French crawling up Flynn's backside. You saved *me* this round."

She stayed silent. He was missing something, he just didn't know what. "You put me on the right track looking for Vos Loo instead of Dmitri," he said. "You told me not to trust the woman I believed was Yvette and you were right. You found the getaway car and you had the sense to bring us here to Villa Bernier." He reached his hand out and touched her fingers with his own. "You're smart and gutsy and a damn fine operative."

The room lightened while she considered him and his words. "I'm ignoring Flynn's orders for now too, but I'm warning you. Regardless of whether he gives us a few more days of grace or not, you get in my way or try to stop me and I'll cut your balls off."

She was serious and Lawson knew it. The wild, reckless, pampered rich girl playing at spy was gone. In her place, a pissed-off woman.

"I'll remember that."

Taking a chance, he ran his thumb over the top of her hand and forced himself to ask the question he knew he should avoid but couldn't. "Regrets about our night together?"

Zara didn't hesitate. Didn't even blink. "No."

Thank you, Jesus. Standing up, he pulled her to her feet. The satin of her nightgown brushed against his chest and belly as he wrapped her in his arms.

His morning erection hardened a little more as he held her against his chest. "Let's go back to bed."

Her body stiffened and she pushed against his chest, shaking her head. "You go back to bed. I'm...dancing this morning."

He glanced at his watch, still on his wrist. "It isn't even six a.m. yet. Dance later."

Tiny lines bracketed her lips as she frowned. "I need to clear my head."

She pivoted away and opened a drawer in the dresser, grabbing some clothes. Throwing them on the bed, she turned her back to him and removed her nightgown.

He stood by the bed, appreciating the view of her naked body but irritated she was leaving. Watching her clipped movements as she pulled on a black leotard and matching leg warmers, he realized she may not have regretted having sex with him, but she was still unsure how she felt about being his partner.

She twisted her hair, clipped it to her head and grabbed a pair of ballet shoes out of the armoire. "I'll be in the studio. Come get me when you're ready to work."

She left him standing in the middle of the room. No parting smile. No goodbye, I'll-see-you-later kiss. Yep, she was still mad.

Rubbing his eyes, he flopped back on the bed and threw the pastel comforter down to the end. The best thing for him to do was let her go. Let her work through her emotions about their relationship. He could get some much-needed sleep and then they could talk again later.

He closed his eyes and threw his arm over his face to block the light now coming in the window. After five minutes, he rolled over onto his stomach, beating his fists into the pillow to rearrange it. The scent of Zara's hair engulfed him.

Swearing, he purposely made his brain think of boring stuff...complex fractions, running a mental exercise of packing a parachute properly. Finally, he dozed off, but even in sleep, she tormented him. In his dream she was running away from him, looking over her shoulder with that determined expression on her face before she was swallowed up in a group of people. He called to her, screamed her name, as he tried to plow through the crowd, but she was lost to him.

He woke up sweating and grabbed his jeans off the miniature table nearby. He convinced himself it was dollhouse-sized furniture, pink walls and lacy bed canopy that made deep sleep impossible. If he stayed in the Tower Room much longer, all the testosterone in his body would evaporate like it'd never been there.

"I'll be dancing like a fairy if I stay here any longer," he murmured, snatching his shirt off the floor where he'd dropped it in his hurry to get into bed with Zara. He didn't bother to put it on before taking the stairs back down to the second floor two at a time.

Zara stretched her arms over her head, took a couple of cleansing breaths and walked over to the CD player. Lawson had said he wasn't going to quit, but she suspected it was because of her. While she should have been pleased he would risk his career to help her resolve her issues with Dmitri, she didn't like feeling responsible for Lawson cutting his own throat.

She shuffled through several CD stacks and selected Christina Aguilera's. The album was full of no-nonsense, hard-hitting songs Zara liked. Their message was clear—*don't mess with me, I can take care of myself.*

She'd lifted the motorcycle key from Lawson's pants before

he woke up and debated taking off after Dmitri in the light of day. The idea pumped adrenaline into her veins, but smacked of stupidity. No matter how much she wanted to confront Dmitri head on again and end his criminal career, walking into the lion's den by herself without a real plan was suicide. Instead, she'd spent an hour memorizing the map of Dmitri's hideout she'd downloaded from Lawson's laptop, loaded her gun, charged her cell phone and hardened her heart. When night came, she'd be ready to do surveillance. With Lawson.

And if the opportunity arose to take out Dmitri, she'd do it.

Sliding the CD into the player, she forwarded the disc to the song she wanted and cranked up the volume. Then she walked confidently back to the mirror.

Synchronizing with the music, she threw several jazz steps in the mix of ballet steps Christian had put together the previous day. Her feet seemed to pick up the flow more readily, and she expanded the repertoire of movements, adding modern dance steps. She flubbed a few because her body was so tired, but she shrugged it off and kept moving.

Completing a small jump, she landed in fifth position with a demi-plié and noted both her feet and hand positions were perfect.

"Yes!" she said aloud, making a fist and pulling her arm into her body.

Get ready, Dmitri. Here I come.

Chapter Twenty-Eight

Lawson stood just outside the studio doors transfixed by Zara's grace and determination.

He'd given up on sleep, showered, charged his cell phone and drank half the carafe of coffee Marie had left for him on a tray outside his room. The shower and caffeine should have helped him shed the weariness in his bones and jumpstart his brain for another day of terrorist-hunting, but it hadn't worked. He didn't want to spend the morning doing his job. What he wanted to do was watch Zara dance.

One of the large doors of the studio had been ajar and he'd opened it another couple of inches so he could see in. Music, heavy on the bass, but slower this song, poured out at him.

In the early morning light, Zara stood at one end of the large, open room, facing a wall-length mirror. She'd shed her leg warmers and Lawson could see a V of perspiration darkening the black leotard between her shoulder blades. While she danced through two songs, he enjoyed the way she changed her movements and steps to match the tempo of the music. She shrugged off frustration over missteps and repeated the combinations until she was satisfied. He smiled when she nailed a landing she was trying so hard to get right.

In that brief moment, he could see her as a young girl, her face set like it was now, pushing herself to do better. Loving the work, the music and the costumes. Unwavering in her dedication. A wonderful blend of spunk and spirit.

He sensed Christian sidle up behind him. "Dancers are a special breed of people," he said, just loud enough for Lawson to hear over the music. "Some of us even admit to being insane."

He glanced over his shoulder at the dance instructor before returning his attention to Zara. She was special, he knew that.

"Insane, huh?"

"We need to be in order to get through the training, the rehearsals and the injuries. To be successful, we have to have an iron will."

In the Navy, Lawson had made it through everything they could throw at him. Then he'd gone on to survive specialized schools for underwater and airborne training so he could successfully complete a rescue in deep water or sky-dive out of a plane at a dangerously high altitude and survive the landing.

Combat medic courses and survival training came next, teaching him advanced EMT skills, weapons handling and evasion and escape techniques. There had been many times when he thought he'd wash out, but he hadn't. He'd made it through all the courses with nothing less than ironclad determination.

Christian viewed Zara over Lawson's shoulder. "She is struggling today, because she's upset about something."

"Flynn wants us to call it quits and return to the States."

"Flynn's ultimatum isn't interfering with her concentration. You are."

As Zara worked through another combination of steps, she faltered trying to hold a pose with one leg stretched out in the air. Catching herself, she made a face, rubbed her knee and tried again. "Isn't it your job to be in there helping her?"

Christian sighed audibly. "She doesn't want help right now. Her struggle is with herself. Until she comes to terms with it, and you, my coaching is wasted."

Lawson stayed quiet, frustrated with Christian's observation, but also lost as to what he could do about it.

Backing up a couple of steps, Christian leaned against the wall. "Have you ever heard the term *'pas de deux'*?"

Inside, the song ended and Zara grabbed a towel to wipe off her face and neck. Lawson could see how tired she was. "No," he murmured so she wouldn't hear him.

Christian lowered his voice as well. "It's French for 'step of two', partnering in ballet. It has advantages for both the man and the woman, you see. By dancing with a partner, the woman can jump higher and perform positions too demanding to do on her own. She can appear to float around the stage as she is carried. The woman in turn allows the man to extend his line and show off his strength. Each of the partners must have a high level of skill on their own, but it is their partnership which creates the most grand and awe-inspiring of dances."

Lawson cut his gaze to Christian. "Your point?"

"Zara is in need of a good partner."

Lawson shook his head. "I can do a lot of things, but I can't dance."

Christian smiled and pushed himself off the wall. "Zara can teach as well as perform. Perhaps if you approached dancing with her with an open mind, you would find it very much worth the effort."

Music again filled the studio, but this time at a lower volume. Christian disappeared down the hall.

Lawson returned to his voyeurism. Zara was back in the spot where she'd been dancing, but now she was sitting on the floor, tugging off her ballet shoes. Her shoulders were slumped over and her fingers worked slowly.

Gathering his courage, he pushed the door open and walked through into the brightly lit room.

Chapter Twenty-Nine

"Tired?"

The sound of Lawson's voice snapped Zara out of her thoughts. He stood near her in his standard jeans and T-shirt, bare feet and scruffy face.

He'd never looked better.

Pulling one of her ballet slippers off, she dropped it on the floor and massaged her foot. "Sleeping Beauty awakens."

He walked past her to the mirror. "How was the workout?"

"Peachy." She pulled off her other slipper and studied her toes. "I suck."

Out of the corner of her eye, she saw him turn to look at her. "You do not suck. I saw you. You're damn good."

She jerked her head up. "You were watching me?"

"I was curious."

Raising her arm, she threw her ballet slipper at him. He flinched and knocked it away. "Hey!"

She reached for the other one. "You jerk. I can't believe you were spying on me."

"You're fun to spy on." He laughed as she threw the other shoe at him.

Her aim was true but he smacked it into the mirror behind him. Plopping down on the floor next to her, he bent his knees and set his elbows on top of them. "Your dancing is incredible."

The hard shell around her heart softened a micron. Hugging her knees to her chest, she wiggled her toes. "You've never seen a ballet performance. How would you know?"

"Because I'm an athlete. I don't know squat about ballet, but I do know what it takes to make your body move and respond the way you want it to. I can appreciate what you're doing with yours even if I don't fully understand the mechanics of it. You're a natural."

Every muscle in Zara's body was warm and tremulous from her workout. Stretched to the max. Knowing Lawson had been watching her impromptu recital made her oddly self-conscious. She wished she didn't care so much that he'd seen her dancing like a crazy woman. She wished her heart would harden up again instead of steadily getting softer.

"Even without my injury, I would never have made it as far as my mother. I'd love to think otherwise"—she dropped her head into her hands—"but it wouldn't have happened in a million years."

"What about choreography like Christian suggested?"

"I don't have the time or the desire. I'm not good enough anyway."

"Sounds self-defeating."

"It's called reality."

A heartbeat of silence passed. "Quitter."

She raised her head and narrowed her eyes at him. "I am not a quitter."

Lawson just smiled at her. A challenge.

She pushed herself off the floor and walked away from him. "How many times do I have to say it? I don't want to be a ballerina."

"A lot of spooks use a regular job as cover."

Regular job? She headed for the back of the studio. "You have no idea the amount of time it takes even to be a choreographer. Besides, top choreography, just like top ballet, demands the ability to dance better than what I did here today."

"You're basing this on one bad practice?"

Zara stopped in front of the barre and placed her hands on her hips. "I'm basing it on knowledge."

Lawson rose off the floor and followed her to the barre. He stopped a foot behind her and met her eyes in the mirror. "What are you scared of, Zara?"

She forced herself to look him in the eye. After a minute, she willed herself to admit the truth. To herself as well as him. "Not being good enough."

"For who? Your mother? Christian?" He shrugged. "Who?"

Everyone. She pinned her gaze on the floor. "Being a good dancer, being a good spy, it doesn't matter. You have to endure the training, survive the politics and force yourself through all kinds of BS. All kinds of hassles. Your family, your friends, your teachers, they all think you're crazy. Sometimes you even think it yourself. But, in dance, when you stand out there on that stage and perform, hear the audience's applause, it's one of the greatest rushes you ever experience. As a field operative, you get the same rush when you stop a leak or put a criminal behind bars."

"I feel the same way when I rescue someone. I don't get applause, but knowing I did my job and saved someone's life makes all the BS and hassles worth it."

At least he could relate. "I bet you've never quit anything, have you?"

He scratched the top of his nose. Sighed. "Actually, I quit Boy Scouts in seventh grade."

"Because of the ugly uniforms?"

His laughter echoed in the room. "No. Because I failed Tracking. Twice. I was never going to make Eagle Scout without that badge."

"The man who never gets lost failed Boy Scout Tracking?"

He offered a sheepish grin. "Now you know my darkest secret."

She looked at him standing there so close she could lean back into him. "Then we're even since you know mine too."

"You mean about not being good enough?"

She nodded and dropped her gaze to the reflection of her feet in the mirror.

Lawson moved, putting himself a step closer, but he didn't touch her. His warm breath danced on her ear. "You're more than good enough, Z. Everything about you is incredible."

Her leg muscles trembled a warning. "There's that adjective again."

"Yes," he murmured into her hair. His hands touched her waist. "Incredible, beautiful, sexy as hell. Perfect."

Feeling self-conscious, she stepped forward. "I don't know what planet you grew up on, but where I'm from I am *so* not perfect."

"You're wrong." His head dipped and he kissed the top of her shoulder.

She kept her gaze down, not wanting to meet his eyes in

the mirror. She had to get away from him before he felt her whole body trembling from his touch. His hands, his lips, even the deep sound of his voice, made every cell in her body tingle with want.

As she shifted to the left, she tried to call up her training to help her out. Some philosophy of Flynn's to help her out. Nothing came and Lawson moved, trapping her.

It still irked her he'd wanted her file just so he could find ways to seduce her, but the truth was she'd wanted him since the first time she'd seen him at the Farm. The seductress persona she'd worn at the airport hadn't just been a test to see how he'd react for the mission's sake...she'd wanted to know how he'd react for her sake. The entire time they'd been together, she'd been flirting, baiting and teasing him for her own selfish, female want.

He lifted a hand and touched her neck. Her gaze locked on his fingers in the mirror as they fell to the top of her shoulder where he'd just kissed her. As he ran his palms down her bare arms and settled them on her waist again, heat spread from his hands, warming her abdomen and fanning outward.

"Your legs are fantastic. Shapely and well-toned and they're topped off with the most incredible as—ahh...butt I've ever had the privilege to touch. And these," he said, cupping her breasts gently, almost reverently, through the Lycra of her suit. "These fill up my hands like they were made for them. And my hands aren't small."

The way his hands brought her breasts together created better cleavage than her Chantelle demi push-up bra. He squeezed and her knees went weak. She parted her lips, closed her eyes and leaned into him. *Just once more before this is over...*

Her bottom brushed against his jeans, and he sucked in his breath. Opening her eyes, she sought his in the mirror. The sexual hunger in them was as dark as the ivy growing up Poseidon's leg in the garden outside. As he released her breasts, he pulled her bottom against his groin and this time it was Zara who sucked in her breath.

"Jesus," he said into her hair. "I'm obsessed with you."

She let out a soft laugh. "Obsessed, huh?"

His hands closed over her breasts again, his fingers pinching her taut nipples. "Hell, yes. I can't get enough of you.

Your awesome body, your sassy mouth. None of it."

"You should see someone about that. The Agency has plenty of therapists, you know."

"No therapist, just you."

She faced him, planting her hands on his chest to push him away, but he cupped her butt cheeks and kept her lower half pressed against his. "Ever been obsessed before?" she asked.

"No." His roaming hands froze, as if it were just dawning on him. "Never."

Zara's heart hammered hard. She looked up at him, at his lips poised just above hers. "Never?"

He took her mouth with such possession, her knees buckled. But he held her firmly and she knew he wouldn't let her fall. "Never," he whispered against her lips.

Chapter Thirty

Annette forced herself to stare down Alexandrov Dmitri, her heart pounding erratically. It was one thing to talk to a terrorist on a phone, quite another in person. Sweat trickled down her spine. "They're at Villa Bernier. Now our deal is complete. I want my sister."

Dmitri wagged a finger at her. "You must deliver Zara Morgan to me. Alive."

Again the bastard changed the rules. She wasn't surprised, only more determined. "That wasn't the deal. I held up my end and kept you informed about Zara's activities and about the CIA's mission to track you down. I dropped your coordinates in her and Lawson's lap. I expect you to hold up your end and get Biaggio to turn my sister loose."

He moved like lightning, his hands going around her throat before she could blink. Her own hands pulled at his wrists, trying to break their steel clamp as he forced her down to her knees.

"You forget, Special Agent Newton," he ground out between his teeth even as he dug his fingers into her neck. "You have no power over me. If you want your sister to leave the Family's clutches, you'll bring Zara Morgan to me. Tonight. My lieutenant will follow you and ensure your cooperation."

His thumbs pushed further into her throat, cutting off her air. "And for your insolence, you'll deliver Vaughn to me as well. Understand?"

She nodded yes, what else could she do? He released her, and she fell to the floor, clutching her bruised neck. She swallowed several times, coughed. Her voice came out hoarse. "Zara's one thing. Vaughn is another. I doubt I can bring him in alive."

Dmitri hauled her to her feet. He brushed at her shirt,

patted her arm and pushed her toward the door. A snap of his finger and the man standing to his right immediately fell into step beside her. "Then bring him in dead. I really don't care. Just do it, or your sister stays exactly where she is."

With Dmitri's lieutenant on her heels, Annette stumbled out the door and past the security goons, rubbing her neck again as she fought back tears. What was she going to do now?

Chapter Thirty-One

Lawson released the clip in his Heckler and Koch and checked it for the third time. Satisfied it was fully loaded, he clicked it back in and slid the gun into the waistband of his jeans. As he sat on the bed, he shoved his feet into his combat boots and began lacing up the right one.

The room was a disaster, owing its current state of disrepair to his and Zara's last round of sex. One sheet was knotted around a bed pole on the headboard. The comforter and pillows were lying in a pile near the flagstone fireplace. One of the potted palm trees sat crookedly in its pot, having been tipped over and then hastily righted. Lawson smiled. It had been a day he wouldn't forget anytime soon. He could still feel the imprint of Zara's teeth on his left shoulder.

It wasn't like him to lose control, to become so careless, but he'd done just that earlier in the dance studio. He'd taken her right there against the mirror, where anyone, including Christian or one of his staff, could have walked in on them. When she'd looked up at him with those big blue eyes, happiness and desire burning in them, he'd been too far gone to stop himself. He'd wanted to bury himself deep inside her and make her even happier.

He was being completely unprofessional. While the majority of people who worked for the CIA were used to pushing the boundaries of protocol, Lawson wasn't. But this kind of craziness with Zara wasn't just a break from protocol, this was something else entirely. This was...this was...

Hell, he didn't know what it was, but he did know he was having the most intense, best sex of his life.

Finishing with the first boot, Lawson went to work tying the second. The smell of Zara and sex wafted around him as the sound of the shower running in the adjacent bathroom filled his ears. He thought about her standing under the running water and damn if heat didn't shoot straight to his groin like a lightning bolt. He shook his head and slammed his booted foot back down on the floor. It had to stop. After the first lovemaking session, and in between lunch and a long nap with Zara tucked securely in his arms, he'd jumped her beautiful bones again. His obsession was going to kill him if he didn't get control. And soon.

Because, even though he didn't want to admit it, she wasn't just a beautiful woman he loved having sex with. She wasn't his fuck buddy any more than she was his girlfriend. She meant something to him, but she was his partner. His *work* partner. Their relationship was only going to get more complicated.

When the mission was over and they returned to America, the alternate reality they were caught in now—working a dangerous mission in a foreign country—would be over. They'd both go back to real life. Zara would stop looking at him with her heart in her eyes. She'd stop wanting him the way he wanted her. She'd return to her life and he'd return to his. Even if she stayed at Langley, he'd probably be lucky to spend more than a minute or two talking to her in the halls. She wasn't the kind of woman who would settle for a man like him.

He heard the shower shut off in the bathroom and pushed off the bed.

For now he had a job to do. Detaching his emotions, he grabbed his leather jacket, slipped it on and began loading the inside pockets with extra clips of ammo, a Swiss Army knife, a pair of high-powered night vision goggles and a small Maglite flashlight.

His clothes and personal effects were already packed. He stuck his digitally encrypted cell phone on his belt buckle and packed his notebook computer and satellite hookup in his travel bag.

Zara emerged from the bathroom dressed in a black sweater and black jeans. As she came to stand next to him, she raked her fingers through her towel-dried hair. Her cheeks were flushed and her lips were shiny with lip gloss, but Lawson noticed her stiff, clipped movements as she kept her distance from him and grabbed the doorknob. "How soon do we leave?"

"Ten minutes."

"Did you talk to Flynn?"

"I left him a message."

Her gaze lingered on him a moment, her eyes hard and edgy. "You understand you're risking your career tonight."

He grinned at her, trying to lessen her concern. "You'll put in a good word for me with Flynn before he stands me up in front of the firing squad, right?"

His attempt at humor didn't work. She reached into her jean pocket, pulled out a key. "You'll need this."

He snagged the motorcycle key out of the air, held it up, looked it over, feeling the sting of betrayal. "You were going to take off without me?"

Her tone was unapologetic. "I considered it. Decided I should play by the rules this once."

"Flynn would be proud of you."

She shrugged as if she no longer cared about Flynn's approval. "I need to say goodbye to Christian. I'll meet you at the barn."

Twenty minutes later, Zara passed by the statue of Poseidon and shivered. The days were pleasantly warm, but the nights in Switzerland were cold. The temperature had dropped twenty degrees since sunset. She'd already had a taste of the night temps on the Ducati when she and Lawson had ridden through the French and Swiss countrysides. She'd literally frozen her naked butt off, but at least then, she'd had her own personal furnace to snuggle up to.

There would be no snuggling tonight. Her partner always became all business the minute he strapped on his gun. That Lawson was different from the one who stole her breath with the simplest of looks and worshipped every curve and indention of her body like a sculptor worshipped his model.

Glancing back at the house, she followed the footpath through the orchard and paused near a statue of Artemis, the Grecian warrior Goddess. She was all professionalism now too, even though her nerves were getting to her right along with the cold. She was about to do surveillance on Dmitri. She was about to sever the carotid artery of her career and possibly Lawson's.

Looking up at the Goddess's powerful face, she said a prayer. *Watch over me, Artemis.*

Catching movement out of the corner of her eye, she was

surprised to see Annette walking toward her from the house, instead of Lawson. As she cleared a line of apple trees, Annette lifted a hand in greeting and another chill spread through Zara's body.

"What are you doing here?" Zara asked. "I thought you went back to Paris with Flynn. He doesn't trust me to come in on my own, does he?"

Annette stopped, her gaze sliding over the garden before circling the back edge of the orchard that was lined with evergreens. Her attention landed on Zara, but darted off again to the side. "I need to take you out of here for your own safety."

Zara's nerves crackled under her skin. "I'll take my chances with the French police and FI. I can't—won't—quit this mission yet."

The FBI agent glanced over her shoulder at Christian's villa. Soft light from the upper-story stained-glass windows filtered into the courtyard. "Dmitri knows you're here. He's coming for you. Tonight."

Her heart jumped. She instinctively scanned the area all around the gardens, taking a step toward the house. "How did he find out I was here?"

Annette ignored her question and gripped her arm, steering her away from the villa. "Where's Lawson?"

"Answer my question, Annette." Zara tried to remove her arm from her friend's grip, but couldn't without hurting her. "What's going on?"

Annette continued to propel her across the grass away from Artemis and the orchard. "Where's Lawson? We don't have much time."

Zara jerked her arm out of Annette's hand. Something was off. Very off. "Did you tell Christian about Dmitri when he let you in? He could be in danger."

Annette took a step forward. "You're the only one in danger right now."

The measured tone of her voice triggered an uncomfortable feeling in Zara's stomach. A feeling that had nothing to do with Alexandrov Dmitri. "You're not telling me everything. Do you know how Dmitri found out I was here?"

Annette sighed audibly and Zara saw her hand move to the gun on her hip. She slipped it out of its holster and pointed it at Zara. "Because I told him, and now I have to deliver you to him and save my sister. So do us both a favor. Tell me where Lawson is."

The sight of the gun made adrenaline rush to her nerve endings. "I don't know," she lied.

Annette raised the gun so it pointed at her face. "Perhaps you'd like to reconsider that answer."

Delude, deceive, distract. "What happened to your sister?"

"Not your concern. I'm taking you and Lawson to Dmitri. I'm sorry, but I don't have any choice."

Zara nodded as though she understood, and then she kicked her right foot up and caught Annette's gun with the heel of her sneaker.

Chapter Thirty-Two

The partially cloudy night didn't offer much light and the dark woods loomed to her right. Zara smelled the bed of slippery pine needles under her feet as she ran along the tree line. She couldn't see more than ten feet ahead of her, but even if the moon had been fully out, she knew she wouldn't be able to see Annette because of the grade of the hill. She ran on.

She should have stayed and fought her, but for all Zara's training, her stubborn psyche had resisted. Her fight-or-flight instinct had ordered flight. *She's my friend. How could I fight her?*

Catching her breath, she slid her hand across the rough bark of a pine tree and slipped farther into the shadows, trying to keep her bearings as she moved in the direction of the barn. Trying to get her bearings as Annette's betrayal sank into her bones.

She froze at a noise in the woods behind her. Her hand shook as she reached under her jacket and pulled the Glock from her waistband. She held her breath, gauging where the noise had come from and listening for it to repeat itself. Her eyes fought to bring the nearby trees into focus, but in the dark, everything blended together.

A minute passed and she heard nothing outside of the breeze rustling the tops of the pines towering above her head. Slowly inching forward, she forced herself to breathe. A deer or some other nocturnal creature deep in the woods had probably stepped on a twig and snapped it.

Only a rookie would believe that.

Or a stupid, pampered rich girl.

Moving forward again, her foot fell on a hard, slippery surface and slid out from under her. She broke the fall with her hands, dropping the Glock on the ground. Swearing under her breath, she patted the bed of pine needles searching for the cool metal.

Her hand stilled as she heard the noise again, closer this time. She lifted her head, looking over her shoulder and sensed something moving toward her. The way it moved told her it was not a four-legged creature, but it was too sizable to be Annette. Dmitri? Too bulky for him.

She jumped to her feet and started to run, dodging trees as best she could. The back of the barn had to be close.

As she cleared the tree line, Zara saw the monstrous two-story horse barn ahead of her. She ran hard, jumping over a water trough and praying the moonlight wouldn't be strong enough to give Annette or her hulk of a friend a clear shot.

Before she'd gotten more than ten feet, she heard a faint whoosh and felt a sharp sting in her right butt cheek. Opening her mouth to scream for Lawson, she took two more running steps before the ground rushed up to meet her.

Chapter Thirty-Three

Cold. She was so cold, it hurt to move.

Zara listened to the rise and fall of voices nearby. With her head pounding and her mouth as dry as cotton, she tried to open her eyes, but her eyelids were too heavy. They refused to obey.

Her drugged sleep beckoned at her, and she let herself drift, not wanting to fully wake and face what was happening. Not face the knowledge lurking on the edge of her consciousness.

A hard shiver ripped through her body and the men's voices jolted her back to wakefulness. Her muscles were limp and she fought to turn over, wanting to get her cheek off the cold floor, but her body wouldn't respond.

Unconsciousness threatened to take her under again and she used all of her will not to give in. Her training told her to pretend unconsciousness and buy time to get her bearings, yet primal instincts pumped adrenaline through her system making her twitch. The fogginess in her brain cleared a fraction, and snippets of the night and what had happened made her heart pound loudly in her ears. She unglued her tongue from the top of her mouth and swallowed.

Low laughter, familiar and devoid of humor, sent goose bumps over her skin that had nothing to do with the physical cold of the floor. She sensed a presence bending over her as hands gripped her arms to roll her over.

Struggling to keep her eyes shut, Zara forced her body to act like dead weight. Her captor wasn't fooled. He shook her and slapped her face, bringing about the flinch that revealed her lucidity. As she stared back at his ice-blue eyes her heart seized and her mouth formed the word "no".

~ ✧ ~

Damn, damn, damn, damn. Lawson punched his fist into the nearest tree and swore a string of curse words. Crouching, he picked Zara's gun up off the ground and bent his head in disgrace. He'd screwed up royally. Someone had kidnapped her right out from under his nose.

He'd been checking the Ducati's gas level when the twitch in his shoulder blades started hammering at him. He'd left the cycle and run back to the house, a surge of unexplained adrenaline pumping his legs as hard as they would go. Inside, he continued to run, through the east wing and to the west, calling Zara as he went. Christian emerged from the library, and seeing Lawson's distress, joined him in his search. The maid, Maria, reported she'd seen Zara and Annette walking in the garden, but now neither was anywhere to be seen. Why had Annette returned and how had she bypassed the gates and front door? Maria assured Christian Annette had never entered the house.

He'd run the length of the property, Christian on his heels, and arrived back at the barn. One of Christian's security team had met them there with news that a guard in the back quarter of the property was dead, his neck sliced ear to ear. Searching the woods around the barn, Lawson discovered the Glock.

No Annette, no Zara. One dead security officer. As he left the woods and showed Christian the gun, his cell phone rang. He almost ignored it, but instinct told him not to. His blood froze, then boiled, as he listened to the voice on the other end.

"She's beautiful, isn't she? So full of life." The man sighed. "At least for now."

Dmitri. How had the son of a bitch found them? How had he kidnapped Zara? Had he kidnapped Annette too? Or had Annette done the kidnapping?

Lawson drew a sharp breath at the reaction his gut had to the thought. There was no point exploring the how of it at the moment. Dmitri had Zara. The details could wait. "What do you want?"

"I have what I want. The Princess. I appreciate you bringing her with you to Switzerland. Our reunion has been bittersweet, and it will be even better when her sister joins us."

Lawson clenched his jaw. Christian's eyes widened as the man came to stand in front of him. "Hurt her or her sister and I swear I'll kill you with my bare hands."

The terrorist laughed. "Yes, well, first, *Monsieur* Vaughn, you have to catch me."

Before Lawson could answer, the connection went dead.

He punched the closest tree.

"My God," Christian said, from behind him. "He's got her, doesn't he? Dmitri's got my Zara again."

Fingering the cell phone, Lawson breathed in and out and tried to keep thoughts of what Dmitri would do to Zara at bay. Zara and Lucie. Jesus, the bastard would be in heaven having both women at his disposal.

Considering the mental map in his head of the estate where Dmitri and Vos Loo were holed up, Lawson ran through his options.

He could save them, but he couldn't walk in with guns blazing and expect a happy outcome. This wasn't a Schwarzenegger movie. He had to fight his impulsive nature and use his head. Failure was not an option.

Surveillance at Dmitri's new estate was tight but he'd spotted at least one weak point. The problem was, he didn't know the layout of the house or where Dmitri would keep hostages. He couldn't sneak into the estate's compound and rescue them without help. And right now, help, in the form of his team, was too freakin' far away.

Turning and striding back toward Christian's house, he punched a speed-dial button and waited for Del Hoffman to pick up.

Chapter Thirty-Four

"Agent Morgan." Alexandrov Dmitri crouched over her. "What a pleasant surprise to find you here."

Zara tore her gaze away from his eyes and brought a shaky hand to her face. This couldn't be happening. It had to be another nightmare. There was no way she could face Alexandrov Dmitri like this—on her back without a weapon or a prayer.

He stood and motioned to one of the four men arranged around the foyer. Each was dressed in black wool pants and a black turtleneck and carrying an automatic weapon. "Help her up, Jean-Paul."

A young man with chubby cherub cheeks slung his gun around to his back and moved toward her. Strong hands hoisted her to her feet. Her knees buckled, and he half-carried her to a straight-backed chair in the adjoining room. He dropped her onto it, and her right butt cheek screamed where the tranquilizer dart had nailed her. Gripping the edge of the seat, she fought to keep herself upright, swallowing the nausea that tightened the muscles in her jaw.

The room was carpeted and furnished with a scattering of expensive pieces, including a magnificent Louis XIII desk and matching chair. Heavy wool drapes were closed against the night. Armed men, again dressed completely in black, stood in the corners.

Dmitri knelt in front of her, the faint odor of his musky aftershave and cigarette smoke teasing her nostrils. His dark hair was longer than the last time she'd seen him, soft curls brushing the straps of his shoulder holster. A thin pink scar ran across the top of his right cheekbone and disappeared into a sideburn. A souvenir from prison?

"You are not easily dissuaded, are you?" he said. The scar

rose on his cheek as he smiled. "I'm beginning to think you like me. Maybe even enjoy being my hostage. Perhaps you get off on fear?"

She refused to be goaded, to play his game. Silence, the ultimate act of defiance, was the one thing he couldn't stand. Pressing her lips together, she stared back at him and watched with satisfaction as his smile faltered a micron.

He thrust his face mere inches from hers. "In prison, I learned several new abuses to add to my list of torture techniques. I haven't had the chance to try them out on anyone yet. You could be the first."

He walked his fingers up one of her thighs, and a thin, gold chain peeked out from his shirt sleeve. Her lost gold necklace encircled his wrist in two loops. His breath touched her cheek. "You are such a pretty girl. Maybe this time I will administer the torture myself. Then we can both get off, huh?"

Anger zinged through her. Hate coiled in her stomach. On reflex, she thrust her elbow sharply at his face, and welcomed the connection of bone to bone. He fell backward, swearing and grabbing his cheek.

Before the armed guards could move, he regained his balance, stepped forward and cold-cocked her, the force of the blow knocking her out of the chair. She landed heavily on the carpeted floor and curled into a ball, ears ringing.

She clamped her eyes shut to hold back the tears.

"Alexandrov," someone said in a warning tone.

Dmitri's booted feet stepped away. Someone snapped his fingers and hands lifted her again into the chair. Her arms were pulled behind her and secured with flexicuffs. Then the cherub-faced youth moved around to the front and tied her legs to the legs of the chair. She blinked several times, keeping her eyes on the top of his head and trying to bring his dark curls into focus.

A man, compact and powerful, with dark skin and hair, moved from behind her and seated himself at the desk. As Zara's eyesight cleared, she saw his suit was vintage Italian silk. Under it, he wore a cashmere sweater. He steepled his fingers in front of his chest and gazed at her impassively from under heavy brows. "Where is your partner?" His accent was almost nonexistent.

She noticed the mole to the left of his finely chiseled nose and knew she was looking at Stefano Biaggio. The head of the new Italian Mafia sect. Varina's boss, lover and business partner. A man who no doubt had a very large chip on his shoulder when it came to Zara and Lawson.

A strange calm settled over her. If Stefano was asking her where Lawson was, that meant they hadn't caught him. He would come for her, all she had to do was buy some time.

"I don't know what you're talking about." Speaking caused pain to radiate from her cheek and jaw where Dmitri's punch had landed. "I don't have any partner."

Stefano tapped his index fingers together. "Then you are a woman of great talent. You have killed four members of my organization, stolen one of my motorcycles and tracked down Alexi all by yourself." He touched a file folder on his desk. "The CIA does not have many men who could accomplish so much in such a short amount of time."

She shrugged one shoulder. "Never send a man to do a woman's job."

Stefano studied her for a long moment, his eyes dropping to her chest and then down to her spread knees. Where Dmitri always went with brute strength, Stefano understood that humiliation could be as effective as a punch from a fist. A normal woman would have instinctively tried to bring her knees together even if the attempt was futile. Zara forced herself not to move a muscle.

He sat forward and flipped the file open. "We know of your partner, Agent Morgan. I have his complete dossier here with yours." Slipping a black and white 8x10 from the papers inside, he held it up for her to see. There, caught by the Ambassador's security camera, was her and Lawson in profile. Stefano pulled out several more photos, shot from different angles. He raised his brows to her, waiting.

She let him wait. She wasn't going to volunteer anything, not even lies. It would end up costing her, that she knew, but the longer she stretched out the interrogation, the better her chances for survival.

"Vaughn has caused more trouble for me in the past forty-eight hours than all the other agents who've tried to bring my empire down combined. I cannot let such offenses go." Stefano sat back in his chair. "You understand?"

Again, she offered only silence.

Stefano glared at her. "Alexi told me you would be

uncooperative. What a shame. Perhaps this will change your mind." Reaching into the file, he pulled out another photo. This one of Zara and Lucie entering the hotel's front lobby.

Not Lucie.

The game suddenly swerved and jumped to a different level. A personal one that went beyond hers or Lawson's safety and survival. The two men in front of her were about to screw with her family. "She has nothing to do with this. Leave her alone."

"Too late," Dmitri said, clapping his hands together and beaming at her. He signaled to one of the men in the back of the room, Zara's chain swinging from his wrist. "Bring the girl."

Sheer terror rose under her skin. Looking over her shoulder, she held her breath.

Lucie appeared in the doorway to the room a minute later, flanked on each side by a guard. Her hands were cuffed behind her back and duct tape covered her mouth.

Zara jerked on her bonds as her sister approached. "Are you hurt?"

Lucie shook her head, and Dmitri shoved her back into the chair. She whipped her head around and pinned her gaze on him. "This is between you and me. Not her."

He thrust his face in front of her. "Then tell me where Vaughn is."

She clenched her teeth together, released them. "I don't know."

"You're lying." He stood erect and motioned his men to bring Lucie forward. He grabbed her by the back of her hair and forced her down to her knees in front of Zara. Pulling his gun out of the holster, he dug the end into Lucie's temple. "Tell me where Lawson Vaughn is, or I'll blow her brains into your lap."

Zara stared into Lucie's frightened eyes, afraid to blink. Her brain sped through her options and the consequences each one might bring.

"He went to Paris to catch up with Conrad Flynn," she lied, grateful Annette wasn't in the room to contradict her. "He left this morning and I haven't seen him since."

"Why?" Stefano asked.

"Director Flynn came for him because of the uproar with the French authorities over Varina and Giovanni's deaths." She willed her voice to stay calm. "We already knew you had set up camp here, and Flynn left me behind to keep an eye on you. He's notified the French and Swiss authorities of your whereabouts."

Stefano snorted. "The French and Swiss have better things to do than bother me, and the United States does not scare me." His eyes narrowed a millimeter and he pointed a finger at her. "You, on the other hand, have killed several members of my organization. That I do not take lightly." He shifted his gaze to Lucie and back to her. "I believe in an eye for an eye."

No, not Lucie. "If you want to prove a point or exact retribution for Varina's death, then kill me. Lucie's death will mean nothing to the CIA or the United States. Mine will."

Stefano drew a deep breath in through his nose, flaring his nostrils as he studied her. "The key to successful warfare is meticulous preparation. I, for one, hate improvisation." He tapped his index fingers together again. "But perhaps, under the circumstances, we can make a deal."

Zara knew her doom was sealed. Whatever deal she made with Stefano and Dmitri would kill her. But if it gave Lucie even the slimmest chance of survival, if she could keep Lucie alive until Lawson arrived, she had to take it.

She looked at her sister and gave her a weak but encouraging smile. "A deal. Of course."

~ ✧ ~

"I have a problem," Lawson said into the phone.

"Yeah, I know." Del snickered. "He's dark and dangerous and knows how to piss off Stone without raising an eyebrow. So what's new?"

"This is a real problem. I need help."

"Okay."

"Dmitri's got Zara."

The line was silent for several seconds. "What do mean, 'got her'?"

"Kidnapped."

"Holy shit," Del whispered. "How did that happen?"

"Long story. Bottom line is I fucked up. Where's Pegasus?"

"Let me check." Lawson heard Del's fingers tap his keyboard. "Looks like they're all here in the States on standby."

"For what?"

"Missing agent. He's been out of contact for three days now, and Pegasus is on call to ship out to Pakistan pending the DCI's orders."

It wasn't optimal, but it could have been worse. His team could have been in Middle or South America involved in a search and rescue. At least if they were in the D.C. area on standby, he had a chance of getting them to Europe within a reasonable timeframe. Especially if they were going to soon be on their way to the Middle East anyway. "I need you to go to Stone and tell him what's happened. I need Pegasus here in Switzerland and I need them ASAP."

"I'm a peon in the beast known as the Agency. I can't go to Michael Stone. You better call Flynn and get him to talk to the big guy. He pisses Stone off, but he also pulls a lot more weight."

Damn. The last thing Lawson wanted to do was explain to Flynn how he'd screwed up and let Zara get kidnapped.

But for her, he would get down on his knees and kiss Flynn's feet if it meant he would get him his team.

Chapter Thirty-Five

Zara sat still as stone in her chair. Lucie was seated on the couch and Dmitri leaned against the wall behind Stefano, staring at Zara. It was meant to unnerve her, so she ignored him.

"Did you know anyone killed in the September eleventh terrorist attacks?" Stefano asked.

While Dmitri was a crafty manipulator who liked to tease and taunt and draw things out, Stefano was a different animal. The Mafia leader preferred to get to the bottom line as quickly and efficiently as possible. A ruthless executive. She wasn't sure where his question was leading, but she answered honestly. "Yes. Several."

Stefano focused on a framed photograph on his desk. "My family as well. Two of my cousins and a half dozen college friends. The bride-to-be of my stepbrother. All lost in the World Trade Center Towers because a minority of men are bent on destroying the West in the name of God." He shook his head. "Those attacks did not just affect Americans. They affected all of us."

Zara glanced at the grandfather clock in the corner. It had already been close to two hours since she'd been kidnapped. Another six before the sun came up. Time, so far, was on her side.

"Islamic fundamentalists are a black mark on the twenty-first century," he continued. "Their followers are ignorant, uncultured peoples who thrive on fanaticism and violence. They have brought their darkness to the United States and they continue to spread the same violence throughout the European community in an effort to make us fear them. This fanaticism has gone unchecked for too long. They should be made to pay for the destruction and killing they have committed. They should be wiped off the face of the Earth."

An eye for an eye. The Mafia way of life. Zara sighed. "The United States and Great Britain are trying to flush out and bring those responsible to just—"

Stefano slammed his hand on the desk. "The United States and Great Britain have done nothing but add fuel to the fire. Many of the Islamic leaders responsible for nine eleven walk free, continuing to pour money into their private militias and planning more attacks, not just on the United States but worldwide."

Dmitri crossed his legs at the ankles. "Two days ago, an al-Qaeda sympathizer drove a car bomb into a canteen of an air base in Belgium, killing over a hundred people. He was a disciple of Osama bin Laden."

Stefano's jowls shook with rage. "The same man was suspected of planning a suicide mission against the U.S. Embassy in Rome last year. He was questioned by the Italian authorities who in turn notified your government and requested help in prosecuting him. The Italian government was told to handle it themselves. The U.S. could not be bothered by such an insignificant matter. Do you know why, Agent Morgan? Because they were too busy sending more troops to Iraq."

Drawing in a deep breath seemingly to calm his rage, he sat back in his chair. "There are highly efficient ways of dealing with these Middle Eastern mongrel races. Ways of eliminating both the fanatic leaders and their followers. My colleagues and I have developed such a way." He exchanged a look with Dmitri. "We will give them exactly what they want."

When he didn't continue, Zara broke her silence again. She needed to keep him talking. "Guns? Bombs? Weapons of mass destruction? How will that help your cause without hurting the innocent?"

Dmitri answered, his voice carrying excitement. "Silent bombs. Highly efficient, but less messy than traditional weapons. Easy to carry and disseminate and extremely deadly."

Zara's brain clicked. "Biological agents. That's why you recruited Dr. Vos Loo."

Stefano nodded. "Genetic engineering of biological agents can alter their incubation periods, the way they are spread and even the clinical syndromes they produce. Bacterium can be mixed with viruses to create the most deadly and the easiest-

spread diseases the world has ever known."

"Vos Loo's father," Dmitri said, warming to the discussion, "dabbled in creating alternate agents back in the 1950's for the Russian Biological Warfare Program. Unfortunately, none of them were used in anything more than laboratory experimentation."

"And all were supposedly destroyed at the end of the Cold War." Stefano held up a finger and tapped it against his temple. "But the doctor kept his own personal notes and hid them in a secret underground lab here in Switzerland. Jon has continued his father's work."

Dmitri pushed off the wall. "It all works out perfectly, you see. The Middle Eastern fanatics want to buy weapons with the capability of distributing fatal diseases to the rest of us. Some of them came to me in the past, but I always turned them down. I didn't want to deal with them. Now, Stefano wants revenge for the senseless deaths of family and friends at the hands of these same fanatics. I find the idea very appealing. So along with Vos Loo's help, I've arranged a deal that gives everybody what they want. I supply the weapons and Vos Loo supplies the anthrax and smallpox agents."

Stefano chuckled softly. "Vos Loo has developed a virus which is fast acting and highly contagious like SARS but contains a deadly strain of a pathogen similar to anthrax. When the deal goes down, our Islamic buyers end up exposing themselves to a deadly disease without even knowing it."

Dmitri chuckled too. "Then the Muslim dogs take it back home with them and our biogenetically engineered version of the plague kills thousands of them, all of them if we're lucky."

"Luck has nothing to do with it," Stefano retorted, the impatient, calculating commander again. "Meticulous planning does. In a few days, we will have justice and achieve what the Superpowers have failed to do with armies, warfare and trials."

In other words, Zara thought, *don't send an egomaniac superpower to do a hit man's job.*

Stefano opened a laminated wood box on his desk and drew out a cigar. "Vos Loo's strain takes twenty-four hours from exposure to full-blown symptoms. However, by the time a high fever and chest congestion appear, it's already too late. The exposed person's white blood cells have dropped significantly. His lungs fill with blood and his fever spikes, causing brain-damaging convulsions. He goes into shock and respiratory failure. All major organs shut down. Within forty-eight hours, the virus will have run its course and the patient will be dead."

"In the meantime," Dmitri said, "he has exposed countless others. His family, the men he prays with at temple, his business associates. All who in turn pass the disease on."

Zara challenged their logic. "As soon as the World Health Organization recognizes the cluster of disease, they'll isolate and quarantine those affected just like they did during the SARS epidemic."

Stefano dismissed her argument. "The WHO moves at a pace comparable to your Congress. By the time they understand the massive scale of the disease, the quarantine will be too late. Plus, it will take them weeks to figure out the antidote. In order to survive the virus, a specific combination of antibiotics and antimicrobials has to be administered within the first twenty-four hour period."

Ethnic cleansing. Dear God, how could they even be talking about such a thing? Zara shifted her gaze between the modern-day versions of Hitler and Milosevic in front of her and once again called on logic to help her out. "Cleansing Europe of Muslims, even if it's only the extremists, is a massive undertaking. You may make a dent in their community, but you will never eliminate the entire Muslim world."

Stefano rolled the cigar between his fingers. "An effective war campaign does not limit itself to striking the enemy on only one front. My plan is in fact multifaceted. As the world deals with the biological attack, new attacks will be initiated, originating from the most unlikely of sources. The Health Ministry itself will unknowingly distribute contaminated antibiotics. Blankets and other supplies provided by humanitarian aide agencies to the refuge camps in Afghanistan and Pakistan will be contaminated with smallpox. The Muslim world will be under siege. Few will survive. Those who do will have nothing to live for."

Scenes of death and disease filled Zara's mind. Her stomach roiled. "How will you keep non-Muslims from contracting the disease? If Dr. Vos Loo's virus runs amok, aren't you putting yourselves and your own families in danger?"

"Adherents to the Islamic faith are a very tight-knit family," Stefano answered. "They keep to themselves. A few innocent people on the fringes may be infected, those who tolerate and accept Muslims into their community, but every war has its collateral damage and anyone who befriends this group of people deserves to die. My network of health administrators here in Europe and in America will be instructed on proper protocol for dealing with the outbreak should it affect large numbers of Europeans. The antidote cocktail will be made available for those I deem appropriate. All of us here are already receiving vaccinations as a precaution."

Zara glanced at Lucie. A deep line creased her sister's forehead, mirroring her own. She glanced back at Dmitri and Stefano. "So how will you expose your buyers to this supervirus Vos Loo's created?"

Dmitri's eyes danced and he rubbed his hands together. "You, Agent Morgan. You are about to become a weapon of mass destruction."

Chapter Thirty-Six

Director Flynn was silent for so long, Lawson was sure the man had either fallen back asleep or the connection had gone dead.

Interrupting the DO's sleep was a bad idea, especially since he was already on his shit list, but Lawson didn't have any choice. He had to have help. He'd roused Flynn out of his slumber and spilled the entire story about Zara's kidnapping in less than thirty seconds. Now he waited for Flynn's response.

Silence didn't bode well. Lawson paced the library floor. "Director?"

"Way to screw up, Vaughn." Lawson could see him swinging his legs over the bed and sitting up. "What's your plan?"

"I'm heading out to do surveillance on the estate where Dmitri's at as we speak, but I can't proceed past that until I have backup. There are approximately thirty well-armed guards and a very sophisticated security system in place. I want my Team here as fast as I can get them."

Another pause which seemed to Lawson to last an hour. "Even if Stone is willing to send your team, it'll be hours before they arrive. What do you plan to do in the meantime?"

"I need at least one more man on the ground who can help me with surveillance until Pegasus arrives. Two or three would be better. If this group breaks camp or if any of the major players leave the compound, I've got no way to follow them. Do you have any Agency-trained operatives in this region?"

"Of a sort," Flynn answered.

The spot between Lawson's shoulder blades twitched. "What sort?"

"Bernier."

This time it was Lawson's turn to let silence hang between

them. "Come again."

"Your host at the Villa."

Like a kaleidoscope, images and snippets of conversations with Christian blended and refocused into a different picture in front of Lawson's eyes. Christian's knowledge of weapons. His detailed background checks and knowledge-gathering of people he didn't know. His extensive wardrobe.

"Holy hell," Lawson said. "You've got to be joking. Zara's ballet teacher is a freakin' spook?"

Flynn cleared his throat. "We've used him occasionally. He's proven to be a good access agent, getting information for us, and his villa's been a safe house for some of our people over the years in exchange for protection of his extensive art collection."

Lawson glanced at the doorway to make sure it was clear and then he lowered his voice. "I don't know squat about art, but shouldn't those pieces be in museums or something?"

"Even the Louvre has had major works of art stolen right off its walls in the middle of the day. Few museums are safer than Bernier's estate."

"Does he have any actual field experience?"

"Of a sort."

"Jesus." Lawson laughed without humor. "You've got to give me more than that."

"I can give you one of the best spies in the business," Flynn said. "Myself. I'll bring my goons from security, and another expert on terrorists who's at my disposal." Lawson thought he heard a moan—a woman's moan—in the background. No wonder Flynn was extra pissed at him. "We'll meet up with you in approximately one hour. While you're waiting, develop a viable op plan for us."

This could not be happening. "*You* are coming into the field with me to rescue Zara."

"Hell yes," Flynn said, sounding irritated. "Got a problem with that?"

A freakin' ballet teacher and his boss were about to become his back-up team. He wasn't sure how the night could get any worse. "Just as long as you understand I'm in charge of the mission. Sir," he added.

Several heartbeats passed and Lawson could have sworn Flynn was smiling. "We'll discuss that when I get there."

Chapter Thirty-Seven

A small circle of orange glowed across from Zara, Dmitri's cigarette seeming to move by invisible hands. They sat in darkness, the bathroom clouding slowly with smoke.

Her hands were still cuffed, this time circling pipes attached to the sink next to her head. The bathroom floor was hard under her butt and she listened to Lucie's steady breathing coming from the corner.

Her tormentor sat comfortably a few feet away, and Zara knew this was her last opportunity to get him to answer the questions circling her brain. "Why didn't you shoot me that night at the farmhouse?"

The tip of the cigarette burned brighter for a few seconds, and then moved to dangle over his knee. "Does it matter?"

"It matters a great deal to me."

"Look no further than the seven deadly sins, my dear." He laughed indifferently. "Greed is my usual motivator. You claimed you knew where my weapons were and I almost believed you. It was worth a chance. Besides, I knew who you were—the daughter of a millionaire. Knew you'd been asking around about me. Taking you hostage was extraordinarily enticing even if you didn't know about my weapons."

Zara straightened her feet out in front of her. "You're lying. You didn't plan to kidnap me for ransom money."

Dmitri laughed under his breath. "All right, I suppose not. But it is still worth contemplating. How much do you think I would have gotten?"

"Enough to make you happy for life."

"Ah, but there is never enough money to make me happy."

"Why did you think Tim Owens knew where your weapons were?"

A pause. "He did."

"He wasn't working your case. He didn't know."

"Is that what he told you?" The cigarette moved to his face, the tip of it illuminating his lips as he took another drag. The orange glow grew darker, retreated. "God, you're gullible. You think I'd trick him into coming to that old farmhouse if he didn't know about my inventory?" He snickered.

For a moment, Zara considered his words. A trickle of renewed anger burned in her stomach. "Why trick Owens to come to the farmhouse then instead of your compound?"

"Do you know who was waiting for me at my camp? Mahmoud Saleh, Prince Abkhahar's second in command. The Prince wanted his missiles and if I didn't show up with them, Mahmoud was prepared to execute me."

Leaning her head against the sink, Zara shut her eyes.

Dmitri continued. "Owens was my last hope of finding those damned weapons. Running was out of the question. Mahmoud and his army would have tracked me down within a couple of days, cut my balls off and left me to bleed to death. I dare say, even now, prison sounds more attractive."

He pulled on his cigarette, blew the smoke out. "And then you showed up, willing to give me what Owens refused to. You were far more interesting than him, and I saw instantly you would be more fun to torture as well."

Zara stayed still, willed herself not to be baited. "How did you get my necklace?"

The lighted cigarette moved in the darkness again. Zara could tell he was fingering her chain. "I pulled it off your neck when we struggled. A little souvenir."

At her silence, he chuckled. "Now my question. Did you know where my missiles were?"

"Yes," Zara lied, already calculating how she'd get her chain back. "What about Annette? How did you get her to help you? Something about her sister?"

The cigarette was almost gone. "Ah, the beautiful Amy. Rogan Janvrin discovered her at Harvard when he was teaching there. Intelligent, witty, she was perfect for Varina's prostitution ring. Janvrin invited her to Italy under the guise of a romantic weekend and Stefano pressed her into work for him. He can be very persuasive, you know. Janvrin routinely seduces young girls like Amy away from the States and gives them to Stefano."

Dmitri threw the butt of the cigarette down between them.

"Your FBI friend was able to figure out what had happened to her sister, but could never uncover enough hard evidence to open an official investigation. When she became aware of the link between myself and Stefano, she offered to be of service."

"She put Lawson and me on your trail here in Switzerland so she could kidnap us."

"It's too bad she didn't fulfill her part of our agreement and bring in Vaughn with you."

Zara figured that meant Annette was dead. That's why she hadn't seen her. Waves of sadness mixed with her anger. "This won't work, you know...me being the carrier for Vos Loo's supervirus. Your Islamic buyers won't touch me. In fact, they'll probably be offended you're offering something so appalling as a Western woman in the form of a bonus."

"You read too much of your own country's propaganda," Dmitri scoffed. "The fanatics who participate in *jihad* are excluded by bin Laden from many of the strict Islamic followings. They smoke Turkish cigarettes, gamble in Las Vegas and dream of raping virgins in Heaven. One look at your pretty blonde hair and blue eyes and they'll be salivating. You'll be the recipient of all their hatred as well as their lust."

He cracked his knuckles. "Besides, even if they don't want to beat and rape you just for fun, they'll still take you. When I tell them you're worth millions in ransom money, they will no doubt ask Allah to bless me tenfold. Even a few thousand dollars can buy them a ship full of weapons."

A sharp rap at the door brought Zara's head up. Light from the hallway poured into the room as a guard opened it. "Breaking camp."

Dmitri stood and brushed off his pants. "Good." Zara flinched at the feel of his fingers on her wrists. "Time to go, Agent Morgan." Over his shoulder, he nodded to the guard. "Get the other one."

The man moved toward Lucie, kicking her awake.

Zara's tingling hands fell weakly into her lap as Dmitri keyed open the cuffs. A surge of panic, strong and harsh, rose under her rib cage. If they moved, Lawson wouldn't be able to find them. "Go where?"

He hauled her to a standing position, jerking her arms behind her and snapping the cuffs back on. He pushed her toward the door. "Jon Vos Loo's father left him more than just the recipes for his biological nightmares. He also left him his lab. A compound about two hundred kilometers from here on the border of Germany. That's where we'll meet our buyers."

As they left the bathroom, Zara saw the men in black walking through the halls and rooms of the estate, wiping down doorknobs and handrails with focused efficiency. Behind a set of French doors, she heard a vacuum. She tried to slow Dmitri's rapid pace, but his pressing grip on her upper arm kept her moving. Lucie and her guard followed close behind.

At the front door, Dmitri placed a strip of duct tape over Zara's mouth. Lucie received the same treatment and then a black bag went over each of their heads. An iron arm— Dmitri's?—gripped Zara just under her lungs and lifted her feet off the ground. She was carried down several steps before being shoved into a running car. The hands pressed her down to the car's floorboard, and she kicked out with her feet and made contact, enough to bring a grunt from her handler. But it was wasted effort. A blow caught her in the ribs and made her gasp for air.

Seconds later, the car shot forward. Raw panic surged through her again, a shameless silent scream echoing in her head. Trying to control her emotions, she breathed deeply and evenly through her nose.

Lawson was out there somewhere. She closed her eyes and willed her mind to block out what was happening and think of him and his superhuman ability to track anyone and never get lost. As the car sped toward the Swiss-German border, Zara told herself to keep the faith. Lawson would find them, she was sure. In the meantime, she just had to keep Lucie alive.

As the third black armor-plated Mercedes limousine rolled by in front of him, Lawson held his breath as well as his trigger finger. Lying in the weeds of the roadside, he was close enough to the car to read the imprint on the front tire. Close enough that one bullet from his gun could blow that tire out and stop the procession of Stefano Biaggio and Alexandrov Dmitri.

And bring the wrath of a dozen or more well-armed men down on him and his ragtag team of pseudo-commandos.

Flynn's solemn voice came through his digitally encrypted Motorola headset. "Don't do anything rash, Commander."

Lawson let out his breath and took his finger off the trigger as the car zoomed past him and another took its place. This was, without a doubt, his worst nightmare. A hostage situation where he couldn't control any of the variables, and the hostage, a woman whose life he had come to value more than his own, within reach but not within access.

Add to that, his boss, twenty-yards away, directing his every move. The other members of his team—Zara's ballet coach, an Air Force colonial who chauffeured Flynn around Europe in a helicopter, three bodyguards from the CIA's Office of Security, and Flynn's wife, a former CIA operative/analyst and now FBI agent who just happened be with Flynn in Paris—men and a woman he had never worked with before.

"Lead car's tracking system activated," bodyguard Dom Spencer said.

One bright spot had come from Del Hoffman. The King of Techies had had the absentminded foresight to send new equipment with Flynn's bodyguards on the off chance they might find time to do a trial run.

Spencer was currently positioned a quarter mile northwest of Lawson and outfitted with a thirteen-inch long Rutger MK II. The sleek .22-caliber gun did not fire bullets from its silenced barrel. This one, CIA-certified and techie-approved, fired small GPS bugs instead that could attach themselves to almost any surface, including armor-plated cars, and like a chameleon, change colors to match the vehicle's paint.

The tiny devices looked like some sort of futuristic insect and, when activated, sent out a clear, pulsing signal to satellites circling above the Earth. A signal that would be tracked from the heart of the enemy's camp into Langley, Virginia. The exact coordinates of an operational base could be passed onto Lawson and his team as well as Pegasus, whose members were now speeding over the Atlantic in a C-130.

Accompanying Pegasus was a SEAL team, because now it wasn't just enough to save one of the CIA's foreign counterintelligence officers. The American, British and French intelligence services had witnessed movement among a dozen different Islamic fundamentalist cells in the past forty-eight hours. Communications intercepted between them and suspected Mafia deputies pointed at a union between the two camps. It appeared the bad guys were joining forces and Lawson and Zara were smack dab in the middle of it.

Lawson didn't care. Not much anyway. Anarchy was brewing in Europe, but his sole focus was Zara. He would chase Alexandrov Dmitri and Jon Vos Loo and a group of Mafia hoods until the last breath left his body, but it wasn't in order to save anyone but her.

In the end, if his team kept Western Europe from some biological nightmare, great. He was all for it. And if he had the opportunity to put a bullet between Dmitri's eyes, he would gladly pull the trigger after he castrated the son of a bitch. No problem.

But the bottom line for Superman on this mission was to save Lois Lane.

Dom Spencer's low voice registered in his ear. "Rear car's tracking system activated."

The taillights of the last vehicle, a black, civilian-styled Hummer, disappeared into the night. "Copy that," he said. "Move out, Team."

Chapter Thirty-Eight

German-Swiss border

Zara had seen a lot of things in her life. The inside of a terrorist's compound was not one of them. While the mock version Flynn had trained her in was similar, she'd have to recommend a few changes when she got back.

If she got back.

Bare, sterile and completely windowless, the structure provided its occupants with the basic necessities of the criminal-designed life—bathrooms, a weapons arsenal and a fully stocked laboratory. Cameras and infrared detection devices had been added since Jon Vos Loo's father built it in the 1950s with funds provided by the German and Russian governments. Remote-controlled doors on the prison cells as well.

Zara pressed her ear against the metal door and listened to sounds echoing outside in the hallway. Footsteps, a toilet flushing, someone whistling. The tension, the urgency that had affected the group when leaving the estate was gone. In its place, a cocky air of success.

No barricades had stopped their caravan as it moved through the Swiss countryside. No international SWAT team had swooped down out of the mountains and hijacked them at sunrise. No one-man army had managed to sneak in amongst the host gang and save her.

She was on her own. Walking her eight-by-six sealed cubicle, she knew she had no choice but to save Lucie herself. She looked for anything she could use as a tool to help her escape. There was a mattress on the floor, a toilet, a sink. A single recessed light and a small air vent in the ceiling. Nothing that would aid her. She took inventory of what she was wearing. Turtleneck, jeans, her Prada jacket, a pair of ugly sneakers. No gun, no cell phone, not even a pack of matches or a tube of lip gloss.

She let out a sigh and sat on the mattress. Her mind was clearer now after several hours of sleep in the car, but MacGyver she was not. She couldn't work up one idea, not even a far-fetched one as to how to escape her prison cell.

Resting her elbows on her knees, she dropped her head into her hands. Her muscles and neck ached from the cramped position she had slept in and she was starving, but at least she was alive and relatively unhurt. It had to be getting close to midmorning, which meant, if she had heard Dmitri right, she had approximately eight hours before the meeting took place. Eight hours. She had to try something.

Even if she completed her part of the deal, Stefano would never let Lucie go. Lucie had seen his face and heard the plan to cleanse Europe and the world of the Muslim population. She could ID him and all of his men. No way would he or Dmitri let her live.

One of Zara's shoestrings was untied. She pulled the shoe off and threw it across the room in frustration. It bounced and landed on the floor. She kicked the other one off and stared at it. *Do something,* her mind demanded. *Move.*

"Okay, okay," she whispered back. She stared at the shoe and drew in a deep breath. "Forget MacGyver. If I were Conrad Flynn, what would I do?"

Flynn would never let himself get in this mess. She picked up the shoe, fingering its dirty lace. She looked over at the toilet and the sink and then down at her mattress. She gave the top of the mattress a couple of pokes with her finger, and the worn-out stuffing gave way easily. She went to the sink, turned on the water and analyzed its flow down the drain.

"But if I were Lawson," she said to herself, shutting off the water, "I'd come up with an operational plan." She shed her jacket and threw it on the mattress. Then she paced the cell again, looking at the door from all angles.

Moving to stand in front of the door next, she examined the room from that angle, pretending to be Dmitri. Trying to think like he would think. Self-assured, unafraid, and, she hoped, unprepared for an ambush. Mentally running through her options, she settled on one for her Plan A.

"First, I have to figure out where Lucie is."

Then all she had to do was evade the twelve men guarding the compound, avoid the infrared detection devices and cameras, make it to the underground garage, hot-wire a car and bust through the compound's outside gate.

"I can do this." She returned to the mattress. "I'm one of Flynn's secret army."

The electronic door to her room slid back noiselessly, and Dmitri stood in the doorway, a tray of food in his hand. He set it on the floor inside the room but didn't venture in. "Breakfast. Eat it."

She felt a ping of satisfaction that he was too nervous to step into the room with her unfettered. "Did you feed Lucie too?"

"She's sleeping."

"You drugged her, didn't you?"

He shrugged. "Of course."

"Why didn't you drug me?"

"Because in a few hours, you'll be receiving a dose of Vos Loo's special virus. He didn't want other drugs in your system, especially after the tranquilizer Annette used. Makes the virus's pathogenicity unreliable."

"A rather big word for you."

Dmitri leaned his shoulder against the doorjamb, taking her bait. "Hang around Dr. Frankenstein long enough, he rubs off on you."

"Frankenstein?"

"Creator of freaks and monsters."

Zara considered his words. "Vos Loo's father experimented on people, didn't he? That's why these cells are here."

"What scientist exists without his research?"

"But Vos Loo updated all of this, so he must have experimented on people as well." She shivered at the thought of the men and women who had paced the cell and sat on the mattress before her, knowing they were going to die. "How many cells are there?"

Dmitri glanced down the hall. "A dozen or so. Only a few are as modernized as this one."

"How long before Vos Loo injects me with the virus?"

He checked his watch, exposing her chain on his wrist. "Four hours. It will take three more after that before you begin to show signs of the disease. Another hour and you'll be dangerously contagious. Before that happens, the deal will be done and you and the Islamic dogs will be on your way."

She stood and walked toward him. His casual demeanor stiffened. "I want my gold chain back," she said, stopping just inches away from him.

The ice-blue eyes mocked her and one corner of his mouth rose in a snarl. "You'll have to kill me for it."

No retreat. No surrender. "Deal."

Chapter Thirty-Nine

"Ah, Germany," Christian said, looking north over the foggy hills. "Europe's problem child and a beer lover's paradise."

Mist fell on Lawson's face as he tugged on a pair of jungle fatigue pants over his jeans. To most people, especially travelers, the weather conditions were less than favorable. For the leader of Team Pegasus, the heavy fog and mist were welcomed. Like camouflage, Mother Nature's handiwork helped to shield his men from the enemy. Nightfall was still hours away, but the weather would allow him and his team to move up the timetable and launch their plan early. He hoped it was early enough.

Donning a matching fatigue jacket, Lawson glanced around at the other men inside their temporary defensive perimeter. Flynn was updating the members of Pegasus on the current situation. Alongside them, five U.S. Navy SEALs and their senior officer also listened and asked questions. Six other SEALs were already in place south of the perimeter doing surveillance on the compound where Dmitri and his group had disappeared. Built into the rocky hill, the enemy encampment was nearly impenetrable.

The group with him today would find a way in. They had to. The worldwide Islamic terror network was on the move. Intelligence services, including the CIA, had noticed a marked increase in chatter over the airwaves during the past twenty-four hours, much of it generating from Pakistan where Osama bin Laden was believed to be hiding out. Conversations between known militants had been intercepted by American and British electronic eavesdroppers.

Britain's specialists in Cheltenham had gathered information indicating preparations for new terrorist attacks, focused in Europe and the Gulf, were well advanced. Several of the communications suggested the militants already possessed surface-to-air missiles for use against targets in the United Kingdom. Others would be receiving weapons soon.

Arrests had been made in Pakistan after local police, assisted by American commandos, had raided a flat. Rifles, maps of Paris, Belgium and Frankfurt, and literature on the dissemination of biological weapons had turned up in the hands of an Afghan and a Yemeni.

In Italy and Spain, the previous chatter between the Italian Mafia deputies and bin Laden's al-Qaeda militants had completely ceased. Another warning bell.

The United Kingdom's alert codes had been raised from yellow to high-risk orange. America's as well. Politicians in France and Germany, as always, refused to raise an alarm until more information about the nature of the threats could be determined.

As he pulled a floppy camouflage hat down over his ears with one hand, Lawson adjusted the headset of his Motorola radio with the other. He secured his HK at his waist, strapped a KA-BAR knife to his ankle and slung the strap of a submachine gun over his shoulder. Armed to the teeth and looking at the men in his company, he suddenly felt better. More in control. He had a job to do and now he had the proper equipment and men to do it.

Flynn finished talking and looked at Lawson. He motioned Lawson over. "Before we go any further with this, I want to establish chain of command."

"Uh-oh," Christian chimed softly in the background.

Lawson locked eyes with the SEAL lieutenant. Both of them were more than qualified to lead the show, and neither would willingly concede control to the other.

Flynn glanced between them. He addressed the SEAL leader. "Normally, I would hand command to you, Lieutenant Redington, because of your experience, but these are not normal circumstances. Commander Vaughn and the Pegasus team have more specific experience with this particular terrorist which gives Vaughn the upper hand this time. As we've already discussed, this is a delicate situation, not only due to the men we're going after but because a very important CIA operative, her sister and possibly an FBI agent, are being held hostage by this group." Glancing between the men again, he continued.

"However, Lieutenant, I'm sure Vaughn and his men would appreciate any input you can offer."

Lieutenant Redington nodded. "My men and I are ready to assist Team Pegasus as needed."

Lawson took Redington's outstretched hand and shook it, feeling another surge of relief. He was in charge. "Let's get down to business."

The rest of the men, including Christian, Flynn's Air Force pilot and the three bodyguards, were brought into the discussion. Intel from Del back at CIA headquarters offered the group a picture of what they were up against.

The structure had been built into the top and side of a steep and wooded hillside, a combination laboratory and bunker. Built and furnished with money from the Russian and German governments, it was suspected of being used intermittently for experimentation of drugs and vaccines on Jews and Muslims since the 1950s. Insertion points were limited to two. An entrance tunnel was located at the top of the hill near a helicopter pad. The other, an underground garage which led to the compound's main entrance, was sealed by electronic doors. These were controlled by keypad.

Security would be tight. Ambushes would be unlikely—the design of the bunker would give Dmitri a false sense of security and he would rely mostly on cameras and infrared detection devices for perimeter breaches—but booby traps were still a possibility.

Using a rough blueprint of the compound Del had provided, Lawson divided the building into three sectors and assigned men to each. The three top snipers from the SEAL and Pegasus teams would take up positions in the hillside as a cover force along with Flynn, his pilot and his bodyguards.

"I want you in a secure position," he said to Flynn, "where you can take in the whole picture and give us direction. In other words, do what you do best."

"Hoffman will be sending us more updates as the day goes on," Flynn said. "I'll relay the pertinent information to you as it becomes available."

Christian piped up from behind Lawson's point man, Johnny Quick. "What about me?"

Lawson blew out a breath and looked Christian straight in the eye. "Stay out of the way and don't get shot. Zara will kill me if anything happens to you."

"Hmph." He tried to look annoyed but only managed to look relieved.

Lawson reminded everyone that once they were inside the bunker, they would encounter both a heavily armed militia and a lab stocked with biological agents. Every man there had been trained in bioterrorism, but Lawson reviewed strategic responses to deal with the expected scenarios anyway. Emergency units in Germany and Switzerland, equipped with biohazard suits and clean-up kits, had already been alerted and were on standby in the event any biological or chemical weapon was released.

After an hour, a solid op plan was in place. The two teams had picked it apart step by step and given themselves several options as back up. Lawson instructed Lieutenant Redington to check in with the men in the field. The SEAL adjusted his lip mike and touched the transmit button in his radio. "Apollo, this is Zeus. Do you copy? Over."

"Zeus, this is Apollo. What's our situation?"

"We're about to move out and hook up with you."

"ETA?"

Redington looked at Lawson. Lawson held up five spread fingers and Redington said into his mike, "Five minutes. Sit?"

The situation report sounded favorable. "No one's moving. Liebe and Priest have circumnavigated the camp. Report footpaths but no tangos. No booby traps. Cameras stationed above garage entrance and on helo pad. Otherwise, security is minimal."

"Roger that, Apollo. We're on our way."

As per Lawson's instructions, the two teams divided up and fanned out, disappearing into the mist.

Chapter Forty

Digging another handful of stuffing out of her mattress, Zara took it to the sink and shoved it into the drain. She turned the water on full blast and watched the sink fill. Satisfied, she returned to the mattress and dug out more of the musty-smelling stuffing. Holding it in her arms, she carried it to the door, knelt down and dumped it on the floor. She kneaded it into the small crack at the bottom, then positioned the mattress at an angle to the door.

Sliding down the far wall until her butt hit the floor, she closed her eyes for a few minutes, running her plan over in her mind. It was simplistic, but the element of surprise would at least gain her freedom from the cell. She estimated she still had two hours before Dmitri or one of his guards came for her.

The sound of water hitting the floor made her open her eyes. She watched a puddle grow on the floor. All her dreams and hopes for the future—returning to Paris to continue her work as a field operative, tackling dance in her off hours again, having a relationship with Lawson—could die with her in a few hours. No one would know how happy she had been the past few days. How alive she had truly felt.

Even Lawson didn't know. She'd never worked up the courage to face the truth herself, much less tell him. He'd become much more to her than a partner, more than just a European fling while caught in the adrenaline-pumping mission. He'd become her friend and she cared deeply what happened to him. She wanted to live—not just to get Lucie out alive, but to spend more time with Lawson. She wanted a relationship. Long-term, preferably, with lots of sex.

Was it love? She didn't know. With unsteady hands, she wiped tears off her cheeks. She probably would never know. For now all she could do was sit tight and wait.

~ ✧ ~

Halfway up the hill, Team Pegasus and their SEAL counterparts met up with the men doing surveillance on the bunker. When everyone was assembled, Lawson and Redington briefed them on the specifics of the mission. Questions were answered and contingencies discussed. Small color snapshots of Alexandrov Dmitri, Jon Vos Loo and Stefano Biaggio were passed around.

The CIA preferred all three to be taken alive. Full-face photos of Zara, Lucie and Annette were also passed around and protocol for getting them out of the line of fire and secured was detailed. All the men had been through similar hostage situations before. All were determined to get the job done safely and efficiently.

The mist turned to solid rain. Lawson gave instructions to his cover force and gave the order for each element to move out. Standard operating procedures, including radio silence, were to be followed until all the teams were in place. Crawling on their bellies because of the slippery footing, Lawson and his men moved slowly to their position on the west side of the helicopter pad.

While they waited for the other teams to check in, he could no longer block thoughts about Zara from his mind. Images of her bruised and battered swam in front of his eyes. He had never had patience for bullies, hated them in fact. Those who lived to inflict pain and suffering on others were worthless in his book. If Dmitri or one of his thugs had hurt her...

At the thought, pure hate crawled into his chest. Like a boa constrictor, it squeezed his lungs and stole his breath. Anger, sharp and white hot, flooded his body. Anger beyond anything he had ever felt before. He wanted to hit something. He wanted to kill someone.

But before he killed them, he wanted to pull their balls out by way of their throat.

Flynn's steady voice cut through the sound of blood pounding in his ears. "Commander Vaughn, I have orders for you to hold your position. Do you copy?"

Lawson forced his anger down a notch in order to answer.

Too much emotion of any kind led to poor judgment calls and at that moment, he couldn't afford to make a bad call. "Orders from whom?" he said. "Over."

"High command. Our Pakistan prisoner is beginning to remember information which may be critical to this mission. Hold your positions until further orders are received."

As far as he was concerned, the men and women of high command, sitting in their comfortable chairs and staring at their computer screens while he was laying on the ground in no-man's land with rain pouring off the brim of his hat, could kiss his ass. The time was right and his group needed to move. Nothing the Pakistani prisoner would tell them would be worth sacrificing Zara's life.

He glanced over at Johnny Quick, lying three yards away painting his face with mud from the ground underneath him. The two exchanged a silent look communicating their frustration. There couldn't possibly be anything worse than having their boss and his bosses calling the shots for them in the field.

The SEAL lieutenant's voice interrupted Lawson's reply. "Teams three and four are in position, Commander, and waiting for your signal."

As someone who had commanded teams of soldiers many times, Lawson knew what it took to be a good leader. It wasn't the extra bar on the sleeve of his uniform. He earned the respect of the men under him by being calculating, decisive and intuitive.

He'd left Flynn in charge of the overall operation because he was the right man for the job. It would have been easy to overrule his boss's orders but undermining Flynn served no purpose. Every good leader knew how to follow the chain of command. "All teams hold position."

Seconds ticked by. Then minutes. The rain continued to pour, its rhythmic sound dulling Lawson's senses. He looked through the scope of his suppressed MP5 to see the entrance near the helo pad. The fog gave them incredibly good cover, but it also cut his visibility to almost nothing. He could barely make out the solid door a scant twenty feet away.

Trying to keep his mind off Zara and what was happening to her, he ran through the infiltration and takedown scenarios again. He knew the other men were doing the same to keep themselves focused and pumped for the job ahead. Rescuing Zara, Lucie and possibly Annette, and subduing the terrorists, was the main objective, but staying alive was too. Everyone needed to be aware of their counterparts, lest they shoot one of their own.

Lawson mentally dissected the interior of the bunker, trying to figure out the most logical place for the women to be held. The blueprint Del had provided was based on a model of other bunker-style laboratories built in Europe around the same time. The cells where human guinea pigs were imprisoned were on the second floor close to the lab itself. The garage and disposal areas were below and living quarters were on the floor above. Lawson and his two teams would work from the top down while Redington and his two teams came through the garage and worked their way up. The scenario was less than ideal for getting to the hostages quickly, but it was the only logical way in.

"Commander Vaughn, I have new information," Flynn said.

Lawson raised his eye from the scope and lowered his mike. "Go ahead."

"Not over the radio. I am sending a man to deliver the information. He will be coming up behind your position."

Lawson felt Johnny's gaze on him. "Not advised, sir." The last thing he needed was for Christian or one of the other men with Flynn to slip on the hillside and alert the terrorists inside the bunker. "I'll send a man to you. Hold your position."

Pointing at Johnny, Lawson motioned for him to retrace their steps and retrieve the message. Johnny nodded and disappeared back down the hill.

While he was gone, Lawson wondered what information was so valuable Flynn refused to give it to him over the radio. They had already determined there was little chance Dmitri, Vos Loo or the other men with them had the technology to decipher their transmissions even if they were monitoring the airwaves. The only reason for Flynn to worry about the secrecy of his latest information was if he believed the Germans or some other country's intelligence service with the proper equipment and technology was listening.

Ten minutes later, Lawson started at Johnny's voice behind him. "Coming up behind you, Commander," he whispered. The man must have double-timed his belly crawl to make it back so fast.

"What have you got?" Lawson asked.

"Pakistan's InterServices Intelligence reports their prisoner broke. He claims a squad of al-Qaeda sub-bosses are headed this way to meet with Biaggio and Dmitri this evening. They're planning on buying biological agents and the weapons to disperse them." Quick looked toward the helo pad. "It's a big deal. Sheikh Jaradh Abdul Mohammed is supposedly among them."

Sheikh Mohammed was described by CIA counterterrorism experts as one of al-Qaeda's operation chiefs. An intimate of bin Laden's, he'd also been instrumental in designing the attacks on the World Trade Center according to some reports.

Lawson shifted his gun. "Why would one of al-Qaeda's most important leaders venture out of hiding?"

"Biaggio insisted he wouldn't work with anyone else. Since he holds the strings in Europe right now on the type of munitions al-Qaeda needs for putting anthrax and other shit into the air, I guess Mohammed didn't have a lot of choice. Plus, here in Switzerland, the antiterrorist laws are pretty weak. The most these guys will get if they're arrested is ten years in jail."

Lawson considered what Flynn and the high command back in the States were planning. Mohammed was the catch of the century if they could pull it off. "Are we sure this prisoner is telling the truth?"

Johnny smiled, his teeth white against his mud-caked face. "Interrogators wired the guy's balls to a 110-volt generator and the minute they turned the crank, he babbled like an auctioneer."

Lawson's scrotum tucked up into his body. "Jesus. I would, too, even if I made it all up."

Johnny raised his hand and made a clamping motion with his thumb and fingers. "Alligator clips. Vietnam-era torture technique."

Torture didn't always work. People would say anything to make the pain stop. "So how long do we wait to see if Sheikh's party shows?"

"Our guy claims before prayer this evening."

Glancing at his watch, Lawson blew out a breath. "If they're running on Eastern Europe time and they plan to have the deal done in time to pray, that means we've potentially got less than an hour."

"Yep. Flynn wants you to reconfigure the groups so there is one to meet the al-Qaeda liaison. Our new primary goal is to take Mohammed alive."

Lawson didn't like what he was hearing. "The minute we descend on the al-Qaeda group, Dmitri will know we're here. We'll lose the element of surprise for taking the bunker."

And getting Zara out alive. The unspoken words ran through Lawson's brain, and he could see by the way Johnny nodded he was thinking the same thing.

The two lay side-by-side for several long minutes. Finally, Lawson told his friend, "I think I'm too close to this one, Johnny. I'm not sure I know what the right call is."

Silence hung in the rain between them as Johnny took awhile to answer. "What's your gut say?"

Lawson chuckled. "My gut says, 'fuck Mohammed'. We don't even know for sure he and his entourage are going to show up. We need to take the bunker and take it now before Dmitri gets wind we're out here. Flynn can take care of the Sheikh."

"I agree."

Lt. Redington's voice half-whispered over both of their headsets. "Tango at four o'clock."

Lawson spoke into his lip mike, "Copy that. What's our boy doing?"

"Sentry duty on the footpath by the perimeter. Southwest side. Cell phone in hand. Probably shitty reception inside the bunker."

Unspoken communication passed between Lawson and Johnny. Lawson spoke again into his mike. "Who is in position to take him out?"

"This is Apollo," came the reply of the SEAL sniper. "I have him in my sights."

He didn't hesitate as he gave the command. "When the tango is out of camera range, take him out even if he's still on his phone. Whoever is closest, conceal the body."

"Roger, Commander," Redington answered.

Ten seconds later, the SEAL lieutenant's voice spoke over Lawson's headset. "Tango down and concealed. Combat vest holds a radio and a remote control garage door opener."

Bingo. There was no reason to use a sledgehammer when you could use a garage door opener. "Where did the tango emerge from, Lieutenant?"

"Funny you should ask, sir." Lawson could tell Redington was smiling. "I think we just found another way into the bunker."

Chapter Forty-One

Zara stood in ankle-deep water with her back up against the wall nearest the door. She'd turned the water down to a trickle and now stood listening for footsteps in the hall. In one hand, she held her Prada jacket. In the other, a jagged piece of plastic tray. Leveraging the tray on the edge of the sink, she'd broken it into several pieces to form a rudimentary knife. It wasn't much of a weapon against an MP60, but Lawson had taught her to use less and still take a man down.

Without a clock or a window, it was impossible for her to know what time it was. The sensory deprivation left her disoriented and exhaustion made her lightheaded. She was also starving. She hadn't eaten the food Dmitri had brought for fear it was drugged. It made sense Vos Loo wouldn't want drugs in her system before he injected his supervirus, but then Dmitri was also a skilled liar. It wasn't worth the chance.

Hearing voices in the hallway, she tensed. Leaning forward, she laid her ear against the door, trying to make out what the men were saying. The conversation in Italian was muffled.

She pressed her ear hard against the cool metal and brought an arm up over her other ear to block out the dripping water. The men drew closer, the tone of their voices low but relaxed, and stopped outside her door. Zara listened, her heart pounding a staccato inside her rib cage.

"The Muslim dogs are on their way. Vos Loo wants the girl."

"We should have a turn at her first, huh? This one would be more fun. She's not doped up. Might put up more of a fight." Rude snickers.

"When will Iacopo be back from his cigarette break?"

"He should have been back fifteen minutes ago, the horse's ass. Go find him."

"What about the girl?"

"I'll take care of her, *stupido.*"

Silence. Then more snickering and a back slap.

Zara lifted her ear from the door and moved back along the wall. *Or maybe, I'll take care of you.*

Across the short expanse of room, a drop of water fell into the sink's pool. One of the guard's footsteps receded down the hall.

As she examined the jacket in her right hand and the primitive knife in her left, her nerves calmed just like they always did right before something major. She'd been priming herself for this moment for hours and finally it was here. She blinked several times, rolled her shoulders and let out her breath.

At the sound of the door sliding open, she tightened her hold on the knife. Water rushed out of the room and the guard expressed surprise with a curse word. Distracted by the water rushing over his boots, he failed to bring up his gun immediately. As he stepped inside the doorway to see what was causing the flood, Zara threw her jacket at his head, blinding him.

He jerked his head and reached for the jacket with his empty hand. She turned and delivered a solid kick to the arm cradling his semi-automatic weapon. The guard went sideways, stumbling on the mattress and losing his balance. The MP60 splashed into the water on the floor.

Dropping her homemade weapon, she dove for the gun. Adrenaline pumping through her body, she grabbed the barrel and swung the butt of the gun down on the guard's head. The man recoiled, still trying to jerk Zara's coat off his face and calling for help. As he rolled away from her, he fell off the mattress, the jacket falling free.

She lunged and brought the butt end of the gun down on his head again, this time connecting with his temple. His body froze for an instant before crumpling into a flaccid heap in the water.

Her arms and legs trembling, Zara stood over him while she caught her breath. She slung the strap of the gun over her head, took a handful of stuffing from the soaked mattress and wedged it in the man's mouth. Bringing her head up, she scanned the opened doorway to be sure no one was approaching.

She had to work fast. Water from the room was still seeping out. She rolled the guard onto his stomach and pulled a shoestring from her jeans pocket. Quickly she tied the man's hands behind his back before she relieved him of the handgun strapped to his ankle and the knife on his belt.

Rolling him over, she tapped his cheek. "Good job, *stupido*."

As she shoved the handgun into the waist of her jeans, she picked up her jacket. She removed the strap of the semi-automatic weapon, stuck her arms into the jacket's sleeves and replaced the strap over her shoulder. The guard's knife fit in the right pocket.

Moving toward the door, she came up short. Annette stood there, taking in Zara's handiwork and fingering the gun in her hand. Zara brought the MP60 up and leveled it at her chest.

Annette slid her gun back into its holster. "Looks like you don't need my help breaking out after all."

Zara kept the gun trained on her. "You're here to break me out?"

Annette's eyes were tired and sad. "I'm sorry, Zara. Biaggio has my sister. I've tried everything over the past six years to find her and get her away from him, but nothing's worked. This was my last hope." She wiped brusquely at the tears in her eyes. "Looks like I've failed again, but at least I can help you and your sister."

"Do you know where Lucie is?"

Annette pointed to the ceiling. "Upstairs. North side. Take the stairs at the end of the hall. Once you've got her, go down to the garage. I left the keys in the Hummer."

"What about you?"

"I have some unfinished business with Biaggio and Dmitri." With that she turned and disappeared down the hallway.

Zara thought about going after her, but she couldn't risk it. In the doorway she let her eyes slide to the left and then to the right. Seeing no one, she stepped into the hall and pressed the lighted button on the remote control pad.

With a soft *whoosh*, the door to her cell closed.

"Hel-*lo*," Lawson whispered, examining the camouflaged

entrance of the tunnel. Tucked in to the northeast side of the hill and out of camera range, the tunnel, Lawson guessed, was Vos Loo's escape route if he were ever cornered.

Flynn's voice crackled in his ear. "What have you got, Commander?"

Lawson exchanged a smile with Lt. Redington and touched the communication button on his radio. "A way into the bunker undetected," he said, keeping his voice low. "Ask our techie friend at HQ if he knows anything about underground escape tunnels."

Flynn was silent for a moment. "Roger. I'll get back to you."

The two leaders moved stealthily into the nearby trees. "I can take two men out of my group," Lt. Redington said, "and send them in ahead of the rest of us to find where the hostages are positioned. They can plant audio-video devices to give us a better picture of what we'll encounter once we're in."

Lawson had already brought Redington up to date on Flynn's orders regarding the arrival of Sheikh Mohammed. He shook his head. "Pegasus will do the infiltration. We can use the tunnel to get in undetected and possibly secure the hostages without raising any alarms. Your men stay here and handle the Sheikh if he shows."

Redington nodded, but gave him a skeptical look. "And if you do raise an alarm?"

Lawson slapped the SEAL leader on the back. "I expect you to come in with guns blazing, Lieutenant, and save my ass."

Redington smiled. "Copy that, sir."

The bottoms of her wet sneakers squeaked on the concrete floor. Zara kicked them off and laid the heavy MP60 on the floor next to them. She needed to move like a cat, quickly and silently. The shoes were too noisy and the MP60 was too awkward in her hands. The brutal power of the weapon was attractive, but the weight and size were an encumbrance.

Removing the guard's handgun from her jacket, a heavy black European 9-millimeter, she checked the safety. It wasn't on. She chambered a round and listened.

Hearing nothing, she ran past the cells—cages, really, with

steel bars from floor to ceiling—and eyed the end of the hall. On each side was a closed door. Annette hadn't said which one was the door to the stairs. *Hang right,* her brain told her. All right turns would eventually lead her in an ever-narrowing circle. She'd be sure not to miss the stairs or Lucie.

Of course, she wouldn't miss the guards either, but maybe if she were very careful, she could dodge them. Zara leaned her back against the wall and checked the clip in the gun. Fourteen bullets and one in the chamber. At least *stupido* had given her that much plus his knife. It was tempting to go back for the semi-automatic weapon but she again ditched the idea. She was much more comfortable with the handgun and her wits.

Pushing off the wall, she reloaded the gun and moved quickly down the hall. Once at the door, she pressed her ear against it and listened. Dmitri would be checking his watch about now and wondering where she and *stupido* were. He might already be on his way to find out what was holding them up.

Hearing no sounds coming from the other side, she turned the knob and pushed the door open, gun at the ready.

Nothing.

Except the most beautiful flight of stairs Zara had ever seen. She took them two at a time.

Chapter Forty-Two

Lawson's point man moved ahead of him in the dark tunnel. The sides were fortified and in decent shape for a structure that seemed ancient. The tunnel had probably been built by someone in a previous century, possibly even as far back as the Romans. The first of the Vos Loo scientists had incorporated it into his compound. Smart man.

Johnny stopped and held up a hand. Lawson stopped behind him and repeated the gesture to communicate to the men bringing up the rear. The noiseless conga line froze.

At first he thought his point man had found a tripwire or some other measure to warn the occupants inside the laboratory of a security breach, but when Johnny motioned him forward, Lawson saw through his night vision goggles that the only thing he'd found was the interior door.

The two men scanned for infrared pinpoint beams and ran their fingers around the entire doorframe feeling for thin lines of copper wire. There were none. Neither was there any kind of keypad or other electronic-verification device requiring a number or thumbprint to access the compound. Johnny exchanged a look with Lawson and the two examined the door again, unable to believe Alexandrov Dmitri would leave himself so open.

But then it wasn't Dmitri's compound. It was Vos Loo's. No doubt Dmitri had sent the guard to cover this one weak spot in the entire operational base. Lucky for Pegasus, the guard just had to talk to his girlfriend.

There was only one way to know for sure if they could walk into the lion's den without detection. Lawson motioned his point man to fall back. He reached for the latch on the wooden door and listened for noise on the other side. Johnny aimed his suppressed MP5 at the space the door covered.

And then he heard it, footsteps. Someone was coming.

Drawing back, Lawson flagged Johnny. The message was conveyed down the line at the speed of light and when the door to the tunnel opened, the guard's eyes never had time to adjust to the darkness before his windpipe was shattered.

As Lawson and his conga line entered the compound, they used the SEAL technique of peeling off man-by-man from the line and clearing a given area of the room they were entering. All they met was fluorescent light, scattered boxes and half-empty shelves. A supply closet.

Two terrorists down, about ten more to go. The conga line reformed and the men moved on.

"Where is your man Antonio?" Dmitri demanded when Stefano entered the lab. "We are still waiting for him. Time is short."

The mafia leader set his newspaper on the stainless-steel table next to a set of vials and gave Dmitri an inpatient look. "He and Francesco should be back. Did you check the monitor?"

Jon Vos Loo turned his small, dark eyes on Stefano. "Do not lay things on my counter." His voice was so low Dmitri barely heard him. With a gloved hand, the biochemist picked up the newspaper and dropped it in a nearby garbage can. "Nothing on my counter," he repeated under his breath.

Dmitri reined in the urge to slap Vos Loo upside the head. God save them all, he would be glad when he was done dealing with the mad scientist. Stefano, too, for that matter.

Walking past the exam table, he strode into a side room where four video monitors sat in a row. Their screens showed no activity inside or out. Dmitri slapped the empty chair where one of Stefano's men should have been stationed. The Mafia leader had been rotating them through security details and two-hour naps to keep boredom and exhaustion at bay, but with his force limited to twelve, he was short of eyes.

As he studied the black and white video screen showing the area of jail cells, Dmitri's pulse rate jumped. There was something on the floor. A liquid? He leaned forward over the empty chair and squinted at the monitor. In the corner of the screen he could see something else. Something solid and dark.

He straightened and glanced at the other three screens. Two showed a view of the outside of the bunker, top and bottom. A third showed multiple views of the stairwell, each picture taking up a quarter of the screen.

A shadow caught his eye.

Checking the screen showing the jail cells, he fingered the gold chain around his wrist. The princess was up to her tricks.

He strode back into the lab. "Come with me," he said to Stefano. "And bring the syringe."

"Lucie," Zara whispered, moving to the side of the bed. There were three rooms on this upper floor, two of which held sleeping men. Their snores vibrated through the walls. The third and smallest room held Zara's sister.

"Lucie," she whispered again. Lucie turned her head and murmured something incomprehensible. Zara stuck the black gun in her waistband and stroked her sister's cheek.

Lucie's wrists were tied to the bedposts, but she was fully clothed and showed no signs of abuse. Zara breathed a sigh of relief. Using the knife, she cut her sister's bonds, grabbed her under the arms and pulled her upright.

"Time to go, sis. Wake up."

"Zara?" Lucie mumbled.

She maneuvered Lucie's legs off the bed. "Come on. We've got to move quickly and quietly."

"*Où?*" Where are we going?

Zara threw Lucie's arm around her neck and hoisted her to her feet. "We're getting the hell out of here."

Her sister only outweighed her by ten or fifteen pounds, but Lucie's near-dead weight was impossible to move. After shuffling her into the adjoining bathroom, Zara held her over the sink and splashed cold water on her face. At first, Lucie's protests were mild. Then, as the sedative receded and gave way to lucidity, her head came up and she shoved at Zara, sputtering and swearing at the cruel treatment.

"Shhh. I know, I know." She steadied Lucie as she swayed.

271

"I'm sorry, but I need you awake and able to move. We're in Dr. Vos Loo's laboratory near the German border and he and Dmitri are looking for me. Do you think you can run?"

Lucie blinked several times before pinning her focus on Zara. Determination fired underneath the haze. "I'll try."

Zara pulled the gun out of her waistband and grabbed her sister's hand. "Come on, then. Let's go."

Chapter Forty-Three

The means to escape sat in the garage. It probably wasn't the only exit out of the bunker, but if Annette was telling the truth, it was the best one. It provided them with wheels.

Leading with the handgun out in front of her, Zara continued her descent down the stairs with her back against the wall. Lucie held her left hand and mimicked her posture, sliding her back along the wall as they took each step. Zara used slow, careful movements to keep Lucie from falling.

Just as she set foot on the second-floor landing, Dmitri's voice echoed on the other side of the metal door. "Goddammit! I will kill that bitch!"

Her heart lurched into her throat. She heard footsteps running toward the door. Squeezing Lucie's hand, she pulled her forward. "Now would be a good time to run."

"*Non merde*," Lucie said, stumbling behind her. No shit.

"Level One, clear," Lawson said into his lip mike. He mentally heard the relieved sigh of the SEALs, Flynn, Christian and the others who were all outside the bunker listening. "Ascending to Level Two."

The basement of the compound was exactly what Del had predicted. A garage, an incinerator and a couple of supply closets. Pegasus had disabled all of the vehicles as a precaution. Any terrorists trying to escape would have to go on foot.

Pegasus was now ready to get down to business. He nodded at Johnny, and the point man pulled open the door to the stairwell.

Because of their limited view and tight quarters, stairs were less than optimum for infiltration. Noises carried like a voice through a bullhorn, and the bullet from a discharged weapon could ricochet, injuring anyone who got in the way. Getting cornered by the enemy on a three-foot-by-three-foot landing was a death sentence.

Lawson had ordered Teddy, C.J. and Rooster to hold back until he and Johnny made it to the second-floor landing. They would act as cover if any of the terrorists picked that moment to use the stairs.

Backs against the wall and weapons sweeping the stairs over their heads, Lawson and Johnny started up.

He'd just placed his foot on the fourth step when all hell broke loose above him.

Chapter Forty-Four

"Come back here," Dmitri snarled from five steps above Zara. "You can't escape."

Lucie had fallen and Zara struggled to get her back on her feet. She raised her gun and pointed it at Dmitri's head, even as she tugged on Lucie's arm. "Stay back or I'll shoot you."

The ice-blue eyes snapped at her and a sinister laugh bubbled up from Dmitri's chest, but he stopped in his tracks. His gaze fell to the black gun in Zara's hand, catching the way it trembled, and he smiled. Then he brought his gaze back up to hers, sizing her up. Debating whether or not she was capable of pulling the trigger.

Just to make it clear, she cocked the hammer.

"You won't shoot me."

Zara guided Lucie forward and swallowed the lump in her throat. If it weren't for her sister, she would have pulled the trigger without hesitation. "Don't bet on it."

Lucie fell again, swearing as she tripped down another stair. Zara reached for her.

She saw him move out of the corner of her eye, and she immediately knew her mistake for what it was. Before she could bring the gun back to bear on him, he was there, knocking her hand away. The gun went off as his body collided with hers, the report so loud it drowned out Zara's cry of pain as she landed with Dmitri on top of her.

Her head smacked against the edge of a stair and pain exploded behind her eyes. The gun fell from her hand and her body rolled with Dmitri's, momentum carrying them over. Air rushed from her lungs as her back hit the concrete, and her knee popped as Dmitri's legs, entwined with her own, twisted her leg in an awkward angle.

She cried out again, pushing him away. He grabbed her

wrist, and as their bodies came to a stop, dealt a sharp blow to her jaw. Pinpricks of light burst under her eyeballs and she tried to pull back.

As he let go of her wrist, he buried his hand in her hair and jerked her to her feet. She stumbled, her knee giving out as Lucie screamed her name.

Dmitri forced her back up the steps. "Don't be stupid, princess. You can't get away from me."

The stairs swam in front of her eyes and her feet fumbled trying to find them. One hand tugged at Dmitri's where he held her hair, the other sought the wall for a brace. Behind her, Lucie gasped.

"Run, Lucie." Flinging her right arm out, she struck at Dmitri's chest. "The garage is right below us. Run!"

He deflected her arm and shoved her, face-forward, against the cold block wall. A new wave of pain engulfed her skull and she sagged.

"She can run," he hissed in her ear, "but she'll never make it. My guards will kill her before she touches the door."

A man's low voice drawled behind them, "Your guards are dead, Dmitri, and if you don't release Agent Morgan, you will be too."

Lawson. Her head ringing, she turned to look over her shoulder at him. He was in camouflage, soaking wet from head to toe, the thick black suppressor of his weapon pointed at Dmitri's head. Greasepaint and mud covered the rugged cheekbones of his face, and his eyes were shadowed by a floppy-brimmed hat. He barely looked like her Lawson, but Zara would know his voice and the hard set of his mouth anywhere.

Three steps behind him was another member of Pegasus, John Quick. Zara remembered him from the farmhouse. His weapon was also trained on Dmitri. Straining her eyes, she saw the top of Lucie's head disappear down the last flight of stairs. Instantly, another man in camouflage took her spot, gun raised.

Lawson and Team Pegasus were there. Lucie was safe. Zara's knees went weak.

Dmitri snatched her off the wall and turned her to shield his body from Lawson. It was déjà vu. One arm went around her neck and he jerked her up a step and onto the landing by the door. Lawson swam in front of her eyes, and she grabbed Dmitri's forearm with both hands, trying to break the band of steel pressing against her windpipe. It was no use. She was too weak to fight him now.

The cool tip of something pricked the side of her neck. The syringe of supervirus. She froze.

"Ah, yes." Dmitri's breath was hot against the side of her head. "Lawson Vaughn, coming to Agent Morgan's rescue again. How Hollywood of you." His voice was calm, poised, as though the arrival of Pegasus was not at all unexpected, but Zara could feel his heart thumping like a fist against her shoulder blades.

Alexandrov Dmitri was scared. The thought brought a moment of satisfaction. "Shoot him," Zara said to Lawson. "Just shoot the son of a bitch."

Lawson's gaze locked on hers from under the brim of his hat for the briefest of seconds before dropping to a point right of her face.

The point where Dmitri was pressing the syringe against her neck.

The terrorist yanked her up another step. "She's as good as dead if you make one move." The cool tip cut in further. "This baby holds five ccs of a supervirus Vos Loo has engineered. A cocktail so deadly, he named it simply *Mors* after the Roman god of death. Rather dull, wouldn't you say? But then our good doctor wasn't hired for his poetic genius."

Lawson didn't move. Didn't blink. Didn't even seem to breathe. But his stillness did not convey apprehension to Zara. If anything, it managed to suggest calm. "The compound is surrounded by a group of U.S. Navy SEALs," he said, as if pure logic could reason with a madman. "You can't escape. Release Agent Morgan and lay down your weapon."

The tip of the syringe dropped from Zara's neck, and she inhaled a deep breath, expecting Dmitri to let go of her. He might be crazy, but he wasn't stupid. He had to know his only chance for survival was to give up peacefully.

Instead he twisted, and she heard the sound of the doorknob turning. Before her brain comprehended, before she could fight back, he jerked the door open and propelled her through it.

"Lawson," she cried, falling to the floor. The door slammed shut and one of Stefano's men, lying in wait to help Dmitri, threw a deadbolt across it.

Dmitri shoved a cap on the syringe and stuck it in his back

pocket before drawing a handgun from his shoulder holster. "Where's Stefano?"

"In the lab," the man answered. He motioned for Dmitri to follow him across the hall. "He said to bring the virus. The entire batch must be destroyed so there is no proof against any of us."

Dmitri stayed put. Footsteps and men's voices echoed on the other side of the door. "I'll join you in a minute."

He grabbed her arm and pulled her down the hall toward the cells. "First I must secure the girl."

The guard gave him a quizzical glance, but nodded before ducking into the lab.

Dmitri jammed his gun into her back. "Let's go."

As her bare feet touched the water in the hall, her knee gave out again. She slipped and fell on the concrete floor only to have Dmitri haul her back up. She heard a woman's voice, the crash of glass, a man's raging scream and a gunshot behind her. The silence immediately following the report was quickly replaced with a jumble of men's voices and then more shots.

Blackness clouded Zara's vision. She stumbled, but Dmitri was ready. His fingers dug into her arm. She tried to summon the energy to fight, but she had nothing left. Her legs and arms were too weak. She trembled all over.

He pushed her toward a barred cell at the end of the hall. The door was partially open and he threw her inside. She collapsed against the putrid mattress as he shoved the toilet out of the way and removed a section of wall from behind it. There were no pipes, only the empty mouth of a dark cavern. He seized her jacket and dragged her across the floor. "Go," he commanded.

Numb, Zara lay on the floor where the toilet had sat and eyed the entrance to Dmitri's escape route. She didn't have the strength to fight him, but she sure as hell wasn't crawling into a dark, scary, cobweb-filled tunnel with him.

After all, she did have her limits.

"Fuck you," she said.

She expected a swift kick from his boot. Instead he laughed. High-pitched and loud, it was the laugh of a man pushed to the breaking point. "'Fuck you'," he mimicked, shaking his head and continuing to laugh, softer now. In the background, Zara heard the door to the stairs splinter. "That's a good one, Agent Morgan. Very original." The laughter died and he grabbed her by the jacket lapels, bringing her face inches from his own. "Now move your skinny American ass." The arms of steel thrust her into the dark.

Dark was an understatement. Crawling on her hands and knees, Zara was claustrophobic as well as disoriented from the total absence of light. She could not discern whether they were moving up or down, and she was repulsed at the musty smell of the earth filling her nostrils and the feel of spider webs against her face. Unseen bugs skittered over her fingers and dropped from the ceiling into her hair. She seesawed between wanting to scream and wanting to vomit.

The only positive about the suffocating darkness was the fact Dmitri couldn't see her pull the five-inch knife from her jacket pocket as she pretended to stumble. The blade had nicked her stomach during their fall on the stairs, but she'd ignored the pain in the ensuing fight. Now she maneuvered it into the sleeve of her jacket as she crawled.

The far-off sound of gunfire met her ears and she paused, listening. Maybe what Lawson had said was true. Maybe the compound was surrounded by commandos. Hope flickered in her chest.

Dmitri's gun poked her butt. "Move it."

She crawled forward again, the thought of rescue dangling in front of her. If Lawson had men stationed outside the compound, she could be leading Dmitri right into their hands. Feeling a jolt of adrenaline, she picked up her pace.

Chapter Forty-Five

Lawson didn't move for several seconds as his eyes took inventory of the scene.

Shelves full of equipment and supplies had been ripped from the walls and thrown on the floor. Stefano Biaggio and half a dozen of his men were dead, broken glass covering them and the floor of the laboratory.

Backing into the hallway, he radioed Flynn about the biohazard mess. Flynn copied the news and asked about the rest of the terrorists. Lawson looked across the faces of the men lined up against the wall under the surveillance of Rooster and C.J. "Everyone but Dmitri and Zara are accounted for."

"Agent Newton?" Flynn asked.

Lawson looked at Annette, sitting on the floor with her back to the wall. Her eyes were glazed and her story was sketchy, something about freeing her sister and punishing Stefano. "Alive, but shocky. We'll bring her out in a minute."

Lawson glanced at Jon Vos Loo, the infamous biochemist. The man sat on the floor, rocking back and forth with his hands secured behind his back.

His gaze danced between Lawson and Annette. "I'm glad she killed him." He halted his rocking. "Biaggio. He tried to ruin everything. All my hard work. Years of research. The bastard was going to destroy it all."

Annette's attention was locked on the floor. Lawson had already asked her where Dmitri had taken Zara, but she'd shaken her head. She didn't know.

"Weapons?" he asked Teddy Winkle. The man held up the agent's semiautomatic and Vos Loo's pouch of scalpels, each bagged and tagged. Lawson threw his hat on the floor and bent down in front of Vos Loo. "Where is Dmitri taking Agent Morgan?"

Vos Loo looked away and began to rock again. "I'm a great scientist. No one touches my work."

Just what I need, a freakin' Rainman. "Alexandrov Dmitri's touching your stuff now, Doctor. He's got your supervirus. Tell me where he is and I'll get it back for you."

Vos Loo, the idiot, ignored him.

Suddenly furious, Lawson grabbed the doctor by the front of his shirt. "You tell me where Dmitri is or I'll make sure your hands are never able to concoct another drug of any sort."

The man's gaze snapped back to his, widening in surprise. "You can't hurt me. The Geneva Convention bans any mistreatment of prisoners." He shook his head. "You can't hurt me."

Before Lawson could yell at Teddy to get him a 110-volt generator and a set of alligator clips, Johnny called to him from the other end of the hall. "Commander, I've got something."

Releasing the squirrelly doctor's shirt, Lawson ran to join his teammate. Johnny pointed at the hole in the wall inside a jail cell. "Secret tunnel," he said. "Just like the other one."

Damn. Dmitri was too smart to allow himself to be trapped. "Where does it come out?"

"Guess we follow it and find out."

Lawson lowered his mike and informed Flynn and Redington of the situation. "I'm going in. Over."

"Not advised," Flynn's voice came back. "If Zara and Dmitri are in the tunnel, we'll retrieve them on this end when they come out. I want you out here to back up the SEALs in capturing our Muslim friends. Do you copy, Commander?"

Lawson looked at Johnny. Johnny shrugged. "Your transmission was pretty broken up, sir. I didn't understand a word he said. Did you?"

Lawson touched his radio button and then ran his thumb over his lip mike. "You're breaking up," he lied to his boss over the thumb-created static. "Your last transmission was unclear. I'll catch up with you outside. Over."

Flipping the Motorola off, he slapped Johnny on the back and shoved his headset off his head to rest on his neck. He called down the hall to the other three men of Pegasus. "Get Agent Newton and the prisoners outside and figure out where the hell this tunnel leads. Quick and I are going in and I expect you guys to be on the other end when we come out."

"Yes, sir!" Teddy, Rooster and C.J. answered.

Nodding at Johnny, Lawson fell to his hands and knees and started to crawl.

~ ✧ ~

Zara could see the light at the end of the tunnel. Literally.

Natural light filtered down to the muddy floor several yards ahead. The walls of the passageway were broadening and the air smelled fresher. She drew in a deep breath and rose to her feet in a crouch. Her knees ached, her injured one screaming in pain, but she ignored it all as she searched for the exit. A few more feet and she would be free.

They entered the circular opening, still six feet underground, and stood up. A metal ladder led to a grate above their heads.

Zara blinked as she looked up at the squares of sunlight shining down. Her feet made soft sucking sounds in the muddy ground. She reached for the ladder, but Dmitri stopped her.

He motioned with his gun for her to back away from the ladder. "This is where we part company."

She took a step back and then another as Dmitri raised the end of the gun to her face. "*Now* you're going to kill me?"

The tip of the gun touched her cheek and Dmitri brought his face close to hers. "You could always beg for your life, princess."

Pressing her back against the earthen wall, Zara coaxed anger to mix with her fear. She was not going to die in this disgusting tunnel. "You heard Commander Vaughn. This place is surrounded by SEALs ready to shoot you the minute you walk out of here. You have to take me with you. I'm your only hope of escape."

"They won't catch me." He placed one hand beside her head and positioned his gun next to her temple. "Especially if you're not slowing me down."

Zara held herself rigid as he pressed his body against hers. "You were an interesting opponent this time. I regret we didn't have more time to play."

She hated him being so close, but if she was going to do any serious damage with the knife, she needed him as vulnerable as she could get him. "Your plan failed and your partners are already under arrest. You have nowhere to go. Cut your losses and turn yourself in."

The terrorist stroked her hair and ran his fingers across her throat. Smiling, he pulled the syringe out of his pocket and waved it in front of her face. "I still have Vos Loo's vaccine, which I'll put on the market and sell to the highest bidder. And I still have my life."

He brought his lips down to hers, and she turned her head and shifted her right hand so the knife point slid into it. His lips brushed her cheek, and he whispered, "The only true failure in life, you stupid girl, is death."

Girl?

She pressed the end of the knife into his stomach. "Then consider yourself a failure."

As Dmitri's eyes widened with realization, Lawson's voice echoed in the underground chamber accompanied by the distinct sound of a gun cocking. "Let her go."

One side of Dmitri's mouth tipped up. He chuckled without humor. "Game over, Agent Morgan."

The needle pricked her skin and a flood of warm fluid oozed into her veins.

She jerked back and as the chamber exploded with gunfire, she dropped to the ground and screamed like the girl she was.

Chapter Forty-Six

As a member of Flynn's secret army, Zara had been trained in wet jobs—the liquidation of an asset—although she'd always hoped and prayed she'd never have to perform one. Terrorists were one thing, a trusted asset another...at least until one betrayed you. As Lawson yelled into his radio that she'd been infected with Vos Loo's virus and he needed immediate medical help, she laughed at the irony. Dmitri had just done a wet job on her.

Goddamn SOB.

Lawson bent in front of her, the muscle in his jaw working overtime as he used an antiseptic wipe to clean the blood from her hands. Dmitri's blood. "Medivac's on the way."

"Your timing could use some work." She looked into his panicked face. The face she loved. "You can't blame faulty communications on this one."

"Yeah, well, you know us Hollywood types," he drawled in attempt to match her *laissez-faire* attitude. "We always wait until the last minute to save the damsel in distress. Makes for a better climax."

Behind them, Quick had already bagged Dmitri's gun and the still-half-full syringe. He bent over and checked Dmitri's lifeless body for anything else of consequence. "Hell of a job you did here, Agent Morgan."

She was so tired she could barely speak. "My plan was to rescue myself."

Lawson wiped at her cheek with a fresh antiseptic pad. His touch was incredibly tender and thorough. "Any broken bones?"

She tipped her face into his fingers. Even with the latex gloves he was wearing, she liked the feel of his fingers, their heat against her skin. "No."

His fingers stilled for a second, and then he continued with his cleaning. "You've got a pretty good bruise on your cheek and it looks like you've got a shiner to go with it. Dmitri?"

She nodded. While her body was being invaded with the supervirus, it seemed like small talk was all she could manage. "I did that elbow-in-your-face move you showed me. Knocked him on his ass. He didn't like it."

"Poor sport, huh?"

"He didn't like a *girl* getting the better of him."

"You're pretty woozy. Any drugs in your system besides the virus?"

"No. I'm dehydrated and I haven't eaten since they kidnapped me."

Lawson's gaze dropped to her clothes. "Looks like I owe you a new jacket."

She looked down and scrunched up her nose. Blood was staining everything and... "Oh God, what is that?"

Lawson wiped at a bloody glob of...of... "Brain matter," he said.

"Dmitri's brains are on my Prada jacket?"

Snapping off his gloves, he pulled out a penlight and checked her eyes. "Pupils are even and responsive to light. Any head injuries?"

His face was so close to hers she could have leaned forward and kissed him. The green and brown camouflage paint on his cheeks had run together and turned to gray. "I cracked my head on the stairs but I think I'm okay. Just don't tell Flynn or he'll have a reason to label me mentally unstable and order a round of psych exams."

Lawson's expression softened slightly. He stared into her eyes. "Any other injuries I should know about? Sexual assault?"

She swallowed and shook her head, wishing he would lose the businesslike approach and at least smile at her. "What about Lucie? Is she all right?"

John Quick raised his head. "Your sister's doing fine. She's with Director Flynn and the others at our base camp. I guess she's been telling everyone how you saved her life." He stood and touched Lawson's shoulder. "I'm going up top to signal Teddy and the helo where to find us. By the way, Mohammed is a no-show. You need help getting Agent Morgan out of here?"

Lawson shook his head. "I've got it covered. Thanks."

John nodded and started up the ladder. The metal grate was rusty and squeaked when he jarred it loose.

As silence settled around them, Zara stared at Lawson. She watched, fascinated, as his shoulders bent, his eyes closed and his head bowed. As if all the life were draining out of him. He drew in a deep breath and released it slowly.

Wanting to reassure him, she laid a hand on his dirty, scruffy jaw. His hand came up to cover hers and they sat like that for several long seconds. When he raised his head, Zara was shocked to see tears filling his eyes.

Lawson Vaughn was about to cry. Her tough, supremely confident, alpha-male partner was about to cry...

Smiling, she leaned forward to press her lips against his. He slid his hands to the side of her face, kissing her back.

She let her breath go. Lawson was kissing her like he loved her.

But then he broke away. "This is my fault," he whispered, resting his forehead against hers. "I've screwed up a few times in my past, Zara, but never like this. I put your life in jeopardy and I'm sorry."

God, she loved him so much it hurt. "It wasn't your fault." She ran a hand through his wet hair. "And I'll be okay. There's an antidote in the lab."

"The lab was destroyed."

"Destroyed?" Zara's stomach fell and a chill ran over her skin. "Tell me Vos Loo's still alive."

Lawson nodded. "He's uncooperative, though. I'll probably have to beat it out of him, but I swear to you, I'll get the antidote."

They stared at each other in silence. She couldn't tease him anymore. She couldn't let him believe this was his fault, but what could she say to keep him from blaming himself? "I'd do it all again just to bring Dmitri down."

Dropping his head in his hands, he rubbed his face. "Zara..."

She forced a grin. "At least my reputation will stay intact this way."

He shook his head. "I've realized I don't work well in a partnership."

Now she grinned for real. "Quitter."

He didn't take her bait. "I'm a whole lot better being the leader of a group."

In the distance, she heard the thump of helicopter blades. It was now or never. "You know about transference, right? With hostages?"

"Yeah." Lawson frowned. "I know what it is."

"At Christian's I started having these weird feelings for you. I thought it was sort of like a crush, you being the guy who rescued me at the farmhouse and then again when you saved me from Varina."

Lawson's frown deepened as though he wasn't particularly happy about that. He leaned back. "You have a crush on me."

Zara knew from his body posture and facial expression she'd said something wrong. "It's not exactly a crush anymore. I'm in love with you, Lawson."

A nerve in his jaw jumped. Before he could respond, John Quick was yelling from the open hole at the top of the ladder. "Heads up, Commander. Director Flynn's here. Wants to talk to you. Helo is due in three."

Lawson gave his teammate a nod and began to busy himself with sealing his gloves in a plastic bag and sticking his penlight in his flak jacket. Avoiding her eyes, he asked, "Can you stand and walk?"

She pulled her knees into her chest and hugged them, confused by his sudden all-business demeanor again. Her body ached, her heart was raw and, even though she was beginning to feel foolish for baring her feelings to him, she still had a yearning to wrap her arms around him and never let him go. "Yes."

He rose to his feet and offered a hand to help her up, his gaze still avoiding hers. She ignored his hand and pushed herself off the floor into a standing position. Even though she weaved like she was drunk, she turned her back on him.

Bending over Dmitri, she ignored the disfigured face and snapped the gold chain, her gold chain, off his wrist. "I've got less than three hours before I become contagious." She could be all business too. "Once I hit that wall, no one can save me. I'd appreciate it if you'd go torture Vos Loo now."

After securing the chain in her pocket, she reached for the ladder and hauled herself up. She didn't miss Lawson setting the timer on his watch.

Chapter Forty-Seven

Conrad Flynn watched Vaughn assist the Medivac EMTs as they lifted Zara into the Army helicopter. He fully expected Vaughn to jump in, even if he had to kick one of the EMTs out to make room, so he could accompany her to the U.S. military hospital in Berlin.

When Vaughn stood back and let the helicopter rise into the air without him, Conrad sensed it was the hardest thing the Commander had ever done in his life.

As the helicopter's noise faded, Vaughn ran back to him. "I need ten minutes alone with Vos Loo."

"I've already downloaded the information on the flash drives to Del. He'll find the antidote."

"Zara doesn't have that much time. Course of treatment needs to start now."

"Vos Loo is zipped up tighter than Fort Knox."

"Ten minutes, that's all I'm asking for." He pleaded with his hands out in front of him. "She's one of yours, Flynn. You can't let her die."

Conrad understood Vaughn's determination, shared the feelings of responsibility for Zara's condition. "Officially, I can't condone torture."

"No, sir. How about unofficially?"

He considered that for all of two seconds. "Unofficially, I want you to do whatever it takes to save my officer."

"That's the op plan."

A few seconds later, Vaughn disappeared into the bunker, John Quick following in his footsteps.

Julia slid up next to Conrad and circled his arm with hers. "I'm surprised you're not in there with him."

"Blame your ex-boyfriend. Stone's turned me into a pansy-ass government official just like he is."

She chose to ignore his dig. "Lawson seems like a competent guy. I think Zara's life is in good hands."

"I sure as hell hope so."

Flynn had given him ten minutes to break Vos Loo. It took him three. Running out of the bunker with the combination of drugs to save Zara's life written on a piece of paper, he found Flynn standing exactly where he'd left him.

"I've already contacted the hospital and spoke to the doctor in charge of Zara's case." He handed Flynn the paper and gave Julia a nod of recognition. "Requesting permission to use your helicopter to follow up in person."

Flynn took the paper and gave Lawson a look of disbelief. "Can Vos Loo walk out on his own or do I need to send in a stretcher?"

"I never touched him, sir."

A smile broke over Julia's face. "How did you get the antidote?"

"I offered him a job."

"A job?" Flynn's sharp voice caught the attention of those nearby.

It was all he could do to stand still and explain that once in a blue moon delicacy worked better than a sledgehammer. "If you don't want him working for someone else, you better put him to work for us."

For a split-second, Flynn just stared at him. Then he chuckled and shook his head. "Good work, Commander. Permission granted. Let's go."

Johnny fell into step with them and as they passed Christian, the man yelled at Lawson. "*Pas de deux*, Lawson. Take care of her."

He nodded at Christian and ran for the helo for all he was worth.

Chapter Forty-Eight

Berlin Army Hospital

For Zara, the hours moved like a mouse inside a snake, stopping and starting in fits. First came chills, then deep, aching pain in her hips and shoulders. Her lungs filled with liquid and she coughed violently for stretches at a time. Her nose bled.

Inside the quarantined room with its white walls, white sheets and hard, linoleum floor, she shook and vomited and bled and cried. The worried faces of nurses and doctors peeked out of biohazard suits as they swarmed in and out of the room, checking her vitals every fifteen minutes and shooting her IV full of drugs.

No one else was allowed in to see her. When the pain got bad enough and Zara was sure she would die, she told the nurse washing her face, "I thought I'd die by bullet or explosion. Something cool, you know? Guess the gossips at Langley will still have something to talk about."

The woman nodded inside her face mask and hurried out of the room.

The next nurse received a litany of orders from Zara. "Tell my mother Lucie can have all my clothes and shoes. Tell my dad I want all my trust fund donated to the South Side Dance Studio in the Bronx." She hugged her stomach and rocked in the bed, trying hard not to whimper. "Tell Flynn there's a safe deposit box in a bank in Naples under the name Anna Zara Pavlova he should retrieve. And tell Lawson..."

Tell Lawson what? What could she will to the man who had risked his own life more than once to save hers? She released a breath as the stomach cramp diminished. "Tell Lawson he was a good partner."

At twelve-oh-six, she gave in to the whimpers and lost

consciousness.

When she woke, she was no longer in the white room. A window admitted bright sunlight. Framed pictures of painted houses decorated the wall next to her bed. Vases and baskets of flowers, balloons and cards covered every surface.

"Welcome back," a nurse in a colorful smock said as she pushed a cart into the room.

"I'm alive?" Zara asked, wiggling her toes for good measure. Her stomach ached and her head felt heavy, but the clawing pain was gone.

"Very much so." The nurse moved to the bed and pushed a button, causing Zara's head to rise. "You're one very lucky gal. It was touch and go for the past couple of days, but the doctors are sure you're no longer contagious or at risk."

She smiled to herself. "I'm alive."

Over the next several hours, her family, including Lucie, came and went, filling her in on the details. Her mother brushed Zara's hair and Lucie applied makeup to Zara's face, a truce having been struck between the two women who both loved her.

Christian brought her a package. She opened it to find a new Prada jacket. "From Lawson," he told her.

Lawson. Where was Lawson?

Director Flynn and his wife, Julia, were the last visitors the nurse would allow that day.

"What am I going to do with you, Tango?" Flynn said, setting a basket on her bedside table. A bottle of Dom was surrounded with packages of Ding Dongs. He tossed a package at her. "You nearly ended my career as DO before I even got started."

She fingered the package and set it on the blanket. "Where's Lawson?"

Flynn and Julia exchanged a look. A look that made Zara's stomach ache again. "Never mind." Tears burned behind her eyes. "I didn't really expect him to be here."

Julia squeezed her arm. "He was here, Zara. He even stole a suit and snuck in here while you were unconscious. He held your hand all night and yelled at the nurses who tried to make him leave."

Zara's stomach dipped again for a completely different

reason. "Then why isn't he here?"

"My fault," Flynn said at Julia's raised brow. "We needed Pegasus in the field."

"Oh."

Flynn stared at her in silence, Julia again giving him a look and a get-to-it nod. He made a face at her and said to Zara, "You coming back to work for me?"

Zara considered his offer. She was a damn good operative, whether she played by the rules or not, and being a spook was the only thing she wanted to do. "Yes, but next time I pick my own partner."

Flynn held out his hand. "Deal."

They shook.

Epilogue

30,000 feet, Eastern Atlantic Ocean
Ten days later

Pegasus was finally going home. As the Learjet sped through clear skies away from the rising sun, Lawson looked out the window at the peach-colored clouds below and tried to relax. He'd been awake for the past forty-eight hours straight and he was mentally and physically exhausted. He'd earned every minute of the two-week leave Flynn and Stone had promised him.

Settling a blanket over his tired body, he closed his eyes and thought of Zara. Her blue eyes and smiling mouth had invaded his every waking moment since he'd put her on the helicopter that whisked her away to Berlin.

Flynn had reported that, even after the antidote saved her life, Zara had been kept for observation and treated for dehydration before being released. The Director of Operations had personally escorted her back to the States forty-eight hours later and debriefed her. She'd been examined again by the specialists at CIA headquarters and vetted clean.

Lawson and his team had also received a standard physical and a psych evaluation in Germany, but what had taken days in Zara's case had been condensed down to hours for them. The morning after she'd been admitted and still lay half-unconscious from the drugs, the CIA had sent them to Yemen.

Lawson had balked, but Flynn insisted the danger had passed for Zara and another person needed his help. So Lawson and Pegasus went to find the lost spook Hoffman had told him about. They found him, but it was too late. The man had had his head cut off.

From Yemen, they'd been sent to Afghanistan where a reporter for NBC had been kidnapped. They had hooked up with Lt. Redington and his SEAL Team and once again, the combined units had pulled off a Hail Mary. Thirty seconds before the reporter was sure to die at the hands of an al-Qaeda lieutenant, Pegasus and the SEALs made a daring rescue.

One man lost. One man saved. When Lawson tallied up his mental scorecard, there were still more in the saved column than the lost. He should have felt good about that. Should have felt pumped after the last rescue.

Instead he felt like crap.

An image of Zara rose in his head. And then another and another. The last one at the end of the tunnel. *Have you ever heard of transference?*

He'd been about to pour out his heart to her, tell her how he couldn't breathe without her, and then she'd told him about her crush. Told him she was in love with him.

Not him, the *hero* who had rescued her. The revelation had sent him for a loop. She said she was in love with him, but he knew she was confused. She was in love with Superman, the leader of Team Pegasus. Not Lawson Vaughn.

Throwing the blanket off, he sat forward and rubbed his eyes with his fists. Hell, he'd always known getting involved with Zara was a bad idea. He'd known he wasn't good enough for her, but even now he still wanted her. He wanted to wrap his arms around her and bury his nose in her sweet-smelling hair. He wanted to watch her sleep, make her laugh, listen to her swear.

He missed her.

The guys of Pegasus were some of the best friends Lawson had ever known. He loved the camaraderie and the competition between them whether they were rescuing an injured pilot or shooting hoops.

But they weren't Zara. Teddy, Rooster, C.J. and Johnny combined could not replace his liberal-viewed, lip-gloss wearing, terrorist-hunting partner.

After unsnapping his seat belt, he moved through the cabin of the plane. Most of his men were snoring, dead to the world. Only Johnny's curious eyes followed him as he walked by.

In the rear of the cabin, he sat next to the SATCOM phone and picked up the handset. He dialed Hoffman and waited for the phone to connect with the nearest satellite.

"How's she doing?" he asked when his favorite techie

answered on the other end.

"Jesus, Law, it's five o'clock in the morning." Del yawned in his ear. "Normal people are still asleep."

"You and I are not normal. We work for the CIA."

"How did you get my home number?"

"I may not be a super geek like you, but I do know how to use the Internet. Now tell me how Zara's doing."

Lawson heard the crunch of bedsprings. "She started her new job for Flynn Monday."

"New job?" Lawson's heart tripped a beat. "He's sending her back into the field already?"

"She's at the Farm. Teaching one-day workshops on hostage survival. Flynn figured her firsthand experience made her the perfect teacher."

Lawson whistled softly under his breath, relieved Zara wasn't going back into the field as a case officer yet and intrigued she would agree to teach a class at the CIA's training center. "She's not going back to Paris?"

"Flynn was going to send her back next week, but Deputy Director Stone wants to keep her out of France for awhile. Give things more time to settle down." Del yawned again. "Rumor has it she's asking for placement in London. She plans to tackle a female Palestinian group the government believes is planning death and destruction on the Arab world."

Lawson smiled to himself. That sounded like the woman he knew. "Anything else?"

"You mean in regard to you? Sorry, Law. All us techies know is that Zara went extreme again and you saved the day."

Lawson grunted. "Truth's more complicated."

"Always is. One more thing you might be interested to know, Zara bought an old house outside Arlington. Some run-down duplex that's been sitting empty. Annette told me she and Lucie are using some of Daddy Morgan's money to open a dance studio for underprivileged kids once they get the place fixed up. Lucie's going to run it."

"Is she living at this house?"

"Why don't you just call her, man? Annette's got her number if you want it."

"What happened with Annette?"

"She's out of a job, but because of the extenuating

circumstances and the fact she helped take out Biaggio and Vos Loo, her jail time will be cushy. Her sister was found and brought back to the States. Annette says she's a little messed up, but she's going to see a good psychotherapist courtesy of Zara."

Lawson sat back in his seat and stared up at the ceiling over his head. He couldn't call Zara. He didn't know what to say. In between rescues, he had called other people to check on her: Christian and even her parents. Sitting forward again, he glanced at his watch. "I'll be checking in at the office at 0800 hours. We'll talk more then."

"I want details, Rebel."

"Done, Yankee."

Lawson replaced the phone as Johnny slid into the seat opposite him. He pointed at the phone. "Zara okay?"

"Sounds like it."

Johnny nodded. "How 'bout her sister? She doing okay too?"

Lawson studied his point man carefully. "Lucie's staying in the States for now. She and Zara are going to open a dance studio."

One eyebrow lifted. "Cool." He glanced out the window. "Where's this studio at?"

"You got something going for Lucie now?"

Johnny blushed and sent his attention around the cabin, checking to see if any of the other men were awake. Satisfied they weren't, he looked at Lawson and said, "We shared a...a *moment*. You know, after the rescue."

"A 'moment', huh?"

"Are you going to bust my balls about this?"

Lawson laughed. "Studio's outside of Arlington. Del says they're fixin' up an old house."

Johnny nodded and went back to staring out the window. After a minute he fidgeted in his seat and shot Lawson a glance. "Think Zara and Lucie might need some help?"

Lawson's spirits began to rise. Love was like a dark tunnel. You went in blind, never knowing what you'd find or where you'd come out. But if you didn't get down on your hands and knees and get dirty with it, you might never see the sunlight at the other end.

"I doubt they need help," he said, giving his friend an understanding smile. "But they might enjoy our company."

The Farm,
Camp Perry, Virginia

"Does anyone know what this is?" Zara held up a thick book with a broken spine and a well-worn cover. There were nine men and three women sitting in her class today. Most of them were fresh out of college. A handful were military commandos who had joined the CIA full time. Zara found it difficult not to think about Lawson every time she looked at one of them with their unsmiling eyes and laced-up boots. She found it hard not to remember how he'd turned brusque and businesslike in the face of her admission of love.

Even though he'd held her hand while she fought for her life, he wasn't there when she woke up. He'd dropped out of her life and left her feeling unbalanced, like she was walking around in some kind of fog. Like her time with him in Europe had been nothing more than a crazy dream. Now she was awake, but she still couldn't seem to get her bearings.

He'd been checking up on her. She knew he'd called everybody *but* her. He obviously cared, but the big dummy was too chicken to face her after she told him she loved him.

That was just too darn bad. He'd have to face her, because eventually, if he didn't come to her, she was going to him. She didn't care if he was in the middle of Timbuktu saving a drowning kitten, she was going to hunt him down and make him face his feelings for her. She'd been through too much to let him walk away. A near-death experience could do that to you.

A near-death experience could do other things to you too. Lucie had attached herself to Zara's hip since the moment she'd come out of the tunnel under Vos Loo's lab. She'd fluctuated between joy at being alive and anger about her ordeal. Zara understood. Her sister was undergoing the same emotional upheaval she had the first time she survived Dmitri. The two now shared a bond that was closer than ever and Zara welcomed it. She hoped Annette and Amy were sharing a similar experience.

Taking a deep breath, she slid her hip off the scarred wooden desk and cleared her mind of thoughts about Lawson. Flynn had given her an important job to do and she didn't want to let him down, or the men and women sitting in front of her.

In the days and months to come the students before her would learn what she had learned here a year ago—how to infiltrate hostile countries, how to communicate in code, how to retrieve messages from dead drops and how to recruit foreign agents to spy for the United States.

Zara's class, however, was not a how-to workshop or a test of physical strength.

"This," she said, waving the book, "is the 1963 version of the CIA's manual of interrogation, the *Kubark Manual*. It is still the most comprehensive and detailed explanation in print on effective coercive methods. The bible of torture techniques.

"If you are ever a prisoner in a foreign country, you will no doubt be subjected to some of the methods described in this manual to extort information out of you. But it isn't only police forces, intelligence services or foreign governments you have to worry about."

She set the book on her desk and picked up a dry erase marker from the tray at the whiteboard. "This class is a case study." She wrote the word *betrayal* in capital letters across the top of the board before turning to look at her students. "And this case study is about me and a terrorist named Alexandrov Dmitri."

Five minutes before class was over, Lawson and Johnny snuck into Zara's room. Her back was to him as she crossed off a word on the whiteboard. When she turned and saw him, she went completely still. She hadn't heard them open the door or enter the room.

She shifted her focus away from him as if he wasn't there and looked over the class. "Any questions?"

Yep, she was mad.

"Yeah, I got one." A guy in the front desk grinned up at her. "You doing anything after class, Professor Morgan?"

The male students snickered and the female students

rolled their eyes. The man jabbed an elbow at a friend seated next to him.

Lawson walked the aisle between the desks. "She's busy."

Passing the young guy, he thunked him on the back of the head with his hand. He stopped in front of her, blocking her view of the classroom, and pushed his sunglasses up on his head to look into her eyes.

Her flinty blue gaze challenged him. "Class dismissed."

They stood locked in place as the classroom slowly emptied out.

Lawson soaked up all the pissed-off energy she was throwing at him, loving every second of it. She was alive. Very alive.

He set the bag he'd brought her on her desk. "Word around Langley is I saved your butt again."

"I know. I'm the one who started that particular rumor."

That brought him up short. "You?"

"Of course. Subterfuge. It's part of my job as one of Flynn's secret army."

He chuckled. "So how are you doing?"

"I'm good."

"You look good."

She scanned his face. "You look tired."

No argument there. He knew he looked like hell warmed over. "Any nightmares?"

She placed the marker on her desk and picked up a pencil instead, shuffled a few papers. "You don't have to worry about me. I'm doing great for a pampered rich girl."

He grinned at her sassiness before glancing over the empty classroom. Johnny had closed the door behind him when he'd left with the others. "Hoffman tells me new enrollees are begging to take this class. Maybe I better get here earlier tomorrow so I can see for myself."

"You're coming back tomorrow?"

"Possibly." He took a step toward her. "If you let me spend the night with you."

She stopped shuffling the papers. "Awfully sure of yourself, aren't you, Commander?"

He took the pencil out of her hands and tossed it on the desk. Then he pulled her against him. "Z, I haven't been sure about anything since the moment Annette stole you out from under my nose."

She tipped her head up. "But you think you can blow me off and then show up when it suits you to sleep with me because I told you I loved you."

He took a deep breath. "Yes. That's what I was hoping."

Her hands pressed against his chest and he let her back away.

But she couldn't go far because of the desk. "No way."

He grabbed her waist and gently lifted her off the floor to deposit her on the desk. She stared at him in surprise, but didn't push him away this time.

Looking down into her eyes, he was suddenly afraid to breathe. "Zara, I..." He stopped and hung his head, trying to find the right words. The moment he'd seen her, he'd wanted to fall down on his knees and tell her he loved her.

She touched the side of his cheek. "What is it, Lawson?"

He turned his head and kissed her palm. Moving closer, he put his hands on the desk on either side of her and leaned into her space, catching her wonderful scent. She smelled like night-blooming jasmine, heart-stopping sex and the Paris countryside. She smelled like the woman who'd stolen his heart.

Clearing his throat, he found the words he wanted to say. "I'm not Superman, Z. I can't leap tall buildings or stop speeding bullets. I'm just a man who makes mistakes and gets scared like everybody else."

He took a breath before continuing. "I'm not a wealthy man, either. I'm not Harvard educated and I know you deserve better than me, but you better get used to me showing up to spend the night, because..." His voice had grown husky and he cleared his throat again. "I love you. So the question is, can you be happy with a poor mortal like me?"

Zara's eyes searched his and came to rest on the outline of his mouth. A faint smile played across her lips. "Can you dance?"

Laughter rose in his chest. "Hell no. But for you, I'll learn."

She kissed him, slow and sweet. Then she whispered against his lips, "Lawson Vaughn, I know exactly who and what you are. I don't need a superhero to make me happy. You'll do just fine."

He took her chin between his fingers and lowered his mouth to hers. Her arms went around his neck and she tugged him closer. Within seconds, the sweet kiss turned hot and needy.

Lawson broke away, breathing hard. He dangled the bag in front of her face. "I got this back for you."

She pulled the red dress out, hugged it to her chest. "My dress."

"I knew it was important to you." The smile that curved her lips made his heart jump. "Maybe you can wear it when we go back to Paris. I still owe you dinner."

Licking her bottom lip, she shook her head. "I can't go to Paris now. As soon as I wrap up this class on Friday, I'm leaving for London for my new assignment."

"Yeah, I talked to Flynn. He offered me a job working alongside you."

"What?" Her back straightened. "I don't need a part...ner..." She trailed off, squinting at him. "Unless you're willing to agree that *I'm* in charge of—"

Lawson cut her off with a kiss. A moment later, she *ahhed* into his mouth. The wildcard spook was once again his partner on a very important mission.

About the Author

Misty lives with her real life hero and hubby, Mark, her twin sons Sam and Ben, and her big dog, Max, in a small town along the Mississippi River. She's a multi-published author who divides her writing time between suspense and paranormal. Once a month, she indulges her love of fashion by blogging at www.solestruckfashions.com.

To learn more about Misty, please visit www.readmistyevans.com. Send an email to Misty at misty@readmistyevans.com to receive her newsletter or join her Yahoo! group to join in the fun with other readers as well as Misty. http://groups.yahoo.com/group/MistyEvansSuspense.

Hotshot spies never die. They just slip undercover.

Operation Sheba
© *2008 Misty Evans*

Julia Torrison—codename Sheba—is keeping secrets.

Seventeen months ago she was a CIA superagent, tracking down dangerous terrorists with her partner and lover, Conrad Flynn. A mission was blown, literally, when a bomb Julia built exploded early and Conrad died.

Yanked back to Langley and given a new identity, she is now the Counterterrorism Center's top analyst, spending her days at CIA headquarters and her nights in the bed of her boss. Her former life as a secret agent has been sealed off. Like her heart.

Conrad Flynn—codename Solomon—has his own secrets. For starters, he's not dead. Going under the deepest cover possible, he faked his death to save Julia's life. Now he must tear her life apart and ask her to help him hunt down a traitor: her new love.

Is Con a rogue agent or just a jealous ex-lover? To find out, Julia will have to enter a web of seduction and betrayal to play the spy game of her life using nothing more than her iPod—and her intuition.

Julia warns: "Beware of sexy spies bearing gifts. Trust no one and sleep with a gun under your pillow." Conrad warns: "Sex, lies and tantalizing suspense...don't worry, I'll protect you."

Available now in ebook and print from Samhain Publishing.

GREAT CHEAP FUN

Discover eBooks!

THE FASTEST WAY TO GET THE HOTTEST NAMES

Get your favorite authors on your favorite reader, long before they're out in print! Ebooks from Samhain go wherever you go, and work with whatever you carry—Palm, PDF, Mobi, and more.

WWW.SAMHAINPUBLISHING.COM

Lightning Source UK Ltd.
Milton Keynes UK
27 January 2010

149183UK00001B/184/P